BULLS OF PARRAL

BULLS OF PARRAL

By

MARGUERITE STEEN

KAYE & WARD · LONDON

First published 1954 (Collins)
Reprinted 1955

Reprinted by Kaye & Ward Ltd
194-200 Bishopsgate, London EC2
1969

SBN 7182 0815 3

Printed in Great Britain by
Lowe & Brydone (Printers) Ltd, London

PART ONE

Chapter One

ON AN evening in July, a couple of years after the end of the Civil War, the autobus chartered for the novillada at Cabrahigos broke down, and its occupants piled out on the roadside, to see what God would send them. There was nothing within sight but an endless patchwork of olive groves and a ragged edge of sierra, above which the sun had left a blur of blood and gangrene. Cabrahigos is a flea-bitten town which can afford but one bull-fight a year, but it is usually a good one; the afición is uproarious, but at the same time sharply critical, and not a few young bullfighters date their advancement from a good showing in the Cabrahigos ring.

In a few minutes it would be dark. Mary Carpenter, weak and sleepy after the fight, subsided into a clump of lavender, and did not even notice the Buick that came humming along, and drew up several yards ahead of the autobus.

"But—why me?" she stammered, when she grasped that she was being offered a lift. She indicated her fellow travellers, who smilingly shook their heads. No, no; la señorita . . . La inglesa.

God knew, the Spanish owed little enough, after their war, to her countrymen. But this was Andalucía, where no bitter herb takes root. Shamed, apologetic, grateful—Mary yielded to friendly compulsion.

Two men—one the chauffeur—were in front. She sat in the back, with a pale, extinguished girl, about her own age, of extraordinary beauty, who supported, face down across her knees, a

7

child whose black hair fell like the wing of an exhausted bird across her flushed cheek. Mary cast a smile of sympathy at the small prostrate figure : it was exactly the way she felt herself—the way everyone feels after the bullfight. The gathering darkness, the smooth movement of the car, the overpowering scent that reached her from the woman's hair and garments, increased her drowsiness. At a bump in the road her head jerked back against the padded seat, and she longed for nothing so much as to leave it there and pass into dreamless sleep—the profound sleep that follows hours of tension. But courtesy required her to struggle a little longer against the demands of nature, and Mary straightened her spine, pressing it into the angle of the seat, and bringing all her will to bear on the present situation.

" You are English, miss ? "—The words were slowly spoken, with a strong Spanish accent.

" Si, señora." She had spoken Spanish so long that her own tongue came clumsily to her.

" You . . . live . . . in Spain ? "

" I came over, during your war, as a journalist."

" You wrote for the English papers . . . about our war ? "

She coloured, as she nodded.

" But now you have—I am not sure how to say it—su propria guerra : a war of your own." She paused, to look down at her gloved hand, which lay on the child's head. She looked at it in surprise, as though wondering what it was doing there, and lifted it, to take a cigarette out of the case which lay on the seat between her and Mary. She lit the cigarette absently, forgetting, or not choosing, to offer the case to her companion. " You do not write about your war," she proposed.

" I—I'm teaching at the Berlitz school : English, and French, and a little German. I started before the war—our war, I mean." Her lips tightened. " I decided, during the war—your war—to remain in Spain, and get really to know a country for which I had so much respect."

" But the English supported the Government." She paused. " All the news the English papers printed was false propaganda. What did you do about that ? "

8

" I—disagreed." Mary smiled, a little grimly. " So I wrote home to my editor—and my family—that I wasn't coming back ; and I managed to get a temporary job in a hospital."

" And what did your family say ? "

She shrugged her shoulders. She was wide awake now.

" Naturally, they were not pleased."

" They say all the women in England, now, are—I don't know the word—reclutadas."

" Conscripted. That's not why I stayed in Spain," said Mary quickly. " My sisters are in the services, and they're naturally disgusted with me, for ' dodging the draft.' If I'd been sure of getting into the censorship, where my languages would have been useful—— ! But that, even in war-time, seems to be a matter of preferencia. I think I'm more use here than I'd be washing dishes, or filling up Government forms, or operating a machine."

" You are very certain of your opinions, miss." A trail of scented smoke drifted across Mary's nostrils. After a silence— " I think it is perhaps difficult for a Protestant people, to understand our Spanish point of view."

" But I'm a Catholic. I was received about four years ago. That had a good deal to do with my decision, to stay on after the Spanish war——"

The child turned over on her mother's knee, brushed away the flake of black hair from her flushed face and murmured :

" Dondé estamos ? "

" Despiertate, chica. Wake up, and speak English. Here is an English miss——"

" Qué fastidio "—She lapsed back, curling herself like a snail into the curve of her mother's arm.

Mary laughed.

" She's tired out. Perhaps," she offered, " she has been to Cabrahigos ? "

" Our name is Parral."

" B-but——" Mary stammered.

Seis toros estupendos de Parral. Her eyes went to the back of a bronzed neck in front of her ; the head it carried was dropped forward ; the brim of a silver-grey Cordobés rested on its wearer's chest. She drew a deep breath. " Permit me to congratulate you, señora ! The fourth bull—the little nevado : one does not often see a bull like that, except in a corrida ! "

" Muchas gracias, señorita. They do not interest me, the bulls."

" Excuse me," muttered Mary ; recognising the snub, she felt herself colouring.

" My husband was, naturally, at the fight. My daughter Aracea goes with her father always. She can speak English—a little. She has other English miss. But we live in the campo. For foreigners it is not like Madrid, or Sevilla, or even Barcelona. It is dull." The wife of Parral tapped the ash off the end of her cigarette. " In Andalucía, the Moorish influence is still very strong. I think Spain alter a great deal, in a few years' time. I wish my child grow up intelligent "—The depth of her emotion showed in the failure of her English phraseology. Speaking slowly and carefully, she had made, so far, no mistakes in the unfamiliar language. A gush of sympathy carried Mary towards this unknown woman, the limitations of whose environment her Spanish experience enabled her to estimate.

" Where do you live, miss ? "—The lights of the town sprang suddenly around them.

" Please don't trouble ; I can easily make my way home from here."

She got out on a plaza. The lily-like head of the wife of Parral bent vaguely towards her. The child looked up, and buried her face again on her mother's knee. The man beside the chauffeur stirred briefly, made some somnambulistic gesture of farewell.

Mary started along the cobbled street to her pensión. " Buenas noches, señorita "—" Muy buenas, la rubia." The lights, the soft voices at the rejas, had stood to her for " home " for two contented years. A shadowy figure opened a door, and she climbed a wooden stair to her little room, with its one, uncertain, blinking light, its pallet bed with the thin mattress of straw, and its rickety table on which were piled her books, her manuscripts and the meagre equipment of her toilette. To-morrow morning—Monday—she must face, at ten o'clock, her first group of pupils : three or four youths who wanted commercial English, a university student, ambitious to read Shakespeare in the original, one of the local guides, and a black-browed, sullen young woman in the thirties, whose stupidity was no less inexplicable than her reasons for joining the class.

She switched her thoughts abruptly to the bullfight : to the nobility of the little Parral bull, to the excellent faena, in the second suerte, by a boy from Santafé—and to her strange encounter. That was certainly something to tell the class : that she had been given a lift home by Don Luis Parral ! And the beautiful girl, and the child who had " an English miss."

When one is poor, and obliged, in a foreign country, to earn one's own living, dignity becomes very valuable. It was difficult to combine dignity with her present way of life. The cheap pensión, the constant preoccupation with tiny sums of money, the forced economies in necessary things like food and clothing were beginning, she recognised, to have a bad effect on her character, and debarred her from many contacts to which, by tradition and upbringing, she was entitled. Andalucían loving-kindness blinded her to it, much of the time, but in more lucid moments she was conscious that an English lady, with a university degree and a good home and family, should not live in the way she was living. Since the end of the Civil War she had slid, somehow, out of the society of the young Falangists who had formerly been her friends : too much of politics—and she was sick of politics. Latterly, she had sought, and found, humanity in the company of tavern-keepers, bullfighters, lace-makers and factory hands ; with these she had formed friendships for which she was deeply grateful, yet, in indulging them, had a sense of disloyalty to her own class, and her own standards of living, that stood between her and the satisfaction of which she was in search. She knew that by the few foreigners of her own social position she, from time to time, contacted, she was regarded as having " gone native," and this roused her resentment, not only on her own behalf, but on behalf of those who, in all innocence and kindness, had befriended her. And she felt she was drifting . . .

She knelt down before the small plaster image of the Macarena and lifted her face to the light. It was a curious face—well-shaped, superficially hard, prematurely lined about the eyes and the corners of a wide yet determined mouth : the face of an individualist, a face of strong, though possibly mistaken, principle.

She prayed, first, for Spain. Then, for all bullfighters. Then, for herself.

II

The brief Andalucían winter passed, and spring warmed into summer. From time to time, from her seat in the sol, Mary saw the Parrales, padre y hija, across the pale sand.

Her seat, and transport to the ring, cost usually several meals. She sat on hot blocks of cement, with a newspaper over her head to preserve her face and neck from the burn of the sun, her tired eyes fixed on the spectacle : on the courage, skill and grace of the man and the nobility of the bull. Out of all this valour, even I can draw valour, to continue my life. " Who among the Delphians," asked Plutarch, "is the Sanctifier?" The Bull, who not only is holy himself, but is so holy that he has power to make others holy. He is the Sanctifier, and sanctifies by his death . . . One of these days, when I've got time and access to libraries, I'll see if I can trace the dithyrambic progression . . .

In October, with the feria of Jaén, the season, for her, ended. She could not afford the journeys to Valencia and Barcelona. Six months, at least, of emptiness lay ahead. Her classes had diminished ; for that she knew she was not to blame. The Andalucían temperament does not lend itself to protracted effort ; a little knowledge is sufficient to build up the boundless Andalucían self-confidence. Several of her delinquents, she learned, with rueful amusement, had set up as teachers themselves : so much the worse for their pupils.

During the fall, when her vitality ran low and she worked

on the book that might or might not achieve publication in London, after the war, she knew she was beaten. She had no money left and must go home—if she could get there. But what prospect was there, in war-time England, for a professed supporter of the Franco government? She saw herself, clinging dumbly by her loyalties; taking refuge in silence from the attacks of those unable to distinguish between Francoist and Hitlerian Fascism; warned off from Fleet Street, and, not improbably, cut by former friends; an object of suspicion—thrust into some form of employment that was sheer waste of her abilities. And what, in war-time, is bitterer than waste?

On an afternoon blind with icy rain, she was summoned to the telephone. An unknown voice informed her that the Señora Parral wished, if convenient, to see her. As the journey was long, and the times of autobuses difficult, a car could be sent.

She made an appointment for the following day, and was interviewed in one of those featureless rooms to which, in private houses, she was accustomed: set pieces of furnishing that bear no trace of habitation, and exist for no purpose, seemingly, other than the storage of superfluous chairs and cabinets. The house itself, reached across kilómetros of rain-lashed country, its distant reaches blotted out in cloud, was an immense, dank shell; in it, the wife of Parral had no more substance than a ghost, or one of those delicate, transparent creatures that shrinkingly inhabit a shell's convolutions; sensitive to a sound, a vibration, the faintest intimation of an alien presence. Taller than Mary, she wove in the dark air, before the latter's eyes.

"I said to you, we have an English miss. My daughter Aracea has become very difficult. I think she finds the miss antipática. My husband says to get a Spanish governess, but I think it is a pity she forget her English. My father was professor in one of your English universities. We were all given English education. It is not very easy, now there is war, to find someone. The misses who came back after our war was over are rather old "—Mary controlled a smile—"and I think it is not good for Aracea to be with old person all the time. Do you ride, Miss— Carpenter?"

13

Mary admitted, with some surprise, that, before she left England, she had been used to horses. A sudden eagerness ran through her—diluted with incredulity. It was unlikely that the immediate future could resolve itself in this simple fashion.

" I am sure you told me you were a Catholic ? "

" A convert ; yes."

There was a cold, subtly antagonistic interview with the dueño ; Mary recognised, and mentally saluted, a courteous enemy. If she got the job, it would be through no goodwill of Don Luis Parral's ! There was no sign of the child, or of the " antipathetic " governess—poor soul. Don Luis sat at his table scowlingly fingering its equipment ; he had narrow, dark brown, very delicate hands. His wife sat motionless in a chair on the far side of the room. Mary felt pressure in the air, and, on the part of Don Luis, increasing boredom. He rose abruptly and crossed the room. As he reached the door, Doña Leandra slowly lifted her drooping head.

" Pues—— ? "

He made a gesture of impatience.

" The matter rests with you," he muttered, and left them alone.

Terms were stated, and accepted without discussion. Before the first thin sun of spring broke the buds on the spraying rose, Mary was installed as a dependant of the house of Parral.

III

It was a full month before she broke down Aracea's antagonism, and her resistance to any form of discipline. She had, often, a strong feeling of sympathy for the departed miss, whose task must have been a heavy one. It was shocking to discover a child of twelve, of a cultured family, who could not read, whose writing resembled that of an infant, struggling left-handedly with pothooks and hangers, who knew nothing of the history or geography of her country. " Where's Málaga ? " asked Mary one day, apparently at random. Aracea shrugged her shoulders.

" No sé." " But you've been there, to the bullfight." Aracea shrugged again. " We go in el Buick " (she pronounced it " Bweek "). " How should I know ? "

That she spoke some English was due alone to her mother's efforts, and to the fact that the " miss's " Spanish was elementary. Aracea had had, it transpired, a great deal of fun out of the unfortunate Miss Baxter's attempts to make herself intelligible. Her disappointment at the withdrawal of this form of amusement was patent.

" You don't make mistakes ! " she complained.

" Why should I ? I've been living in Spain for years."

" You should have hear Miss Bax ! "—Aracea proceeded to give an imitation, which Mary cut short.

" You should ' have hear ' yourself ! Did you ever hear the saying, ' Dijá la sarten á la caldera, Tiate allá, cul negra ' ? " —Aracea chuckled unexpectedly. " Well, go on ; put that into English."

" No puedo," she mumbled, wriggling her shoulders.

" We say it more shortly : ' Pot calling the kettle black '."

This for some reason captured Aracea's fancy ; she took it up in a chant.

" Pot calling the kettle black, pot calling the kettle——" She interrupted herself ; turning crimson, she stamped her foot. " I am not a pot ! You have no business to call me ' pot ' ! "

" Nor have you any business to ridicule Miss Baxter," said Mary calmly. Aracea blinked ; she was not used to people coming back on her.

" Tell me the names of the bulls," said Mary, another day.

" Why ? " asked Aracea, suspicious, as always, when they were in the schoolroom.

" It doesn't matter, if you can't remember them," Mary was cunning enough to reply, which, as she had foreseen, instantly kindled Aracea's vanity and her pride as the daughter of Parral.

" Of course I remember them ! "—She poured out a stream of names, only breaking off for want of breath. Mary was writing something carefully at the head of a sheet of paper. " What are you writing ? " asked Aracea curiously.

" The name of Capanegra."

" Why ? "

" Because you are going to copy it."

" No, I'm not." Aracea drew back.

" Of course you are. You can write the name of your favourite little bull ? "

Aracea learned to write, because, instead of trite combinations of English words, she was allowed to copy the names of bulls. Then of bullfighters. Then lines from the bills : " Seis Toros Estupendos de Parral." So long as instruction was linked with her ruling passion, she was amenable. Mary discovered that she was exceptionally quick, and her memory phenomenal—even for a child of her age. She brushed aside with contempt her former lesson books—the translations of *Cinderella* and *Red Riding Hood*, from which the unfortunate Miss Baxter had in vain striven to make her read—but struggled through the captions in old numbers of *Clarin* and *La Lidia* until she was able to read the notices themselves. Mary was in something of a quandary about this exploit, for the contributors to the bullfighting press used the andaluz, and Doña Leandra had expressed the wish that her daughter should learn the castellano. This, however, she consoled herself, could come later ; it was something to have conquered Aracea's aversion to the printed word. When introduced to classic literature, the child of Andalucía, to Mary's amusement, was as much defeated by the castilian as by the English idiom.

" But you have to learn el castellano."

" Why ? "

" Because all the famous books about bulls are written in castilian. You want to read Belmonte's life—about how he used to swim the river by moonlight, as a little boy, to fight the bulls. And Ibañez's great bullfighter story, *Sangre y Arena*——"

She knew she was guilty of not fulfilling one of the terms of her engagement : to distract Aracea's mind from its tauromaquían fixation. But it was soon evident that that mind, in some respects babyish, in others prematurely developed, was not to be distracted, and that the only way to rouse it to any scholastic effort was through appeal to her main interest.

She soon discovered it was useless to plan out a timetable. Lessons—if they could be called such—had to be slipped in between such vital matters as feeding time—for the cows in calf, for the calves themselves, and for the bulls brought down from the pastures to be readied for the ring. She learned to obey the sign from Aracea that commanded silence when the brave bulls came up mildly to their troughs; not to move, or to make a sound in departure from those sanctuaries that enshrined the future glory of the ring. She learned better than to plan work for mornings when the calves were to be branded, or they were testing the young stock.

The first time Mary saw a heifer come up twenty times to take the stab of the iron, and afterwards worked with the cape, she was thrilled as she had seldom been thrilled at the ringside.

" But I'd no idea they tested the cows, as well as the bulls ! "

Convinced, by then, of the honesty of Mary's interest, Aracea gave her a benevolent look.

" But of course, Miss Mary. The cow must be as brave as the bull, because of their children.—Ay-ay: did you see that? She nearly caught Juan. She will make great sons," concluded Aracea, with satisfaction. During the ride back to the house, she treated Mary to some interesting and variegated information on the art of breeding that enlightened the latter as to one of the possible causes of Miss Baxter's nervous breakdown.

" How do you know all this ? " she ventured to inquire, after a startling description involving a bull which, on the eve of the fight, got away and wasted itself in an amorous episode that disqualified it temporarily for the ring.

" I learn it from the boys, naturally. The boys know everything—more than the mayoral. I don't like the mayoral," she confided, " and when the bulls are mine, I shall get rid of him."

It was no use, reflected Mary, bringing English prejudice to bear on a case like this. English farm children probably knew as much about the processes of nature as Aracea. But she was beginning to understand the misgivings of Doña Leandra.

Sometimes there were long rides to distant uplands from which, through the binoculars, glimpses were to be had of the herd, slowly moving in its wooded pastures. Across the plain, infinitely far away, tiny as ants, moved the men on horseback, the bulls that were being separated and brought down to the feeding lots, and the steers that helped in their safe conduct. The pellucid light, the sense of distance and the tension transformed it, for Mary, into a colour film.

" Caramba, look there ! "

A bull charged out at one of the horsemen. She watched the horse stretch itself into a gallop, while, urged from behind, the steers spread to collect the bull. It was no wonder, thought Mary, that Don Luis refused to take his daughter on such expeditions.

Her greatest and most unexpected delight came on the eve of a novillada, when she was summoned to Doña Leandra's room. It had been an exhausting day ; frantic at the prospects of the bullfight, Aracea had been more than usually intractable; Mary had just succeeded in getting her to bed.

" Miss Mary "—she had become Miss Mary to the household : Miss Carpenter was too troublesome a combination of syllables—" Will it inconvenience you, to-morrow, to go to the bullfight in my place ? "

" I'd be delighted." She was reminded, by the look of distaste on Leandra's face, that her enthusiasm was misplaced.

" My husband will be in the President's box, or on the barrera. Some of our friends will be in the palco, but there will be room for you and Aracea."

" Many thanks, señora," said Mary meekly—wondering what it would be like, to view the ring from such exalted seats. She had hoped to be offered a seat in the Buick, but expected to have to shift for herself, on arrival at the bullring.

" I do not wish, please, my daughter to go at the back of the ring. Sometimes my husband wishes to take her, but I do not like it. It did not matter, while she was chiquitilla, but it is not a place for little girls."

"No, certainly. We'll come straight home, when the fight is over."

For Mary, it was the beginning of a rapturous season. She learned to take for granted the luxury of arriving in the Parral car, the prestige of being conducted to a box, instead of milling for a slab of concrete in the sun. Her one regret was that, from the distance of the palcos, one lost the intimate contact with the fight to which she was accustomed. She envied Don Luis and his cronies, down on the barrera.

But the small, excited body beside her acted as a conductor for all the emotions. If Parral bulls were in the ring, Aracea became uncontrollable. People turned to look and laugh at the beautiful, overwrought child whose shouts betrayed a familiarity with bullfighting vernacular not considered becoming to her sex. Mary was obliged, not seldom, to quell her.

"Be quiet! Girls don't say those things. They belong to the rough people over there in the sun."

Driving home, Aracea's head lay, often, on her knee, and Mary, on the edge of sleep, recalled the road from Cabrahigos. On one such drive, she saw Aracea's eye glinting darkly through a flake of hair, and patted the silken head.

"I thought you were asleep, chica."

To her astonishment, Aracea wriggled up on her knees, and flung her arms round her neck.

"Te quiero—mucho!"

It was long since she had heard the words "I love you." Hugging the hot little body to her, she wondered if she had the right to so much happiness.

Summer died into winter, and when mist lay deep across the pastures and the house of Parral was enrolled in cloud, Mary managed to establish some kind of routine. She took much pains to make the lessons interesting, and the results were gratifying. Long before spring swept its sheaves of frail lavender, blue and pink across the low-lying meadows, Aracea was reading fluently in both Spanish and English. She had completed, to her immense satisfaction, a large drawing of the map of Spain, which Mary helped her to colour, and on which all the principal bullrings were marked with red circles, and the lesser ones with blue. Grasslands and grainlands—equally important—were appropriately coloured. Mountain ranges linked into the grave question of transport, and working out distances with the help of an old Michelin guide broke down, to some degree, Aracea's resistance to "sums." The masterpiece, when completed, was proudly exhibited to Don Luis, who pronounced it estupendo, embraced his daughter a great many times, and, with Aracea perched on his knee, offered his felicitations to the miss—together with the grave hope that her pupil was not being overworked. Mary replied, with equal gravity, that there was no danger of that.

There were plenty of escapades, to interrupt the progress of learning. When missing, Aracea was usually to be found in one of the big, cold, empty rooms lit only through an iron-barred square of window, controlling with cape or muleta the rushes of the " bull " impersonated by one of the half-dozen or more small boys, sons of the herdsmen, who formed her faithful entourage. Mary was as little aggressive as possible in breaking up these sessions ; she would wait until the practice was over, and even, to Aracea's delight, take a turn or two with the cape, before sending the boys back to their quarters. But they disturbed her. She knew she was not doing her duty in countenancing them.

On days when the wind screamed round the house, the rooms filled themselves with the stinging smoke of olive wood and it was too cold to open the windows, she tried to organise games ; she tried to make Aracea and the children drill and do exercises —of which they soon tired. Secretly, she sympathised with them. Of what value was this bending and arm-swinging and jumping, from their point of view ? It led to nothing and achieved nothing. It made one warm, perhaps ; but it was easier and more comfortable, to get warm over the brasero or under the blankets—and what was the point of exhausting one-self in that way ?

With the return of spring chaos again reigned in the school-room. Wild with the sun, the sense of quickening life and the acceleration of tempo as the days moved towards Easter, Aracea was uncontrollable. Aided and abetted by her father, she snatched at any pretext for avoiding lessons.

After its winter sleep, the ranch was like a hive preparing to swarm. It was further enlivened by Don Luis's visitors : some on business, others frivolous—taking advantage of the balmy days to drive out, to enjoy the hospitality of Parral and the famous Parral manzanilla ; to discuss the prospects of the season and—in privileged cases—to watch the tientas. By all of these Aracea was much petted and flattered : which increased the problem of keeping her in order.

Behind the house stretched its vast walled garden, its terraces and cinnamon coloured palms, its countless little pools lined and encircled with azulejo, its fountains that never played, because water was precious. The ponds were crusted with scum, through which swam pale, blotched fish of incalculable age, or mosaicked with the dark jade of lily leaves, supporting the small, crippled cups of rose, or white, or orange. A tangle of deteriorated vine, rose, wisteria and plumbago smothered the paths ; weeds sprang shoulder-high from the cracked marble of rotundas. Rotting lemons and pomegranates added their scent to the pungent emanations of germinating verdure that converted the garden where once the ladies of Parral had taken their leisure into a gigantic compost-heap, breeding-ground of insect and vermin. Since the death of Don Luis's mother, no one had cared for the lovely garden, which had gone back to wilderness under the eyes of its present owner.

Unable to resist the silver shafts of lilies that rose star-like through patches of weed, Mary foolishly descended, to fill a basket with flowers. The air reeked of syringa and myrtle, whose incense filled the rooms.

A mosquito started up an old infection, and she spent two days in bed, dosing herself with quinine. On the third day she came dizzily to her feet, but knew she was not fit to ride out to the tienta. This was why, fortunately for her temperature, she did not witness the incident with Capanegra.

Chapter Two

I

THE LITTLE bull splathered through an opening in the stone wall of the corral, collected himself, and stood still, adjusting to his surroundings. He was the colour of an over-ripe mulberry, and the transparent light picked out the layers of immature muscle in thin plates of steel. He bore on his right hindquarters the brand of the ranch and on his flank the number 7. His ears were clipped and his tail had grown into a skein of floss silk after the clipping. His name, derived from a famous ancestor, was Capanegra, and he knew the sound of it ; the humans who brought him up, kept on repeating it, and he stored it in his shrewd brain, conditioned by impeccable breeding.

" Is that the one ? "—Indifferent as beauty can be to disapproval, and insensitive to tensions which so far as her companions were concerned, blotted her out as completely as though she ceased to exist—the señorita Gloria Meléndez y de Larra flashed her teeth at the child by her side. Like most of Don Luis's female visitors, she detested the spoilt only daughter of the dueño ; like all of them, she knew it paid to show attention to one who would eventually inherit one of the richest estates in Andalucía ; the child Aracea, who stood like a lad, her legs encased in leather chaps copied from those of her father's herdsmen, her black brows gathered in a scowl under the brim of the miniature cordobés, whose chinstrap bedded itself in the soft flesh of a stubborn jaw.

" Is that your little bull, Aracea ?—the one you brought up yourself ?—E' bonico."

" Shut up ! " hissed Aracea furiously.

Gloria Meléndez raised her brows, laughed, and threw a glance at Don Luis. He, naturally, would not put his spoiled brat in her place, but there was no excuse for his apparent blindness, as well as deafness, to all but that ridiculous animal in the middle of the enclosure.

Gloria folded her arms and allowed her hip to sag ; the vermilion petal of her lower lip, which sullenly covered the splendid double line of her teeth, fell away in a yawn. She had had enough of standing on a camion, watching the young stock come up for the tests. The reason for submitting herself to this boredom—Don Luis Parral—stood at her elbow. She could feel him in her veins, in the stream of her blood. It amused her, in an angry fashion, to have him standing there, immune as though encased in stone, pouring the whole of himself into those absurd little creatures that came up, one after another, to take their pricks from the vara. He should pay for it later on, she promised herself, and, under pretext of drawing her cigarette case from the pocket of her silken shirt, allowed her bare arm to brush the back of his hand. She drew back with a quick affectation of modesty.

" Perdone—— ! "

" Por dios, señorita ! " burst through the clenched teeth of Aracea. " *Can't* you keep still ? "

The little bull had his head up, looking at the group of humans on the lorry. They did not scare or enrage him. He had a misty memory of a hand that held the milk-bottle to his mouth, before he was weaned and turned out to grass. He stood in the sun, with the light running over him like water—looking grave, looking noble ; thoughtfully regarding the two-legged beings whose eyes were fixed on him. There was complete silence. Beyond the walls of the corral stretched the desploblado, with its shining verdure and scattered masses of rock and clumps of cactus and aloe, and beyond that the line of the sierra, tearing the hard, bright sky into a ragged fringe.

Capanegra felt he would prefer to return to his pasture. He swung towards the opening through which he had just been driven into the corral, and, in turning, sighted something he had not noticed before.

It was not the first time he had seen the man-horse : that strange, four-legged, two headed being that appeared, sometimes, out in the long grass or under the trees of the grazing grounds. He had seen it, the first time, with a shock of mistrust, but, like a wise little bull, taking his cue from his companions, had ignored it. But seeing it at a distance, separated from it by a long stretch of earth and familiar trees, and the bodies of other cattle, was different from being isolated with it between four stone walls.

A sensation he had never experienced stirred under Capanegra's shoulder-blades, an irritable, ant-like crawling that forced the flesh up into a perceptible swelling. It was the first time he had been aware of his morillo—the hump at the base of the neck of all fighting bulls that signals the excitation of the combative instinct. Too well-bred to engage in premature dramatics, he waited, while the man-horse slowly advanced, with a silly, teetering motion that seemed, to Capanegra, to be making mock of him.

Choosing his moment, he ran, and received, to his surprise, a sharp prick in the shoulder—qué barbaridad !

Taken aback, but completely fearless, and much offended, he shook himself back, took a trot round the corral—his eye fixed always on the object of his resentment—and launched himself suddenly, at an angle. Again sharpness sank into his shoulder, and the blood of seven generations of brave bulls rose in Capanegra's veins. He went in like an expreso, head down, tail brandishing : saw the insensate, four-legged, two-headed object rush past him—and heard a shrill sound, which he did not recognise as human laughter, but knew to be derisive.

Someone yelled " Look out ! " as his head took the edge of the camion with the force of a tractor. Out of a confusion of staggering bodies, of female shrieks and masculine shouts, the body of Aracea Parral described a parabola in air and came down on all fours on the grit of the corral.

Capanegra stood perfectly still, confused by the yelling— unaware of people rushing up behind him with spread capes.

Aracea dragged herself to her knees. She was no more than a couple of yards from the young bull. The bleeding palms of her hands beat the air.

" Papá ! Papá ! Don't let them spoil him ! "

The peónes checked at Don Luis's demented gesture. The life of the padrone's daughter was at stake, but everyone there, with the probable exception of the señorita Meléndez, knew that to show the cape to a two-year-old bull is to ruin him. In a sick silence, that none dared in the presence of Parral himself to interrupt, the child staggered to her feet.

Capanegra stood with his head down, still thinking, still angry. But puzzled. Something was there that nature bade him destroy. But he was not sure about it, as he was sure about the man-horse and the wooden thing on wheels.

" Capanegra. Capanegra my son."

That word belonged to him. That sound was associated with the sweet, forgotten taste of milk, and a comfortable friction on his brow and between his ears. The sensation at the base of his neck had subsided, but his shoulder was a little sore, and wanted comforting. He took a doubtful step forward, dropping his head.

" Capanegra. Hijo mio."

The feeling he remembered registered itself under the stiff hairs, in the hard bone of his brow ; crawled up between the spread of his horns ; worked gently but strongly down again ; lingered softly round his muzzle—long enough for him to smell it, to smell the warm, human flesh associated in his memory with tenderness and care.

In a silence deeper than death, the child and the bull, leaning shoulder to shoulder, crossed the corral, and, crushed close together, passed out through the gap in the wall. Aracea drew back, while Capanegra lifted his head, saw before him the limitless ranges of his familiar grasslands, and, with a mere playful toss of the horn towards his companion, strode out towards freedom.

" E' un bravo, Papá ! "

His limbs dissolving, the sweat pouring down his face, Don

Luis laughed and stammered as he clutched the child against him.

" You said he'd be no good, because I brought him up myself, and he used to follow me like a little dog, before he went out to the pastures."

" I was wrong," muttered Don Luis—who would have died before admitting it to anyone but his daughter.

" It was all the fault of that fool, for laughing at him——"

" Be quiet," mumbled Don Luis, whose natural good manners would not allow his guests to be insulted, whatever his private opinion of their conduct might be. But he had his own formula of insult; the kiss he dropped on the back of Gloria's hand, as she slid into the driving seat of the long, cream-painted Mercedez-Benz she had brought, in defiance of rules, right up to the testing ground, was so casual as to be an insult in itself. He did not even trouble to lift his eyes as she dragged her hand away.

" Many thanks, Luis, I have guests." She rejected his insincere offer of hospitality, flashed him a murderous smile, let in the clutch and the car leapt forward with a roar that took the horses up in the air. The spectators exchanged glances as the dueño stood there, with the smile on his lips that meant bad health for somebody ! La Meléndez had gone a little too far— even for Luis—this time. Like the majority of breeders, he did not hold with allowing his bulls to get the smell of petrol before the time came for loading them into the trucks.

" What an uncle," observed Aracea disgustedly, and spat dust. " What did she come for ? She doesn't know anything about bulls."

The sun beat strongly in their faces, before taking its final plunge below the folded line of the plain in whose secret hollows moved the famous herds of Parral, whose name had made history for three generations. Don Luis threw his daughter up on her horse, and the pair of them headed the cortége of guests and peónes that rode down the walled lane from the corrales. Father and daughter rode with the easy " give " that belongs to those bred to the saddle. Aracea's hands stung, and the coagulating blood was sticky on the reins, but she was too proud to complain of it. She ducked her head to peer under the brim of her father's hat.

" What is it ? "—He spoke kindly but absently, for he had much on his mind.

" Our bulls are the best bulls, Papá."—It was not a query, but a statement.

" Claro." To every breeder, his bulls are the best bulls. The commissions he had booked for the season bore out Don Luis's opinion : but he sometimes wondered what his grandfather would have made of the small, light animals that carried the famous devisa into the rings of Madrid, Sevilla, Barcelona and Jérez. Because Parrales were small and short of horn, they were popular with post-war fighters. Managements took trouble to secure them for the engagements of the stars. Brave bulls, they had all the nobility of their high, broad-branched forebears ; but Don Luis's conscience pricked him, when he wondered if he had betrayed the tradition of the breed. Well—Miuras had lost credit, because the matadores did not like them, and one must breed to popular demand, or lose money. The technique had altered since the great days of Joselito (whom Don Luis was too young to remember, but whose memory he had been brought up to honour) and Belmonte, whose impeccable art stood to Don Luis's generation for the apotheosis of all that is noble and seemly in the ring, and whose most famous faena was executed at Cordóba, with a Parral bull.

Aracea's little bull was going to be too large ; it was almost certainly predestined to the novilladas—and no breeder can afford to depend on those.

His mayoral came floundering up on a rawboned black horse as they reached the brick posts that defined, without guarding, the beginning of the carriage way. The posts and the drive itself—actually, no more than a track of beaten earth—acted in the old days as a point of assembly for the cavalcades which, there converging from their various points of departure, formed themselves into a procession to approach the house. Pepe the mayoral, thrusting his way to the dueño's side, said :

" Chombo has eight of them, ready to be looked at to-morrow, at the spring beyond Las Hormigas."

Aracea pricked her ears. Don Luis did not turn his head.

" How are they ? "

" As you said : three good ones, and the bragado that hurt his horn in the branding." Don Luis scowled ; he did not care to be reminded of accidents. " It's not bad. The left point is a little short, but he's not timid on that side."

" And the others ? "

Pepe rocked his outspread palm.

" Regular."

" Take out the bragado."

" As you say." He hitched his shoulders. " But——"

" Don Amadeo is a friend."

" They don't pay much, at Maderas," shrugged the mayoral.

" Some day, perhaps, they will pay more."

" Or they'll make the ring into a football ground."

" Take out the bragado, and put in its place the bull Negrito."

His henchman exploded unprintably.

" We're keeping that for Jérez ! "

" Let them, for once, see decent animals at Maderas. Oiga : it will pay us, to build up the prestige of that ring. Maderas is not on the tourist route, but it is not impossible, from Sevilla or Ronda."

" And where are the tourists ? " mumbled Pepe.

" Hombre, the war is not going on for ever. The prudent man looks at the horizon. People who come to Sevilla for the Easter fights have to wait until the twenty-fifth for the feria at Lorca, and till the twenty-ninth for Jérez. They might well fill in with a good novillada at Maderas. Don Amadeo will agree with me."

" Then we go out to-morrow," sulked Pepe, " and look at bulls."

" Go out—where ? "

" I said it—beyond Las Hormigas."

" And we get there—how ? " was the smooth inquiry.

" Pues—señor—— ! "

"It has perhaps escaped your memory, that Amadeo Ribera, formerly Cigarrón, took the cornada in 1932 ?—that a man who has been nailed through the hip to the barrera is incapable of riding long distances ?—God gave you brains, man ; use them," said Don Luis, with dubious sweetness.

"And the auto ?—and the binoculars ? "—Pepe Frías, head herdsman to Don Luis Parral, was too young to share his employer's respect for the name of Cigarrón, and, like all who followed the fights, held the Maderas ring in contempt. He saw no reason they should go to the trouble of fetching the bulls down to the near pastures for the little profit Maderas offered.

"Don Amadeo does not buy bulls through the binoculars," Don Luis told him, and bade him go with God.

Aracea pressed eagerly forward to her father's side, as the black horse wheeled away.

"Is Don Amadeo coming to-morrow, Papá?—Is Paco coming with him ?—Can we cape the baby bulls ? "

II

She got much the same pleasure of looking at her father as Don Luis got out of looking at his bulls. If details escaped her immature eye, she was very conscious of the whole : of the tight cap of lightly silvered hair, drawn down towards a thick black line of eyebrow, and the dark orange tan of skin that had hardly started to sag—Don Luis was in his mid-forties—above the fine bone-structure of his handsome face.

Like the majority of Andalucíans, he was short, but made up for want of inches by a fineness of bearing that earned him the sobriquet of El Grande. After the fashion of an Andalucían gentleman, he wore a fine linen shirt and collar, with no tie. His short jacket moulded itself like paste to broad shoulders that fanned out from a narrow waist, to which trousers tailored in the high-pointed Andalucían style did full justice. These he wore on the ranch, sometimes supplemented by chaps of soft, bronze leather. When he went to town, Don Luis dressed like an ordinary business man; his broad grey cordobés was canted over his eyes, to shield them from the sun—not over one eye, after the fashion of the youths who swaggered along Las Delicias, and, in the days of tourism, were pointed out to naive victims of local guides as " muy típico." The mere notion of being " típico " would have frozen Don Luis—save at feria time, when, dressed in the height of tradition, he drove his fine mule-team down the illuminated alleys of the fair, taking as much, or more, pride in his beasts than in the young women, chosen for their beauty, who sat on the hood of the open carriage, their crisp ruffles spread out like tails of peacocks, their fans beating the air like moths' wings under their significant eyes.

Some day, thought Aracea, she too would be lovely, and would displace the young women who shared, for the present, Don Luis's casual favour. That would be a day, when the Parrales, padre y hija, drove under the festoons of coloured lights—king and queen elect of the feria !

" Papá : when you are dead, who's going to look after the bulls ? "

Don Luis flung back his head and let out a roar of laughter. He took death in his stride. Life is short and death eternal, so you make the most of life while it lasts—as you make the most of a fine wine, a romance you know to be fleeting, a solea (ay, dios : there are songs one must regret, and voices—" *Clareando viene el día* "—the silenced voice of Yerbabuena. He was a boy when his father took him to Granada, cradle of the cante jondo. At forty-five one is old enough to have memories). He answered shortly :

" What puts that into your head ? "

" The widow of Don Félix Gómez ; the widow of Concha y Sierra ; the sons of Don Eduardo Miura." She quoted rapidly from the posters. " Will it some day be me—' the daughter of Parral y de la Cerna ' ? "

" What do you know about breeding bulls ? " he teased her.

" I'll know everything, by the time I'm grown-up ! To me the bulls are important : more important than anything—except you, Papá," she assured him earnestly.

"Much obliged. It pleases me, to be as important as a bull."
He hid his gratification under a show of irony. But he was
touched, more deeply than he cared about. It was his punishment—for what he did not know—that he had begotten no son,
to carry on the tradition of Parral.

In his youth, Don Luis Parral was a stylish amateur. When
he lay in hospital, with his first cogida, his father, Don Lucifero,
came to visit him.

"You may now choose which is better : to kill bulls as
Cagancho killed them"—the blood poured into Luis's cheeks,
for he knew how Cagancho killed his bulls : dishonourably, and
in deadly fear—" or," continued his father imperturbably, " to
breed great bulls for great fighters to kill with honour.

"You are a fenómeno, my son," said Don Lucifero, "and
it has cost me much money, to make you a fenómeno. You are
admirable with the cape and you do me credit with the banderillas.
But with the muleta "—he wagged a finger—" you have had
much luck. I would rather be the father of a live breeder than
of a dead bullfighter."

"It is an honourable thing—to be the father of a dead
bullfighter ! "

"Not of necessity." Don Lucifero stuck out his lower lip,
spread the fingers of his right hand and slewed his wrist from
left to right and back again. " It takes much honour, to make
it worth while. You have valour. But you need not have taken
a ride on the horn the other day."

Because this was unpleasantly true, and because Don Luis
knew in his heart that he had not the makings of a great matador,
he gave in. Far from being a coward, he had hated his first
cornada. He knew all about bullfighters who, from that first
unpleasant experience, take into the ring a terror that robs them
of their little skill. As a monied amateur, he was intelligent
enough to recognise that his only justification for remaining in
the ring lay in adding something to the tradition of Joselito and
Belmonte : and he was sufficiently honest to admit he had
nothing to add.

So he surrendered to a tradition as noble, in its way, as the tradition of the fighter. For three generations, Parrales had bred brave bulls. He accepted his heritage and his duty—which was to marry and beget sons to carry on the family strain. And the fruit of his marriage was this girl, who lifted her burning face and eyes of vague aspiration to his.

" No woman can breed bulls."

" That's not true, Papá! What about Murubes?—and de la Covas ? "

Don Luis scowled; it was disagreeable, to be reminded of his feminine rivals.

" You had better find me a son-in-law, to take the business over."

" I'm not going to do as any husband tells me; *I'm* Parral; when you're dead the bulls belong to *me* ! "—She continued after a pause, " Is Paco coming to-morrow, with his father ? "

Don Luis's lip twitched.

" Caramba; is Paco your novio ? "

Aracea, who had not reached the age of blushing, dismissed paternal jesting with a hitch of the shoulder.

" Can we practise our capes," she persisted, " with the calves Pepe's got penned in the old riding school ? "

" Oye," said Don Luis. " Your mother does not like you to play with the animals."

" There's no need for her to know ! I'm as good as Paco," she boasted. " Ildefonso's been working me with the horns all winter. I keep my feet still now, and the cape low down. And Tío Juan says my recorte's muy macho ! "

Don Luis let out a snort of laughter and converted it to a scowl; " muy macho " is not a term that applies to ladies.

" You had better show your hands to the miss," he muttered, " and get them bandaged."

They were within sight of the house which, from this aspect, had the squareness and bleakness of a fortress. Two entrances broke into its façade : one square and low, enclosed by double doors of blistered olive wood, the other, an imposing archway, bearing over its lintel the arms of Parral. Two or three lancets, heavily barred with iron, alone gave access to the apartments on the ground level; above them, a row of tall windows with iron balconies were permanently shuttered behind panes of glass, The shutters had not been opened in Aracea's life-time; in the days of her grandfather, the ladies of Parral, with their dueñas, had watched from the balconies equestrian spectacles devised for their amusement on the broad circle of beaten earth that fronted the mansion.

Father and daughter rode under the arch into a cobbled patio, disturbing the pigeons that rose, like flakes of rusty silver, to settle on the jutting, orange-coloured roofs. Round the patio ran a dark stone colonnade, into which descended, in two sweeping curves, the stone staircase that led from the gallery. As usual, in houses of the type, the whole of the ground floor surrounding the first patio was given over to storage—of grain, of bedding and fodder for the horses, the gentle sound of whose hooves and dragging of their chains sounded by day and night through the house of Parral. At one end of the main gallery, with its floor of waxed tiles, was a wooden balustrade, overlooking the patio of the horses, their stalls and the stalls of the domestic cattle. The whole of this patio, and the principal one, and another that served the domestic quarters, was enclosed within the deep walls of the old house, and defended by wooden doors, studded with iron and barred with shafts of teak it took two men to lift.

Only the initiate dared launch himeslf, without safe conduct, on those convoluted interiors, deriving light only from windows opening on passages: passages that led, in the majority of cases, to blank walls. There swarmed the innumerable dependants of the house of Parral: cobweb-like ancients who claimed its hospitality along some tenuous line of relationship to the dueño or his staff. Some had not seen the sun for twenty years; sheltered, warmed and fed, each had his ambiguous corner. Hordes of children flourished there like mice. It was Aracea's favourite, and forbidden, playground.

Of the extravagance entailed in the maintenance of his household Don Luis had his suspicions, and shrugged them away. Was he feeding ten, twenty, fifty or a hundred people?—Dios

sabe. He waived responsibility. The only expense on which he
could put his finger, and which constantly irritated him, was the
English governess. That Miss Mary! Claro, the daughter of
Parral must be educated ; but why by an Englishwoman ? That
she was a Catholic, and an aficionada of the bulls, was no
reasonable excuse for her imposition on his household. He had
weakly given in—because there are occasions when one is bound
to propitiate a woman. Even a wife. Was it going to be worth
while ? Was there the smallest possibility of Leandra's giving
him a son—— ? Ay-ay ; he had miscalculated, over his marriage.
He should have taken his choice among the gay, grey-eyed,
Andalucían daughters who offered themselves—though delicately,
with the grace of their breeding—to the son of Parral : to the
girls with mouths like pomegranates and lazy eyelids, who only
asked to be relieved of their virginity. And some witchery—
some brujería—had led him astray, had betrayed him to a pale
Castilian, with a dangerous background and upbringing—
dangerous, that is to say, to a son of the vine-stock, whose
claims are simple, explicit and fully understood by his own kind.

A brief vision of Gloria Meléndez, of her sultry eyes and
sullen lips, floated across the inner eye of Don Luis, as he
shouted for someone to take his horse. Round the patio were
ranged the cars of his guests ; in his office were the bottles of
manzanilla and coñac and anis, the plates of ham, olives and
anchovies that stood for the traditional hospitality of Parral.
They were coming, in, clattering after him. He composed his
expected smile of welcome . . .

Aracea slid from her horse, threw the reins on its neck, and,
hitching her chaps, swaggered towards the old woman who
detached herself from the shadows of the colonnade at their
entrance.

" Olá, tía Candelaria. Have the goodness to tell Ildefonso
I want him."

Chapter Three

MARY FINISHED reading her letter—which had been heavily censored—and replaced it in her handbag. She looked round the room to which, though by now familiar, she invariably found herself summoning up resistance. It was like no other room she had seen in a private house, during the whole of her time in Spain.

The walls, from floor to ceiling, were covered with books, with the most extraordinary conglomeration of books, thrust on the shelves with no attempt at order or classification. Novels in half a dozen languages jostled calf-bound volumes in which VII took precedence of II, and I, III and IV were lost, or had strayed elsewhere. A block was given to works on philosophy, in tattered, paper-backed editions ; three bound in tooled leather whose gilt lettering leapt from the sombre background : *Filosofía y Actualidad*—Ramiro de la Cerna. Between the honey-coloured parchment spines of fifteenth century monasterial records were stabbed modern bindings in green, red and orange. Broken-backed copies of Tauchnitz shouldered crushed morocco, loaded with gold leaf. Unamuno, Baroja, Thomas Wolfe, Sinclair Lewis, Pierre Louÿs, Gide, Proust, Maeztu, Edgar Wallace and Hugh Walpole completed a scene of bibliophilic disorder that smote the breath from Mary's lungs, when she first set eyes on it. Qué barbaridad !

A refectory table three yards long was littered with magazines —many still in their postal wrappings : with papers and writing materials. At these, on her arrival, she had caught hopefully, as evidence of a taste conforming with her own ; but they lay there, week after week, the feather brooms of servants passing over without disturbing them. It was Mary who, once or twice, washed out and refilled the bottles, in which the ink was crusted with the heat; as it was Mary who threw out the dead flowers which were left to wither on a chair, or in a vase that no one troubled to fill with water.

On another table lay a broken-stringed guitar, and piles of yellowed music. On the floor, in which were repeated, in black and white marble, the interwoven crests of Parral and de la Cerna, were spread some Persian rugs, of indisputable antiquity. In the corners, on pedestals of ebony, were vast porcelain jars that vaguely recalled the legend of Ali Baba. There were various divans, heaped with cushions covered in dark, ecclesiastical brocades. The room was darkened by ilex, and by the elaborate rejas that formed a grille above the terrace that, on a lower level, provided a clearing between the tangled garden and the house.

The wife of Parral leaned against a table—doing nothing. Thin as paper, thin as air, with the lost look of a girl in an ilex wood, she was just visible in the dark twilight—doing nothing. It would not occur to her to switch on lamps, which, as Mary lifted her hand, cast, with their shades of purple brocade and dark, tarnished fringes, isolated pools of light among the heavy furniture, leaving the rest of the room in darkness.

Leandra Parral turned her long neck slowly; the carriage of her head was that of a doe—proud, yet timid, But, thought Mary, there is no timidity in her; she would stand still, with high head and level brows, to receive the shot in her indifferent heart.

" You are better, Miss Mary ? "

" Thank you ; I'm quite well now."

"You have read your letters. They are still bombing London ? "

" Yes."

" You must be glad, not to be there."

Her face burned.

" I'd better find Aracea. There won't be much time for reading, before supper."

As she spoke, the red glow caught in the branches of ilex changed, as though some celestial electrician had shot a sheet of talc between them and the setting sun.

" Shall we read in here, or in your bedroom ? "

" I think," said Leandra, " I will not read with you any longer. I think it is better I not. Perhaps you have not observed it ; but Aracea prefers I am not there. Es lógico. She does not care to be a little girl, with two grown-up people who talk about things she cannot understand."

" That will do her no harm. She's getting rather too much attention these days——"

A shriek interrupted her, and carried both women to the window.

Down on the terrace, lit by electric bulbs, crouched a small boy, gripping the horns of a bull. Aracea was facing him, the magenta and yellow folds of an old fighting cape bunched in her hands. It was too heavy, and she could not hold it properly, but her stance, as she waited for the " bull," was as gravely classical as the maestro's, and the suavity of the movement with which she passed the horns within an inch of her hip drew a smothered chorus of Olés from a hidden audience.

" Caramba ; the de frente por detrás ! " smiled Mary.

" Stop it ! I insist you stop it ! "

Mary turned slowly.

" You know Aracea only obeys me because I'm interested in the bulls."

" You—an inglesa—— ! "

" But for the bulls, señora, I should not be here ; have you forgotten the road from Cabrahigos ? "

" It's unnatural—it's horribly uncivilised—for a girl—to live for nothing but bulls and the bullfight ! " Dragging open the window, Leandra cried through the rejas to the children below.

There was silence, followed by a scuffle. Then nothing but the chirping of cicadas in a tangle of myrtle. Darkness surged up from below with the extinction of the lights.

" It is only play, señora. It is healthy for the child and gives her exercise. I have thought it wise, so far, not to check——"

"It was not for that you were engaged, Miss Mary." The frostiness of the reply caught her breath. There were many things she could have said: "Do you want to make her life as empty as your own?" and, "If you take this from her, what do you propose to put in its place?" But she bit her lip.

Presently she answered, in a low voice:

"The little I've accomplished, so far, is mainly due to her dependence on my sympathy with the things she cares about."

"But it is not English, to like the bullfight!"

Mary grimaced and spread out her hands.

"Pues, señora—from that point of view—I'm not English! But you knew that," she pointed out, "when you engaged me. And nothing would make Aracea into an 'English' little girl. I am sure you would not wish it—any more than Don Luis."

"My husband and I do not think alike on all things." Mary lowered her eyes; it was not for her to say that this, self-evident, added to her personal difficulties. "What," asked Leandra suddenly, "do you mean to do with your life, Miss Mary?"

"That's a strange question to put, just now, to any English-woman!" She forced herself to speak lightly.

"The war will be over—this year, or next."

"Ojalá!" breathed Mary fervently.

"Then you will go back to England, and perhaps you will get married," suggested Leandra.

She laughed. Like all normal women, she wished to get married, and knew no Spaniard married a woman—least of all a foreigner—over the age of thirty. Yet what kind of a husband, she wondered, am I, without money or social standing, likely to discover in post-war England? She wondered, not for the first time, whether spinsterhood would be more tolerable in her own country, or in Spain.

"There are other things beside marriage. I have a friend who runs a school; she might give me employment, as a start." She glanced at her watch. "Con su permiso—I must find Aracea. There's hardly time for our reading, before supper."

She went out on the shadowy gallery, with its endless doors opening on blacked-out rooms. Already the sky was crowded with stars, and the air loaded with the scent of dung. She could not resist the impulse to run along and look over the wooden balcony into the patio of horses. A sweet smell of hay, a contented champing, rose from the stalls; it was too dark to see, but here and there came a faint gleam from a polished flank; a chain dragged, a hoof beat softly on the cobbles. Under the balcony there was a rustle and a murmur; another of the innumerable children of the house of Parral was probably being begotten down there, in the warm, dark straw. A stab went through her heart, at the thought of leaving it. Her long sojourn in Spain had cleared up the sentimental illusions that clog the perception of the foreigner. Accepting its limitations, she knew distinctly, that this was the country to which her heart belonged. Loyalty and affinity are two different emotions. I have seen the worst and the best of Spain, she thought, and I would rather live here than anywhere else in the world.

Retracing her steps along the gallery, she heard the purr of an engine. Leaning over the balustrade, she recognised the long, pale shape of the Mercédès belonging to Carlos de la Cerna, the cousin of the dueña. Round the single electric bulb strung on its cable across the patio, bats were whirling; her arms crossed on the carved railing, she stared at the light and the blur of wings until her eyes were dazzled. She became aware of a whisper, a shuffle and a giggle.

" Aracea," she called quietly.

Suddenly the engine roared; there was a screech of gears, repeated; a scuffle as of innumerable rats. The unlighted car plunged forward, and, with a crash that resounded from the dark arcades to the tiles where the pigeons slumbered, scattering them in a whirr of wings, hit the stone pillar immediately below where Mary was standing.

There was a yell; a door slammed open, shooting a rectangle of light across the cobbles—and Aracea scrambled on all fours up the stairs. Mary caught and jerked her upright. A childish scream sounded through a bellow of masculine voices.

" What have you been doing? "

" Nada—nada ! " Aracea tried to twist herself free of Mary's grip. What a lovely child it was: miniature, feminine reproduction of the father.

" What were you doing with the car ? "

" Nada—let me go, Miss Mary ! We were working our capes——"

" You've been told not to bring the boys into the patio."

" Mamá sent us off the terrace, and——"

" Come, get out of those trousers and into the bath ; you smell like a ganadero—and what's the matter with your hands ? "

Preoccupied with examining the deeply-scored palms for grit, she paid little attention to Aracea's flamboyant account of her adventure. She pressed a wad of lint, soaked in disinfectant, into the sores, and Aracea let out a shriek ; it was not worth while being stoical, for an audience of one.

" Ai-ee—that hurts ! "

" You don't want to get tetanus, do you ? What a mess. You should have come in at once and had it attended to." She sent her with a little slap towards the bathroom.

" Oiga, Miss Mary : Capanegra is a brave bull. He could have given me the horn, but he knew me. Wait till you see him in his corrida ! "

Mary looked at her curiously.

" You love Capanegra, don't you ? "

" Claro. He is my own little bull. I love him."

" But it won't grieve you, to watch him die ? "

" Por qué ? " The dark eyes met hers without understanding. " All brave bulls are born to die."

How lofty is the Spanish attitude to death. She remembered making this comment to an English acquaintance, and her fury at the flippant reply : " I suppose so : so long as it isn't their own." " It's a pity you weren't here to watch them through their Civil War," was the answer, which, like most good answers, came to her too late. In any case, it would not have convinced her compatriot. But she knew that if she had raised a little bull, she could not have borne to watch his ordeal in the ring. She felt the curious humility towards her pupil which, she supposed, balanced their relationship.

While a servant brushed Aracea's hair, Mary read the pages which Aracea stumblingly translated into English. The short lesson over, Mary laid down the book, and smiled into the mutinous eyes of the child.

"That was not bad. Now we can talk Spanish."

"And you are not bad!" Aracea's teeth flashed between her curving lips. "And we will talk English, so this old boba does not know what we are saying. Tío! Granuja!" she shrieked jerking her head away from the brush. "You're hurting me!" she hurled at the meek soul who muttered a prayer for forgiveness.

"Haven't you been told that's not the way to speak to servants?"

"It is what they are used to. Now I will tell you something. To-morrow comes Don Amadeo Ribera, to look at bulls. You know who is Don Amadeo?"

"Por cierto; he is Cigarrón, who took the alternativa in '32—or perhaps it was '33. He fought two seasons and got the cornada on Resurrection Sunday just before the war." Mary came out with it pat.

"Olé la aficionada! And he is the father of Paco; you remember Paco?"

Out of some scores of Pacos, Mary recalled a handsome, well-mannered little boy who had come several times to the palco, to bow and shake hands, and present Aracea with a bag of sugared almonds or a branch of oranges; and, the courtesy accomplished, took care to snatch a handful of sweets before thrusting and bouncing his way down to rejoin his father on the barrera.

"And Papá says we may cape the becerros—the baby calves."

A scream came from below. And another. And another.

"What's that?" Mary ran out on the gallery.

The car had been pushed back from the pillar, but no one appeared in answer to her cry of "Qué es eso?" Only thuds, gasps and smothered shrieks.

She turned back into the lighted room, where Aracea leaned

towards the looking glass, pushing her hair into a wave over her brows, in imitation of her mother's.

" What was that about ? "

" It sounded like somebody being beaten," she observed indifferently.

" Who ? "

" How should I know ? "

" What were you doing in the patio ? "

" Pues—I told you : working our capes."

" You—and who else ? "

" Ildefonso—and me—and some of the other boys."

Mary continued to look at her. Manifestly some means must be found of putting a stop to this kind of thing. Someone was always getting punished for infringement of the rules that included prohibition, to the children, of the main courtyard. If the boys had actually, as Aracea claimed, been playing there, it could only be by her invitation, or command. As for the likelihood of their laying a finger on the car—Mary knew enough to dismiss it. The older boys, including Ildefonso, were too anxious not to forfeit their privileges, of which the first and foremost was that of living close to the fabulous bulls ; as they grew up, of being allowed to try their skill with the novillos, and, at all times, of profiting by the largesse of visitors to the house of Parral. Indulgent as the Spanish commonly are to the young, the indulgence of Don Luis or his friends would not extend to damage done to their property and punishments were apt to be as excessive as tolerations.

Mary closed the door, walked slowly to the window and gazed at the stars.

" To-morrow morning we will learn that poem you were supposed to have finished yesterday."

" To-morrow—you forget, Miss Mary ! " Aracea spoke hastily—" come Don Amadeo and Paco. There will not be time for lessons."

" Al contrario ; there won't be time for little bulls."

" I can learn my poem any day, but Don Amadeo——"

" Don't tire yourself with giving voice." Mary spoke crisply in Spanish. " You will not cape the bulls to-morrow."

" Mi papá says——"

" What your father says makes, for once, no account. It was you who meddled with the car, wasn't it ? It is time you learned the difference between naughtiness and dishonesty."

" I didn't—I never——"

Mary took the shrill whine with calm. She had learned not to apply English standards to dealings with her pupil. Naturally, if you are accused of something, you lie the first time ! She had sought, on several occasions, some means of convincing Aracea that truthfulness paid ; so far, she had not discovered it. Truthfulness, as Aracea might well inform her, did *not* pay, with her countrymen. Meanwhile, to punish the child each time she told a lie would be to involve them in continual ill-feeling. She would not, however, lower herself to argument.

" I thought Ildefonso was a friend of yours."

" Claro, es mi amigo."

" But you don't mind him getting flogged."

" They can't flog a girl ! "

Mary concealed a smile at the ingenuous admission.

" Then you did it."

Aracea jerked her head away. Presently she muttered, through the dark curtain of her hair :

" And I shall cape the calves to-morrow."

" No, you will not," said Mary, very calmly.

" I shall ask mi papá ! " shrieked Aracea.

" Don't give yourself the trouble ; I am going to speak to him myself."

Before Aracea reached the door, Mary was through it, and slipped the outer bar across it.

The house of Parral echoed with yells, with poundings on wood, with a vocabulary that made Mary reflect there was much in the señora's objection to her daughter's spending so much of her time with the herdsmen. The staircase and gallery filled themselves with dark, anxious faces.

" Por dios, qué pasa ? "—" Josú qué pasa con la chiquitilla ? "

" The chiquitilla has behaved badly. Pay no attention to her." Their mute reproaches followed her down the stairs.

When she tapped on the door of the office and entered, the dim-lit room was full of smoke. Expecting to find the dueño alone—the Mercédès was the only car that remained in the patio —she was taken aback when several heads were turned towards her. One or two of the men removed their hats and cigars ; all stared with the stony reserve, nor far removed from insolence, which is the attitude of the Spanish male to a woman of " a certain age," a stranger, a foreigner and a dependent. One, Carlos de la Cerna, smiled, and addressed her, showing off his English before the others.

" Good evening, Miss Carpenter. I hope you have recovered from your illness ? "

" Thank you." She collected herself quickly, and addressed herself to Don Luis, who did not trouble to rise from his chair. " Con su permiso, señor—I will return later."

" You wished to speak to me, señorita ? " In his surprise, he did not address her as " miss." She decided to press her advantage.

" I understand, from Aracea, there is a becerrada to-morrow."

A smile ran round the room. La inglesa was not much to look at, but she was simpática ! The nearest man, in whose dress and bearing she recognised the almost extinct type of the rejoneadores, the horseback fighters, addressed himself to her, giving her the full benefit of a set of gold-capped dentures.

" La señorita es aficionada ? "

" Si—señor ! " She made the two words into one of three syllables, with the accent on the last, and flashed a smile back at him. It was not the first time her smile had done her good service, and she felt the atmosphere change, from antagonism to approval.

" What's this ?—Parral gives a becerrada and does not invite his friends ? "

Don Luis took their raillery with a grudging smile.

" A misunderstanding, amigos. Cigarrón and his boy are

44

coming to-morrow. I shall allow the children to play with the calves."

" Olé tu hija. Olé la matadora ! "—They were flattering him, and he knew it, for not one held with the appearance of women in the ring. Inclining his head in acceptance of the compliment, he addressed himself coldly to Mary.

" The señorita is at liberty, if she chooses, to watch the children playing with the bulls."

" Many thanks, señor ; but——"

He gave her a stony stare that made her lower her eyes. Thank goodness, she had learned, by now, the tricks of dealing with her employer.

" I would naturally not presume to interfere without the señor's authority ; but, until her hands are healed, Aracea won't have much control of the cape," she said, with hypocritical meekness, which he, master of the arts of hypocrisy, she knew would value for what it was worth.

It was clever, because it afforded Don Luis an opening for boasting of his daughter's prowess. She remained demurely silent during a running commentary of compliments and laughter. " Olé el padre. Olé la chica—she has all the salt of the Old One ! " The glasses filled themselves with manzanilla, of which Don Luis and his guests had already had plenty—and Mary was relieved to know that Aracea was out of earshot while they drank her health.

Carlos de la Cerna limped up to her. A black eye-patch enhanced the rakish brilliance of his face. She felt the usual impulse of attraction, as she smilingly waved away the glass he offered her.

" Do you refuse to ' toast ' your pupil ?—I expect she gives you a great deal of trouble."

" Not so much as she has just given you," she answered, under cover of the laughter. " Is the car much damaged ? "

He stared, flung back his head and roared with laughter.

" So it was that little pícaro—— ! "

" You might have waited to be sure, before beating up the boy."

" It is not my custom to beat people ; I employ others to do it," he told her, with loftiness.

She repressed a smile as she turned to Don Luis.

" So I have your permission, señor, to tell Aracea she is not to cape the calves to-morrow ? "

Don Luis checked a chuckle, to pinch his lower lip vexedly between his fingers. He had looked forward to displaying his daughter's skill before his friend El Cigarrón.

" The wounds are bad ? "

" Bad enough ; a lot of dirt got into them." She hoped heaven would pardon her a little exaggeration. " The señor is as well aware as I am of the danger of infection."

The word " infection " brought its desired reaction ; no member of that audience had not seen infection end on a mortuary slab.

Having gained her point and expressed her thanks, Mary slipped out into the patio. She went to look at the car ; so far as could be seen in the faint light, the only damage was a twisted bumper ; it had evidently hit the pillar fair and square, probably in top gear—which would stop the engine. The great stars blazed overhead ; she pressed her fingers to her aching temples.

She had gained her point—so far as establishing her authority with Aracea was concerned—but gained it dishonestly : as, unfortunately, so many advantages had to be gained, that involved Don Luis and his daughter. Yet what was the alternative ? Don Luis would have laughed and shrugged at the accident, would have offered to pay for it, and would have been either amused or impatient with Mary's concern over a miscarriage of justice that affected the small son of one of his herdsmen. And Doña Leandra, although, in principle, she would have taken Mary's part, was as likely to question the need to take seriously so trivial a matter.

Submerged in one of the brief waves of pessimism that sometimes overcame her, Mary wondered whether the task she had undertaken was, in the end, worth while ; whether the principles she strove to implant in the mind of her pupil could ever take root in soil so profoundly alien, irrigated by so many discouraging influences ; and whether, in the long run, she was justified in trying to impose on the child of one nation the moral code of another.

Something stirred in the darkness beside her, and her groping hand touched something that shrank. Her fingers curled themselves instinctively into a bunch of thin cotton material.

" Ildefonso. Hombre—qué pasa ? "

She pulled into the dim light of the patio a youth of fifteen or sixteen, in a paper-thin cotton shirt that hung in strips over his trousers. Against the sun-bleached stuff his skin was nearly as dark as that of a Negro, and so dragged over the frail, bony foundation as to give the effect of a cadaver.

She caught her breath at the sight of weals, faintly pin-pointed with dried blood, along the curve of the spine. She touched them, and the boy winced.

" It hurts ? "

" Sí, señorita."

" Come with me."

" No." He managed, with an unexpected movement, to twist himself out of her grip, but did not run away. Under his drawn brows, he had the wary look of a little bull, that might drop its head and charge, but waits for the moment.

" Who beat you ? "

He was silent.

" Did you touch the car ? "

He burst into incoherencies. How should he do it—he, that did not know one part of an auto from another ? To drive one would give him a fear like the sea ! Bulls, after all, are creatures, with blood and hearts and intestines like human beings ; but the demonio that feeds on goma and gasoline is not to be approached save by those who are educated to it.

" No hay quien pueda decir nada de mí, porque soy un hombre de vien ! " he claimed with passion.

" Eres muy hombre, Ildefonso," said Mary. She touched him softly on the shoulder, and left him to his pride and his pain.

Chapter Four

I

IN THE yard behind the white-washed barn a boy strutted for the benefit of an audience—his spine hollowed, small buttocks well thrust out, montera pulled low on his smiling brow. (Ay, hombre, you won't be wearing that smile when you go out to meet your first bull!) His right elbow curved out from his side, his left was rolled into the embroidered satin of a miniature parade cape. Olé matador. Olé tu madre. Olé Niño de Maderas. An appreciative chorus rumbled in the shadow of the barn, making a pale frieze against the gilded darkness.

The hard, intense faces, split into smiles, were marked, in most cases, by their owners' occupation. No fatal accident had taken place on the Parral ranch in the time of Don Luis, but few of his herdsmen had escaped such minor disasters as being flung headlong into cactus—which might carve out an eye, or leave its eternal brand between chin and cheekbone—or getting the bull's horn in shoulder or backside, or breaking a limb or two through the shying of a panicked horse. Each was intimate with fear, and each could remember when he was sound and proud and gay, like the stripling who strutted out there in the sun. Several were rejects of the ring itself, and to them the spectacle was like the ghost of their youth—though none had been like Paco Ribera, sleek and self-confident, with a father, once a famous matador, now the prosperous proprietor of a dry-goods store, who could afford to stuff him with fresh meat and buy him suits from Manfredi's to mess up—just for the fun of the thing! The ghosts of their own starved, ragged youth rose beside the figure in the sun, and their eyes narrowed in speculation. With Paco's advantages, each felt, without malice, that he might to-day be the owner of a comfortable banking account, a business, a fine town house and a radio-gramophone. Alternatively, he might be crawling round selling lottery tickets, or he might be dead. On the whole, it was better to be a herdsman on the Parral ranch, feeding a wife and a dozen children on garbanzos and hoping a lucky number would turn up one day, than to be a Paco, with all his trouble ahead of him.

A little apart, supported by his sticks, stood Don Amadeo Ribera—El Cigarrón—trying not to look fatuous, and his friend, Don Luis, chuckling, but not much. A bitterness of envy soured his appreciation of the scene. The perfect balance of young limbs, straight back, well-muscled thighs and light yet sturdy calves cut into him.

"Show me your arm," he said abruptly. With a flash of teeth, the boy held out his right arm. As he smiled up in Don Luis's face, his eyes were like dates floating on blue-white enamel, the flesh on his cheeks ran like brown cream over the neat bones, his mouth was of red wax and his teeth matched the whites of his eyes. Handsome and proud, he aimed his beauty like an arrow at Don Luis's heart, as the dueño's thumb and forefinger bit into the stiff satin of the sleeve.

"A good arm for the sword and flannel."

"Such an arm," growled the father, "is not developed by kicking a ball about."

Recovering himself, Don Luis threw back his head and roared with laughter. The other turned on him.

"Na, Luis! What is there in putting a lump of leather between two sticks ?—The diestros of el futbol are persons without honour or breeding ; they are not caballero—and a great many are communists," concluded Don Amadeo, with vicious satisfaction.

"Olé matador," observed Don Luis politely. He signed to one of the men, who went towards the barrier behind which the dewy muzzles and rough backs of the little calves were milling and tossing. The gentlemen withdrew, to sit on the shafts of a wagon, and a thin boy moved forward, with a smile of exquisite and respectful shyness, to take the " matador's " cape and offer him in exchange the small magenta and yellow fighting cape he bore, folded, across his arm.

" You look fine, Paco." He spoked with gentle envy.

Gratified, Paco was too grand to show it, and frowned past the speaker's shoulder at the bunch of small boys who were edging eagerly forward, their serious faces straining towards him with hopeful impatience, bumping him, touching him, each trying to make sure he would not be overlooked by this glorious Paco, the personification of their dreams. Their excited bodies stank of dirt and hunger ; Paco, who was fastidious, brushed the sweaty small hands away ; he had not put on his new suit to be mauled by the kids, and he was already annoyed and disappointed by Aracea's absence.

" Don't mess me !—Pues, Ildefonso, you're my peón de confianza, and you, Rafael, go in first. Nobody else is to come in the ring unless I give permission "—a wave of bitter disappointment passed over the straining faces, but Paco meant to dominate. "You, Gatito, can carry the water—and mind you're there when I want you "—a virtually naked gnome, rejoicing in the name of Little Tom-Cat, cut a hilarious caper at this mark of favour—" and Rogelio can hand me the swords, for once. Mind you fix the rag properly——"

The rest had turned away, downcast—but a shrill squeal went up from Little Tom-Cat, galloping across to the shed for the pipote of water, which had been left in the shade.

" Olá ! Ya viene Aracea ! "

All the way there in the car he had been smiling to himself, thinking how she would look, and what she would say, when she saw him in his " suit of lights." He had managed, with great difficulty to keep the secret at their last meeting ; bursting to tell her about the colour, and the embroidery and the deference paid by the famous house of Manfredi to the son of El Cigarrón, he had, by means of supernatural restraint, contented himself with rousing her curiosity. " I'll have a great surprise for you, next time you invite me ! " Resisting her pleading and her petulance made him feel manly, as he laughed and waved her good-bye.

" Give me those things," he muttered, as he snatched the cape and montera back from Ildefonso, crammed the latter on his head, wriggled his elbow into the former, and, as Aracea reined her horse at the corner of the barn, took half a dozen smart steps forward, rose on his toes, lifted the montera and held it up towards her—the attitude of the dedication—with a radiant smile.

Mary wished she had a colour camera. The sky, the blue sierra, the green plain pouring down to the white buildings, the chalky-jade clumps of cactus, the groups of pale figures dyed to the colour of the roseate earth—all made a painted backcloth to the kingfisher-bright figure stabbed like an exclamation point in the centre of the bright dust ; the sun blazed a line of steel down the small, polished head, and drew a shadow sharply at the feet.

As the audience started laughingly to applaud, Paco's attitude of unconscious nobility became a swagger. Clapping the montera back on his head, he strutted up to the horse and offered his hand with a flourish, to help Aracea descend.

Ordinarily she would have disdained assistance, but transported, even dazed, by her playmate's magnificence, eyes blank with admiration—she reached slowly down to place her bandaged hand on the brown fist. Eyes still fixed, as in a trance, on Paco, she pulled her leg absently over the pommel, but remained standing, one foot in the stirrup, until Paco, fully conscious of the admiring audience, placed his hands on her waist, the way he had seen gentlemen do for ladies, and swung her down. It was his first exercise in the courtesy, and it was due at least as much to Aracea's agility as to his skill that the pair of them did not roll on the ground ; but a chorus of Olés rolled from the barn as the children stood face to face, their eyes reflecting each other : his with smiling pride, hers stricken into unsmiling respect.

" Qué guapo eres tu," breathed Aracea.

II

Mary strolled towards the shade, discreetly acknowledging the salute of the gentlemen, but not joining them. Had she been foolish, to relent, and let the child have the treat to which she had so much looked forward? She did not believe in labouring punishments, and the stormy night was succeeded by a peaceful morning. Aracea was too intelligent to sulk, and had learned the futility of appeal against her governess's decisions. After breakfast, she went meekly to the schoolroom, and accepted in silence her allotted task: *The Donkey*, by Gilbert Chesterton. Words like "errant" and "parody" were additions to her vocabulary, and, thought Mary, something of the pain and pity of the verses might penetrate her heart. Having a memory like a parrot, she knew it well enough to rattle it off at the end of half an hour, and accepted corrections of her pronunciation with more grace than usual.

" 'Parody' is something to make you laugh," she said glibly, "and 'errant'—that's like Don Quijote. But it's silly," she objected. "How can ears be 'errant'?—And Don Quijote didn't have long ears like a donkey!"

Having done her best to combat the literalism of her pupil's mind, Mary picked up her needlework.

"Now write it out. And you can ask me when you're not sure about the spelling."

Aracea cast a doleful glance at the clock, opened her lips, and closed them, after a glance at Mary's calm face. With a deep sigh, she picked up her pen. Presently she pulled a face, leaned back, and nursed her right hand pitifully with her left.

"It hurts."

"Then you're holding the pen too tightly."

"No, it hurts where I bend it."

"Nonsense." Mary smothered a smile. "It's your left hand you cut; you've only got a few little scratches on that one."

With a look of limitless reproach, Aracea wrote a few more

words, wincing from time to time and drawing her breath through her teeth, as proof she was suffering.

" May I have a rest, now ? "

As Mary, threading her needle, made no reply, she waited before resuming coaxingly.

" Miss Mary. When I have finished writing about the burro, can we go down and watch Paco with the calves ? "—She put down her pen and went to lean against Mary.

She had never done that kind of thing with " Miss Bax," but this was different. When Miss Mary was angry, she neither raised her voice nor lost her temper : which, impressing Aracea in the beginning by its strangeness, ended by gaining her respect. Another odd thing about Miss Mary was that, for good or ill, she kept her word. For some curious reason, she also took it for granted that other people kept theirs—which put one, some-times, in embarrassing positions. If she had raged, or cried, on finding she was mistaken, it would have been funny, but she never showed anything but a cool surprise, that in some way stung one's pride.

Aracea hesitated, then dropped the top of her head against Mary's cheek, like a little cat inviting caresses. She was not used to fondling or being fondled, and usually stiffened up and wriggled away from attempted contacts, but there was something fresh and clean about Miss Mary that reminded one of nuzzling into spring grass.

" Oiga ; I am good now. And I want to see how Paco is with the rag and the sword. I know I can beat him with the cape——"

This time Mary allowed her smile to come, broad and generous, as she slipped her arm round the childish body. Looping her needle into the stuff, she took Aracea's chin between her finger and thumb and looked straight in the child's eyes.

" So you're good now, are you ? "

" Sí-sí," nodded Aracea emphatically.

" Then—when you've finished your work—you may watch : on a condition. That you tell your father it was you, and not Ildefonso, who damaged the car."

" Of course ! "—Aracea gave a joyful skip, that ended in a shrug. " I will, if you like. But it won't matter, to Papá."

" It mattered a good deal to Ildefonso. His back is very sore this morning."

" I expect Capanegra's back is sore too. But the pricks were very tiny, weren't they ? " she asked anxiously. " And I think he was too angry to notice much, at the time. I hope the flies aren't bothering him.—Please, Miss Mary," she begged, " while I finish my writing, will you tell Concepción to put out my calzones, and order the horses ? "—She threw another distracted glance at the clock. " We'll miss it if we don't make haste."

III

" I've got something of importance to tell you after."

Aracea, who had recovered from her awe, was displeased that Paco had overlooked her bandages. She drew them to his attention.

" Oh yes," said Paco carelessly, " Don Luis said something about scratching your hands——"

" You suppose I wear bandages for a few scratches ? "

Paco took this with fine, masculine off-handedness.

" Come now ! You know if a man gets the horn up his arse, we call it a scratch !—But you must have had a near squeak——" The fury in her face warned him to atone for his flippancy. " Qué miedo. I wouldn't like to have lain like that, right under the bull's nose," he was kind enough to admit.

Mollified, Aracea began to preen and to boast.

" The horn was here "—she pointed, untruthfully, to her chest. The colour changed faintly under the boy's skin ; he had more imagination than Aracea, and one does not much want to think of things like that, just before facing a lively becerro. " And you know what I did ?—I put my hand," she said slowly, " the bloody one—on the bull's horn, and pushed it aside, like that——"

" Muy noble," muttered Paco, genuinely impressed.

54

" Listen ! and I called him," pursued Aracea, now fully launched on her romance. " ' Capanegra,' I called him : ' hijo mio.' Because he's my own little bull : the one I fed with the bottle. And though he'd had his pricks, he let me put my arm round his neck and lead him out of the lot. How is that for a brave bull ? "

Someone shouted for " Música " and ripped a string of chords from a guitar—recalling Paco to his duty. As he slipped past, he flung at her across his shoulder :

" Anyhow, I'm going to fight in a *real* becerrada the week after next ! "—recapturing his superiority, and leaving Aracea with the breath smitten from her lungs.

She obeyed without spirit the summons of her father. Mary, watching the deadly stillness of her face, wondered what Paco had said ; what had gone wrong.

The first calf that came floundering out of the pen pranced round like a goat, and was far too inebriated by its new-found liberty to pay attention to the small boy who tore out, cutting the dust with an old fighting cape. The spectators roared with laughter. Paco bit his lip, while the luckless Rafael ran himself to a standstill in the effort to gain the calf's attention. Puffing and blowing, he cast an agonized eye at his leader for permission to desist, but a furious gesture from Paco sent him back to his doleful occupation. Worn out at last, the inevitable happened ; he tripped over the cape and fell flat on his face, thus, for the first time, drawing the eye of his quarry, who, galloping up, dealt him a cheerful dunt in the buttock with a horn-bud, then, apparently shocked by his yells, capered away, while the victim scrambled to his feet and, holding his bottom, made full pelt for the safety of the barn.

" It's a manso," muttered Paco disgustedly. No one could do himself justice with a manso, or tame calf, which, continuing to conduct itself like a ballet dancer, had again lost interest in the business in hand.

" Shall I take it, Paco ? "—Ildefonso offered himself humbly, and Paco nodded. It is the business of the cuadrilla to spare its maestro the indignities of the fight. The thin boy moved out on the dust, and waited for a moment, gravely, before shaking out his cape. The calf stood still.

" Who is it ?—He looks like a gipsy," rumbled Don Amadio. Don Luis shook his head.

" The son of one of my herdsmen. His brother fought a couple of seasons—but this one is better."

Their experienced eyes narrowed on the frail figure in the sun ; skeletal, under-developed, the nodules of the vertebrae showing all down the scarred, uncovered spine—something came off it only to be recognised by the initiate. Relaxed almost to limpness, Ildefonso stood, his head drooping towards the left shoulder, regarding the bull out of the corner of his eyes with an effect only of semi-attention ; but the yard had ceased to be a circus. Sensing the change, the calf dropped its head, backed a pace or two and scraped up the dust.

" Ildefonso is my daughter's maestro." Don Luis chuckled quietly, and nudged the child at his side. " That's the truth, isn't it, hija ? "

Aracea nodded absently. She did not care about the calf, or Ildefonso. Her eyes were on Paco. Why should she, who could cape him out of the ring, be debarred, on account of her sex, from wearing the suit of lights ? Why should Paco be given his début with the becerros, while she sat in the schoolroom, learning stupid poems about burros ? She felt so sick with Paco, so furious and so jealous, that she would have liked to stalk away ; leave him to his calves ; show her indifference to his suit of lights. But her father would probably regard that as an insult to Don Amadeo. There was nothing for it but to stay in her place. She stayed there, sullen and smouldering, dodging the pressure of Don Luis's hand on her shoulder.

Ildefonso wheeled slowly, to face the calf. The limpness was gone. He murmured " Huy, toro," and stamped his foot.

The change came with astonishing suddenness. A rusty flash crossed the dust and was taken into the fold of the cape that received and passed it on smoothly and calmly : Why hurry, little bull ?

Taken aback, but gallant as a brave calf should be, it recovered

56

almost instantly and came in again—to be received and dismissed in the same quiet fashion that roused at once its anger and its curiosity. The second rush brought a murmur—as much for the bull as the boy—"Así un bravo. Así un Parral." Flattery for the dueño. Don Luis sat woodenfaced, but was glad his little animal had not let him down in front of his visitors.

Paco was edging up impatiently; he did not wish to share the honours with an underling. He saw, to his annoyance, Ildefonso gathering the cape towards his hip with the right hand, and shortening the swing. The media-veronica ?—What cheek ! But he would only make a fool of himself, and get bumped; then Paco would go out, and, after a suitable preparation, show them how it should be done.

The calf came in so close, this time, that its shoulder brushed Ildefonso's hip as it turned in passing. And stopped dead. Olé torero.

His back to the motionless calf, Ildefonso spoke sweetly.

"There you are, Paco; he's yours. And he's as sweet as the sea."—He moved modestly away, to avoid the applause.

"Mucho estílo," grunted Don Amadeo, with his eyes on his son, but referring to Ildefonso. If Paco gave a performance as neat as that—hands low, and all the movements as slow as music —there would be something to be proud of.

Paco went in with a great flourish. He had got to efface Ildefonso's impression and prove himself in every respect a better torero—for honour of the new suit and the family name. You couldn't depend on little bulls, but this one was smart and straight running, and might give one a chance to pull a trick or two. After a few passes with the cape, he would end up, not, like Ildefonso, with the media veronica and recorte, but with the much more showy revolera, in which you spin with the bull, letting the cape fly out from one hand. Even if it didn't quite come off, it would look well, and finish the act in style. His father might laugh, but it would be admiring laughter—the kind that awards a plucky effort. Huy toro.

The calf looked at him slightingly. And trotted away.

Paco turned purple with mortification. He raced after the

calf, shouted, stamped his feet, jumped up and down, shook the cape and ended by slapping it across the calf's nose, in the vain endeavour to rouse its spirit. He called, in desperation, the whole of the cuadrilla into the ring ; they yelled and stamped, offered the calf indignities, like pulling its tail and tweaking its ears. Ildefonso, approaching it on his knees, shaking the cape right under its nose, got no reaction but a muffled bellow and some hoof-scraping. It was dazed. Alas, it was not a brave bull. Don Luis apologised vexedly to Don Amadio, who assured him, with sympathy, that these things happen in the best of herds.

Tears were steaming down Paco's face, as Ildefonso spoke to him gently.

" Mala suerte, hombre ; but the next will be good. It was bad luck you should get a manso."

" You just about cut it in half with that turn you gave it," snarled Paco. " If you don't know more about becerros than twisting their guts before they've been five minutes in the ring you'd better be a carpenter." Ildefonso hung his head ; his character was so humble that he accepted the blame without question. The day went dark for him.

On the second, after some scrambling and scuffling, Paco was able to retrieve his credit. To a chorus of Olés (flattery for El Cigarrón) he brought off his revolera. His work with the muleta and wooden sword was acknowledged to be in the tradition, he showed courage, skill and grace, the primary qualifications of the torero. Don Amadeo received with graciousness the felicitations of Don Luis, and Paco, radiant, received so much praise that his ill-temper was forgotten. He flung his arm across Ildefonso's shoulders.

" You shall help me to undress, chico—and praise God the new suit didn't get spoiled ! " he lowered his voice to add. Ildefonso, smiling and colouring with pleasure at the mark of restored favour, went to collect the capes and the swords. Don Luis signed for the car, and told Paco, who was streaming with sweat, to get in. Don Amadeo was helped to his seat, and Ildefonso, clutching his bundle, perched perilously on the back bumper. The car set off slowly, in a cloud of dust, followed by the children, running, yelling and letting off steam in the fashion of small boys obliged for too long to comport themselves in accordance with adult standards of behaviour.

Having waited for the dust to settle, Mary and Aracea followed the procession back to the house.

" Well ; what did you think of Paco ? "

After a pause, Aracea answered soberly :

" Very good. Very good indeed. Muchos cojones."

" That will do ! Because you play with the boys, there is no excuse for copying their language."

Aracea's eyes were absently fixed across the ears of her horse. She paid no regard to the reproof.

" But Ildefonso is best."

Mary gave her a quick look of commendation.

" I'm glad you agree with me."

" He does everything the right way," said Aracea slowly.

" Paco's ayudados are very pretty ; I think he's better with the muleta than the cape."

" Yes, he snatches," frowned Aracea. " Ildefonso keeps it quiet—the way he teaches me. He will be a great bullfighter some day."

" And Paco—— ? "

" Paco will have to be a great bullfighter ; he is the son of Cigarrón." She ended with an impatient sigh.

" What's the matter, chica ? " asked Mary tenderly.

" Papá never gives me a chance. He promised he'd let me ride in the tientas this year, but he didn't ; he made me go on the wagon, and that's how I got this "—she jerked her wrists impatiently. " He's only let me cape the becerros once or twice. It isn't fair "—She caught her lower lip in her teeth.

" But, chica, you're not going to be a bullfighter—— "

" Why not ? "—Aracea flung up her head. " Mi tía Carmela—— "

Mary's heart sank. She knew all about " mi tía Carmela " whose portrait—a shocking, mid-nineteenth century daub—had been removed, at Aracea's request, from the antesala to the schoolroom. " Mi tía Carmela " had been, according to legend,

a famous amateur rejóneadora, a well-known performer at charity
fights organised and patronised by the fashionable world of her
day. Unlike the majority of adults, Mary did not take childish
aspirations lightly ; she knew that bitterness and disappointment
lay ahead, and wondered what mitigation could be found.

" And who would look after the bulls, if you became a
fighter ? "

When they reached the house, she was told Doña Leandra
wished to speak to her.

Leandra was walking slowly up and down, with a cigarette
between her fingers. In the white peignoir, with her falling plait
of hair, she looked like a distracted schoolgirl.

" I shall take Aracea to town this afternoon. Will you please
tell her to be ready, about five o'clock."

" I'll see that she is.—The señora has remembered, of course,
that her friend Paco is here," Mary ventured to observe. Leandra
turned and fixed her with her large, dreary eyes.

" I think perhaps it is time she not play so much with the
boys."

Mary, who had, for some time, seen this coming, was silent.

" It is different in England, but our children grow up more
quickly."

" I realise that."

" She knows that other little girls don't spend their time
playing with servants' children and waving capes."

" If the señora will excuse me—she doesn't have much
opportunity of finding out what other girls do ; I mean, girls
of her own class."

" That is why I am going to town. We will have tea with
the de Gaulas. The marquesa's children are about Aracea's age.
They learn dancing. I arrange for her to join the classes."

It might be worse, reflected Mary. However much she
scorned the company of her own sex, Aracea might enjoy the
dancing.

" Has she anything to put on ? "

" I'll find out. She's been growing out of everything lately ;
I meant to speak to you about it."

" Do me the favour, Miss Mary, to tell Concepción to bring all her dresses in here, and send Aracea to me."

Aracea, clinging to the rejas of the schoolroom, was shouting to one of the boys on the terrace.

" Tell Paco I'm up here, when he's had his bath."

Mary laid her hand on her shoulder.

" Come along, your mother wants you."

" Por qué ? "

" I think she wants you to try on some dresses. You'd better get out of your calzones and let me put on some clean bandages."

" I can't. Paco's here."

" Be quick "—Mary pushed her towards the bathroom— " Put on your peignoir, and I'll look after Paco until you come back."

Muttering rebelliously, Aracea wriggled out of her breeches, swore as she knotted her dressing gown cord, and thudded furiously on bare feet to her mother's room.

. . . At five minutes to five, the Buick rolled into the patio. At twenty minutes past, a servant came down the stairs, with the embroidered linen covers which were buttoned over the seats when Leandra and her friends used the car. At half-past, drawing on her gloves, Leandra descended. Her hair and face gleamed like pearl through the cage of net that enclosed her small, high head and little cap of flowers.

" Where is Aracea ? "

" No sé, señora ! "

" Find her, and tell her I am ready."

The woman came running back ; the chica was not to be found.

" Ask the miss to speak to me."

The summons was unnecessary ; Mary was already hurrying down the stairs.

" I am sorry, señora. She was ready an hour ago. The telephone rang, and, as no one seemed to hear, I went to answer it. I left her in the schoolroom, looking at a magazine, and when I came back I took for granted she was with you. Conchita

61

has gone to look for her "—for once, she felt furious with Aracea, for putting her in a ridiculous position.

The servant she had sent in search of her leaned over the gallery to shriek :

" No está ! "—The one thing really intolerable about servants was their habit of making drama out of trifles.

" I had better go myself. I'm sorry you have been kept waiting, señora," she said vexedly.

" I will not wait," said Leandra, with languid impatience. " You will please find her, miss. I do not wish she spend the afternoon with her father and his friends."

Mary flushed ; it was one thing, to be treated as a servant by some of Leandra's visitors, another to be spoken to in that fashion before a sly-eyed chauffeur and an alert maid. She turned and went sharply up the stairs. She was going to find Aracea and teach her a lesson, this time ! But—she caught herself up— is my annoyance concerned with her silly prank, or is it on account of being humiliated before the servants ? Coming to the conclusion it was mainly the latter, she waited a few moments, to gain control of herself, before starting on a search which, at the end of half an hour, had yielded no trace of the culprit.

In the heart of the jungle that had once been garden, Aracea and Paco giggled, and she held up her finger at the sound of the horn.

" That's Tomás, blowing the children out of the way. Bueno ; now we can do as we please ! "—She twitched the muslin frill of her collar from the clutch of a rose that scattered its blood-coloured drops on her dark hair, and plunged her hand into her bosom to scratch. Both children were already devoured by the mosquitoes that bred in the rank pools. Paco was tearing at his bare legs, and slapping away the flies that settled on his neck.

" Gracias a dios, we can now get out ! "

She took a flying bound, followed by Paco, into the shoulder-high weeds—and let out a shriek. In her eagerness to escape, she had forgotten the shallow tank in their midst. A revolting stench of rotted vegetable matter mingled with the hot smell of herbage, and Aracea staggered out, with green slime wreathed round her ankles and spattering the short hem of her white dress.

" Mierda ! " she spluttered, for some drops of the disgusting water had splashed into her mouth. Looking down, she saw a bracelet of leeches round her shin. " Take them off—take the filthy bichos off ! " she screamed hysterically. Fortunately they had not had time to imbed themselves ; Paco plucked them off, with masculine contempt.

" You've made a fine mess of your dress. And women don't say ' Mierda ' ; you'll have to confess that on Sunday. I suppose Padre Gerónimo will give you a penance," he told her, self-righteously.

" Mierda to Padre Gerónimo." She grinned at him, recovering her assurance. " Do you like my dress ? "—Her head on one side, she coquetted at him through her lashes. Paco burst out laughing.

" Like it ! You should see yourself—— ! " He doubled up with laughter, but Aracea, pouting, persisted.

" You saw it before ! You saw it before ! "—In her eagerness she jumped up and down. " You like it ! Go on ; say you like it."

Worn down by feminine obstinacy, Paco mumbled :

" Muy linda. Anyhow, it makes you look like a girl."

" I don't care about looking like a girl ! "

" And I wouldn't like my friends in Maderas to see you on the plaza in your calzones ! " retorted Paco. " You look like a maricón ! "

" What's a maricón ? "—She snatched eagerly at the new word : but Paco, realising he had gone too far, and would get into trouble with his papa if it came out he had introduced the term to Aracea, mumbled :

" Something dirty. And if you tell that word to Padre Gerónimo, he'll probably say you'll go to hell."

Storing the word in her memory for future use, Aracea decided it was wiser to drop the subject, and observed :

" Anyhow, I don't walk on the plaza in my calzones—and I've never even been to Maderas."

" It's a fine town and ours is the finest house in it!" boasted Paco. " From our mirador you can see right into the ring."

" Plaza de Toros de Maderas ! " scoffed Aracea, who knew exactly the status held by Maderas in the bullfighting calendar.

The boy turned white.

" It's the best ring in Spain !—except "—he gulped ; one did not lie about things like that—" the Monumental and—and the Maestranza !—at least," he corrected himself, " it will be, when I've fought in it."

Something warned Aracea she had carried her teasing too far. Dragging herself free from the weeds, she sidled up to him and slid her bandaged hand into his.

" Will you dedicate your first bull to me ? "

" I—might." His surprised tone showed that he had never thought of it. He opened his eyes widely, but not on Aracea. Like all boys who follow the bulls, he saw ahead of him the sacred Vision : the fabulous hour, the crowded arena, the waving arms, the lifted trumpet, the opening of the door of the toril . . .

" Will you promise ? "

" If you like—I will.—' I dedicate this noble bull ' "—he stepped away from her. He lifted an imaginary montera to a visionary spectator. " ' I dedicate this noble bull to the incomparable señorita Aracea, daughter of Parral ' "—The words died on his lips ; his head was lifted, his cheeks quivering with emotion—and the vision passed. He dropped his head ; his body went limp ; the sidelong smile he turned on her was sly and sweet.

" Ay—*Paco* ! " breathed Aracea.

The evening light turned her face to beauty and blotted out the stains on her white dress. For the first time in her life, she felt contented to be a girl. The contentment might not last, but, for the moment it was there, like a purring kitten curled into her breast.

They had reached the edge of the jungle, where the old house cast its shadow upon them. The shadow was chill ; she shivered, but was happy. They turned and smiled at each other.

" You had better be my novia," said Paco off-handedly.

Chapter Five

" THEY'VE HAD a shocking time at my niece's factory. Of course, she can't write any details——"

" My family got into the country, but they've not got a stick left ! Not a stick ! "

Sipping her coffee, Mary listened to the interruptions, to the boasting, as each staked her vicarious claim on the horrors " at home." She had just finished reading the short, stiff letter from her sister, an officer in the WAAF, telling her that the friend to whom, on her (Mary's) departure for Spain, she had given power of attorney had been killed in the raid on Portsmouth. " I suppose," wrote Ann, " you'll want to appoint someone else, as you say nothing about coming home ? "

" Well, what about my niece Monica—in her last year at the Royal College ? It's iniquitous, to put a music student on the lathe ; think of her hands ! "

" It's terrible, to think of all those shattered careers. Doesn't *anybody* care about the future ? "

" Who says there's going to be a future ? " came in a raucous honk from the end of the table.

" Oh Potter, you know you don't *mean* that," in a frightened squeak.

" I see they've extended the call-up again."

" That'll catch a few more shirkers "—with vicious satisfaction.

" Surely there aren't any left, by now ? I can't imagine anybody worth her British name not wanting to do her bit— regardless of age groups."

" Yet here we sit in comfort "—The speaker flushed crimson and brought her hand hard down on the table. " I don't care what any of you say : it's *damnable*, to be old."

" I can picture circumstances in which it's more damnable to be young ! "—The woman who had spoken of " shirkers " lifted her voice. " Nobody can say of any of us that *we* haven't got an honest excuse, Potter ! "

The few Spanish in the tearoom lifted their heads with curiosity as " La Rubia " crossed to the table in the window. Four English faces met hers with a bitter antagonism. She looked down at the frowsy heads, the ancient English hats, the shabby tailor-mades of the " misses " who, since 1939, had drifted back, with their Spanish employers, from Biarritz and St. Jean de Luz.

" If you've finished talking at me, perhaps I may be allowed to say something ?—

" Long before the Spanish war you were drawing your living out of this country. You called yourself supporters of the Nationalists, but you didn't make much effort to stand by the cause to which you paid lip-service, did you ? "

" Our first duty was to our employers," came in a strong Lancashire accent from the head of the table.

" That's a good answer, Miss Harris—except in war time ! Why not say it's pretty difficult for someone of your age to justify her existence in the middle of a civil war ? I'm not blaming you ; but I do take exception to your sniping at someone who stood by her principles and paid a pretty steep price for it."

" In the shape of a comfortable job ? "

" In the shape of forfeiting her credit with her own countrymen," snapped Mary. " I understand your attitude ; it's no more than a foretaste of what I'll run into, if I go home and try to get myself a job to-day. Censorship, broadcasting, a responsible post in the Ministries—anything I'm really fitted for—they'll all be closed to me, on account of my Nationalist affiliations between '36 and '39."

" And the Forces ?—And the factories ? "

"I'm surprised," she said slowly, "that you subscribe, as educationalists, to the waste of literate material. There seems to be enough of that already. Miss Ferguson was talking, just now, about shattered careers ; Miss Monck was deploring—and I agree with her—the drafting of a music student into a factory. There are thousands of illiterates and play-girls to man the factories and drill on barrack squares : why should I, who have something valuable to contribute, make one of them ? It wouldn't liberate Miss Monck's niece, or prevent an art student from being called up, or some wretched, sensitive girl from deserting from a job she's totally unfitted for.

"I know how you feel," she concluded, "and I honour you for it. You resent being out of the war picture—through no fault of your own. But that doesn't give you the right to push me in, as proxy !—' I stand for sacrifice ; The rest aloof are the Dardanian wives, With bleared visages, come forth to view The issue of the exploit ! '—You can play the Dardanian wife if you like, Miss Potter : but you'll have to find another sacrifice ; I've thrown up the part."

She had no right to be so angry—and the " Dardanian wives " line was sheer brutality. She turned away, her heart filled with shame, and pity for those grey sisters whose lips had never known a lover's kiss. Steady, now, steady : that was forbidden ground. For four years she had disciplined herself never to think of love, or of a mutilated body stretched on a sidewalk, that stood for the end of her womanhood.

Her heart beating quickly, she paid her bill and walked down the stairs.

A long tourer shot in to the curb with a shrieking of brakes and furious clanging from the street car under whose bows it had cut.

"Muy buenas, Miss Carpenter."

She started, then smiled doubtfully, conscious of observation from the window overhead. One more black mark against her ! The name of Don Carlos de la Cerna, related to all the families of Sevilla, and linked into most of the scandals that stirred behind the rejas of the great sevillan mansions, was, to the misses, synonymous with that of Don Juan Tenorio.

" Good afternoon, Don Carlos."

" What are you doing here—all alone ? "

His smile and everything about him, she thought objectively, was charming ; even the black eye-patch. His looks, before a shell-spinter nipped out that eye, were probably a little too spectacular. Lounging in the driving seat, his other disability, which had taken him out of the Cavalry, did not show. She had heard from Aracea the story of the hand grenade that killed his horse under him, and reduced his left leg from the knee-cap down to pulp. An artificial limb had replaced it and in the eyes of most people, contributed to the romantic halo surrounding the handsome bachelor in his late thirties, whose bone-thin face, prematurely lined, wore a permanent mask of gaiety.

" I'm taking a little holiday," she smiled back at him.

" You are staying in town ? "

" Oh no ; I'm going out on the autobus—presently."

" I am going out too," he told her quickly. " I hope you will give me the pleasure of your company."

" I expect you'll be leaving too late."

" Too late for what ? "—His eye twinkled at her.

" Too late for me," said Mary primly. She had no business to be flirting with the dueña's cousin, and there were other reasons, she reminded herself, why she should not encourage his attentions. So—" Hasta la vista," she concluded, and made to turn away.

" Please, Miss Carpenter ! "

His English was better than Leandra's, and he never addressed her, as most people did, as " Miss Mary," or " Miss." It is a pity, she thought ; we might have been friends. Since taking up her duties in the house of Parral she had gone very short of friendships ; apart from its isolation, and the ambiguity of her position in the eyes of Leandra's visitors, she had felt no affinities among the few who deigned to take notice of her—with the exception of Carlos de la Cerna : and this exception, her instinct warned her, was a dangerous one.

" I expect we shall meet at supper, Don Carlos."

" I have only to do a little shopping, and see a friend. Please let me pick you up in—say "—he pushed back the glove from a wrist darkly coated with smooth hair—" an hour's time. I hate driving alone ; please be kind ! "

The temptation to exchange the jolting and crowded autobus for a high-powered car, not to have to walk the last half-mile from the dusty parada, was irresistible. She gave in—hoping her hesitation had not been interpreted as coquetry.

" May I give you a cocktail first ? "

No—a thousand noes ! The news would be round Sevilla in an hour, that the " miss " from the house of Parrai had been seen in a bar with Carlos de la Cerna.

" No, thanks—I'm going to the Cathedral. I'll meet you at the Puerta de Oriente, at half-past six," she said hastily.

The green dusk was gathering and the bats flying low. The little fawn-coloured hawks that swing about the Giralda had settled for the night. As she strolled across the plaza, where the gardeners were watering the beds of zinnia, she was conscious of the privilege of seeing a great tourist centre divested of its foreign element : Sevilla, purely and perfectly itself, with its own intensive pre-occupations.

With the return of its aristocracy, the blooming of its patios, and lights burning behind rejas that had been dark for two whole years, it had managed to recapture its ebullience—finer and more delicate in quality than that displayed for the foreigner. Networks of scaffolding crawled over ancient façades or indicated the site of new buildings ; fabricas were in process of construction ; there was talk of the revival of the glories of the feria, of a fine new casino to replace the old, flea-bitten Kursaal. Presently when the European war was over, the shutters would come down from all those windows along Sierpes, Franco and Tetuan ; the shops that sold paper fans and castañuelas and machine-made shawls and mantillas, and metal plaques of the Macarena, and horrid little plaster models of the Torre del Oro and the Giralda would resume their trade with the multitudes of tourists on whom so much of the local prosperity depended.

For the present, Sevilla was pure and calm—a chalice brimming with the essence of its past. As she set foot on the worn slabs of stone that give access to the Patio de las Naranjas, she paused to visualise the scene, when Yusuf Abu Ya'kub's Court of Ablutions covered this noble space, and the voice of muezzin fell from the minaret yet uncrowned by the symbol of Christian faith. The sky behind the Giralda was an emerald veil faintly pierced by small, pale stars, and the foliage of the orange trees hung dead, each leaf cut and polished in ophidian. Her feet stirred a dust of blossom and sent a withered ball rolling towards one of those immemorial figures, intrinsic to the Spanish scene, that sit hunched on the brim of fountains. Starvation looked at her out of a pair of bleared eyes. Begging was now forbidden, but Mary dropped alms into a trembling claw, and received a whispered blessing.

She knelt in the chapel of Nuestra Señora del Pilár, said her prayers : first giving thanks for Spain's deliverance from the powers of evil and the restoration of its ideals ; then asking God to look after her own country, continue it in strength and deliver it from its afflictions. Then she sat quietly for a while in the near-dark, embroidered with golden candle-flames ; and, when she judged the time had come, went to the Eastern door where, something to her surprise, she found Carlos waiting.

II

" Do you enjoy your life on the ranch, Miss Carpenter ? "

" Very much." (What did he expect her to say ?)

" And Aracea ? "—He chuckled.

" She's a dear child. I'm devoted to her."

" That's very fortunate. She did not precisely—what is the word ?—endear herself to her former governesses," was the dry response.

" It's rather difficult, to be ' endearing ' to people who don't understand you."

" I was going to say something very impertinent "—He was still laughing quietly ; his delicate hands swung the wheel with an admirable precision that made light of the act of driving.

" Then don't say it," she cut in on him.

This time he laughed openly, throwing back his head and taking the balmy air on his long throat. They were cruising through the outskirts of the town, caught from time to time in the headlights of a car that roared past them.

" I am sure you, as an Englishwoman, are more than equal to impertinences ! " he teased her.

" Very well ; then *I'll* be impertinent ! " She had recovered her assurance. " It's the first time, in this country, I've driven with anyone who doesn't take it as a reflection on his personal honour if he doesn't tear the life out of his engine."

To her amusement, he took this seriously.

" We can go as fast as you like ! This car will do 200 k.p.h. Do you want me to show you ? "

" Thank you ; I much prefer it as we are."

" You are an extraordinary person," he burst out.

" For liking to drive at a speed that allows me to appreciate my surroundings ? " she taunted him.

" You are not at all the ' English governess.' You are much too young—and too good-looking."

" Don Carlos." This required taking in hand ; she stiffened herself. " I have lived long enough in Spain to appreciate the piropo. A compliment which is completely inoffensive in Spanish takes on another significance when it is translated into my language. This is a matter," she went on hurriedly, " that I couldn't possibly explain to you ; it's one of those things deep-buried in the convolutions of English character ! " She allowed herself to smile. " If you want to pay me a compliment, pay it in Spanish ; in that way I can accept it, as part of the natural courtesy of your people."

" Por dios, you mean the English do not pay compliments ?—Vaya, Miss Carpenter ! I have many friends in England ! "

" The connotation is different," said Mary primly.

"But I speak very good English!" he protested.

"Excellent English," she agreed. "I only hope Aracea will speak as well, by the time I have finished with her."

"We have many English affiliations. My family, as you know, are vine growers; Leandra belongs to the intellectual branch—Madrid and Segovia. She is very beautiful—mi prima —isn't she? It's a pity she is so delicate. She has never recovered from my uncle's death. It's a psychiatric thing—no? She was a little in love with her father. Bad luck for Luis! And perhaps " —he flashed his teeth at her—" good luck for me."

She felt herself recoil.

But Carlos went on light-heartedly:

"You know the reason I spend so much time at the ranch? Luis, naturally, is worried there is no son to succeed him. If anything happens to him before Aracea is married, there is nobody to look after the bulls."

Relieved, she asked:

"And what about your vine-growing?"

"Carai—I am the youngest of four brothers! My career was to be the army. This little matter "—he flicked the artificial leg —" put paid to that! So now I must find myself another occupation, and, like Luis, I am fond of the bulls."

He braked suddenly beside a white-washed wall, swarmed over with bougainvillæa.

"Here we can get a glass of good wine. We are very early; shall we stop a little, Miss Carpenter?"

In a myrtle arbour, on the edge of a patio of trodden earth, they sat at a marble-topped table. A gipsy boy in a white jacket brought glasses, and a bottle of La Riva wine. Some one out of sight was plucking the strings of a guitar; a sudden strain of flamenco broke on the starlight and moonlight. Something rose in Mary's throat and strangled her.

At this very moment, in England, people were living in deadly fear. There was the thunder of guns, the noise that is like the ripping of a vast sheet of linen, the crash, the cries, the clouds of dust. What right had she to her immunity?

"Tell me about yourself," Carlos was saying.

"There's not much to tell. I fell foul of the censorship during the war, and resigned my job."

"Whose censorship—ours, or yours ? "

"Both. You know Press reports were fine-combed before they left the Teléfonica : that's just a war-time hazard. Your censorship was doing its job—according to its lights. But it was different our end. I oughtn't to be saying these things—but I happen to know about some of the letters that were written, protesting against reports that were pure Red propaganda—and never got printed. I used to be proud of my profession ; the whole essence of journalistic honour was check up, check up. You know what that means ?—Make sure of your authority before you print a line. That went by the board. I was ashamed to be a reporter—and Guernica finished it.—Do you mind," she burst out, " if we don't talk about it ? "

Her teeth clicked on the rim of the glass and her hands were shaking. Carlos said quietly :

"You were brave to stay on. The Reuter's man and two of the Americans had to get out. Delaprée of the *Paris-Soir* was murdered and Dautun of the *Petit Parisien* got away by the skin of his teeth."

"It wasn't courage. By then—I'd begun to care about Spain. It's fatal—in that kind of a job—to get emotionally involved ! "

"Who looked after you ? "

"Oh—I'd got a few friends. They sponsored me into a hospital job. I was determined to stay on," said Mary slowly. "All the literates, the articulate people seemed to be on the Government side ; we—so few in comparison with them !—had no time to express ourselves, except through action. I thought, if I saw the whole thing through, I might be able to write something that would stand—with intelligent people—for refutation of the lies our papers circulated, at home. That's why I became a Catholic. Nobody in England seemed to realise it was essentially a religious war."

"What happened after that ? "

"Well, I got ill—and the rest is rather confused. I thought, after the war, I wouldn't have much trouble, in finding work.

But it didn't work out that way. It's fairly tricky, holding an obsolete British passport——"

"You must have failed "—he frowned—" to make the right contacts."

"I was well in with the Falange—if you mean that. But, as an Englishwoman, naturally I can't subscribe whole-heartedly to a dictatorship, except as a stepping-stone to the restoration of the monarchy."

"But your monarchy," he reminded her, "is only a figurehead."

"That's true," she agreed. "A figurehead, maintained by national sentiment. It's a symbol—like the hammer and sickle. And you know how powerful a symbol can be."

"We need more than a symbol. The Spanish, Miss Carpenter, are rationalists; we are not governed, like your people, by sentiment."

"Yet," she said quickly, "you accept the symbol of the Cross."

After a brief silence, he lifted his hand to summon the waiter.

"Chico: who's playing the guitar?"

"My brother; does he molest the señores?" asked the boy, with the quick sensitivity of the gipsy.

"Ni na ni na. Tell him to play the malagueña.—You like flamenco, don't you?" he asked Mary, as he refilled her glass.

"I don't know very much about it," she admitted. "Sometimes I hear them singing in the village, and, of course, Don Luis's friends, when they have a tertulia——"

"I suppose my cousin never plays now?"

"Doña Leandra?—I've seen an old guitar, but I did not know it was hers."

"She was a superb guitarrista, a pupil of Segovia. You should have been at the musical parties at my uncle's house in Segovia. Everyone came—the maestro himself, once or twice; Granados and all the great amateurs of the cante jondo. Falla dedicated one of his best works—I've forgotten which—to my cousin. And one summer the Argentina came, with her company; carai, that was a famous night! I was only a boy of

ten or eleven, but I fell madly in love with her; I wanted to
kill everyone who went near her. It is not many that can boast
they have danced the sevillana with La Argentina!"—He was
smiling, twisting the glass between the thumb and forefinger of
his impossibly narrow hand. He had placed her on his left, so
that the eyepatch was hidden behind the immaculate sculpture
of his profile, and she had a brief vision of the beautiful child,
transported with passion for the dancer. He must indeed have
been wonderful to look at, in his youth: the blue-black hair, the
long-lashed grey Andalucían eye, the bitter-sweet mouth and fine
polished skin drawn tight over the jawbone . . . She said
hurriedly:

"I think it is time we were going"—to which he paid no
attention, turning sharply to clap his hands. The boy came
running.

"Su servidor."

"Tell the guitarrista to come here. Dance," said Carlos
curtly. "This boy," he informed Mary, "is a famous dancer;
one of the few remaining."

A semi-circle had formed itself as by magic: the blind guitar
player, his guide, a slick youth in a city suit who carried a
bandurría, some landworkers from the tavern at the end of the
patio, the padrón and his wife, and some old women who stood
modestly in the background. Mary thought, This is crazy; I was
mad to come. There was little hope, now, of concealing her
innocent escapade from her employers.

The players bent over their instruments and let out a sudden
fury; "Olé," muttered Carlos, and started to clap out the
rhythm; the others copied him.

The boy, who had pulled off his white coat, leapt into the
crescent formed by the audience; from the crown of his head
to his heels his body described a lithe S; the crack of castanets
came from his fingers that dropped before his lowered brow;
his hair was like a wild bird's wing as his feet drummed the earth.
Anda niño. Olé. Toma. Así se baila. Olé gitano.

III

She found herself staggering across the patio. One of the old women opened the cancela for her. On the road white with moonlight the long, pale car waited, guarded by several youths. The old woman shuffled after her. Mary opened her handbag automatically, to drop a few coppers in the palsied hand.

" Dios se lo pague. The señorita will come again.

" The chico dances well. But——" She bent her head to catch the whisper—" the señorita should have seen Don Carlos —ay ay, qué lastima ! He was the best dancer of them all."

Carlos limped out and handed her into her seat.

" You are very silent, Miss Carpenter."

" I'm sorry ; I was thinking."

" We are perhaps going too fast ? "

" No, not at all," said Mary hurriedly. If travelling like a comet could save her credit with the house of Parral, she was willing to risk it.

" We shall be there before ten," he told her carelessly. " There are not many places now, where you can hear the flamenco. The radio is exterminating all that. What a perfidious invention ! " he muttered—and laughed. " I pay them not to instal it at that place. It is rather an expensive arrangement," he confided, " but it is worth while—to preserve for a little something of the essence of our soil."

" Then—is flamenco dying out .

" It will not ' die out,' any more than the bulls, but it is like a person suffering from poison—the poison of the cinema, the radio, the ' swing ' from New York. The young guitarristas now play ' Slow boat to China ' and ' Begin the béguine,' instead of the solea, the seguidilla and the martinete ! The boys and girls dance the foxtrot and most of them don't know the sevillana. It is difficult to find a patio that is not within earshot of some pestilential loud-speaker.—I think I am giving you the impression I am old-fashioned ? " he interrupted himself, and continued through her disclaimer, " It is not that at all. I used to go to dances three or four times a week ; I danced the foxtrot with young ladies who visited my mamma, and the Black Bottom with the ones who didn't ! "

" You must miss that very much."

" Ca—*that* is not the dancing I miss." (" He was the best dancer of them all "—the whisper came back to her.) " But a little mishap like this "—he rapped his artificial leg—" leaves one with time for thinking. Although the Church has been restored to us, there are still many evil influences at work in Spain."

" Do you think, then, it's deliberate ? "—She was startled.

The hum of the engine filled a pause. He said slowly :

" Obviously, the jazz, and the crooning, and the señoritas exhibiting themselves on the pelota courts in little dresses that show off their breasts and bottoms are what people call ' signs of the times ' ; there is no real harm in them—any more than there is harm in Aracea going about in breeches, for which she would have been locked up in her grandmother's day !—But the geniuses who directed our enemies during the war know how these apparently harmless things can be forged into weapons.— Excuse me, I think I am boring you——"

" Indeed you are not."

" In my country," he told her, " we have always lived for and by our arts. The bullfight, music, the dance—with these a man can live. Without a roof over his head or a meal in his stomach, he can *live* ! " he repeated passionately. " Our arts are the momentum of our existence ; they have survived through all our tribulations, and they carry the same message to-day that they carried in the days of Bibirambla. They are there as an outlet for all our frustrated passions and an embodiment of our dreams. They are universal ; there is no question of monopoly by one class or another. I would say, a man is Spanish in direct ratio to his appreciation for the arts of his country. If I am told Fulano de Tal is a Red, but he is a lover of flamenco and a follower of the bulls, I can take him by the hand and damn his politics. I know he is an honest fellow who has come under a bad influence, but for whom there is hope."

" There is at least some comfort in that. I suppose art is the one incorruptible thing——".

She started, as his face turned towards her with fury.

" Be sure the Russians know what our arts stand for to us ! —that through weakening their hold on us as a nation the whole of our racial ethic may gradually be destroyed ! You may take my word for it, Miss Carpenter : the infiltration of Hollywood films and juke-boxes and dances out of Harlem is no matter of ' progression with the times.' It is a brilliant propaganda, whose first object is to destroy us morally, then to drive a wedge between us and our past ; so that, when the moment comes, we shall be like scattered sheep, rushing about with no sense of direction ; at the mercy of the first dogs that come along to drive us into the Russian fold."

They had left the highroad, and, lurching and bumping over the rutted surfaces, Mary was obliged to clutch at the upholstery to prevent herself from being flung against him. The great moonlit blur of the pastures stretched before them, and a few faintly twinkling lights signalled the approach to the ranch.

" So what you really need," she gasped, " is a revival of your ancient art forms——"

" Revival ! "—To her surprise, he chuckled. " What an English word ! Hot Gospellers—Salvation Army—Pentecostal Pilgrims : no ? "

" What an extraordinary knowledge you have—— ! " She could not help echoing his laugh.

" Oh, we were brought up to read everything," was the careless reply. " My uncle Ramiro was very anglophile, and his opinions had a great deal of influence with the younger generation. My parents did not exactly approve, but I was allowed to spend most of my holidays in Segovia, and there were always English boys there—students from my uncle's university. Leandra fell in love with one of them. I mean it. Seriously ! "

" She must have been absolutely beautiful. I am sure they all fell in love with her."

" Naturally. It is a pity. She might have been quite happy, married to an Englishman."

" I suppose the family didn't approve ? "

" He was Protestant." Carlos shrugged his shoulders. " Leandra was always a little foolish. There were several nice boys of good Catholic families ; it really was not necessary to choose the heretic."

" What happened ? "

" Oh, there was a frightful scene ; my aunt was extremely religious, and, between ourselves, uncle Ramiro was inclined to be atheistical. That is to say, he got a great deal of fun out of teasing my aunt and arguing with the clergy. He always came back chuckling from confession ; I believe he used to make up monstrous stories to shock his confessor, and end up by admitting they were all romances—you know : like the libros de caballería ! But I suppose he decided it was carrying a joke too far, to allow his only daughter to marry a heretic."

She was again aware of his face turned towards hers.

" You must please forgive me for talking so much, Miss Carpenter !—but it is so exceptional, to meet a woman who is interested, and simpática, like yourself."

" I have enjoyed it very much." She added, before she could check the words, " I knew someone, once, whose ideas were very much like yours "—and could have bitten her tongue out, for he came back at her quickly :

" A Spaniard ? "

She nodded, frowning.

" He was killed in the war ? "

Resenting the intuition she herself had aroused, she answered shortly :

" I don't talk about it "—and thought how childish it sounded ; but he said calmly, after a little silence :

" You must find it very dull, at the ranch. Luis is a fine fellow, but he thinks of little but his bulls. And as for my poor cousin——"

" It is unfortunate, that she is so delicate." She hoped her quick interruption would warn him to entertain her with no more gossip about the household.

" It is not very cheerful for Luis !—However, I dare say we will liven things up a little, when I settle down to my job."

" What job is that ? " she prompted, as he paused.

" Haven't you heard ? "—He seemed surprised. " Luis is going to train me up in the business. It may surprise you to hear," he teased her, " that there is a good deal more to breeding cattle than branding them and turning them out to grass ! "

" Even I know more than that ! I talk to the mayoral, and once or twice I've helped Don Luis with his accounts."

" Caramba, you must be in his good graces."

" As a matter of fact, I'm not—really. But I happen to be good at arithmetic."

" Por dios—you must help me ! Luis threatens to turn the books over to me, and I am hopeless at paper-work."

" I shall be very glad to help—if I'm needed," said Mary demurely.

" I shall hold you to that promise.—Ay, isn't it beautiful ? " —He flung up his head and sniffed the balmy air. " Do you know what I'd like to do now ?—Get on a horse, and ride away between those folds in the hills——"

" Are you able to ride now ? "

" They have made me a special saddle. I can't do much at present but jog along the roads, but in a week or two you will see me handling my animal like a rejóneador ! "—A blare of radio came from the mayoral's house as they passed it. " Qué barbaridad !—Thank God Luis doesn't have it, except in the office."

" So you are really going into business with him," She hoped she did not sound too pleased, but the continual presence of Carlos would help to relieve some of the longueurs of the house of Parral.

" That depends. I can't afford a partnership at present, and that, of course, is what Luis would like. It is a misfortune he has no son, to carry on the name and the tradition."

The iron lanterns on either side of the main extrance showed them that the doors were shut. Carlos gave two blasts on the horn, and they waited in the moonlight. As the inner bolts clanged and the great leaves of the door grated back the car slid through into the patio and braked at the foot of the staircase.

" So I shall stay until I've learned all Luis wishes me to know," concluded Carlos, as he opened the door for her, " perhaps three or four years—and then——" He looked across her shoulder and grinned. Following the direction of his eyes, Mary saw Aracea, in her dressing gown standing at the top of the stairs. " And then," grinned Carlos, raising his voice, " I shall marry Aracea ! "

" Where have you been, Miss Mary ! "—Aracea ignored the jest.

" I'm sorry I'm late, chica——"

" But where have you *been* ? "—Aracea stamped her foot. Carlos, with a wave of the hand, vanished into the office. Mary bent to kiss her, reproaching herself for the fact that the child's face was burning and her eyes glittering with excitement. Aracea flung her arms round her neck and returned the kiss, but maintained her note of injury. " It is very wicked of you, to be so late, and made us all worry ! "

" Why should you worry ? I'm old enough to look after myself. Come, I must change my dress——"

" But what were you doing with Carlos ? '

" I went to the Cathedral—and I missed the bus."

" But the autobus goes at half-past five, and it's after ten o'clock ! "

" I know, chica—I'm sorry."

" Why didn't you take a coche ? "

" Coches are very expensive." She had been seen arriving with Carlos, and there was nothing but to tell the truth, or part of the truth ; it was to be hoped the interlude at the tavern did not come out, it would certainly increase the bad impression her unpunctuality had made. " Luckily, Don Carlos was passing, and he offered to bring me out—but he had several things to do, and I had to wait.—Now get into bed and I'll come and tuck you up when I've changed. Look, I brought you some turrón ; but you're only to eat one bit, and mind you clean your teeth."

The grey-and-white check, or the silk fantaisie ?—The latter

81

was new, and she had been "saving" it for some unspecified occasion; apart from fiesta days and the bullfight, she had seldom an excuse for dressing up. She felt its softness under her hand, and the innumerable little ruchings that made it softer and more feminine than most of her dresses. If she looked nice at supper, it might help to disarm criticism of her unprecedented conduct.

What a hypocrite I'm becoming—even to myself! she thought, as she snatched it from its hanger. As if I cared about their criticism!

When she had finished, the dim lights on her dressing table were kind; her reflection in the glass startled her a little—it was so long since she had looked like that: like the girl who came out in 1936 with a glowing heart and soul shining with ambition, eager to prove herself worthy of her first important assignment.

The soft, gingery hair which had gained her the title of La Rubia lay across a brow from which the faint light had blotted out the lines; her eyes burned brightly in their deep setting; her lips, no longer drawn and compressed, opened softly in a shy, incredulous smile. The shape of the dress made her look light and young and disguised her scrawniness; as she pinned her only brooch into the draped folds that gave her, for once, a "bosom," she realised her hands were shaking.

"Miss Mary—qué guapa!"—Leaping to her knees in bed, Aracea greeted her with a grin of admiration. "I've never seen you in that dress before."

"It was the first I got hold of. (God forgive me, how I'm lying to-night.) Come, lie down—oh Aracea! You've eaten all that candy—after what I told you——"

"Vaya—you're much too pretty to be cross. Do you know what I think, Miss Mary?"—Her smile showed the tip of her tongue and the whole of the entrancing little face sparkled with mischief. "I think you're in love with Carlos!"—With a triumphant shriek Aracea dragged the sheet over her head.

It was like a slap in the face. Controlling herself, Mary spoke coldly:

" I do not like that joke ; it is rude and it is not very funny. Now I am going to put out the light."

" I'm thirsty," whined Aracea. " I want some water."

" There you are "—she filled a glass and put the terra cotta jar within reach of the child's hand. " Now you are to settle down and go to sleep."

" I'm much awake," mumbled Aracea.

" Wide awake," Mary corrected her mechanically.

Her lips curling into a smile over the edge of the glass, Aracea shut one eye at her governess. Mary turned away her head quickly. It was an imp and a darling, and indeed it was difficult not to spoil it. She switched off the light.

" Miss Mary."

" And now what ? "

" Sabes que Carlos ha dado calabazas a la novia muchas veces ? "

She slammed the door before she had time to think. The impudence of it !—" Do you know Carlos has jilted lots of girls ? " Then her sense of humour revived. She smothered a laugh as she ran back to her room for a handkerchief. The night was warm ; it would be stuffy in the comedor. She pulled open a drawer, to choose a .fan from the little paper-and-palm-leaf collection she had accumulated in the South.

" Con su permiso, señorita ? "—The oldest of the servants stood there : one of those angel-faced ancients, beautified by devotion to the house where she was born.

" Do me the favour to fasten these two little buttons, Concepción. I suppose I'm late for supper."

The old woman made a gesture of obedience, but did not at once move to perform her task.

" The señora charges me to say that the señorita must be tired after her journey." (She used the word " rendida," which conveys more than tiredness ; Mary wondered why she was supposed to be exhausted after a few hours in Sevilla.) " The señora proposes the senorita should eat in her own room."

When she had recovered her breath, Mary answered :

" The señora is very good. Give her my thanks."

" Su servidora." She lifted her hands to the unbuttoned wristband, Mary drew her arm back sharply.

" No, it doesn't matter."

" Good night, señorita ; that the señorita may sleep well." The gentle presence withdrew, noiselessly closing the door.

So she was to be punished ! Really, this was ludicrous. It would in any case have been ludicrous, but from one young woman to another of practically the same age—— ! It was not the first time she had been brushed by that languid autocracy. Socially the equal of her employer, she had understood and accepted from the beginning the post of inferiority that the governess occupies in the Spanish household, and had taken pains never to infringe the boundaries of her situation. This had been made easier for her because Leandra usually made a point, in public, of showing her a courtesy which influenced at any rate the less thick-skinned of her social circle.

A hot flame of anger stung the blood into Mary's face. Was she supposed not to be trusted with Carlos de la Cerna ?—she who, on occasion, had played chaperon to Leandra herself, since it was still, in old-fashioned families like the Parrales and de la Cernas, considered indiscreet for a woman to go about alone.

But by the time they brought her supper, anger had given way to the pain of disappointment. For the first time since her arrival at the house of Parral she had enjoyed the companionship of an intelligent and attractive man. It struck her, now, how very isolated and wanting in stimulus her life had been, during the past twelve months ; how, apart from her duties, she had lived literally from bullfight to bullfight ; how badly she lacked an outlet for her thoughts and speculations. At nights, she had worked on her book, but, having reduced the notes that covered her time in Spain to something like order, she found herself unable to formulate the philosophy that was to link them together. For want of a human whetstone, her mental qualities had lost their edge ; her brain worked sluggishly—a fact of which she had been keenly aware while talking to Carlos de la Cerna.

Nor did her honesty, once started, stop at this. Had her

84

pleasure in his company been wholly intellectual?—Of course not. They had spoken briefly on a number of occasions, but always their encounters had taken place in the company of other people, who would have looked askance on any disposition on the part of Carlos and the governess to enter into private conversation.

She had, however, sensed his interest, and allowed him, more or less involuntarily, to be aware of her own; taking care both for her own sake and his to keep such intimations well within the bounds of discretion—not only in the presence of their equals, but before servants, with whom, invariably, the germ of gossip begins. It had not been easy. She was drawn physically as well as mentally towards Carlos de la Cerna, and it had seemed to her that the wound of her loss during the Civil War was a little numbed, since he crossed a corner of her life.

Her face burned again, at the realisation that Carlos, by now, must know of her " disgrace." If it was intended to lower her in his esteem, no doubt it had succeeded. Bitterer still was the knowledge that it made impossible any continuance of their acquaintance; each of his visits would resolve itself, for her, into a problem of avoidance.

What a fool—to dress up for the benefit of a man who had found you amusing for a few hours! That illusion of prettiness given her by her looking glass—indeed it was illusion! She knocked the paper shade off one of the lamps and, dragging back the hair from her brow, stared at her face as at the face of an enemy. What a fool. The septicaemia that set in while she was in hospital, nursing venereal cases—that had taken care of her looks, for good. The weeks she spent, mostly in hiding, before they got her away from Madrid—living on coñac and bad potatoes and the scraps of food her friends managed to smuggle to her (because the distribution of meal vouchers was in the hands of the trades unions)—unable, eventually, to keep anything down— had destroyed her digestion; it had been months before she was able to enjoy the rich and plentiful food of the house of Parral.

Yes, the marks of all that were on her face and her body. How could you possibly think, she asked her reflection bitterly, that a face and a body like that could attract a man like Carlos de la Cerna?—that they would tempt him to invite the disapproval, and possibly the derision, of his family, for the sake of pursuing an acquaintance?

Chapter Six

I

ALL OF Maderas was on the plaza; all of its tenebrous, back-street population, its beggars, its cripples, its old men and old women with faces of grievous humility—jostled by the señoritos in flashy, light-coloured suits with the shoulders padded out to unlikely proportions. Demure groups of girls, wearing their velos and clasping their books of devotions, streamed from the church door, to stroll up and down between the nisperos and the house-fronts on the shady side. A hot scent of frying oil was in the air, crowds collected round the lottery wheels, the trays of bitter and sugared almonds, the stalls of the gaseosa-sellers. But the biggest crowd was collected round the entrance to the Hotel Duquesa, whose patio resembled a hive of bees about to swarm. It was the day of the bullfight, and the espadas were putting up, as usual, at the Duquesa, so everyone who had the slightest excuse—and some scores who had none—crushed into the patio in the hope of getting a preview of the heroes.

In spite of repeated blasts on the horn, the Buick would have had small chance of penetrating the solid block of human bodies that formed a living barrier along the front of the Duquesa but for the intervention of the mounted police drafted in specially for the occasion, and themselves sufficient of a novelty to create an impression on the natives. Aracea, wild with excitement, pressed her nose to the closed windows, while Mary leaned back, wiping the sweat from her brow. The drive through the cork forests and through the shadeless mountains had been long and dusty ; their clothes were sticking to them with heat and she longed to wash and change into the fresh linen that was folded in a suitcase at the back of the car.

As Don Luis descended, Don Amadeo struggled forward, propped by his sticks, to receive his distinguished guests.

" Where's Paco ?—Why isn't Paco here to meet us ? " cried Aracea, struggling against Mary's restraining hand. In the babel of salute that greeted Don Luis, neither caught the reply, but Tomás evidently had his orders. Regardless of Aracea's protests, the Buick nosed its way out of the square into the calle Real— scarcely less broad than the plaza itself—at the far end of which stands the bullring.

" Where are we going, Tomás ? " shrieked Aracea.

He answered across his shoulder :

" To the house of Don Amadeo—the Casa Cigarrón : those were the orders of the dueño."

" Oiga, Luis," Don Amadeo was saying ; the pair of them had withdrawn into the cool dimness of the hotel. " We are in trouble."

" Como ? "—Don Luis's attention was less upon his friend than upon the drink someone, unasked, had put into his hand ; he mopped his neck fastidiously, tossed his hat in a chair and fixed his eye critically on the poster he happened to be facing : the name of Parral could have been given more striking representation.

" You know what we've got : Escorpio, Camacho and the boy from Medina that Gómez sold me on the strength of that novillada at Jérez de Marquesada. The Medina kid's been on the bottle for weeks, and Gómez is busy, now, trying to talk him out of this afternoon's show. It's murder to put him in the ring with those bulls of yours."

" Escorpio's all right ; he's taking the alternativa next week."

" Ya lo creo ! So he won't take on four Parrales this after-noon, instead of two. Na, Luis, times have changed ! You remember 1932—when the kid from Santafé undertook to kill six bulls, as a compliment to his province ? "

"Yes, and I remember them unpinning him from the barrera," said Don Luis dryly. "I remember what went on in Granada that night—and I remember we might have had one more matador, if Atarfeño hadn't been a fool."

"Sure." Don Amadeo chewed a hangnail as he muttered, "But I have to consider the credit of my ring."

"Camacho's not bad. It'll help his cartel if he takes on a couple more."

Don Amadeo exploded.

"And what'll the customers say?—I only put in the Medina kid because they expect three, and he was cheap!"

"Hombre!"—Don Luis's eyes narrowed; he despised economy in this connection, and, on the strength of old acquaintance, permitted himself badinage. "You do not, por ejemplo, propose to put me in, in the place of Niño de Medina?"

Don Amadeo ignored the jest. He muttered.

"I have always said my son should not work the novillos."

Don Luis gaped.

"You're thinking of the boy——?"

"I'm thinking of my ring. As between friends: what is your opinion of Paco?"

"He has much courage—hell!" said Don Luis; he was gravely taken aback. "You can't expect a boy of that age to kill Parrales."

The two men looked at each other in silence. Outside went on the uproar of the patio. In the eyes of each was reflected a boy with a skin of polished brown silk, the mouth of a rose and limbs that had yet to mature.

"He did well at Antequera with the becerros. Those children at Malaga—in '33, or '34—you remember——?"

"The younger one was a year older than Paco."

"They'd got less training. They weren't in condition, the way Paco is——"

"Vamos." Don Luis laid his arm kindly across Don Amadeo's shoulder. "Let's go and look at the Niño. A dose of cold water has done the trick before now!—and he can kill bulls, when he's sober. Now I come to think of it, I saw him——"

They were mounting the stairs, very slowly, because of Don Amadeo's infirmity—so the yell that split the plaza came to them only as an echo. But Don Amadeo, in the hypersensitive position of the manager whose credit is at stake, stood still, his cheeks whitening.

" What is that ? "

On one of the balconies of the Duquesa, overlooking the plaza, a wooden shutter crashed back and, its ancient hinge giving, sagged at an angle across the iron railing. Maderas held its breath long enough for the sound of voices and of breakage to reach the spectators on the square.

Nude to the waist, his hair on end like a porcupine's quills, a youth plunged on to the balcony, aiming, as he came, a back-hand blow at someone within. He was so tall that it seemed as though his rush would carry him over the rail. The screams of women were drowned in a yell of " Niño ! "

Bursting through the window behind him, a short, grey-haired man made a grab at the boy from Medina, who shrieked, wriggled like an eel, and, despite the grip of the other, managed to lift the bottle he was carrying to his mouth. The gin spurted out, over his face, over his chin, down his bare chest across which ran parallel lines of bone, and into his mouth. He went on triumphantly holding it until the last drop was gone, then tossed it out over the crowd, which yelled and ducked. The crash of glass on the cobbles added itself to pandemonium. Several other people now appeared on the balcony, to struggle with the tall youth whose drunkenness appeared to lend him demoniac strength, for he actually flung one of them over the balcony. While those nearest crowded round the victim, another shout went up—" Parral ! "

There were few who did not recognise the celebrated person, who, plunging through the window, flung his arms from behind round the maniac figure, and, after a short struggle, in which weight and muscle told, heaved it back into the room, and threw it with a crash that resounded below, on the marble floor.

Don Luis straightened his pale suit distastefully and touched his tie.

" I'm sorry, Amadeo. That has finished it."

" Mucho aburrimiento for the management," was the verdict from the plaza, and five youths, with the light of hope in their eyes, flung themselves on the mob and started beating their way towards the patio. It is through accidents like these that one may get one's chance in the ring.

II

Since the mass ended, the room behind the shop had filled itself with friends and relatives—elder sons with their wives, uncles and aunts, innumerable children. There were bottles of manzanilla and anis del mono on the table, and stone jars filled with the local riojo. There was garlic sausage, cut in paper-thin slices, and dishes of small pickled cucumber and tomatoes, cut in half and sprinkled with oil. There were plates of fat green olives, anchovies and strips of Trevéllez ham.

They had changed their clothes rapidly in a parlour that opened, conveniently, into a bathroom, and Aracea, coached in advance, had made her curtsey to Doña Amalia, the wife of Ribera ; to the wife of the alcalde, and to various other of the pale, bloated, lard-faced women who clumped themselves in corners, watching their men. Instantly clustered about by little girls, she brushed them off, and forced her way into a clump of boys surrounding Paco, who smiled at her with some embarrassment.

" Olá."

" Olá. I want to look at the bullring."

" The bullring—— ? " faltered Paco. Some of his companions sniggered.

" You said, from your house you could see the bullring."

" You can—from upstairs," he muttered. " But I'm going to the hotel. I'm being presented to Escorpio ! " he told her proudly.

" Oh—I'm coming with you ! "

" No, you aren't," said Paco hastily. " Girls can't go there."
He paused, for her eyes had filled with tears. " Por dios don't
cry ! I'll soon be back, and then it will be time to eat. Then
we'll go to the fight. We've got fine places—over the door,
close to the President's box : much better than the palcos," he
assured her, looking under his eyelashes to see whether his
friends were watching. It was all right at the ranch, where
everybody knew them, and Aracea was an important person ;
but here in Maderas he did not want to be teased. He was
obliged by politeness to speak to her, although he would much
have preferred to avoid or to dismiss her with a nod.

He was also uncomfortably aware of the difference between
Aracea and the Maderas girls, who, bunched like their mothers
in corners, flirted their plaits and bows and wriggled their
bottoms to shoot out the flounces of their Sunday frocks. Aracea
was too tall, and she strode about like a boy—although, God be
thanked, she was not wearing her calzones, but a little jacket
and pleated skirt of rose-pink linen. Her two short plaits were
turned up and bunched behind her ears with pink ribbon. Paco,
in a new pale grey suit and a flaming tie, supposed sullenly that
she looked nice, but resented the fact that she was making him
conspicuous. Mary, taking pity on him, was about to draw her
away, when one of the young men who served behind Don
Amadeo's counters rushed into the room.

" The Niño's out of it ! "

He was instantly surrounded by the men and boys, while
Paco slipped away ; none of the women except Aracea and Mary
took much notice. Aracea tugged at Mary's sleeve.

" What did he say ? "

" I didn't catch it ; something about Niño de Medina——"
Aracea darted back into the crowd before she could snatch her.

" What is it ? What is it about Niño de Medina ? "

Somebody turned, laughed, and turned back. Another,
recognising the daughter of Parral, answered her question.

" He's out of the fight."

" Por dios—but who'll take his place ? "

The earnest inquiry brought another laugh, this time of sympathy.

" Qué salero tiene—la niña ! Don't molest yourself, Aracita ! We have plenty of bullfighters in Maderas."

Doña Amalia and her daughters bustled away, to supervise the preparation of the meal—more important than any bullfight ; the men had gone out, and the countrywomen drew themselves together, shy of the inglesa.

" Miss Mary ; it will be too bad, if the bullfight is spoiled."

" It won't be. There is Escorpio, and Camacho ; they say he's very promising."

" Lets's go and light a candle."

They passed through the darkened shop, with its thick odours of cotton goods, garlic and fats, into the hot street. A stream of youths was running towards the Duquesa. Pale, ragged, set in their intention, each had known the kid from Medina was drunk from the moment of his arrival ; each had hung about the house of Ribera since crack of dawn, to offer himself in place of the novillero who, for some reason, had gone to pieces ; each was convinced he was known to Cigarrón, and that he could depend on the sympathy of an ex-matador, to get his chance. The fact that Don Amadeo had sedulously refused to see any of them had done nothing to reduce the optimism which is the chief stock-in-trade of the aspirant torero. They were off, now, hot-foot, to put in their claims ; several had bundles of red flannel under their arms. Mary's heart ached for each of the young, desperate faces, white with ambition, that flashed past. She recognised in one an espontáneo who had flung himself into the ring at Jérez, and whom she had saved, by paying the fine, from expiating his crime of valour in the Jérez jail. She decided, on impulse, to light a candle for him ; though she did not know his name, God would know.

They found the sacristan, bought their candles, and had the satisfaction of seeing them stabbed on the points of the iron bracket at the side of the altar. Then they walked back, in the simmering heat, to the house of Ribera.

Slowly the men started to drift back. They smoked puros

and drank, while an immense meal spread itself on the table :
soup, thickened with eggs, two vast pots, giving off an aroma
of wine and herbs—one of rabbit, with a rich wine sauce, the
other filled with jointed chicken, sausages, ham, veal bones,
onions and breasts of pigeon. The already hot room filled itself
with an overwhelming scent of hot, rich food. The guests
scraped their chairs across the stone floor, and Doña Amalia,
arrogant behind a pile of deep plates, ladle in hand, addressed
her eldest son.

" Y tu padre ? "

" Mi papá says to eat." He avoided his mother's eye. " He
will be back shortly, with Don Luis."

" And Paco ? "

" He is coming with Father," mumbled the youth.

" That is a fine thing, for a boy of his age, to go without his
food while grown-up people gossip ! " grumbled Doña Amalia,
as she plunged the ladle into the bowl and passed down the
steaming plates of soup. There was silence, broken only by the
noises of eating. One of the sons walked round the table, filling
glasses with red wine. " Gracias." " Salud."

But it's not like a luncheon before a bullfight, thought Mary :
or am I imagining ?—No jokes, no laughter, no compliments.
Heads bent over plates. Eyes that avoid encounter.

The tension was broken, eventually, by the entrance of Don
Amadeo and Don Luis. Olá, Don Luis ! Don Luis, with a tight
smile on his face, sat down in the seat of honour that was
reserved for him. Doña Amalia, filling a plate for her distinguished guest, was accosted by her husband. " Ven," said
Don Amadeo, and his sticks swung him towards the kitchen.
She followed obediently.

" Where's Paco ? " Aracea called to her father.

" He is coming, presently."

The words were interrupted by a shriek from the kitchen.
Two of the women leapt up ; the men exchanged glances.
Wailing came from the kitchen. Aracea jumped up and ran to
her father.

" What is it ? "

" Nada, nada. Paco is fighting this afternoon," muttered Don Luis.

Tongues were let loose; the table roared with comment, with discussion, with the drama of the day. One of the daughters went round, to remove the empty plates. Another took her mother's place at the head of the table. Heaped dishes were placed in front of Mary and Aracea; she saw Aracea pick up her knife and fork, and lay them down again.

" Do you feel sick ? " she asked, under cover of the noise.

Aracea shook her head. Mary looked at her. The soft, childish face wore a mask of reserve that aged it curiously.

Paco came in. But a different Paco. His parted lips acknowledged with a smile the roar of congratulation. There was no swagger left, but a strange aloofness. He bent his head over the plate his sister put before him, and ate in gulps. His face seemed to have thinned and he shrank a little from the boisterous shoulder-clappings of his neighbours. All the time his face wore that set smile.

Aracea looked at her one-time playmate. She did not want to eat. All she wanted, for the present, was to contemplate that new and strange Paco, translated on to a plane on which she had no place. Pieces of the past and the future slipped about in her brain, as in a kaleidoscope. It had come so suddenly. To-day, Paco's going to fight a bull. A grown bull. One of our bulls. Will he remember his promise, to dedicate his first bull to me ?

Paco lifted his head and looked at her across the table. But his eyes were two flat discs of black glass.

For the rest of the afternoon, the house of Ribera echoed with the lamentations of Doña Amalia. The scene resolved itself into a wake. Clustered about by the women, she gave vent to her resentment, her sorrow and her fear—under the scornful eyes of Aracea, who, leaning against Mary, expressed in every line of her small, contemptuous countenance her opinion of this female chicken-heartedness.

" Qué tonta ! She knows Paco is meant to be a bullfighter."

" Hush. Perhaps some day you will be upset, when somebody you care about is going into the ring."

"I never shall! It is the most noble thing anyone can do—to face a brave bull."

She groped into the neck of her embroidered blouse.

"Miss Mary. I'd like Paco to have my medal."

"All right. We'll find some way of getting it to him."

III

Up the stairs streamed the fans, the pressmen, the members of the Medina kid's cuadrilla, who, at the eleventh hour, had to make acquaintance of a new master; everyone who, by favour or persuasion, could claim entrance to the house of Ribera. Don Amadeo was up there, and Don Luis, contributing what they could of their wisdom and their experience to the boy who, half in a trance, and with only a few hours warning, was to make his début as a novillero, with Parral bulls. As they helped him into his jacket, Don Amadeo inquired anxiously:

"Is that comfortable?"

"It is a little tight, Papá; I think I may have grown."

Don Amadeo motioned to the dresser, who picked up his scissors, snipped a few stitches, and Paco drew a breath of relief. Someone came in and put a thin coil of chain into his hand.

"That is from the señorita Aracea."

Paco smiled, as he hung the medal round his neck, poking it down inside his collar.

From the seats over the doorway, usually reserved for the Press, or for distinguished supporters of the fight, Mary viewed the surroundings. Maderas was a small and shabby ring; there were no elegant costumes, no mantillas in the palcos. The tiers were crowded with countrymen, armed with leather bottles of wine and water, with family parties, with young men accompanied by whores, and, in solid blocks, the members of the local casino. There was a lot of scrimmaging up and down the tiers, and fights between people who disputed each other's rights to the nominally reserved seats.

Aracea, in her pink suit, sat very still. Mary had never known her so still. Usually she was jumping to her feet, waving to friends, acting up for attention. But to-day she was still. She started as the band broke into the pasodoble, for she had not seen the handkerchief drop, or heard, above the strident hum of voices, the sound of the clarin.

As the parade set out across the sand, her eyes went straight to the shortest of the three figures—to the boy in the middle, in kingfisher blue who, because it was his début in the ring, carried his montera in his hand. A roar went up for Paco Ribera, Niño de Maderas !—answered by a bellow from the supporters of Escorpio, many of whom had travelled a hundred miles, to be present at his last appearance as a novillero, before receiving the accolade in Madrid.

Paco looked good, very good. Smaller than the others, but sturdy. His face wasn't tight, and he didn't seem to be nervous. As he passed into the callejon he grinned at the sword-boy, who took the parade cape he tossed from his shoulders.

Escorpio looked, as usual, stupendous—though he was as yellow as a guinea and thin as a streak of lightning. He stood up, his narrow body curved backwards in a bow, and shot water from the pipote into his mouth in a silver stream ; swigged it round and spat it out. He ignored the people along the barrera, at whom Paco smiled shyly. Several leaned over and patted Paco on the shoulder ; he was their own boy, the boy of Maderas, and they were proud to watch his début. Mucha suerte, hombre.

Camacho, small, fat, as bullfighters go middle-aged, also had his supporters ; but they were not many. He stood stolidly, in a yellow suit that had evidently seen much service. He should have been able to afford another.

Someone came leaping up the gradas, with a cape bunched over his arm. Aracea held her breath, as the encrusted folds of gold and satin were spread on the rail before her. She had envied other women this compliment ; it was the first time it had come to her. Pride, shyness and excitement forced the blood into her face. She wished Paco would look up—but the back of his head was presented to her, with the coleta, worn for the first time, sticking out like a little pig's tail from the clip and button that held it to a flake of his hair.

Escorpio took the first bull—Encrestado III. If it had shown promise of fulfilling its high lineage, it would not have been offered, as a novillo, to the Maderas public; but it was calm, compact, and showed itself in its first run swift as a greyhound. Aracea gave a sigh of satisfaction, and threw a glance at Don Luis in the President's box.

. . . Of course they gave Escorpio the ears; it was his last fight as a novillero, and he deserved it, with his gipsy-like grace, and his valour that was not gipsy at all, but derived from the valour of the young Parral bull. When Aracea explained this to her companions, four pairs of brown female eyes stared at her with glassy noncomprehension. Qué barbaridad! The Ribera women were only there to see Paco. They clutched at each other as Paco walked out on the sand.

" That was very good, very close," ventured Mary.

" He's still snatching," was the implacable reply. A deep Olé! broke from the tiers; they were eager to applaud him— the boy from Maderas—but Paco was doing very well, with the cape and a young bull whose character was not so good as that of Encrestado. " Olé! " yelled the crowd; Paco had just pulled the bull round him in a media veronica that left it standing. He rested his hand for a moment between the horns and walked away with an uncertain smile. Maderas yelled its head off.

" You must admit, he's doing very well! "

" Regular," scowled Aracea. " He's got the banderillas— but he may make up for that with the muleta."

Paco placed one pair only of the darts and nearly made a mull of it. The bull's horn tore off a foot of the embroidery on his sleeve; he yanked it off savagely and stamped it into the sand. Escorpio went in to plant the other pairs; it was his great suerte. The ring rang with applause.

Paco's face was white like milk when he took the muleta and sword from the mozo. They were almost face to face with him; Mary guessed he resented the intrusion of Escorpio upon his own sphere of glory. As, montera in hand, he wheeled towards the President's box, to present his formal salutation, a hush fell on the ring. Mary saw Don Amadeo's face, a little to her left, a grey-green bladder; a frightful smile, a smile of bravado tore it. She felt in her bowels the intimate agony of one who watches his boy walk out, for the first time, in the face of death.

In the silence, the piping voice of adolescence rose to their seats.

" I dedicate this noble bull to the señorita Aracea, daughter of Parral."

The montera skimmed through the air and was caught by someone in the alley. Profiling towards the bull, which waited, head down, bunched with pink, green and yellow, in a distant part of the ring, Paco prepared his ayudado por bajo—the two-handed pass that gives the fighter control of the animal it now becomes his duty to kill.

Mary, to her dismay, began to feel sick. A quick look at Aracea showed her the child's face, white and set as stone.

The bull was troublesome, and Paco, patiently, was chopping it from side to side; he was infinitely more skilful with the muleta than with the cape. When at last he managed to draw it past him, a great breath went up from the ranks. It was not so difficult, after that, to lift it into the paso de pecho, but little as there was in it, the Olés cracked the blue ceiling over the ring. Maderas was determined to encourage its son, who, having given the bull time to turn round, put it quickly, and perhaps rashly, through a series of naturales that gained him genuine applause.

" Caramba," she heard Aracea murmur, " es muy macho. That is *bullfighting* ! "—She was right; and Maderas rewarded Paco with the triple Olé which is the most moving of all sounds that accompany prowess in the ring.

He left the bull admirably fixed, slowly withdrew the sword from the red heart of the muleta, and went in, volapié, without preparation. It was a novice's courage—the courage of one who had never before met the moment of truth. Ignoring the ritual of death, Paco went in to meet it, straight over the horns. It is to be doubted he remembered the position of the muleta—across him and to the right—or anything but the distance he had to cover, which he had just paused to measure before launching himself. The ring sucked in its breath as the blue figure flashed across the sand ; all but the idiot minority recognised the folly of it, for the bull, as commonly happens in the novilladas, was still full of life and cunning. Paco knew it, and his eye was on the clock. He knew he was getting tired, and that, if it came to a test of endurance, the bull might win.

His left foot carried him while the sword sank to its hilt between the shoulder-blades. Letting go, he staggered on. When he reeled round, the bull was sagging to its knees. He could not believe it. Truly he could not believe it. Talk of beginner's luck.

Somebody prodded him into doing the right thing. He went back to the barrera and collected his cape and montera. He was not conscious of the handkerchiefs flapping, or of the tolerant nod that awarded him the ear—because this was Maderas, and he was the son of El Cigarrón, and this was his first appearance in the ring ! Somebody pushed the warm bunch of fur into his hand and he stood, staring at it stupidly, wondering what to do with it, until a push from the peón de confianza sent him, still dazed, on his clockwise round of the ring, in a shower of hats, wineskins, flowers and cigars (there were a few bottles and cushions as well, from supporters of Escorpio, who paid for their partisanship in a ring solidly in favour of local talent). Paco was blind to it all. He was blind to a girl in a pink suit—standing up, beating her hands together and crying in a transport to all within earshot——

" That was *my* bull ! Era lo mio ! He dedicated it to me ! "

Olé, niño. Olé el papá ! Qué imprevisto. It was a barbaridad, that killing. To the young and frenzied majority, another Manolete had risen, who would blazon the name of Maderas across the scroll of the nation's glory. The old hands murmured that it took more than that to make a torero.

Camacho had his usual bad luck, with a crowd that had lost interest, and an inferior bull. After the interval, Escorpio dealt admirably, if cautiously, with his second—and when his turn came, Paco stepped from behind the burladero and acknowledged with a brief, brilliant smile the round of applause. Then he gave his full attention to the bull Negrito, which, having chivvied the cuadrilla across the barrier, was trotting leisurely round the edge of the ring, getting his bearings. Así un Parral! On the small side—it would have taken him another twelve months to furnish up to the statutory 370 kilos demanded by better-class rings—he was a pattern of the young fighting bull : coloured like dark steel, his untouched horns (never would Parral subscribe to the infamous modern custom of shaving down the tips) curving outward and slightly forward from a broad brow full of nobility and wisdom. From the well-muscled hind quarters his weight went forward to the morillo, which, fully risen, imparted a sinister distortion to the lines of pure taurian beauty. A killer in every line ; but an honest killer, as Parrales are bred to be.

"Qué bravo !" muttered Aracea—and bit her lip as Paco spread the cape. If only he wouldn't snatch !

Paco thought, Josú, this is a bull. This is a *bull* !

It was five less twenty-seven when Paco went out to meet the bull Negrito, number 34 of the ganadería of Parral. At five less twenty-five he was spinning through the air.

IV

The kingfisher-blue suit was badly damaged ; not so Paco, who, face down on a slab in the infirmary, cursed because, during the time it took to stitch up the tear in his buttock, Camacho was reaping the glory that should have been his. By the time they lifted him off the table, cleaned up, padded and strapped ("Man, you're lucky !" the surgeon told him. "A clean horn and a glancing blow ; another centímetro and he'd have got you through the tail. Not many people that have lain on this table come off so well ") the infirmary was filled with his friends and admirers—flinging their arms round his neck, beating his back, kissing him, almost dragging his arms out with the violence of their enthusiasm. He let out a yell as they hoisted him to their shoulders—" Look out for my backside ! "—and bore him out into the sun.

Camacho, he reflected, was performing to an all but empty ring. All round the bullring and down the calle Real crowds waited to acclaim the hero. Viva—viva el Niño de Maderas ! Clutching the necks of his supporters, his head swam, above the little running boys, and the familiar faces of his school fellows, and the grinning faces of the police, as they cleared the way for him.

On the balcony, over which they had already thrown shawls and rugs and curtains, his mother, supported by her friends, was waving and screaming and laughing and crying, all at once. It made him want to laugh. Then a youth with his shirt and trousers spattered with blood was dancing backwards in front of him, shouting and holding up something that looked like a wet bag of purple leather. A roar of laughter went up from the crowd— " Los huevos—the eggs ! " " He doesn't want eggs," shouted some wag in the depths of the crowd, " he's got plenty of his own ! " A cheer went up, for everyone knew that the classical ritual would take place now, in the Casa Ribera : the eating of the bull's testicles, that confer virility on those privileged to eat them.

It was a pity the distance to the house was so short ! With final slaps and bangs of good feeling, they sent him stumbling into the arms of his mother. He was lost in a wave of women— sisters, sisters-in-law, servants. He laughed hysterically, as he tried to thrust them off.

With difficulty Mary had prevented Aracea from following the swirl of the crowd towards the exits.

" You must wait ! Look—they're quite crazy ; we'll be knocked down if we get into that mob.—Madre mia, this is nearly as bad as the bullring," she groaned, as they pushed between the shrouded counters towards a roar of voices. " It sounds as if the whole of Maderas is here. Don't stop too long talking to Paco : I'm going to find your father, and see what time he intends to start back."

It was by no means easy to isolate Paco in the jubilant crowd, but Mary managed at last to signal to him, and he came towards them, his eyes glittering and his cheeks patched with crimson : moving stiffly, with the parade cape pulled round him to conceal the tear in his breeches.

" How do you feel ? " she smiled at him.

" Very well, thank you, señorita."

" You made us very proud of you."

" Muy agradecido."—(He had already caught something of the arrogance of the professional !)

" Will you look after Aracea for a moment, while I find Don Luis ? "

" Encantado ! "—As Niño de Maderas, he could afford, without shame, to show politeness to a little girl.

They looked at each other across an infinite distance. He thought, She's just a kid, and was puzzled to find that this gave him a kind of compassion for her.

She thought, He's altered. It's almost like meeting a stranger. *Why don't we say anything?* She stammered :

" I lit a candle——" and swallowed. It was funny that lighting of the candle ; she had never done such a thing for anyone before. And she hadn't even known . . .

" Bueno ; and it worked ! As a matter of fact, I lit one myself." His brother had run across to the church and brought one ; stupefied with excitement, he had not thought of it for himself. His hand had shaken as he lit it before the Virgin on his bureau, and he had muttered a prayer.

" And my medal ? "

" It's here, round my neck ; do you want it back ? "

" Of course not "—her face turned crimson. " And I'll send you a present—later," she concluded stiffly. She wished to show him she was quite conversant with the etiquette of the dedication.

" Thanks." That was to be taken for granted ! (Mary had slipped, on Aracea's behalf, a `few notes to the mozo who collected the cape, which Paco, on receiving, had grandly swept aside. " Keep it ; the señorita is a friend of mine ! ") " I sent you my cape, didn't I ? "—He did not add that, but for her being the daughter of Parral, he might have found it expedient to " forget." One does not dedicate bulls to little girls with bare knees and pigtails. " And what did you think of me ? " He reminded her poutingly that she had not complimented him.

" You're still too sharp with the cape. Why can't you remember what Ildefonso showed us—— ? "

His face flamed.

" Is that all you've got to say ? "

Her temper took fire from his.

" Do you want me to say you're a Joselito, or a Belmonte ? " she blazed at him. " What nerve ! They say all bullfighters are conceited, but por dios that goes a little too far ! Because they gave you three Olés for your naturales——"

He would have borne it from no one else, but from Aracea, who was his friend. . . . He was shrewd enough, too, to respect her judgment. She had seen, probably, more bullfights than he, and she was the daughter of Parral. His eyes prickled, and his bottom was hurting ; the sweat-soaked fighting suit, which he ought to have changed immediately, felt clammy on his ribs. He turned his head away to mutter :

· " So you think I was no good."

" Oh, you were good ! " she told him earnestly. " I shall tell Ildefonso how good you were. And your naturales *are* better than Escorpio's : he's too long and thin and he does ridiculous things with his legs—I wouldn't be surprised if he got the bronca in Madrid," she concluded, laying cunning balm to his pride by depreciating his rival.

" Anything more ? "—He refused stiffly to be mollified.

" Pues—you did your good things well, as usual, and the bad things were about the same. You wouldn't have got the horn if you'd——"

" Perhaps next time," said Paco, with biting slowness, " you'll join the cuadrilla and cape my bulls for me ? " He stood for a moment, biting his lip ; she was so right, so deadly right ! " And how about the sword ? "—Jesus and Mary, she *should* praise him, if they went on arguing all night !

" Josú—that was something ! "

" So I can kill bulls—yes ? "

" It was the best thing in the whole afternoon," she assured him, with so patent a sincerity that his grim face relaxed into a smile.

" Well, I'm glad I did something to please you ! "

" What are you going to do next ? " she asked eagerly.

" I don't know. Papá doesn't want me to go on in the novilladas. He's going to try and buy me into somebody's cuadrilla for the rest of the season. Gómez says——"

" Who's Gómez ? "

" I thought you knew everybody in the business ! " he mocked her. " Gómez is Niño de Medina's manager, and now that one's finished he's lost his meal-ticket. He's been round licking my boots ! " boasted Paco. " He says he could get me in with Montoya."

" Are you going to let him manage you ? "

" What—with Papá to look after me ? And I don't want Montoya ; he's getting on, and he's been talking of retiring ever since the war. I'd rather wait till I can get with one of the younger lot. I must keep my eye open for some tientas, to keep me in practice.—Well "—he glanced over his shoulder—" all these people are waiting to talk to me. Hasta luego—I'll send you my notices ; I bet Garzón will spread himself to-morrow in the *Correo*."

" Hasta luego." She held out her hand. " You looked fine in the blue suit, Paco," she said, wistfully.

His temper fully recovered, he laughed as he swung away.

" That black bicho of yours has cost me a new pair of breeches ! Tell your Papá I'll take the price of them out in working his little bulls ! "

A lump came up in Aracea's throat ; she swallowed it. But it was like saying Good-bye to somebody for ever. Paco had grown up, and she was still a little girl.

Chapter Seven

SHE FOUND Concepción at her bedside with the tray, and saw, to her surprise, it was nine o'clock.

" The chica still sleeps, señorita."

" Let her sleep ; she had a long day yesterday. You had better make some more coffee, she'll be thirsty when she wakes up."

It was ten, when a pale, languid and still drowsy Aracea stumbled, in her dressing gown, into Mary's room. Mary, who had taken the rare opportunity of staying in bed, dropped her book.

" Olá ; are you ready for desayúno ? "

" I don't want any."

And no wonder, thought Mary, after Doña Amalia's pollo. She got up, found the fruit salts, mixed a fizzy dose and held it out.

" This will liven you up."

" I don't want livening "—but she took the glass and sipped slowly with grimaces. Presently she thrust it back at Mary. " It tastes nasty."

" Because you've let it go flat." She gave it another stir. " Drink up, and we'll ring for breakfast."

" I've got a pain."

" Where ? "

Aracea indicated vaguely, and Mary cast a quick glance at the peaked little face. She had been expecting this for some weeks, and no doubt the journey, the excitement, the heat and the rich food had brought it on. Fortunately she had prepared the child, who gave her a sidelong look as she asked wisely, " I suppose it means I'm growing up ? "

After she had dressed, Mary went to give the news to Doña Leandra.

" This makes it more difficult——"

Mary inclined her head ; she knew perfectly Leandra's meaning. This put a definite stop to the hobnobbing with the boys in the basement ; it also added to her responsibilities as chaperon.

By midday, the origin of Aracea's pain was well defined, and she was unusually meek about lying on the divan in the sala and being read to. It was very hot, and the windows and the double doors on the gallery were open to catch what little air stirred between the garden and the patio. A short, grey-suited figure passing the doors made Aracea start up.

" Was that Don Alejandro ?—Who's ill ? "

" I don't know ; perhaps one of the servants."

" Or Mamá. It's not surprising she gets sick, spending all her time indoors, among these stuffy old books. Qué fastidio. Why can't she come riding with us ?—She never goes anywhere but into town, to visit the shops and have tea with the marquesa. It's that beastly old Tía Carmela—perhaps," said Aracea cheerfully, " Tía Carmela's ill ; perhaps she's going to die ! I wish she would ; she's like a nasty old insect, crawling round the house."

Mary was conscious that her reproof lacked conviction. She felt very much as Aracea did about Tía Carmela—the skull-faced old woman, crippled with arthritis, who occupied a place of unpleasant privilege in the household. Tía Carmela had accompanied Leandra on her bridal journey from the north, her vicious fidelity accepting transplantation from her Castilian earth to the foreign soil of which she hated every grain. Isolation had tightened her grip on the one to whom she had devoted herself; from bodyservant she had made herself into friend and confidante, existing like a parasite on the unhappy girl whose every secret she knew. Mary had begun by wondering how Don Luis tolerated her presence, but had come to realise that his toleration was only part of the indolent indifference he showed towards his wife. She felt that if any act of hers could serve to loosen the unhealthy clutch of Tía Carmela on the wife of Parral, she was ready to perform it.

The week of indisposition that curtailed Aracea's usual activities offered opportunities that Mary decided to use in the cultivation of a closer relationship between the child and her mother. If Leandra showed no pleasure in their companionship, she made no effort to avoid it. She wandered about the sala, picking up a book and putting it down, starting to write a letter and abandoning it—did she ever finish anything? wondered Mary; and wondered whether any attempt to interest her in her daughter's occupations would be taken amiss.

One of their most successful diversions was the scrapbook Mary had instigated through the winter months. Since the beginning of the season great bundles of clippings had accumulated, and Aracea was temporarily contented with scissors and paste-pot, making a great mess on the floor—which, as it was nearly her supper time, Mary told her to clear up.

" No ! " said Aracea, with a scowl meant as a reminder that she was an invalid.

" Nonsense ; a little exercise will do you good."

" The servants will do it ; it is their business."

" Would you like "—Leandra had drifted to the table ; she averted her eyes from the picture of a particularly bloody bull, bristling with darts, which occupied the centre of the page— " would you like to go to Segovia ? "

Aracea stared.

" Segovia ? There's no afición worth talking about in Segovia."

" Chica, I was not thinking about bulls. You know Segovia is my home. You have never been there."

" I know ; where they murdered my grandfather." Mary caught her breath ; truly, it was an impossible child sometimes. " I'd like to go there some time. But there's Jaén on the fifteenth and Taragona on the twenty-fourth. And then there's Málaga and Colmenar and a lot of little fights I can't remember without my book. So we couldn't go until the end of the month. Oh yes ! "—She clapped her hands. " Then we'd be up there for the feria at Valladolid, wouldn't we ? I've never seen that ! And so long as we were back in time for San Miguel——"

" Aracea ! "—Mary could hold her tongue no longer.

" What's the matter ? "

Leandra said, after a pause :

" I can't wait until the end of the month."

" Why not ? "

" Because "—she moisted her lips—" you may have a brother, or sister, some time in the autumn."

Her daughter gaped at her.

" But—that can't be true, Mamá ! You're not a bit fat : you're not even as fat as Gloria Meléndez ! "

" Don Alejandro says I must have a little change of air."

" Is Papá going ? "

" I don't suppose so, on account of the business."

" Then I'm afraid I can't, either." Aracea shook her head gravely. " You'd better take Miss Mary. I'll stop here and look after Papá and Carlos. I'm grown-up now," she reminded them, and, to put an end to the discussion, jumped up and ran out of the room.

In silence, Mary began to clear the litter on the table. Leandra sat, gazing at her outspread hands. Mary ventured :

" It seems to be an excellent idea." Leandra shrugged her shoulders. " I will do what I can," promised Mary, " to make Aracea behave sensibly. It is time she, too, had a change of surroundings."

Supposing a son were born : how would it affect Aracea ? How soon would she realise her displacement ?—These and other conjectures came between Mary and her sleep ; but, when morning dawned, and a completely recovered Aracea was heard shouting to the groom, it was obvious that the information had not yet penetrated her consciousness.

The pink glow of sunrise had not lifted from the ˙pasture when they cantered out, and the arch of the sky was still dappled with red, tulip-like clouds.

" Let's go through the village and out towards Sanjorje."

" The village " was the double row of labourers' cottages that formed a cobbled gully between the estate and the beginning of the cork-forests : a favourite excursion for pleasure-riders, for, beyond it, the road rose softly, deep in orange-coloured dust, until it melted into the forest tracks. But since the war they had been warned not to venture too far into the deep glades, which were said to harbour undesirables.

They nodded to the usual greetings. Everyone knew Aracita had not been out for a week, and everyone knew the reason. Dark-eyed girls and women sent smiling glances of complicity to one who had been received into the great secret society of their sex. Aracea exchanged cheerful Olás with her friends, and broke off with a shout. " Papá ! "

Following the direction in which her whip was pointing, Mary recognised the bay horse, with the Parral groom, standing outside the tavern.

" And look—Miguel's got the grey—the new one ! "— Impatiently, but mindful of the cobbles, she thrust ahead of Mary. " What luck—now I can try it. Olá, Miguel ! Where's Papá ? " —She flung herself out of the saddle, to run her hand approvingly over the silver flank of the horse, which flung up its wild head and mane, flared its nostrils and plunged sidelong. Aracea took the reins out of the groom's hand and Mary backed her horse a yard or two, watching the small, confident figure, as it gentled the animal back to stillness.

" Isn't he beautiful !—What is he called ? " Aracea asked the youth, who grinned sheepishly.

" No sé, señorita."

She laid her forehead gently against a tremulous muzzle.

" You're lovely. Your mane is like a white flag. Papá shall give you to me, and you shall be called Bandera ! " she was murmuring, as Don Luis appeared in the door of the tavern.

He saw Mary first—she was directly in front of him—and the look of distaste, almost of offence, to which she was accustomed, settled into blankness on his handsome face. He wished her " Buen' día'," and was obviously taken aback when Aracea flung herself into his arms.

" Papá—how lovely—the new one ! "

" Sí, es bonico." Mary wondered why he should employ the slighting term of an obviously magnificent animal.

" Superior ! "—Aracea indignantly disclaimed his tepidity. " Come, let's be off ! "—She lifted her foot to the stirrup and Don Luis laid his hand smilingly on her shoulder.

" No, hija ! Another day—perhaps. This animal is not ready for you yet."

" What do you tell me ?—That I cannot ride a horse ? "

" That you cannot ride this horse," he corrected her. " Anda ; hasta la vista." Mary caught a look from the corner of his eye which she interpreted as an order to remove herself and her charge out of the way. Easier said than done.

Working up for one of her rages, Aracea stood her ground. The two began to shout at each other, and Mary hastily wheeled her horse out of the way while the groom struggled with the grey. Through the roar of Parral voices—which drew an interested audience—the sound of a car, lurching down the gully, was unheard.

Mary was the first to see the brilliant head of Gloria Meléndez, the flash of her teeth, as she braked, and looked amusedly at the scene between father and daughter. She got out, a figure of spectacular elegance, wearing the Andalucían riding habit, cut like a man's, in a light chestnut brown ; a broad sash of black satin defined the slimness of her waist, and emphasised the rich thrust of her bosom under the pleated shirt. She was carrying the whip, a pair of doeskin gloves and the black cordobés, which she put on, clipping the chinstrap negligently above her ear, while she smilingly surveyed the combatants, too deeply involved, by now, to mark her approach. As usual, she ignored the governess's presence. It was absurdly like a colour film, thought Mary.

" Olá, Luis."

The Parrales spun round ; Don Luis's face was a picture.

" Olá," observed Gloria negligently to Aracea, as she gave

her hand to the father. She nodded towards the grey, and laughed. " It looks as if we're going to have as much fun this morning as we had yesterday! "—Pulling on her gloves, she walked round, passed some sharp comment on the grooming, and with a vault like a youth's was into the saddle. The boy sprang back with a yell as the grey went up in the air, but the girl on its back only laughed as she mastered it. Avoiding the eyes of his daughter, Don Luis mounted. The two gave a superb display of horsemanship, as they galloped towards the forest.

During all this, Aracea stood like a stone, not even moving when threatened by the lashing of the horses' heels. She remained —cut to the heart, Mary knew, by the cruel satisfaction of the two swaying backs, the echo of laughter that bespoke an intimacy from which she was excluded.

" Come, chica," said Mary gently.

Aracea swung herself into the saddle and, with set lips and jaw, thrust past her, in the direction from which they had come. It was useless to say anything. Mary let her ride alone.

At the gateposts they came face to face with Carlos de la Cerna. It was weeks since he and Mary had exchanged more than a casual word; she knew herself guilty, virtually of snubbing him. But of what good was it, to prolong an acquaintanceship that could bring no satisfaction to either?

" Buenos días "—Mary drew rein, but Aracea, without a look or a sign, rode on. " It is nice, to see you are getting on with your riding."

His unshuttered eye twinkled at her.

" I promise you, in a month I shall be riding the bulls down for Luis! "—He nodded towards the departing figure of Aracea and lifted his brows. " What is the matter?—Am I in her bad books this morning? "

" She has had "—Mary hesitated—" a disappointment."

" Ah? "

" She was hoping to ride with her father."

Carlos's lips pursed themselves and his eyebrows, rising even higher, pushed the smooth skin of his forehead towards the shining line of his hair. Then he burst into laughter.

" Miss Carpenter ! You really need not be so *terribly* discreet. If I had known you were resuming your morning rides, I would have suggested you should avoid the road to Sanjorje."

She felt herself colouring and knew his bold eye was on her face. He bent a little towards her, and the levity of his expression vanished as he murmured :

" That is so charming ! Spanish women do not blush much ; it makes you look like a little girl." Before she had recovered from his impudence, he continued, " But surely you knew about Luís and Gloria ?—It has been going on a very long time."

" Please——! " she stammered. " You forget my position here. I really cannot listen to gossip ! "

" Por dios, what else is there to listen to in the house of Parral ? " he shrugged. " You have not been very kind to me, Miss Carpenter ; if you have forgotten our pleasant evening, I have not. I hoped we might have repeated it."

" There have been no opportunities," she answered primly. " I am a busy person, and so, I think, are you."

" Opportunities do not ' occur,' they are made. If I can arrange one, will you avail yourself of it ? "

" Don Carlos." She gave him the full level glance of her eyes. " I think you know you are suggesting something which, in the circumstances, is quite impossible."

" Vaya—now you talk like a Spanish woman ! Ladies in England do not behave in that silly fashion."

" That's quite true, and if we were in England I should accept your proposition with pleasure : first, because I should enjoy it, and, second, because there wouldn't need to be any secrecy about it. But, placed as I am, I couldn't possibly entertain any project that would put me in a false position with Doña Leandra."

" That is quite evident ; but—you know my cousin leads a very secluded life. Surely, next time you are in town, we could meet and drive out somewhere ? I can show you some delightful places——"

" No," she said firmly.

He looked at her, half smiling, half frowning.

" ' No ' is a dangerous word to use to a man of my disposition," he warned her—and changed the subject by asking abruptly if she was going to Segovia.

" So far as I know, it hasn't been suggested."

" The chica won't be so pleased to miss the corrida at Málaga."

" She refuses to go."

Carlos nodded his head wisely.

" She will go. Gloria will see to that."

" What can it possibly have to do with the señorita Meléndez?" asked Mary indignantly.

He gave her a mocking grimace.

" What do you suppose Luis does, when we go to town ?— I am left at the club, while Luis takes himself to the Moresco——"

" The Moresco—— ? " she faltered.

" You must know the Meléndez house, near the park ? "

" But—surely—that's impossible ! "

" You are a little behind the times, Miss Carpenter ! " he smiled. " The old Catholic families, like mine, are still strict, but the young, fashionable crowd—the moderns—have begun to imitate the cosmopolitans. Naturally Luis and his amiga never meet by themselves ; but Luis rings Gloria and she gets together a few young married people, close friends—you understand ? Sometimes they go out to some place and dance, but usually they stay at the Moresco and play cards, or have cocktails and music. The old casa Meléndez lends itself admirably to—h'm ! " He repeated his little, secret smile. " My dear Miss Carpenter, it is all over Sevilla, that Luis is completely infatuated—and I think you have had a sample this morning." He looked at her shrewdly. " Luis has never been known to allow anyone but himself to break in a new horse, but—well, Gloria is a magnificent horse-woman, and she has been here every morning for the last week. Naturally, the little one is mortified."

" All the same "—she forced the conversation back to the previous topic—" I cannot imagine Don Luis's accepting the intervention of an outsider, in a matter concerning his daughter."

" Evidently, you don't know the meaning of infatuation ! " —He sounded much amused. " Now Aracita is about again, do you suppose he'll allow himself to be cheated of his pleasure? You may be sure they are both counting on Segovia!—and you and Aracea will not be at all welcome, for the present, on those morning rides. Please do not look so offended! I am only telling you to spare everyone embarrassment."

She pitied the child, as the days went on. Aracea was quiet and spiritless, sedulously avoiding the preparations for the visit to Segovia, of which she could not but be aware. More surprisingly, she showed no inclination to seek the company of her former playmates. Suffering, perhaps, from a touch of compunction, Don Luis made a more than usually boisterous fuss of his daughter, and Aracea took it with a quiet dignity which, Mary could see, puzzled and even annoyed him. She had emerged from childhood, and had become a young girl, already troubled by intimations of the future.

One afternoon Mary found her writing a letter, and wondered to whom she was writing. At long intervals, and under pressure, she wrote, by her mother's wish, to Segovia; to people she had never met—elderly relatives who sent back long, unintelligible epistles full of Catholic admonition, which Mary read aloud to a scornful listener. Segovia offered no bright prospect to Aracea. In pity, Mary asked her:

"Would you like to come into town and see the new picture? —Tomás tells me he isn't wanted this afternoon; I can ask your mother if we may have the car."

To her relief, Aracea brightened.

"Yes; and we could buy a present for Paco. I'd forgotten —but I've just been writing to him." She proudly exhibited the result of her labours.

"Quite good; only two mistakes.—Well, go and change your dress."

Half an hour later she went to Aracea's room. The girl was standing in the middle of the floor, sullenly watching the servants who, under Concepción's direction, were laying out the contents of her drawers and wardrobe. She turned to Mary and spoke loudly and deliberately in Spanish.

"You may tell these fools I am not going to Segovia—not for

you, or Mamá, or anybody. I am staying here, to look after the house for Papá."

The previous night Leandra had returned to the subject.

" You will come with us to Segovia, Miss Mary ? "

" As you wish." She hesitated, " How long, señora, are you proposing to stay ? "

Leandra shrugged her shoulders.

" I do not know ; perhaps a month, or more. The house is close to the Guadarramas ; it is high up ; we get much air."

" That sounds agreeable.—I wonder if, while you are there, I might take a fortnight's holiday ? "—It was the first time she had suggested one since coming to the house of Parral ; she felt she needed it. She might find a little parador in the sierras and work quietly on her neglected book. Leandra showed a faint surprise, but concurred with the request.

" Then you will tell Aracea—it is settled, we are going."

She blamed herself for having postponed the delivery of the message, as she saw the child's face.

" Come, we will talk about it on the way into town."

Aracea's mouth set stubbornly, but she stumped before Mary along the gallery and threw herself into the car.

" I won't. I shan't," she repeated, all the way into the suburbs, until Mary laid her hand on her knee.

" Well, if you won't, you won't ; but we need not spoil this pleasant outing—need we ? "

They found a confitería with a back room looking out on a little patio filled with green plants and withered lilies ; over the consumption of ices, Aracea recovered from her ill-temper. The hunt for Paco's present led them from shop to shop down Sierpes and Tetuan, until Mary, exhausted, suggested that a wallet was the kind of thing he could keep and show to his friends. Aracea, agreeing, made unerring selection of the most revolting piece of leatherwork the shopkeeper produced, bearing in coloured alto-rilievo the figure of a bullfighter : an almost perfect example of the horrific designed for the tourist. As the corners were slightly scuffed, Mary guessed it had been there since before the Civil War. She herself had discovered a handsome

case in crimson calf ; she drew this to Aracea's attention, remark-
ing that the other was a little " cursi."

" Oh no, it's exactly what Paco would like !—And," she
concluded, " it looks much more expensive than the other ; he'll
like that as well."

More time passed in composing an inscription—" It can be
a facsimile of the señorita's own writing, if she prefers "—a
suggestion which, it went without saying, entranced Aracea,
who took much persuasion before agreeing that " Recuerdos,"
and the names and dates, were quite enough, without the flowery
dedication on which her heart was set. "And is it to be sent to
Paco ? " smiled the assistant.

" Oh no ; I must see it first. Do me the favour to take
the address," said Aracea politely. Mary, on the point of saying
that the Segovia address had better be given, bit back the
words.

" I'm afraid we've missed the first part of the picture," said
Mary, as they hurried along the tram-lines. " Oh "—as they
reached the front of the cinema—" it's not the one I thought ;
we've seen this. How stupid of me. Chica, I'm sorry."

" I don't care," said Aracea, whose purchase had put her in
a high good humour.

" We can see it again, if you like——"

" I don't want to see that stupid Yanquí película again !
Miss Mary "—she clutched her companion's arm—" I've had a
marvellous idea. Truly, it's wonderful ! Let's tell Tomás to
take us out to Tío Felipe's place. You've never been, have you ?
—and I haven't been for ages. Oh please, Miss Mary, let's do
that ! It's much nicer, on a hot summer evening, than sitting
in a stuffy cine."

Inwardly agreeing with her, Mary pointed out that it was not
very polite to call on the family of Tío Felipe without giving
them notice : which Aracea brushed aside.

" Tío Felipe and I are muy amigos," she boasted, " and you
know quite well you're a favourite of his, Miss Mary ! He calls
you ' La primera inglesa andaluza ' ! "

Mary chuckled at the memory of the nut-faced little man,

locally famous as a flamenco singer, and a frequent visitor to
the house of Parral, who was always trying to trip her up with
phrases spoken in the most unintelligible andaluz, and roaring
with glee when she failed to interpret them. An old friend of
Don Luis, the friendship did not, however, extend to their wives ;
there could be nothing in common between the daughter of
Ramiro de la Cerna and the rich, country-born and bred señora
who formed a cushiony background to her husband's ebullience.
" Los Felipe," as Aracea called them, were not the equals, socially,
of the Parrales, but, as Carlos had said, there is no distinction
between lovers of the bulls, good music, good wine and good
dance. Don Luis had frequently taken his daughter to the casa
Felipe, so it was to be assumed there was no reason, apart from
the conventional one, why she should not give in to Aracea's
suggestion.

" Well, I think you should ring Doña Vittoria, and tell her
we are coming."

They had drifted back to the plaza, and Aracea was delighted
to skip into the Hotel Inglaterra and request the use of the
telephone. She emerged radiantly from the office.

" They're encantados."

" Did you speak to Doña Vittoria herself ? "

" No, I left a message "—a certain evasiveness made Mary
look at her sharply.

" With whom ? "

" Vaya—what does it matter ? Somebody who answered the
telephone. Oh, Miss Mary, don't fuss—let's go quickly ! It's
quite a long way."

During the journey, Mary was entertained by a description
of the charms of the casa Felipe : of which the chief was the small
ring where, for the amusement of his friends, Don Felipe occasionally put on an amateur bullfight. " It's lovely, Miss Mary !—we
sit all round on a sort of balcony, and there are lights, and the
servants go round with wine and things to eat, and anybody
who likes can go down and cape the bulls. The bulls aren't
much—they're regular "—she rocked her outspread palm with
a perfect reproduction of Don Luis's favourite gesture—" but

it's fun—and there's music, and sometimes Tío Felipe has the gipsies in, to dance. Una noche muy andaluz ! "

The deep, honey-sweet dusk closed in on them ; through the open windows of the car the air brushed their cheekbones and lifted the hair from their temples. It was almost dark by the time Aracea cried out, " Look—there's the house ! And here are the gates. Muy buenas ! " she leaned out to cry to the old woman who hobbled out of the porter's lodge to push back the big screens of ironwork that closed the entrance to the house of Felipe.

Several cars, pushed into the shadow at the end of the drive, filled Mary with misgiving. Strings of coloured electric bulbs, festooned under the arcades that fronted the house itself, increased it.

" It looks as though they were giving a party ; are you sure they are expecting us ? "

" Por cierto ! " Aracea insisted stoutly, as she leapt out of the car. A servant appeared at the door ; Mary asked for Doña Vittoria.

" La señora está fuera," she was told.

" Did you know Doña Vittoria was away ? " she turned on Aracea to inquire. Aracea hunched her shoulder.

" What does it matter ?—Tía Vittoria is a bore, but we've come to see Tío Felipe.—Por dondé están los señores ? " she demanded, and led the way into the house.

There was evidently some sort of entertainment afoot. Mary noted, with embarrassment, tables laid with glasses, titbits and the usual equipment of a cocktail party. A hum of voices ahead added to her misgiving—but left Aracea undaunted. She shouted joyfully, " Tío Felipe ! " as a small, shrivelled figure appeared in an archway, and started with surprise.

" Olá, la guapa !—las guapas," he amended, as he caught sight of Mary. She realised in a flash that he had not had Aracea's message—if indeed she had sent it. She sent a suspicious glance towards her pupil, whose arm was flung, with confidence round Don Felipe's waist. He rose to the occasion in the manner worthy of an Andalucían, and kissed Mary's hand. " Madre mia

—la señorita—la Rubia—la primera inglesa andaluza ! A star strikes me in the eyes—Josú, I am blind——! "

Blind in another sense, thought Mary, ironically. Early though it was, Don Felipe had evidently been celebrating. How to extract herself and Aracea from the embarrassing situation became her major preoccupation. Aracea had no such misgivings.

" We were in town, Tío Felipe—and we were going to the ciné—and it was an old picture—and I wanted to show Miss Mary your house ! Aren't you pleased to see us ? "—With the confidence of established privilege, Aracea ran to the archway—and stopped dead. Mary moved up quickly behind her.

" Papá ! "

Don Luis turned from the group of men and women clustered in the small patio. Beside him stood—it went without saying—Gloria Meléndez. The women, with flowers in their hair, bearing furs or shawls, were dressed, evidently, for a party ; among them the insolent beauty of the Meléndez glowed like a carnation, in a flame-coloured manila shawl that left exposed the whiteness of her bosom. Of the women, she alone wore nothing in her hair, confident, with reason, of its midnight splendour.

" Carai, it's the chica," she observed idly.

A look of sheer murder crossed, for a moment, Aracea's face, though her eyes were riveted on her father. Don Luis's face, also, was formidable, although, in deference to the company, he permitted himself a formal smile.

" What's all this ? "

" We came to see Tío Felipe," she stammered.

He muttered something to his companion, and came quickly towards them. His look at Mary was poisonous ; offended, she stiffened herself.

" Ven," he said to Aracea. His hand on her shoulder, he turned her towards the archway. Somebody cried, " Na, Luis—let her stay ! " Aracea, seemingly half stunned, submitted to being pushed back into the house. Don Felipe had disappeared. Mary felt a fool as she followed them. But she rallied her dignity to say :

" We rang up ; we were given to understand we would be

welcome." It was foolish, perhaps, to assume part of the blame, but loyalty to the child obliged her to do it.

" I am displeased," was all he vouchsafed in reply.

Infuriated by his pompousness, it was on the tip of her tongue politely to inquire in what way they had displeased him; but Aracea whirled on her father.

" What have you to be displeased about? You have brought me here many a time; you know Tío Felipe and I are friends. But that's not why you're vexed. You're vexed because you've got that *puta* with you. That's what she is: a *puta*! "

Don Luis Parral turned as white as ice; gave one look at his daughter, and returned to his friends.

Well, thought Mary, I may as well start my packing. And as for you—she looked at the girl, tumbled, weeping, into the corner of the car: alas, my poor Aracea! You're as good as on the train to Segovia already.

Chapter Eight

I

" YOU HAVEN'T explained how you managed about things like permits?—Your passport must have expired, or the war must have invalidated it, years ago."

Mary turned to smile at the slim, grey-haired, but youthful and well-groomed woman who watched the smoke streaming upwards from the cigarette between her thin fingers.

" Of course. I ought to have explained that.—Well, it's really too long a story; but I suppose I built up credit, of a kind, during the war, and I made one or two influential friends or *their* friends were influential; I forget which! My permiso de residencia keeps on getting renewed—more or less under the counter; and, of course, it helps, now I'm living with the Parrales.—What are you staring at?"

"I'm wondering what brand of fanaticism it is," said Adela Hallat slowly, "that makes a woman with your background and upbringing sacrifice herself, morally and materially, for a country which, a few years ago, you'd not even seen."

"That's too difficult a question." She leaned forward to take a light from the other's cigarette. "It might have been a different story, if the opposite side had won.—I suppose"—she made her voice cool "as you married an American, you sided with the Government."

"Let's not talk politics—and you'd better not say anything about 'under the counter' to Grosvenor."

"I quite understand; the Embassy must be above suspicion."

"Well, we've been trying to do a little discreet wire-pulling, on your behalf. I rather gathered, round Madrid, that you were probably starving in some frightful slum! And—don't mind my mentioning it—you look as if you've been very ill."

"That was years back; there's nothing wrong with me now, except an occasional mild bout of fever. Yes; I suppose I 'look my age'—and then some!"

"You used to be such a little tough." She paused, stubbing out her cigarette in the hotel ash-tray. "Mary," she said, with hesitation, "there's plenty of work, now, for intelligent people, in Madrid."

"There must be. It must be terribly exciting."

"Well—it depends what you call excitement. For the present we're up to our eyes in gasoline. I suppose you know Iberia Airlines will have to close down unless the State Department ratifies our agreement with the English? They've got to get petrol from somewhere—and that's poor Gro's main headache. He spends most of his time with the Ambassador, trying to bawl horse sense across the Atlantic. And, of course, we're his other headache."

"We——?"

"The British. Now, Mary, don't jump down my throat. Being married to an American doesn't change one's whole habit of thought—though it's expected to. The time Grosvenor isn't pacing the marble halls of Castellana like a caged panther, he's losing weight over our opposite number. I must say Sir Samuel was more oncoming than we expected—as well he might be, with Great Britain screaming for iron and potash—but most of the time we're operating in front of a thick, black screen that stands for British diplomacy. All the Spanish are aware of it, and every possible advantage is taken of what looks like a split in our ranks."

" The Spanish stayed neutral, in spite of overwhelming inducement to do the opposite," said Mary quickly.

" I know; and in spite of Suñer," agreed Adela. " There are still plenty of pro-Axis gentry in Madrid, but we've got them taped. Neutrality's all very well, Mary; but there's a difference between the passive and the benevolent kind, and the last is what we're working for. If the British Embassy would take its head out of the bag, the war might be shortened by months.—Don't you *want* to come in on the side of your own people ? " she urged.

Mary answered, after a silence :

" All you've been saying helps me to see the war as I have been trying to see it : as a thing that concerns the whole world ; not England, particularly, or Spain. Being here, after the years I've spent in the South, is like being in the engine-room of a great ship, with controls going out in every direction. What we're doing—what France and Germany and Russia and America and Japan are doing—isn't just words on paper ; it comes right in *here* ! " She smote her hand under her breasts. " But, for the present, I'm too hopelessly confused. In our war—I mean, the Spanish war—I threw in my lot with Spain, against my own country. My emotions—call them, if you like, my passions—are centred here ; outside of Spain, I've only got my cold sense of right and wrong to guide me."

" Isn't that enough ? "

Mary looked at her in silence.

" I shall have to tell you all the rest," she said at length.

" So *this* is where the story begins.—Sweet mercy ! " gasped

Adela, looking at her watch. " I'm supposed to be at a committee ! We're putting on a tremendous show at the Embassy— just to show them what American hospitality is like when we get down to it !—all the grandees and the Big Brass and the panjandrums of literature and the arts. You'll have to come ! It's more your pigeon than mine."

" I'd shrivel away. I've forgotten my party drill—and I have nothing to wear," said Mary, as she helped her visitor to collect her scattered belongings.

" Never mind about that ; come and have dinner to-night. It will be rather a bunch of stiffs—one of Grosvenor's sub-committees—gasoline running out of their ears and noses—but no wives, thank God. When we've finished eating, you and I can tuck ourselves up in my room and talk the moon down the sky ! "

Waiting for the commissionaire to find the Embassy car, Mary, looking out on the bright and prosperous-seeming traffic, felt herself being sucked back into a dream. Was it possible she had looked on this same street only a few short years ago, and seen it littered with glass and blood, its balconies twisted, flames and smoke pouring through its shattered roofs ? "

" What are you thinking about ? "

" The war. I mean, our war."

" I was in London the week before last. They were having raids every few hours. I saw places crumble up and slide down in clouds of dust. I watched ambulances picking up pieces of people."

" Go on."

" I'm sorry."

" Why ? No one is called upon to justify herself, except to her own soul." She added presently, " What are they saying ? Do they think it will be over soon ? "

" There's a certain degree of silly optimism.—Oh Mary." Adela Hallatt's face was twisted ; she turned it quickly away. " I'm American, by marriage—but there are times when one can't help feeling and thinking as an Englishwoman. My uncle —Uncle Bay—says that after-the-war will be worse than the war

itself. No money. The minimum of food. Collapse of industry—
that means strikes. Devaluation. Class warfare. All the soil,"
she murmured, " manured and ready, to receive the Russian
seed."

" *That's* when I shall go back."

Was it her own voice that spoke ? Was it to her that decision
had come, suddenly, on the steps of a Madrid hotel, above a
crowded street ? Sudden light spread through and around her.

" To put your thumb in the dyke ? "—The words were ironic,
but the voice tender, as Adela kissed her and got into the car.
" You *idiot* ! " she muttered through the window. " You look
as though you had received the Annunciation ! "

II

" Of course I see it now—your point of view."

They were stretched in long cane chairs above the golden
glow of Madrid, which rose to meet the immense stars. The hum
of Madrid sounded beyond the dark green silence of the Retiro.
Never had the constellations seemed so close and so bright as,
with starlight on her face and hands locked behind her head,
Mary recited the saga of Aracea.

" Where is she now ? "

" In Segovia, with her mother and some elderly relatives—
being immensely spoiled ! "

" She must miss you——"

" The de la Cernas are one of the ' big ' families. Though
there aren't many children, they seem to know plenty of
youngsters. It's Aracea's first glimpse of ' society '—and I must
say she takes to it better than I expected."

" When do you go back ? "

" In about a fortnight. I expect I'll have to bring her in
for one of the bullfights."

" That child—— ! "

" Come ! She's grown up on a ranch—not *a* ranch, but one
of the famous ranches in Spain."

" I can't help it ; it's revolting. They put up a charity fight last week and Gro and I were obliged to go ; we were both nearly sick. I can't imagine how you tolerate it ! "

" Doña Leandra would agree with you," said Mary mildly. " But it's a matter of taste.—Is Elizabeth still running her school ? "—It seemed better to change the subject.

" Indeed she is ! You'd hardly know it." Adela's laugh came softly through the starlight. " Do you remember how we started—on my legacy from Aunt Isobel ?—with the Basingstoke children, and two or three others ? And we had to borrow from Uncle Bay at the end of the second term ? I don't remember if we told you about buying Elmcott Manor : it was a crazy venture, but Elizabeth was always more venturesome than I. Later on, I begged her to sell, but she was much too stubborn, and—to be candid—from the moment I pulled out and got married, it began to flourish. And the war did the rest."

" I suppose, because it's in a safe area."

" Partly that, partly because Elizabeth is a brilliant organiser. The sad part is "—She checked herself. " I have no right to call it the ' sad ' part. The truth is, it's grown right beyond our original intention : ' a Catholic school for children of good family, too delicate to take the usual convent training.' There's special care, of course, for the ' delicate ' ones, but we now have swimming, riding, tennis, lacrosse—like any other big boarding-school. I've, naturally, retained an ' interest ' ; and Elizabeth's still the secular Head."

" Secular ? "

" At the beginning of the war, we got permission to amal-gamate with the local convent, which was having to close down for want of suitable premises. Mother Mary Joseph and Elizabeth get on perfectly together ; it's an admirable arrange-ment.—Mary ! " she broke off. " Don't say you're thinking of sending your bullfighting child there ! We've got plenty of stamina, but I don't think it's fair to the nuns, to have to cope with that kind of thing ! "

" Don't be alarmed ; her parents wouldn't hear of it. But I'd like to ask Elizabeth to recommend me some books, and advise me a little. I feel I should read some psychology : I need some guidance, now Aracea is growing up."

"From what you tell me, affection will go farther than psychology. Candidly, your description of the set-up shocks me."

"It's not as bad as you think. The mother's—pathetic : a woman of thirty, worn out with pregnancies by a man she knows is unfaithful——"

"He sounds like a monster."

Mary shook her head.

"It's not like that at all. He's selfish, of course : most husbands are, even in our country ! But she irritates him with her melancholy. Andalucíans don't understand that kind of thing—or that flaccid languor, mental as much as physical, for which the doctors can discover no reason. I thought it was tubercular, when I first saw her, but it appears I'm wrong. The family doctor is an old-fashioned Catholic, who no doubt holds that it is her duty and her husband's right to continue inter-course——"

"I suppose it'll end up by killing her."

"Aracea worships her father ; his workers respect him—and he's immensely popular, with both men and women. He dislikes me ; why should I hold that against him ? In the main he's courteous—but he lets me see I'm there on sufferance ! "

"What has he got against you ? "

"Mainly my nationality. Like a good many Spanish, he has not forgiven us for our attitude through the Civil War. He knows I supported the Nationalists, and disassociated myself completely from the British view-point ; but he does not trust me—as he does not trust Socialists, or Communists, or the trade unions. I respect his principles, and do my best not to annoy him. I am particularly careful not to interfere in any way in his relationship with Aracea."

"What a devilish time you are having," muttered Adela.

She answered quickly :

"Would you be surprised to hear I'm very happy ?—Perhaps happier than I have a right to be. I have a feeling that I'm doing something worth while. And whatever I have to endure," she added in a low voice, " I have deserved worse."

She spent, on Adela's suggestion, some days at one of the little summer resorts in the Guadarramas. Her temperature had been flaring up again, and she allowed Adela to persuade her of the folly of isolating herself in some remote parador where, if she got ill, neither nursing nor medical aid would be available. She knew enough of the primitive conditions that prevailed in the wilder regions to establish herself in the annex of a small hotel, where most of her time was spent on a balcony, inhaling the cool, pine-scented air—unspeakably invigorating after the sweltering heat of the South.

Her book did not progress, for she spent much of the time thinking about her decision to return to England when the war was ended. It was not difficult to visualise a war-ravaged country, with no strong spiritual directive, lending itself out of sheer lassitude to the forces of evil—as the tired and disillusioned warrior turns in his bitterness to a courtesan. Who was it said that a man and a nation are weakest in their hour of triumph ? There seemed little doubt, now, that the Axis was losing ; but what about the war behind the war ?—what about the Wooden Horse, with its concealed brand of the hammer and sickle ?

Carlos said, They get at us through our arts, which are our life-force. How about the recrudescence in English art, which, curiously, had formed an obbligato to the war ?—the Russia-inspired work of some of the young painters, which was being passed on to the schools ? What about the self-appointed, notoriously Leftist body, which had taken upon itself the direction of public taste in music, painting and sculpture ? *They get at us through our arts.* And England has no Catholic Church to stand between it and its betrayers.

She had found her way at last, through her few conversations with Adela and Grosvenor, to forgiveness of England for its betrayal of Spain, and, with forgiveness, came renewal of love for the country of her birth, her upbringing and traditions ; and she prayed each morning and each night that, in upholding the things of the spirit, in supporting law and order against anarchism, she might be allowed, on her return, to expiate her own sin of desertion.

III

When she returned to Segovia, her absence, brief as it had been, seemed to have given her a new perspective on the child ; it hardly seemed possible that a mere fortnight could have affected so marked an alteration.

Sharp to perceive the impression she was making on other people, and greedy, always, for admiration—Aracea had quickly grasped that the girls with whom she now associated were not impressed, or amused, but offended by her off-hand manners, and that the boys made fun of her behind her back. Aracea was not used to ridicule, and resented it, but was intelligent enough to know that the remedy lay in her own hands. The one form in which she might have demonstrated her superiority, her riding, was denied her ; for, since the Civil War, no one appeared to ride except a few of the officers of the garrison, and strenuous inquiries failed to produce anything that was fit for the saddle.

In the garden of one of the houses where she was allowed to visit was a frontón, and she learned to play a kind of pelota with tennis rackets, and soon beat all the girls, who had neither her strength nor her powers of endurance. They played early in the morning, before the heat set in, and the boys who hid in the plumbago at the top of the wall, to jeer at this emasculated version of their game, were reduced to whispers of approval by the prowess of the visitor. " Lo viste ?—qué villano ! "

It took some tact and persuasion on Mary's part, to get permission to teach Aracea and two or three of her companions to swim, but persistence carried the day. Supported by old motor tyres, the little girls splashed and screamed among the tadpoles of the Moorish tank, which summer drought had reduced to a mere three or four of its statutory twenty feet. The others were too timid to dispense with their floats, but on the second day Aracea kicked away her tyre and crossed the tank, arriving blown and waterlogged, but triumphant. Within the week she was racing Mary down the full length, and increased her number of lengths each day, to the admiration of her less courageous companions.

One curious, and, to her guardians, gratifying result of the visit to Segovia was that it brought about, naturally, and with no ill-feeling, that separation between the sexes that Mary had doubted her ability to conduct at home. In the more modernised cities, which had begun to come under cosmopolitan and non-Catholic influence, a certain degree of laxity was creeping in; but in this stern Castilian stronghold, where every child could recite the heroic last words of the boy hero Luis Moscardo of Toledo—" Long live Spain, long live Christ the King ! "—the ancient principles held good. Boys and girls, as they reached adolescence, retreated to opposite sides of a gulf, to cross which labelled a boy an effeminate and a girl a wanton. Nothing but the sexual urge warranted, for the boy, the infringement of that well-marked boundary, and it was understood that, for his satisfaction, he should seek, not his former playmates, but the vast feminine community whose justification was to preserve the innocence of their protected sisters.

From the day of her arrival in Segovia, Aracea hardly spoke to a boy : strange situation for one who had consistently despised and avoided her own sex. Wherever she went, she was crowded about by girls, whose flattery—when she began to earn it—ended by wearing down her objections to their society. She began to take interest in the subjects that monopolised their minds : clothes, social behaviour, titbits of scandal gleaned from manicurists or servants—and again clothes. Leandra was languidly pleased, and surprised, on the day her daughter remarked it was time she had some new dresses, and submitted herself, within a ring of admiring and critical adults, to the hands of the family modista. She had no suggestions to offer, but was content to preen herself in the results.

Another contribution to her personal dignity was her de la Cerna blood. She was deeply impressed when shown the marble bust, mounted on a high stone plinth, that marked the spot where the noble and illustrious Don Ramiro Blasco de la Cerna, author, philosopher and professor of Spanish languages and literature at the University of Oxford, Inglaterra, was assassinated by Communists in the summer of 1938 ; and her respect for her grandfather's memory rose near to idolatry when, in an alcove panelled with lacería, which, through its horse-shoe window, commanded an incomparable view of the Guadarramas and the rolling Castilian plain, she discovered a set of engravings, on which she swooped with delight.

" But Miss Mary ! *He* loved the bulls as well ! "

Mary smiled, and made a mental note that a visit to the Prado must be included in their promised trip to Madrid.

" Those are by Goya, one of your greatest painters ; they are reproductions of the Tauromaquía. His motto," she murmured, " was ' aún aprendo ' "—an observation lost on Aracea, who, nevertheless, was not to be torn away until the light died on the pictures.

An uncommonly sedate Aracea, in a silk frock that came half-way to her ankles, instead of ending at her knees, accompanied Mary to Madrid, where they had permission to stay overnight, as the journey was to be taken by train ; to have gone by car through the mountains would have been faster and more pleasant, but the de la Cernas would not hear of it ; there were still many " mala gente " in the mountains. It was only on Mary's insistence to Leandra that to deprive Aracea of this promised treat, as a reward for her good behaviour at Segovia, would be an injustice to the child, that they were allowed to undertake the expedition at all. A heavy cloud of disapprobation lay on the household, on the eve of their departure, and Mary knew she was in disgrace for encouraging this deplorable interest on the part of her pupil.

But their spirits were unclouded when they set out. The high spot for them of the charity corrida for which Mary had managed to get seats was the appearance of Paco Ribera, as a member of the cuadrilla of Marcial Zarcillo, one of the brighter stars of the novillero galaxy. Of this they had been informed in a letter enclosing a really frightful hand-coloured postcard of Paco, autographed in purple ink—which Aracea snatched up and concealed. That made Mary a little uneasy; it would have been more like her to flaunt it on her dressing table. Still, it might be a discreet tribute to public opinion. There were no photographs of bullfighters around the house of de la Cerna !

It was a bad fight.

When Aracea had got over the excitement of finding herself in the First Bullring in Spain—whose tiers, on the sombra, were not more than three parts full, as the tickets were expensive and there were no names on the bills that drew the selective Madrid public—she settled down to be critical.

Working with a cuadrilla all older and more experienced than himself, Paco was given no opportunities. He brought off a useful pass, that drew the bull away from the man and turned it neatly into the horse—but the bulls were sluggish and the audience captious. The bullfighters worked themselves to a standstill, to a running accompaniment of irony from the crowd. Down on the sand, the kingfisher-blue figure looked lost and forlorn. It was an afternoon of hard work, much abuse and no glory. Mary was sorry that the girl's first view of the Monumental should be under such inauspicious conditions. " Mucho trabajo, poco éxito," as Aracea observed, justly.

They had sent a note to Paco's boarding-house—he was not, of course, at the grand hotel, with the stars—saying they hoped to see him after the fight. But either the note had not been delivered, or, in the nervous excitement, Paco had forgotten about it. When they got around to the back-street pension to which they were directed, they were informed that the cuadrilla had left. "They've got a fight at Valladolid to-morrow." Aracea took her disappointment with philosophy.

" There wasn't much to say, was there ?—and Paco would be in a bad temper. So now we can go and see your friends."

In Adela's sala they sat demurely. Aracea contributed her share to the conversation with self-possession. When complimented on her English, she replied calmly,

" Yes, it is very good. I have learned it all from Miss Mary."

"That's not quite true," protested Mary, through Adela's laughter. "What about Miss Baxter?"

"Miss Baxter was a fool, and I did not learn anything at all from her."

"You've certainly got your hands full," observed Adela, while they were, briefly alone. "But I agree with you: it's well worth while. She's going to be beautiful, isn't she?—And, while I remember, here's Elizabeth's address; but don't let her fill you up with psychology. I feel, somehow, that regimented ideas won't give you much help with that one."

The following morning, in accordance with their plans, was spent at the Prado, where, on the strength of the Tauromaquía, Aracea was induced to pay attention to the Goya rotunda, and to express approval of Las Meniñas; but a course of Velásquez, El Greco and Veronese led her to observe that she wished to have her hair cut, and be given a permanente: which so took Mary aback that she returned without a murmur to the hotel, in whose peluqería, by the miracle of a cancellation, the señorita was able to have immediate attention. Any interest shown by Aracea, at this stage, in her appearance seemed worth encouragement—even at the expense of culture. But Mary felt startled, and a little sad, when, at the end of three hours, she was joined in the lounge by a barely recognisable version of her pupil. Not only had Aracea's hair been cut short, and set into a violent wave, but her nails, which she displayed with pride, had been varnished blood red.

"Do you think they'll last until we get home?" she asked anxiously. "I want Papá to see them!"

Hoping secretly that the enamel would soon crack off, and the rapidity of the growth of Aracea's hair dispose of those disastrous waves—she smilingly told the child she was "guapísima," and that they had better hurry up and get some food, before catching the train for Segovia.

Settled into the corner of their first-class compartment, Aracea said:

"Miss Mary. Is there really going to be a baby?"

"Si dios quiere." Although startled—it was the first time

Aracea had mentioned the subject—she made herself answer calmly.

" I suppose I'll have to teach him to use the cape," came drowsily from the corner. Mary half-extended her arm.

" Do you want to put your head on my shoulder ? "

" No—gracias."

Naturally not ; a señorita with permanented hair and varnished fingernails does not cuddle down like a baby. Aracea folded her arms, put her head back and prepared to go to sleep in that dignified position.

IV

" Miss Carpenter ! "

Mary, leaning over the balustrade above the patio of the horses, started violently. It was the evening following their return from Segovia, and she was still tired, after an unusually peaceful day. Aracea, who, on their arrival, had clung to her father, sobbing with weariness and joy to be home, had been out with Don Luis all day. After luncheon, the household retired to bed ; for the full blast of summer was now on them, and the least movement started the perspiration flowing. With the heat came the curse of flies—almost unendurable in the house of Parral, with its equine inhabitants. Shutters were closed and the Flit-gun used in living and sleeping rooms. From now on, until the heat was over, they would live in darkness. Why, thought Mary, had Spain never discovered the means of making summer life tolerable ? She had asked for, and been given, mosquito nets for her bed and Aracea's. Other people, apparently, were not troubled by the flies.

" Miss Carpenter ! "

The voice came, obviously, from the roof, but, craning over the rail, she could see no one between herself and the stars.

" Can you hear me ? "

" Yes ; what is it ? "

" If you go along the passage to your left, you will find something you haven't seen before ! "

What nonsense was this? While she was making up her mind to return to her room, mockery fell from the air.

"Are you afraid, Miss Carpenter?"

"What is there to be afraid of?" she answered, rather sharply. How many ears were listening? What tale would go round the kitchens and stables and barns in the morning?

"Please don't say you are not curious! That is as much as to say you are not a woman!"

Irritated, yet amused, she took a step back, to look along the passage which led, so far as she knew, only past a toilet and two or three windowless rooms that owed their existence to the nonchalance of Spanish builders, to a blank wall, which she had never examined closely. She saw, to her surprise, a faint light, which appeared to be that of a torch, streaming down an uneven flight of wooden steps—and knew instantly where they led: to a mirador she had noticed, sometimes, from a distance, wondering where the access to it lay.

"What in the world are you doing up there?" she whispered cautiously, wondering how he, with his artificial leg, had managed to negotiate the steep flight, at the top of which, by the sound of his voice, he was standing.

"I want to show you something I am sure you have never seen since you came to the house of Parral!"

Fully conscious of imprudence, she stumbled up the stairs, and found herself in a small, square room of glass and wood. The wood was warped, and most of the glass broken. A mere bird-cage of laths existed between her and the stars. The beam of the torch showed spider webs, dead moths, pigeon droppings. She grimaced with distaste.

"I don't think this is very attractive," she was beginning—when he switched off the torch. With a gasp, she found herself looking into the fair face of the moon—almost, it seemed, within hand's reach; the moon that poured a sappy whiteness across the rolling lands of Parral, and paled the surrounding stars. The silence was that of another world.

"You're right," she breathed. "It's wonderful."

Presently he offered her a cigarette; she wondered, as she

accepted it, whether the burning tip might not be marked by one of the thousand eyes that watched over the house of Parral by night. Carlos, apparently, had no such misgivings.

" Well ; did you enjoy your holiday ? "

" We had a delightful time."

" And you ? " he pressed her.

" I too, of course—especially in Madrid."

" You heard no news in Madrid."

" News ? "—Her mind leapt instantly to the war ; could there have been anything——? Had she missed it in the papers ? " I don't know what news you mean."

" Perhaps it hasn't yet been announced." He was enjoying her apprehension. She realised, impatiently, his meaning.

" Oh—social news. I wasn't moving in *those* circles ! "

" It's over," he told her dramatically.

" What is over ? "

" Luis and Gloria."

" Oh—what a mercy. What happened ? "

" It is really rather amusing.—I think you could safely sit on that ledge, Miss Carpenter "—he tested it with his hand. Mary sat, but said hurriedly, " We mustn't stop up here "— then wished she had said " I " instead of " we," which suggested complicity.

" It seems there was a family arrangement which nobody knew about : when she came of age, Gloria was to marry the eldest son of a madrileño family—fabulously wealthy ! A matter of business, of the welding together of two fortunes. La Meléndez is very fond of money ! So she decided—or perhaps it was decided for her—that this romance had gone on long enough. Poor Luis !—it hit him like a bomb. The boy from Madrid is staying at the Moresco, and Gloria, under the paternal wing, is behaving like a girl fresh from her convent ; no more gay parties or rides to Ṣanjorje ! They are being married in the cathedral—and that is the end of the comedy. I have missed you," he ended abruptly.

" That is absurd." She struggled through clouds of relief

towards realisation of what he was saying. " You don't ' miss ' somebody you seldom meet," she braced herself to reply.

" Some people make you think of them whether you meet them or not."

Paralysed on the ledge under the great, white, aphrodisiac moon, she told herself this was madness : sheer, sinful madness, that she must confess to-morrow. There was a sensation in the tips of her fingers, as though they were closing on the fine cloth of his coat ; a sensation in her lips, as though they were brushing his hair, with its sharp, pleasing scent of lemon verbena. The effort she made to rise to her feet was like the tearing of her limbs. She said, through a choking sensation in her throat— " Good night " : and moved towards the stairs.

" Mary." His arms were round her. " Tell me something. Does my black patch revolt you ? "

She could only shake her head.

" And my foolish leg ? "

" Of course not. Ah—please—— ! "

She felt her lips enfolded into his, and his hands pressing her into his body. It was the first time, since she became a Catholic, that she had surrendered to a carnal embrace, and while her conscience shrank, everything else in her flowed out to meet it. It was like coming on a spring in the desert. She gulped like one kneeling to drink in an oasis.

" The moon shines out of your face," he told her gravely.

" Do you remember," he asked her, " that I warned you it was dangerous to say ' No ' to a man of my disposition ? "

She had just sufficient will left to push away the hands that sought greater privileges.

Never, never, she told herself, as she locked her bedroom door, should it happen again. Thank God it was Saturday to-morrow, and the priest was coming to hear confessions. Sinking on her knees, she made a long act of preparation for her penance.

Chapter Nine

I

LIKE ALL men of his temperament, Don Luis Parral burned the candle at both ends. The Meléndez episode ended—and, in a way, he was relieved—naturally, there were others. There were few nights when he did not set out, alone or with Carlos, who had grown into his boon companion, to return a little red in the face, a little puffy round the eyes, only in time to take a bath and ride out with his daughter.

But there was not a detail on the ranch that escaped his personal supervision. He would walk into the feeding lots and scoop up a handful of grain, smelling and tasting it, to make sure it was not being mixed with inferior stuff, and the people in charge getting themselves a rake-off by the sale of the pure corn. When the bulls were brought in off the pastures, to be readied for the ring, he rode always with his vaqueros. He supervised in person their loading into the boxes for transport. He shared with his head man the duty of watching the seed bulls mount the cows, and was not unfrequently present at the delivery of the calves. He had a habit of making surprise descents on people he suspected of shirking their duties, and the younger fry, who threw away their pitillos at his approach, took care to be busy at their carpentry, or bellows-blowing, or wall-mending, at a mere hint that the dueño was in the offing. He knew to a litre the amount of gasolina and oil there should be in his pumps, and made periodical checks on the gauges of the petrol-driven vehicles used on the estate, to make sure his drivers were not stealing joy-rides on their off-duty hours.

All these duties, which many breeders would have left to their mayorales, he undertook because his heart was truly in the business. Carlos, ostensibly his helper, was more often left in the office, with his ear glued to the telephone, his eye on the clock to catch a fight in Barcelona or Asturias, his brow knitted over accounts whose complications were increased by Don Luis's sly aversion to taking his cousin by marriage completely into his confidence. He excused himself for so often leaving the disagreeable end of the business to Carlos by pointing out that the latter was not yet in condition to spend hours in the saddle. " Hombre!" protested Carlos. " I could get about just as well, and faster than you, in one of the cars ! " No, no ; Don Luis vetoed this quickly. Gasolina was dear enough and hard enough to come by not to be wasted when horses were available.

To Aracea's great joy, her father had given her the grey horse, on which she had bestowed the name Bandera. From the time of their return from Segovia, it was taken for granted she should accompany Don Luis on his morning rides, which took him to the farthest pastures : examining boundaries for weak places, and the pipelines that carried the precious water from the springs across kilómetros of dried-up earth to the drinking troughs. She learned to be sharp in recognising the distinction between lawful wear-and-tear and sabotage, of which, since the war, there had been plenty. She shared his anxieties : of drought, and of an outbreak of foot-and-mouth, that decimated a herd less than fifty kilómetros away ; of a valuable cow that slipped her calf, and whether she would carry next time. And his problems : whether or not to sell a two-year-old cow to a breeder who wanted to enrich his strain, but whose reputation was not equal to his pocket—the latter very tempting to one whose banking account declined as his expenses rose ; whether to take a gamble on the old seed bull, Camarista, and let him serve another season, for the sake of the glorious progeny he had begotten over his long span of years, or to dispense with his services in favour of one of the youngsters who had yet to prove his quality as a sire.

He talked to her as though she were a man, sometimes forgetting she was not a man, as she swung beside him with the long mane of Bandera blowing back across her knuckles. Then something she said reminded him she was not a man, and he turned quickly to feast his eyes on this female child, fruit of his loins, who rode her horse like a rejóneadora and responded with eagerness to his every mood.

" What is it, Papá ? "

" You are very beautiful," he muttered, as he turned away.

It was true ; during the following months Aracea stretched out so fast that before Christmas came she was nearly as tall as her father. As her puppy-fat vanished, and bosom, hips and waist defined themselves into that sinuous and super-feminine pattern that is typical of her race, her face also thinned, and its bones were those of her father's people, exquisitely related to the proportions of her body. Aware of all this, Don Luis bit his lip ; his wife was about to present him with another child—a prospect he regarded without optimism ; it was too likely to be only one in the progression of stillborn infants that had thwarted his efforts to provide an heir to Parral.

With this in mind, he said to her one day :

" Carlos will make you a good husband."

She gaped, then laughed aloud, clear as a bell. Qué chiste ! This was fooling indeed—after the manner of Tío Felipe.

" And so will Tonio Tuerto ! "—she named the oldest of the old, retired vaqueros, who, blind in one eye and crippled by a thrust into the hip, spent his days sitting in the sun. " They're both wise about bulls—no, Papá ? "

" Carlos is very fond of you."

She gave him a look ; for a moment apprehension trembled behind the grey Andalucían eye, then she recovered her insouciance.

" Qué disparate ! Carlos is old enough to be my father."

Don Luis's lips narrowed into a thin line.

" Apart from accidents, the property will come to you. Evidently you can't manage it by yourself. Nor can anyone who does not know the business. Why do you suppose I have taken Carlos as my assistant ? "

" No," said Aracea. The syllable was like a flint flung against a rock, but it left its scar. "I'm not going to marry Carlos de la Cerna, even for the sake of the bulls. Vaya, Papá! We don't do things that way now. Perhaps in grandfather's time—but not now," she concluded, with assurance.

So this, he thought, was the outcome of the English miss. This was what came of giving in to the whim of a wife brought up on foreign ideas. Only an Englishwoman would encourage a girl in rebellion against the will of her father.

He had not objected to the earlier ones—the elderly, scared misses who held him in awe, and whisked about like frightened mice pursued by their uproarious pupil. But in Mary Carpenter he had recognised at a glance a being of different calibre. He now bitterly regretted that he had not put his foot down, there and then. But it was not yet too late.

II

Mary had gone to church—to the little chapel of San Miguel, where once a month the priest from Sanjorje hurried through a mass and heard the confessions of the estate workers. It was icily cold, neglected and dirty; the petticoats of the hermaphrodite saint had surrendered their gaudy colours to years of grime, which blackened the galloon and crusted the mock jewels on the vest. Across the horns of the bull whose head was nailed above the chancel arch a spider had spun a thick web, which, hammock for the dust, sagged into a veil of mourning before the eyes and brow. During the war the glass had been smashed in the various niches, and the figures they contained were powdered with dust to the colour of the surrounding stone, so they were invisible, except as shadows. Vermin had gorged themselves on the altar frontal, until it was no more than a fretwork of powdery tissue.

Mary entered it, always, with a profound sense of shock and pity, for it seemed incredible that any Catholic community could allow its place of worship to fall into such a state of dereliction; yet it bore out what she had heard—that in the distanter country regions, where there was no resident priest, active Catholicism was confined to the ancients; the young, brought up in the secular schools of the period immediately before the war, inoculated with scepticism, paid only lip-service to their parents' beliefs; and as for the children—a church that did not regale them with processions and firecrackers on days of fiesta could not regain ground against the indifference of their elders.

She had made one or two tentative attempts to bring the state of the poor little chapel to Leandra's notice, but her efforts were of no avail. On Sundays and days of obligation, the dueña drove into town; she had probably never set foot across the threshold of San Miguel, although it was within a few kilómetros of her own door.

She spread her handkerchief on the ground. It did not take her long to say the rosary, and she had no disposition to linger in that smell of mould and dirt. The sky had become deeply overcast, and she intended to ride back quickly before the rain began. As she lifted the leather curtain, from whose aged greasiness her fingers shrank, it was snatched out of her hand.

" We seem to meet in some strange places." Carlos was standing between her and the door.

She stammered, looking across his shoulders at the blackening sky.

" I think it's going to pour."

" Not yet."

Then she was in his arms, his lips taking possession of hers, as they had done in the mirador. She felt the pressure of the artificial leg, and his arms, no less hard, binding her to him. Suddenly, into her blinded senses, shot the thought of the many others who must have surrendered themselves to Carlos de la Cerna. But even that failed to subdue the craving he had again awakened. Pride, principle and dignity melted, as she thought with despondency, Now I am truly among the damned. And all the while her trembling limbs obeyed his compulsion.

" Why have you been so unkind to me ?—You have made me very miserable." He was doing as he pleased. She thought, No matter ; the thing is done.

She lost sense of time. Reeling there in the half-dark, her mind split itself, she became two people, one delivered to passion, the other looking on. Why, thought the spectator-self, are you doing this ?—Why are you putting yourself to the torment of this sterile experience, in which there can be no satisfaction ?—And to what depth have you sunk, that you are willing to accept physical passion in the place of love ?

" Mary—gloria mía——" he was muttering. Suddenly, with a gasp, he thrust her away from him, still gripping her ; she could feel the bruises forming on her upper arms. " Mary—to-night ? "

A faint roll of thunder restored, in part, her sanity. Dragging herself free, she muttered :

" I must get back to Aracea——"

" Promise me : *to-night.*"

Laying the palm of her hand flat against his questing mouth, she thrust it away and staggered out into the heavy air. Her fingers struggled weakly with the reins she had knotted into an iron ring on the outer wall of the chapel. Carlos came to her assistance. As the uneasy horse pulled back, he looked at the sky.

" In a minute it will be pouring. You must wait until it's over "—But Mary was already in the saddle. Her face felt shrivelled as she looked down on him, still holding the reins.

" Give me your word ; to-night."

She muttered something and jerked the reins from his hands. At the tap of the whip the horse broke into a gallop. The drops of rain, the size of pesetas, were beating on her head, the back of her neck, the thin stuff of her blouse, making the latter transparent. The horses—Don Luis's and Aracea's—were standing in the patio : they had evidently just got in. A groom ran forward as she clattered under the archway—the rain was now streaming down in rods. Head down, she ran up the stairs, as Aracea rushed out on the gallery.

" Por dios, you are soaked ! Come and let me help you—you'd better have a bath."

Although she wanted nothing more than to be alone, the

girl's insistence was not to be gainsaid. While Concepción ran the bath, Aracea, chattering with excitement, helped to strip off the dripping garments. While Mary was in the bath, Aracea remained in the room adjoining, chattering like a magpie.

"When you come out of there I've got something to tell you !—What in the world do you think, Miss Mary ? " she burst out as Mary rejoined her. "Papá wants me to marry Carlos ! Have you ever heard such nonsense ? "

"He was joking," Mary forced the reply through chattering teeth. Aracea shook her head wisely.

"Oh no, he wasn't ; I know my papá, when he is in earnest. But there's going to be nothing of that sort ! Me—marry myself with that one-eyed, one-legged pícaro "—Mary felt herself wincing from the brutality of youth—" who's had every girl on the estate ! I could point you out two—no, three—of Carlos's children——"

"Aracea ! How do you know these things ? "

"Never mind ; I know them." She tossed her head. "And I can tell you one thing ; nobody's going to force me into a marriage with anyone, until I choose someone for myself."

Mary sat down quickly ; her head was spinning. "And then I shall marry Aracea ! " Why had she not taken the jest seriously ? All, now, seemed so foolishly obvious : Carlos's introduction to the business, the terms of intimacy he enjoyed with Don Luis, his position of privilege in the house. But surely they could not force the child into a marriage against her inclination ? Mary's tongue and throat went dry. She knew, only too well, that they *could*.

"You look awfully sick, Miss Mary," Aracea was saying, in accents of surprise. "Would you like some brandy ? "

"No—I'd like to lie down for a little while—I'd like to be by myself."

Did Leandra know of the preposterous suggestion ?—She must ! And, without doubt, she accepted it. Was she (Mary) the only one to perceive the ugliness of this projected mating between a handsome, middle-aged rake and a girl in her early teens ?

Even his mutilations turned now, in Mary's mind, against one to whom, previously, they had contributed a morbid attraction. A man in his thirties, with one eye and one leg, for that beautiful child?—qué barbaridad. A man whose vagrant desires he would never hesitate to gratify, at the expense of Aracea's pride and her pain? A man whose infirmities, it was safe to assume, did not stop at the sacrifice he had made to his country?

In the rush of scandalised indignation on behalf of Aracea, she became slowly conscious of the cauterisation of the canker in her soul. Like one swimming back out of an anæsthetic, she realised there was nothing left of that ugly growth but a small, burning wound that would quickly heal. A genuine revulsion took the place of her former emotion, as the face which so long had fascinated her became, in her imagination, repulsive: the face of a cheap Mephistopheles, gloating over his secret triumph! *Dame tu palabra: esta noche.* She found herself anticipating his defeat with an acrid satisfaction. Never. To the impure experiences which Carlos de la Cerna carried to his marriage bed, whether with Aracea—which, sweet Mother of God, forbid!— or another, she would contribute no more.

III

" Memorare, O piisima Virgo Maria, non esse auditum a saeculo, quemquam ad tua currentum praesidia, tua implorantem auxilia, tua penitentem suffragia, esse derelictum . . . Mater, curro; ad te venio; coram te gemens peccator assisto . . ."

She lifted her head. Her watch told her it was after midnight. She had been on her knees since leaving the supper table, across which the eyes of Carlos smouldering with anticipation, affected her so little that she was able to take a bolder share than usual in the conversation. Even Don Luis deigned to smile, when the miss parried the shafts of Carlos's wit with some dry observation of her own.

She rose stiffly, to unfasten her dress. A sound behind

her made her whirl around—thankfully remembering the bolted door. She saw the latch lift, and fall again. While she rejoiced in his defeat, the palm of a hand battered softly on the door.

That could not be Carlos! Along the gallery, at this hour, were always some curled-up bodies; he would not risk an indiscretion of that kind. But she hesitated before calling out—" Quién es ? "

A voice murmured something about " la señora."

" Is it you, Concepción ? "

" Sí, señorita." As Mary threw open the door, the old servant stood there, her face of ivory framed in a black shawl. " The señorita will pardon me for molesting her. Mi ama está de parto. Will the señorita have the goodness to telephone for the doctor ? "

" I'll come at once."

So the baby was coming—prematurely! It was not due, so far as she had gathered, for another six weeks. Knotting the cord of her dressing gown, Mary ran to the sala. It took a long time to get the connection. Then a confused voice told her that Don Alejandro was " fuera." She impressed on the speaker the urgency of the call, and, hoping for the best, knocked hesitatingly on the door of Leandra's bedroom.

" Concepción, do you need any help ? Do you know what to do ? "

" Sí, señorita "—the voice was as serene as ever, but the dark eyes were uneasy. " If God wills that the doctor is here soon——"

As she returned to the gallery, she could see its darkness thickly populated; the news that the dueña was in labour had spread through the house of Parral. She sent two women to the porter's lodge, to have the gates open and the patio lit, before Don Alejandro arrived, and turned, to find Carlos standing behind her.

" Qué pasa ? "

" The child is being born. If you know where to find Don Luis, get him as fast as you can," she said brusquely—wondering what she had ever found sinister, in this thin, lame man ; what she had found attractive.

The door of Aracea's bedroom burst open and she came flying out, barefooted and in pyjamas, to fling herself into Mary's arms.

" What is it ?—What is happening ?

" It's all right, darling." She held her tightly. "The baby is coming, and we are waiting for Don Alejandro."

She felt Aracea tremble as they stood there, hearing the car roar out. Then she sent for Aracea's dressing gown, took the child into the sala and tucked her up on the divan, whose cushions still bore the imprint of Leandra's faint limbs.

" Miss Mary. Can't I go and see Mamá ? "

" Not just yet."

" How long will the baby take to be born ? "

" Not too long—we hope."

" The others took ages." Mary looked at her ; she had forgotten that Aracea must have been aware of those other births, and must have watched the little coffins being borne along the gallery. " But they all died ! " she concluded

" Would you like to pray that this one lives ? "

After an almost imperceptible hesitation, Aracea crawled off the divan and she and Mary went on their knees. Mary began to recite as much as she could remember of the Litany of Loreto, ending with the prayer :

" Defend, O Lord, we beseech thee, by the intercession of Blessed Mary ever virgin, this thy family from adversity ; and mercifully protect us who prostrate ourselves before thee with all our hearts, from the snares of the enemy. Through Christ our Lord . . . May the divine assistance remain always with us——"

The door burst open and one of the women fluttered into the room, beating her head.

" Ay dios—ay dios—Concepción says it's very bad, very bad ! "

Gently loosening herself from Aracea's clutch, Mary hurried back to the bedroom. The light was bad, the bed a holocaust ;

the sweat, streaming down Concepción's face as she held her mistress's hands, made it luminous.

" Ay dios, señorita ; when will the doctor come ? "

Hours passed—or seemed to pass. Shuttling between the bedroom and the sala, Mary could hardly believe the clock, that marked only the hour of two. Concepción called in some more of the women to help her ; the opening doors let out sounds that quickened the beat of Mary's heart. Was it her duty to offer to help ? She knew nothing of midwifery, and felt it was better to remain with Aracea, of whom, curled up in the corner of the divan, nothing was visible but a section of flushed cheek. Suddenly she muttered :

" If it's a boy, he'll have the bulls, won't he ? "

" And you'll have a brother to look after you, when he's grown up "—an idiotic reply, but no other came to her. Aracea proved her awareness of its folly with a snort.

" By the time he's grown up, I'll have a husband to look after me ! One thing I can tell you : I'm not going to nurse a baby."

" You probably won't be asked to ; but a baby might be just as much fun to nurse as a little bull."

" They're *quite* different." Aracea yawned and stretched herself. " I think I'll go to bed. One thing's certain : if it's a girl, Tía Carmela will look after it—as she looked after the others ! "

" What on earth do you mean ? "

Aracea, strangling a yawn, said calmly :

"I was the only one she didn't manage to kill, because I was the first, and there was a hospital nurse there to look after me."

" You simply must not say such things," whispered Mary, with horror.

" Why not ?—Everybody knows," asserted Aracea, " except Papá, I suppose, and very likely Mamá. Tía Carmela hates all of us, except Mamá, and she wants to have Mamá to herself. She hates Papá most, so she kills the babies, to spite him. There will be quite a to-do, if it's a boy, and she kills him ! " she ended with a laugh.

" Aracea. You must put those wicked thoughts right out of your mind."—But her blood froze; she had seen the old woman crouched in the darkness on the farther side of the bed. While Concepción was there—that good angel!—all would be well; but suppose Concepción were to leave the room?—What, are *you* subscribing to this evil folly? she scourged herself, as she turned back to the child. " You have been doing what I have forbidden," she said sternly. " You've been gossiping with the servants. How many times must I tell you that they are stupid, ignorant beings, and that it is a disgrace to listen to them—let alone to repeat their nonsense? "

" All the same, Tía Carmela *is* a witch," insisted Aracea.

" Padre Gerónimo has told you there are no such things as witches. Witch-stories are an invention of the Devil, to scare people into evil actions," said Mary. " And you had better ask God to forgive you for saying bad things about Tía Carmela."

The sound of a car rushed them both on to the gallery; but it was only Don Luis and Carlos who lifted their disturbed faces to Mary, as she met them at the head of the stairs.

" Is it over? "

" No; we are still waiting for the doctor."

" We will wait downstairs," said Don Luis heavily, and the two men descended to the office. She heard the door close, and the radio switched on—some foreign station. Evidently Don Luis was availing himself of the instrument he loathed, to smother his apprehension.

A thin grey light lay over the house of Parral when Don Alejandro arrived, and relief swept through the household, as though Death took a step back in acknowledgment of his authority. Mary made Aracea take a bath, and had one herself; they both got dressed, in readiness for—what? Whether it were death, or birth, or both, it was more seemly to receive it with one's clothes on.

But it was after midday when, with a last, faint effort, Leandra gave the heir to Parral to the light.

As she looked upon the deplorable scrap of human flesh, Mary's first thought was, Thank God; now Aracea will not

148

have to marry Carlos de la Cerna. Transported with triumph and delight, Don Luis cried out :

" Where is my daughter ?—She should be here, to welcome her brother."

Pity help the welcome, thought Mary, as she went to break the news to Aracea. The girl gave her a strange look, but followed her, to cast a dispassionate glance at the object, hardly longer than the palm of her hand, that lay in hideous limpness in the folds of a pillow. She muttered, " How ugly," and turned into her father's rapturous embrace. Don Luis was impatient to be out, to spread the glad tidings and receive the congratulation of the countryside ; he took it for granted Aracea would accompany him, but she excused herself politely. He was too excited to make anything of her refusal, but shouted to Carlos to order the horses.

With her elbows on the gallery rail, Aracea watched the pair of them ride under the archway. A curious smile played round her lips. Mary laid her hand on the girl's shoulder, guessing the bitterness of this moment.

" It's all right ; it won't live."

" Aracea—— ! "—Mary recoiled.

Aracea nodded her head. " You will see." And marched before her into the schoolroom.

Mary remembered the grim prophecy when, having sustained six months of fluttering life, that infected all who looked upon it save, seemingly, Don Luis, with misgiving—the son of Parral died of a meningitis.

Who, wondered Mary, could have wished survival for the poor human fragment, too feeble to move or wail, that lay on its pillow like a small effigy of patient woe ? She had seen in it, at times, a terrifying likeness to its mother. A mature suffering existed behind its clouded eyes.

There was mourning in the house of Parral, and all over the estate. There was mourning in Mary's heart—but not for the infant or its parents. The little shield was gone—Aracea's frail protection from the shadow that, once more, drew near. She was sure that, as soon as he recovered from his bereavement,

Don Luis's first act would be to tell his daughter that she must consider herself pledged to Carlos de la Cerna.

One strange incident occurred, to challenge the solemnity of the atmosphere. The morning after they buried the baby, Tía Carmela was found dead in her bed. Mary was told of it by Concepción, as she laid the breakfast tray on Mary's knee.

" The old woman is dead," she murmured, with her usual high serenity.

" *Who* is dead, Concepción ? "

" Pues—Doña Carmela."

Looking into the old servant's fathomless eyes, Mary felt the same cold contraction that went through her on the night that Aracea dispassionately informed her that Tía Carmela was a witch. She was aware of dark undercurrents, to explore which would imperil her soul. She said no more ; but when she took the news of Tía Carmela's death to Aracea, the girl said, in the most matter-of-fact way :

" But naturally. All the servants adore Papá, and it was really going too far—to kill my little brother ! "

Chapter Ten

I

A YEAR went by : of which the sensation was the début of a youth called Ildefonso Garcia, and nothing was heard of the Boy from Maderas. You have no chance, as the member of a cuadrilla, of making your name, and Don Amadeo continued adamant about not allowing his son to fight the novillos. Paco read, with bitter envy, the notices of his friend's successes at Orcina, Barbastro, Lorca, Villanueva del Arzobispo : none of them " great " places, but it depended on the cartel. One good name might draw the critics, and you might be lucky enough to snatch some of the limelight. Somebody—he suspected Don Luis Parral—must be backing Ildefonso; a penniless youth could not start out for himself, with all the expenses of travel, cuadrilla and personal upkeep to pay out of his small and hazardous gains.

Well, they were booked for the Easter feria at Sevilla, and, after that—vamos á ver. It was a wonderful thing—it almost stopped one's heart—to be appearing on the same bill with Manolete, even as a peón; but it wasn't so fine to be caping for a sprucer like Zarcillo—whose credit, during the season, had gone slowly down and down. He was lucky to have got the Sevilla booking; it was about his last chance. If he didn't pull it off at Sevilla—adios, Zarcillo.

As, on the eve of the fight, they got out of the big car in front of the Inglaterra, and the crowd pushed round—not a very big crowd, but a matador, after all, is a matador, and Zarcillo, not having fought for a long time in Sevilla, still had his fans— something struck Paco softly on the ear and fell at his feet. Wondering if it had been meant for him, or for Zarcillo, he bent to pick up the carnation, and looking up, saw to his astonishment, Aracea and Mary, on the balcony above him. He grinned, she gestured wildly—and they met in the patio sown with deep chairs and little tables.

Paco was wearing a light suit and a flowery tie; he looked so grown-up that she felt shy in extending her hand to him. Por dios, he was good-looking! A deep, unaccustomed thrill ran through Aracea; she was fifteen; he must be nearly eighteen. She wondered whether he remembered asking her to be his novia! Such childish jests were now, of course, out of place, but they lingered in the back of Aracea's mind, as the pair of them drew closer to chatter on the sofa. Mary, in her armchair, tactfully opened a newspaper. Paco, signing to a waiter, asked grandly what they would drink.

"What are you going to have?" asked Aracea, after Mary had chosen a Tío Pepe.

"I shall have a cocktail: a Dama Blanca," said Paco, showing off.

" What's that ?—I'll have the same," said Aracea recklessly.
" Well : how many fights have you got this season ? "

He looked at her sidelong, and scowled at his narrow hand.

" I don't know. Father is coming to-morrow. I want to
have a talk with him. I've had enough of caping bulls for other
people."

" Zarcillo has had very good notices," she said politely. He
guessed she knew as much as he did, of what the afición said of
Zarcillo.

" Josú—who wouldn't, that oils the Press the way he does ? "
He threw a cautious glance across his shoulder, to see if any of
Zarcillo's friends were in the offing, and bent towards her. " I
suppose you heard about Bilbao ? "

" I read the papers."

" Nice, weren't they ? Well, they threw everything at us but
the seats they were sitting on, and gave us the bronca from there
to Madrid."

Her eyes widened ; she had not known it was as bad as that.

" But I went in the office and listened to the radio—— ! "

" Ca ! Ten thousand pesetas we were supposed to get for
that fight, and all of it went to shut people's mouths. None of
us got our money until we threatened to walk out."

" Do you think he'll be all right to-morrow ? "—She felt very
grown-up and important at receiving Paco's confidence.

" He'd better !—or we're out. Papá's got to buy me into
another cuadrilla or start me on my own. I don't suppose he'll
be pleased at the idea of putting up any more cash, but he can't
stand out any longer against the novilladas."

He stared glumly ahead of him, lost to the girl who watched
him with a precociously maternal look on her face. Paco. To-
morrow, at this hour, he would not be sitting in the patio of the
Ingleterra, drinking Damas Blancas. She guessed, rightly, that
fear, which is the price paid by all bullfighters for advancement
in their profession, had not yet made good its grip on Paco. But
to-morrow, at this hour, he would probably be feeling very sick,
having left most of his dinner, and smoked a great many cigarettes.

" Do you remember Capanegra ? "

" Yes ; he's not among to-morrow's lot, is he ? "

" No ; Ildefonso killed him last week, at Rio Riojo."

" That's a one-horse place to fight," said Paco, with a stab of jealousy.

" Capanegra was a brave bull, but he was too big for the first-class rings. The matadores are frightened of them ! They say even Manolete only fights little, easy bulls," she teased him. She wondered if she had gone too far, when Paco's face turned white.

" That's a lie ! " he shouted—bringing Mary's head up rather suddenly. " Perdone, señorita," he muttered, but his eyes glittered with furious tears. " Esta chica says that Manolete only fights easy bulls—Manolete—lo más valiente, lo más noble de todo ! "

" That was a foolish thing to say," Mary reproached her.

Aracea giggled.

" You know our bulls used to be twice as big as they are now ; they've had to be bred down, because the fighters were afraid of them ! " she defied her.

" And you know as well as I do that the technique of fighting has altered, and that the present-day public expects very different things than they expected from the Gallo, and Estudiante, and Sanchez Mejías."

The slow fall of Aracea's left eyelid checked her.

Paco continued furiously :

" And if you're capable of making remarks like that, I shall take care not to introduce you to any of my friends."

Aracea threw back her head and let out a clear laugh.

" What a loss ! It's a pity you couldn't have introduced them to Capanegra, and seen what they made of a *real* Parral bull."

He got up quickly, made a bow to Mary—" Su servidor "— and, ignoring Aracea, walked with quick, short steps across the tiled floor.

" Why do you tease Paco like that ?—It isn't kind."

Aracea turned her head, with a sweet, wise smile.

" It is kind, Miss Mary. Didn't you see ?—Paco is nervous about to-morrow, because he knows Zarcillo is a bad bullfighter, and he doesn't want to have to be ashamed of him in the Maestranza. It is much better he should go to bed angry with me than that he should worry for what Zarcillo will do in the ring."

She stopped and gathered from the floor the carnation that had fallen from Paco's lapel. She held it tenderly, smiling at it, as though she and the flower, between them, held a secret.

On their way to the escalator, as they approached the swing doors, one of the latter was flung violently back. Paco, returning, stopped dead in his tracks as he came face to face with Mary and Aracea.

"Have you forgotten something?—Was it this?" asked Aracea sweetly, and calmly offered him the crumpled flower.

He snatched it from her without a word and rushed out again. The smile on her lips was a reflection of the smile in her heart.

The de Gaula house, where Aracea and Mary were staying (Don Luis and Carlos were at the Inglaterra), was alive with the buzz and hum of excited young people, who, for the last six weeks, had thought of very little else than Easter and the feria. In the traditional gowns of flounced and spotted muslin, the three girls, including Aracea, were to ride behind the Parral mule-team, driven, of course, by Don Luis : a signal and much coveted honour, for the Parral turn-out had no equal on the parade-ground. In the morning parade, the elder de Gaula girl, Brigida, was to ride pillion behind her father, in the ancient style of the romería, wearing another magnificent ruffled gown, and Catalina, the younger, was to partner her elder brother. Aracea took it for granted she would ride behind her father ; she had provided herself with a rose-red frock for the occasion, patterned with little silvery moons ; although still, conventionally, in mourning for her brother, the feria gave her license, for once, to abandon her dark dresses.

"Aracita ! Guess who's been here ! " she was greeted, when she and Mary came in. " Carlos de la Cerna. Heavens, what a fascinating creature ! " gasped Brigida, who had reached the age when every man is fascinating, and kept her dueña in a perpetual state of frenzy. " You know who he reminds me of ?—El Gran

Mutilado. I'm sure he's done the most frightful and wonderful things—just like Millán Astray ! "

Aracea gave a scornful guffaw.

" Carlos ? He's my cousin—there's nothing particular about him. And anyhow the Gran Mutilado's got a pair of legs that he doesn't take off when he goes to bed ! "

" Vaya ! You know every girl in Sevilla is crazy about el capitán de la Cerna, and when they hear, they'll be ready to kill you——"

" What on earth for ? " stared Aracea.

" You're to ride behind him at the feria ! " shrieked the girls.

" That I won't." Aracea turned crimson.

Nothing would budge her from her flat refusal.

" Me—ride behind that old pícaro ! I'd rather die," she asserted, to the stupefaction of her friends. Mary's heart sank ; she knew this would lead to more trouble with Don Luis, of which, latterly, there had been enough. " Who's Papá going to ride with, if not with me ? "

Brigida de Gaula tittered ; if she knew nothing about the private life of de la Cerna, she knew quite a few things about Aracea's father. It was all over the town about Don Luis Parral and the brilliant young dancer engaged for the season at the casino. La Mariposa had challenged Don Luis publicly, to partner her in the parade, and like a caballero and an Andalucían gallant, he had accepted the challenge. A look at Aracea's face warned Brigida, however, to keep her information to herself for the present, so she hurriedly said she really did not know, and retired to sigh with envy for those who did not know when they were lucky. The very idea, of not wanting to be seen in the parade with Carlos de la Cerna !

" Now, Papá ! "—Aracea had latterly acquired some finesse in dealing with Don Luis ; when he appeared in the morning, to escort her and Mary to church, she fluttered her eyelashes at him across her fan. She was wearing the high comb and mantilla for the first time, because it was Easter Sunday ; she knew she looked very attractive in her long, black, pleated gown, with her first pair of high-heeled slippers and white kid gloves, and she

knew he agreed with and was proud of her handsomeness.
" What is all this, about my riding with Carlos ? "

As he was silent, biting his lip, she continued gravely :

" I'm sure Mamá and the rest of the family wouldn't approve
of it. Of course, everyone knows we are cousins, but a great
many strangers will imagine I am comprometida ! I suppose that
hadn't occurred to you ? "

" Carlos wishes you to be engaged to him."

" Don't let's start that nonsense again, Papá ! " she retorted
gaily ; but she was more nervous than she appeared.

" He promises to make you a good husband."

" And I will promise something else : Carlos shall be padrino
to the first of my children, after I'm married !—Don't let's
quarrel on the Sunday of the Resurrection, Papá. Come ; if we
don't start at once we shall not get a good place in the cathedral."

All the town had wakened to the pealing of the Easter Bells ;
the shining air trembled with green and bronze notes ; the scent
of orange-flower and jasmine pervaded the streets that had not
yet surrendered their morning freshness to the heat of noon.
Half of Sevilla had not even been to bed ; Mary had had difficulty
in persuading the girls off the balcony at two in the morning,
where they sat gossiping in their dressing gowns, listening to the
guitars and inventing romances about the coming week. The
sweet, gay, feminine atmosphere, so different from that of her
own home, brought out all the feminine in Aracea ; she was no
less earnest than her companions about the rituals of hair-setting,
face-creaming and manicure that had taken up most of their time
after supper.

After the High Mass—when they had watched the figures
that wove before the inimitable retablo like a bed of mystical
carnations—they left by the Puerto de Legrato, and stood for a
moment in the Court of the Oranges, greeting and chatting with
their friends. Suddenly Mary caught sight of Paco ; he was
standing shyly and awkwardly in the shadow of the cloisters,
looking towards them, and she smiled and beckoned him. He
hesitated for a moment, than came over ; as he bowed over their
hands, his eyes asked their pardon for the previous evening. Don

Luis turned genially ; he was still uneasy and displeased with his daughter, but it was part of his tenue to be genial in public. The arrival of Paco would set him free to join his friends in the Inglaterra while the ladies waited for the car that was to take them back to the house. He and Paco shook hands, and it occurred to Don Luis to pay a compliment to his friend Don Amadeo.

" Your father is lunching with me, hombre ; you had better join us."

Paco accepted, not without embarrassment, and Aracea cried :

" Then we may come too, may we not, Papá—Miss Mary and I ? "

Seeing the doubt on Don Luis's face, Mary intervened. All of the de Gaula family, with herself and Aracea, had been to the early mass, as well as to the celebration at the Cathedral, and she had planned to get Aracea to bed immediately after luncheon, for a rest, if not a sleep, before the bullfight.

" I think perhaps we would be out of place, chica, in a party of gentlemen."

" Oh, there are ladies as well," Aracea instantly informed her. " Paco's mother is here, with Don Amadeo—and one of his sisters, with her husband : isn't that so ? "—She appealed to Paco, who nodded. " And you haven't forgotten, Papá, that you invited Tío Felipe and Tía Vittoria, last Sunday, when they came out to see us ? "

In the face of the inconvenient length of Aracea's memory, Don Luis could hardly refuse an invitation to his daughter and her governess, to join his luncheon party. They must first drive home, Mary insisted, and excuse themselves to the marquesa de Gaula and the girls—no, a message would *not* do !—and would be at the Inglaterra by half-past one.

The comedor of the Inglaterra was crowded ; an old-fashioned hotel with a solid reputation, it did not cater for the smart or flashy element, but for people who took things like Easter, the bulls and the bullfight seriously. There were many family parties. Zarcillo was there, with his narrow, foxy face, in a party of foreigners—mainly South Americans. He looked sick ; he looked sick to death, thought Aracea. Don Luis's party was accommodated at an immense round table, where Aracea took pains to seat herself promptly, next to Paco—having submitted to the embraces and compliments of Tía Vittoriana. Tío Felipe distributed the piropo lavishly among the ladies—reserving his more florid efforts, as usual, for Mary. Doña Amalia, as usual, was lachrymose; her great melancholy eyes were fixed on Paco, as though for the last time. Carlos had slipped casually into the chair beside Aracea's; she gave him a look, dismissed him with a shrug and turned to Paco.

"Did you go down to look at the bulls this morning?"

"Of course."

"What has Zarcillo drawn?"

He muttered the numbers. The daughter of Parral nodded gravely.

"Twenty-eight is good. The other—regular." (And "regular," for a Parral bull, meant good; meant the top of any other category.) She paused, and lied for Paco's sake. "And Zarcillo looks good. He will do well this afternoon."

"You're loca. He looks like hell." He cast a quick look across her head and lowered his voice to speak under the strong babble of voices. "Don't tell anyone: we've been told to murder the bulls. Nieto and Curro—that's the pics,—have had their orders. We're to break them in two, so Zarcillo'll have nothing to do but walk in and nail them. I'm only telling you because you don't have to think it's my idea of the way to handle Parral bulls."

Her eyes covered him with benevolence.

"Eat something, and don't bother with the rest. Strength comes from the stomach, and nobody can fight if he's hungry," she told him calmly.

He gulped, and gave her a slow, distant smile. He would rather not have been at this luncheon party, among these important people—being only a peón in the cuadrilla of the least considerable fighter on the bill. But, slowly, he was passing into his hypnosis.

It had only begun recently. Once he felt nothing before the

fight but excitement and a few qualms in the bowels; but he
had too often watched the advance of death across the sand; he
had had too much practice in dodging behind burladeros and
scrambling over barreras an inch ahead of the horns. The icy
realities of bullfighting had displaced its thrill. He had one hope
only: that, in the moment before he went into the ring, he
might get the chance to press his two feet into the holy prints
of Manolete, and perhaps some virtue would rise from them,
rise up inside him like a cloud of light! "Then let me do
something—only *something*!" The chances of that were small
indeed; no matador allows his workers to snatch a crumb of
his jealously reserved glory, and no experienced peón lets himself
in for trouble by seeking to draw attention to his own exploits.
Bullfighters are dispensable, and too easily replaced, until they
reach the upper brackets.

Aracea thought, I love him. That's it. I'm in love with
Paco. And I'm going to marry him.

II

When the bull took up its querencía on the spot where
previously one of the horses had been killed, a groan went up
from the crowd. They were fed up with Zarcillo, anyhow, and
more than a few rude remarks were directed at the management
for engaging a fighter of that calibre for the Resurrection Sunday
fight at Sevilla.

Zarcillo had cut a fair amount of dash with the cape, but the
bull had been pic-ed to hell in the second suerte. Like a wise
bull of Parral, it had developed its querencía at the beginning
of the suerte of the darts, and nothing, short of magic, would
draw it from the spot in which it had invested its safety.

Under his cold brows the maestro watched and the peónes
sweated. Time was going on. The blood ran down and made
a deep pool from the bull's massacred shoulder. This was the
moment for Zarcillo's big act—the nailing of the banderillas—
that he never left to anyone else; his sole justification, to-day,

for his presence in the Maestranza. And he couldn't bring it off, unless the bull could be induced to leave that little patch of sand.

There is nothing more tedious, more agonising and more sick-making to the spectators, than the sight of the man trying to draw the bull out of its chosen spot. Aracea pressed both hands, clasping her fan, into the soft place under her ribs, as she watched Paco go in, dropping his cape under the bull's nose, dragging it a few inches, while only the head and the horns moved, and the feet remained implacably planted in the sand. She saw the other peónes wiping the sweat out of their eyes on their embroidered sleeves, and saw Zarcillo waiting furiously, with the first pair of darts in his hands. And she saw Paco walk right in, like a lunatic, and, still trailing his cape, slap the bull across the nose with the palm of his hand.

She did not know that she had yelled with the rest as the bull charged. The spin that carried Paco out of reach of the horns left it enough room to sweep clear of the magic circle. It was surrounded by a flapping of magenta and yellow. A flash of salmon-pink crossed the sand, and Zarcillo nailed his first pair —which he owed to Paco. The audience shouted its applause— for Zarcillo—and the cuadrilla was working like mad to prevent the bull's return to its patch of safety. Zarcillo snatched his second pair, and nailed them with a precision that brought another round of applause. He missed with one of the third-placed just as the trumpet sounded—but the suerte was saved. And the credit was Paco's. She looked agonizedly, to see whether anybody but herself recognised it, and met the sympathetic eyes of Mary. They exchanged smiles.

She could see Paco's face, white as a cerecloth, as he slid through into the callejón. He ducked his head and went to stand alone. In a few more years, she thought, you won't feel that way. You won't carry the maestro's shame visibly on your shoulders. What you really mind is, it's happening in front of Manolete. And, in a minute, they'll all have forgotten Zarcillo. They're only here for Manolete . . .

The other girls were wearing white mantillas with their

flowery dresses; a little envious of their glory, Aracea was unconscious of the fact that her black gown and the half-moon of white camellias in front of her comb singled her out against that brilliant background. Her black silk mantón embroidered in white had the central place among the sheaves of lemon-yellow, carnation and turquoise that draped the front of the palco. She was the youngest, and, without knowing it, the loveliest and most conspicuous of the galaxy of youth and beauty that, in the interval, focused the opera glasses of the tendidos and the barrera seats where the fans and the toughs were collected.

She was sorry Paco was wearing that dark-violet suit—intended, no doubt, to enchance the salmon-pink and silver worn by Zarcillo, who was said to object to his cuadrilla's wearing colours that challenged his own appearance in the ring.

But now no one had eyes for anything but Manolete—for the King, wearing his mystical and tragical crown, separated from his companions by an aura of the supernatural that invested the applause with reverence.

Of the majestic and lethal ballet that followed, Aracea, for once, saw little; even the solemnity of the triple Olé failed to draw her mind and her heart away from the figure that rested its chin on its arms which were folded on the top of the barrier. Paco stood still as a cold, china figure, paying no attention to anything but the god-like being on the sand. The violet suit looked like a bruise.

The eighth and last bull was again Zarcillo's. Zarcillo's face was a dirty yellow, and he looked as if he had a bad taste in his mouth. He knew he had earned the disapprobation, not only of the public, but of his cuadrilla, and under his breath he was cursing every manjack of them to hell. But he meant to save his face. If he did not succeed in doing so, this would be his last appearance in the Maestranza. You can't buy off the Sevillan critics as you can in the smaller towns. If he got a dirty Press here, its echoes would follow him for the rest of the season, and prejudice his reputation in the Argentine.

Aracea watched Paco pick up the cape, and holding it bunched in his left hand, set off at a run across the sand. Parallel with him ran his partner. After a hush, a dark grey Parral bull trotted, with no appearance of speed, down the gangway from the toril. Neat, collected, with head high and forward, it swerved right and made for the barrera. The flash of pink that had enticed it promptly vanished. It paused, turned, and saw across the sand another fan of pink. It made for it with a rush like an express train.

Paco watched it coming. His face was still white, but he had managed to dismiss from his mind all but his immediate duty : an unpleasant one, for the peón is not supposed to show grace or form during this act, which is designed only to demonstrate the disposition of the bull to the watching maestro ; the peón must run, scuffle and be prepared to go like a scalded cat for the barrera. The bull, at its freshest and most imponderable, is there to make a fool of him, and he must take care not to shock or twist it, as he passes it backwards and forwards between himself and his partner.

The bull was very fast, very sharp in its turns between charges, and was hooking on different levels. As it left him for a moment to rush at Santos, he saw out of the corner of his eye Zarcillo, just inside the burlador. Zarcillo looked mean, looked like poison, and his left hand went to his ear. Paco swore under his breath ; that meant *twist it*.

Twist it yourself, you sod, thought Paco, as he ran over towards the tablas which, after his next turn, the bull should be facing. The pale, still face of Manolete was in his consciousness. So Zarcillo wanted his bull handed to him tied up in a basket, did he ? So he wanted it easy—did he ? Already the crowd, tired of waiting, was shouting for the matador. All right, said Paco, and wished he had a big, long chin, like Belmonte's, to stretch towards the oncoming bull. He was sick of leaping about like a grasshopper and running like a hare. So he spread the cape very deliberately, thinking of Ildefonso.

As the bull went through, it struck him that he had not really expected the veronica to come off. The bull was still fully levantado, it had not begun to accept the domination of the capes. He distinctly felt its heat as he pivoted on to his right foot, in readiness for its return. It was crazy with a bull like that, but some compulsion was behind him. The bull came through again, and all his instinct told him to trick it—to make a quick sidestep out and another back when the horns had gone past. But the knowledge of a pair of sad, death-delivered eyes behind him forced him to hold his ground. This time the bull's shoulders actually dunted his ribs and almost lost him his balance, and a ragged Olé went up. Once more, thought Paco breathlessly, and Zarcillo can put his foot up my arse and find himself another peón.

He could see Zarcillo, in the corner of his eye, dodging out, mad as hell—and then see nothing but the bull, coming back for the third time: and, somehow, the cape had got itself bunched on his left hip, and there was a short swing instead of a long one, and the bull was left standing.

The Olé this time was solid, a big chunk of noise, tossed above the yellow and white brickwork and the flags, into the yellowing sky. Running towards the barrera, avoiding the shaft of Zarcillo's eye, Paco strangled a laugh of delight. He had stolen an Olé in the Maestranza on Resurrection Sunday; stolen it from Zarcillo under the nose of Manolete and—a sunflower burst in his brain—Aracea had seen it. She always said his capework wasn't good enough; now what would she have to say!

A furious shout made him spin round. The ring was in disorder and all the peónes were running in. A ragged youth who had appeared from nowhere was citing the bull—to the rage of the audience, the matador and the cuadrilla that spread to catch the intruder. Zarcillo was surely having bad luck, thought Paco as he ran back; he was a stinking bullfighter, who, for the last couple of seasons, had got away with murder—but this was sheer bad luck.

By the time they got the espontáneo out of the ring and the Civil Guard had hustled him round to the lock-up, Zarcillo's frame of mind was visible not only to his cuadrilla but to the spectators. He was murderous, and took it out in insults to the bull. The trumpet went before he got himself collected. He shrugged his shoulders, made wide gestures of " What more can I do ? " and brought his fury back to the tablas as the horses came in.

The Parral bull, by now, was tired of being caped. Its brain of a killer had steadied itself, and, without a moment's hesitation, it launched its thirty-two arrobas of deadly intention straight at the horse. As the horse went up, with its forelegs dangling, the pic went in—half-way down the spine. A yell of outrage rose from the tiers as the bull tipped horse and man over and the capes closed in. When it went for the second horse, pandemonium broke out. It was plain that Zarcillo's picadores had had their orders to mutilate the bull in the most barbarous fashion, and the crowd took it out of them and their master as only a bullfight crowd can do. When the suerte ended, the bull's shoulder looked like a bucket of crimson jelly ; it stood with its ribs heaving, and one of the de Gaula girls was sick.

Apparently transported beyond the abuse of the crowd, Zarcillo went out with a swagger for the suerte of the darts. As he came up on his toes, holding the sticks high, his body took the curve of a cobra preparing to strike. Huy toro. The Parral bull looked at it.

Man and bull started towards each other simultaneously, Zarcillo zig-zagging his way—and all the cuadrilla and most of the crowd saw he was not going to make it. Three things happened, so close together that they seemed like one : the nearest man sailed his cape out, there was an angry cry from Zarcillo, and Zarcillo was riding the horn, the banderillas still in his extended arms, the look on his face and the posture of his body alike ridiculous. Then he dropped the sticks and tried to grip the horn to lift himself—to relieve the shaft of agony that was tearing its way into his vitals.

Paco thought, That's fixed me, for the present.

III

I'm lucky; por dios, I'm lucky, flashed into Paco's mind.
He was tired and very limp, but he had had a bath and a rub-
down and hung out his sodden suit to dry and air; peónes,
unlike matadores, have to look after their own things.

He had not, to-night, to share the miseries and misdoubts
of the rest of the cuadrilla—all chewing it over; all wondering
where the next job was to come from, and whether they would
ever see their wages for the afternoon's work. He was thankful
to be able to escape their company, for, at times like these, the
son of Don Amadeo Ribera was made to feel—if not precisely
an outsider, one who had no genuine stake in the gamble that
held them together. He had a home, a father in affluent circumstances, and no wife or children. Their envy licked out at him
in short, sour remarks. Curro, he guessed, would be the first to
borrow money; Curro who was supposed to maintain a family
of eleven on a picador's pay. He did not mind lending money,
but he did not see why he should be sneered at for lending it.
Curro was owing him plenty already; so were Lagarta, and
Santos, and others. Lagarta used most of his to buy girls. He
and the other boys jeered at Paco for avoiding the brothels;
they did not know he had had a fright, a few months ago, that
had decided him to lay off—for the present. When he had
graduated from the novillero ranks and had reached the grandeur
and glory of the matador—may be he could afford to let up and
take all the fun that offered.

He had had a brief word with his father at the end of the
fight; the Riberas, who had chartered a coche for the occasion,
were returning to Maderas the same night; not even the Easter
fiestas could justify the absence of Don Amadeo and his son-in-
law from the business for more than twenty-four hours.

" Your mamá says, you'll be coming back with us, hijo ? "

Paco shook his head. Don Amadeo gave him a regretful, if
understanding, look; naturally, at Paco's age, he would have

wanted to stay on to the end of the feria, to snatch the holiday fate had obligingly dropped in his lap.

" I want to have a look round, to see if anything's going. I don't want to be out of work until the end of the season," he excused himself—judging that it was not the moment to propose setting himself up independently. Don Amadeo approved of this —more than he approved of Paco's hint that he would require some money. Notes passed, however—together with the reminder that the dry goods store did not exist in order to subsidise young men bent on cutting a dash in feria week—and Paco returned to his lodging.

He had promised to join the other boys at a wineshop near the cockpit, where, he supposed, they would all bemoan their ill-fortune, and Paco, as usual, would pay. He did not mind paying, but a reluctance to join their sour company slowed his steps as he threaded his way through the narrow lanes in the direction of the rendezvous : not bothering much about where he was going, taking loops and by-passing streets he knew for the sake of putting on time. He was not familiar with the by-ways of Sevilla, and when he found himself on a flowery plaza, surrounded by mansions whose zaguanes led to elaborate grilles that afforded glimpses of lights and fountains, he realised he was lost.

" How does it call itself, this plaza, hombre ? " He accosted a passing youth.

" San Antonio, señor," was the surprised answer.

" Many thanks," muttered Paco—and wondered in which of these fine houses Aracea was staying. She had given him the address, and pressed him, with her customary warmth, to visit them, but the boy from Maderas knew better than to thrust his company on the household of the marqués de Gaula. If he had been a matador, it would have been a different thing ; he would have had no hesitation about swaggering through the zaguan, to ring the bell of the cancela and announce himself as a visitor. But as the wretched member of an out-of-work cuadrilla, pride forbade him to avail himself of Aracea's invitation.

The more he thought of it, however, the more he wanted to

see her. It was a pity she was not staying at the Inglaterra with her father. He stood by the fountain in the middle of the plaza, sullenly kicking a pebble. It was very warm and dark; bats whirled round him; and very silent. Once again his glance went slowly round the tall houses, in some of which lights gleamed behind the drawn persianas. He made another tour of the square.

On an unlit balcony, a figure stood in the darkness; he took it for a servant. But as he came below, a voice whispered softly, positively—" Paco ! "

" Olá," he answered, also in a whisper; for he guessed she would get into trouble for a trick like this.

" I knew it was you !—Come in, come up ! " she urged him.

" No." He shook his head, smiling in the darkness; it was nice to have found her. " I just thought I'd say—Buenas noches."

" Wait; I'm coming down," she muttered, and vanished.

Paco waited, feeling doubtful. He was not anxious to be caught by someone of the house, talking to Aracea at the reja; but he leaned against the stone archway, keeping his eyes on the lights at the far end of the zaguan. He saw her come fluttering down a staircase and through the massed flowers of the patio, and then, to his astonishment, the cancela opened, and she was by his side.

" Something told me you'd come; I've been watching for the last hour," she said as she clasped his hand. " Come; come upstairs—we're all playing games and dancing. They'll love to meet a bullfighter ! "

" *No*." He tugged his hand away. " And you'll get into a row for coming outside like this. How did you get the gate open ? " he asked with curiosity, knowing it was not the custom, in houses like this, not to have a porter who checked on all the incomings and outgoings of the household.

She shrugged the query aside.

" How's Zarcillo ? "

" Muy malo." He grinned. " They say he's got a kilómetro of tubing inside him and his guts are mashed to porridge. He won't fight again this season."

" If you won't come in, I'm coming out," she pouted. As he hesitated, aghast, she caught him by the arm. " Come on! There's a little shop, just round the corner, where the girls and I sometimes buy sweets ; they'll let us sit there, and talk."

But for an oil-lamp, the shop was in darkness, tenanted by an old woman who nodded in a corner, unaware of their entrance.

" She's blind," whispered Aracea, " and pretty nearly deaf— old Tía Ana! She won't care about us being here ; I suppose the others are out."

Although he was aware of the indiscretion of this adventure, which would involve both him and Aracea in grave trouble if they were caught, Paco's uneasiness faded as he looked at the lovely girl, her beauty enhanced by the dim light and the low-necked gown and cross of pearls she was wearing on a band of velvet round her slim throat. He said shyly :

" I like your dress—and that thing "—he touched the cross with a nervous finger. " Muy maja ! "

" And I liked you to-day, in the ring ! Ay-ay ; you caped that bull like an angel. Ildefonso should have seen you."

He was so pleased that he felt, to his dismay, tears come to his eyes.

" What are you going to do now ? "

" Give you a kiss."—Holy Mother of God, what had put such a thought into his mind ? By heaven's grace he had not said it, but Aracea was taken aback by the look of horror on his face.

" Wh-what's the matter ? " she faltered.

" Nada.—I suppose I'll go home for a while. I've got to coax Papá into starting me on my own. It's probably not too late to pick up a few fights. The main thing is to keep in practice ; it won't do to sit down in Maderas, and get fat and slow."

" You'd better ask Papá to let you come out to us and work the cows ! "

" Perhaps I will——"

" Por dios, I've got something to tell you." She smothered

her laughter behind her fan. "Papá's plaguing me to marry Carlos."

"Como?"

"Si—verdad! Did you ever hear such nonsense?—Between ourselves," she continued seriously, "I think Papá has gone a little crazy, since the baby died. He's certainly got a spider in his ceiling about marrying me off. *Carlos!* He used to ride me on his knee, when I was about a year old."

"You won't marry *him*."

"What do you take me for?"—Her laughter made a peal of scornful gaiety between the blackened walls; the old woman looked up dumbly, and dropped her head again. "Muchas gracias! When I marry, I want somebody with two eyes and two legs——"

"Like me." Their two hearts, beating, silenced both. Aracea's eyes widened; she moistened her lips, began to say something and stopped; lowered her eyes, and fingered the gold bangle on her wrist nervously.

"Don't you remember—the day you fell in the pond and got leeches all over your legs—and you said you'd be my novia?"

"It was a joke," she whispered.

"And now it is not a joke." He was almost shocked, to discover how little of a joke it was. "They won't let us marry until I've made plenty of money, but we can be comprometidos, now." His voice was deep, tense and not quite steady. He was conscious of the soft curves of her neck and bosom, of her small ear nestling in a wave of dark silk. He wanted desperately to touch her, but custom and his country training were, fortunately, too strong. You don't touch—like that—the girl you are going to marry, until the wedding night.

"I don't suppose they'll even let us be engaged," said Aracea; her voice, also, trembled a little, but she spoke with feminine coolness. "So we'll keep it a secret. Yes, Paco, I'll be your novia!"—She leaned slightly towards him, and the scent of the orange flowers thrust into the innocent opening of her gown made him think of girls who wear strong, heady scents that are part of their art of seduction. The stars swung for a moment, and he pressed his hands hard down on the wooden shelf by which they were standing. "We will wait until Papá has forgotten his foolish ideas about Carlos, and then I will choose a good moment to tell him."

"Aracea—te adoro!" he muttered hoarsely.

She gave him a look as though she were about to fling herself into his arms, and he felt himself shrink—knowing he could not trust himself if his fingers made contact with her lovely flesh. But in her, also, training conquered desire. Holding herself away from him, she laid her lips quickly and delicately to his cheek and sprang out of the little shop.

"I must go, or they'll be looking for me. Adios—Paco—mio!"

"Adios—corazón!"

She ran through the cancela—straight into Mary.

"Where have you been?"

"Only round the corner—to get some sweets." The too glib reply, together with the fact that her hands were empty, told Mary she was lying. Mary's heart sank sickeningly.

"You have been meeting Paco."

Aracea's brows arched themselves with simulated innocence, but her sharp eyes warned her of the folly of proceeding with her deceit. She descended to cajolery, wreathing her arm round Mary's waist. Mary pushed her away.

"If this happens again, you will go straight home."

"I asked him to come in, Miss Mary, but he was too shy! He only came to tell me about Zarcillo, and—and say good night!"

"It was a most improper way to behave, and I have a good mind to tell your father. Whatever Paco does, you are much too old to act in this stupid way, and it's very rude to the people you are staying with. What do you suppose your mother would say, if she knew you ran out of the marquesa's house, to meet a bullfighter?"

"It's not a bullfighter," pouted Aracea. "It's Paco—who I've known all my life."

"It makes no difference. Now you go straight to bed."

" But——"

" If you say any more, I'll ring up the Inglaterra and get Paco into trouble."

She had found, at last, a winning card. Well aware that if her father heard of this escapade, there would be no more invitations to Paco from the house of Parral, Aracea slid meekly past the sounds of merriment from the sala, went into her bedroom, and closed the door. Let them dance ! Let them laugh and sing ! She was comprometida to Paco Ribera.

Chapter Eleven

I

LIFE, that spring, was anything but peaceful in the house of Parral. A smothered enmity that developed between Aracea and Carlos took the shape, on his part, of a chaffing approach that stung her dignity, and to which her only means of retort was rudeness. Leandra spoke to her daughter.

" Chica, you are behaving very foolishly."

" Carlos is insupportable ! "

" He is only teasing you."

" Yes, because he knows Papá is on his side."

" I have warned you——"

" If they think they've got anything to gain by getting rid of Miss Mary," interrupted Aracea in a loud voice, " they're much mistaken. I won't be forced into marriage with anybody, Mamá—and nothing will persuade me to marry Carlos."

" You forget something. When the war is over, Miss Mary will go back to her own country, to her family——"

Aracea's face grew crimson.

" She won't ! Miss Mary will stop with me—you'll see she

will ! She has *got* to look after me—*I've* got nothing to do with the war."

Mary was startled when the girl hurled herself into her bedroom.

" Miss Mary ; you won't go back to England after the war, will you ? "

Taken by surprise, Mary tried to beg the question.

" You're getting too old for a governess—surely ! "

" I'm too old now, for a ' governess,' " retorted Aracea. " But I've got to have someone to look after me, haven't I ? Mamá isn't strong enough to go about with me—and I don't suppose I've finished my education, yet," she ended—an observation that drew a smile from Mary.

The war, it seemed, was bound to end that year, and she was pledged. It made no difference that the pledge was only to her own conscience : or, rather, it made all the difference. Had it been to another person, she might have temporised without dishonour ; *but she who betrays herself is by herself betrayed.*

" Chica "—it was a long time since she had used the childish name—" you are nearly grown-up. People cannot always choose their own lives. If I could choose mine perhaps I'd remain here with you——"

Aracea's arms were clasped round her neck.

" To keep you here, I'd even tell Papá I would marry Carlos ! "

" God forbid ! "—The words were out before she could restrain them, and Mary felt guilty of disloyalty to her trust as she listened to Aracea's delighted laughter.

" That doesn't say I'd do it ! ' Palabra inglesa and palabra española ' ; you know ! When I promise you something, it's palabra inglesa—no ? But when I talk to Papá—we understand each other. I tell him something that will please him so that I get something I want ; and he does the same with me. I love my Papá very much," said Aracea seriously, " so it is better sometimes to say something one does not mean, and not make a quarrel."

It seemed an unanswerable logic, of which Mary felt unequal, at the moment, to questioning the morality; but she had felt for some time that her continuance in the house of Parral hung by a thread, and only hoped that the ending of the war would enable her to leave without a formal dismissal.

A load of mischief on the ranch spared her, temporarily, the inimical attention of Don Luis. Four bulls being readied for the ring got sick. One of the men was horned, bringing another lot down from the pastures. After this every conceivable thing went wrong: a bull destined for Cordoba damaged itself in the loading. The engine of one of the trucks failed, a hundred and seventy kilómetros into the sierra; the breakdown gang that came out stood them up on account of exceptional risks, and they lost ten hours on the journey—in effect, they lost the bull, which mashed itself up during the delay and made an abominable showing at the other end. There was a bad report on two cows sent to Mexico, that stuck in the dueño's gullet. Don Narciso, who bought them, was an old friend, and one does not let down a friend—especially at a time when, owing to the monopoly of transport by war-material, the cost of freightage was trebled. Don Luis fretted himself sick about those two heifers, which according to the letter, were more likely to end in the matadero than as mothers of future bravos.

Sickness broke out among the calves, and for several weeks the stench of burning carcases rolled across the baked earth and in at the windows of Parral. An outbreak of local sabotage damaged some kilómetros of pipe-line and fired three of the trucks, the smithy and a shedful of machinery. Old Camarista had proved not worth his keep. There was an astronomical account for gasolina, and the insurance company was holding back, pending investigation. Don Luis—who had not had time to see a bullfight since Easter—had an unpleasant interview with his bank manager. So far, the season had brought little kudos and no profit; and, to top it all, Don Luis became involved in a law-suit, that necessitated his departure for Alicante. Carlos was left in charge of the reconstructions which were proceeding languidly, on the smithy and the pipe-line.

"Papá's very silly," Aracea confided to Mary, as they rode

out on the morning after Don Luis's departure. " Carlos hasn't a thought in his head, at present, but señorita Josefa ! "—the nurse who, after the baby's death, had stayed on to look after Leandra, and by now seemed to have established herself as a permanent member of the household : young, pretty and noisy, with varnished nails and a wide moist, painted mouth. " He talks to her every night through the rejas—I've heard them !— and I wouldn't be surprised if she lets him into her room. Caramba, and that's the man I'm supposed to marry ! What sort of an idiot am I supposed to be, Miss Mary ? "

They had reached the burnt-out smithy. One man was idly chipping the corners off a pile of bricks, the rest, sitting round on the charred timbers with cigarettes in their mouths, grinned at Aracea and Mary. " Buenas," they allowed themselves to observe amiably.

" You see ?—He ought to be here," muttered Aracea. " Dame una teja," she said sharply to one of the men, who grinned, but presently got up, as though humouring the chica, and shambled over with a tile in his hand. " Basura," she muttered, when she had examined it. She pushed it in the pocket of the loose coat she was wearing. " Papá didn't order those."

" Are you sure ? I believe that's the load that came in yesterday, before he left," said Mary doubtfully.

" He hadn't time to look at them; Carlos was supposed to be here when they were unloading. Now Papá will get a bill, and the work will have to be done over again, and that will cost *more* money."

As they rode into the patio, the telephone was ringing in the office. There was evidently no one there to answer it. Aracea threw herself off the horse, ran in and snatched the receiver.

" Casa de Parral. No, Don Luis is away ; it is his daughter speaking. Sí-señor ; certainly I have authority.

" For the eighteenth ?—But it's very short notice. Four bulls ? Ay, señor—I feel it much ; it can't be done ! Si, entiendo—entiendo . . . Oiga," said Aracea, at the end of a long harangue, " I will speak to the mayoral. I think it is impossible, but we will call you back."

"Buenas," said Carlos, behind Mary. "I thought I heard the telephone."

Aracea turned on him.

"You'd better look up the credit of Sanpedro. See what they pay."

"What's this?"—Carlos was grinning.

"Is there anything ready to fight?"

"Naturally not."—He spun the wheel of his lighter and offered Mary a cigarette, which she brushed aside.

"Look, Carlos: they want bulls for the eighteenth. Something must have slipped up. People don't order bulls from *us*—at the last minute!"

"People don't bother about Sanpedro." Still smiling at Mary, he slid languidly into a chair.

"Sanpedro would pay for the tiles on the smithy. Look at that muck"—she tossed the lump of curved clay towards him. "That's the manure they've loaded on us—because Papá wasn't here to keep an eye on them. Am I going to talk to Pepe Frías, or are you?"

It was the dueña of Parral speaking: someone far outside of and beyond Mary's authority. She recognised it. She felt she had no right to be listening to the altercation that followed.

A strange atmosphere brooded over the luncheon table. All the authority appeared suddenly to be vested in the girl at the end of the table—the little girl, using her knife and fork in a primitive fashion, for one of the things she had failed to instil in Aracea was table manners: clapping her hands, ordering the servants about, thrusting a dish away and snatching at another. Carlos preserved an ironic silence.

"We'll have coffee in the sala," muttered Aracea, "because I'm expecting a telephone call."

It came as they crossed the threshold.

"Bueno. Bueno. Hasta pronto.—That was Pepe. They're bringing four bulls down this afternoon." She and Mary were alone; Leandra had gone to her room, and Carlos remained, no doubt to flirt with the nurse.

"You're sending them to Sanpedro?"

" Carlos checked up. It's all right; they'll pay. They've been having bad weather at Sanpedro, and the fight was cancelled, but now it's fine and the afición got mad; it's very strong, down there, at Sanpedro.—Well, I must go and tell them about the horses."

" Where are you going?"

" But up to the pastures, naturally—with Pepe."

" To fetch the bulls down?—You can't. You're never permitted."

" Papá always goes, and Carlos can't ride well enough. Tonio can't go, because he's not riding yet after his cornada——"

" Aracea; you can't take Bandera out on the range; he's not used to the bulls."

" I'm not taking Bandera," said Aracea scornfully. " I'll have Tonio's horse. I shan't *do* anything, Miss Mary! I'm only going to keep an eye on them, as Papá does——"

" And what about me?"—With all her ease in the saddle and her familiarity with the bulls, she could not see herself riding side by side with horned death, down from the pastures. But it seemed out of the question that Aracea should go alone.

Aracea burst out laughing.

" You will stay here and read the new English novel to Mamá!—Please don't make a fuss, Miss Mary. I promise you I will do exactly as Pepe tells me, and there isn't the least bit more danger than there is in a tienta."

I cannot handle this, thought Mary. She went in search of Carlos, and found him, by a stroke of luck, in the forecourt, talking to the mayoral.

" Aracea can't go up with the men this afternoon!"

" Are you going to stop her, Miss Carpenter?"—He raised his brows sarcastically.

" You know perfectly well I can't; but you could."

" You flatter me. I am the last to claim authority over my little cousin—at present," he ended, significantly.

" Her father has never allowed her to go up on the range."

He shrugged his shoulders.

" Miss Carpenter; you have had charge of Aracea for—what

is it ? Two or three years ? You know by now "—he lowered his eyelids at her and stuck a cigarette in his mouth—" that she does not take kindly to discipline. There is another thing you know. In Luis's absence, I'm master here. I think it might be a good thing if you put that to Aracea—rather strongly. It might save a good deal of unpleasantness, because I shall not in future take orders from the chiquitilla."

" I think," she said, after a pause, " that you are annoyed because, in the present instance—about the bricks, and the work that's going on, or is supposed to be going on, at the smithy—Aracea happens to be right."

" Caramba "—he removed the cigarette from his lips and his one eye covered her with malice—" you have taught the chica a good deal, haven't you—apart from her lessons ?—Let me give you a word of warning. The manners Aracea displayed this morning in the office are not greatly admired in this country, señorita. I mention it only because—it might not be convenient for you to have to make other arrangements, rather suddenly."

" Have you the impertinence to threaten *me* ? "—He had taken her breath away.

" Threaten ?—Come ; what a word to use ! In spite of your unfriendliness to me, I promise you my intentions towards you are of the best. And in what position am I, to ' threaten ' ? " He spread out his hands in a gesture that put him at her mercy. Realising she had nothing to gain by prolonging the conversation and disgusted by his hypocrisy, she turned away. He called after her, " You need not be anxious about Aracea, Miss Carpenter ! She may not know her manners with human beings, but she knows how to behave herself with bulls ! "

" You will promise to obey Pepe ? "—She met the girl on the gallery, hitching an old pair of leather chaps into her belt.

" Yes, Miss Mary—I promise : palabra inglesa ! "

The child is not indulging in what she looks on as an escapade ; she is doing what she conceives to be her duty. Mary murmured, " Go with God."

II

The clouds lay low over the pastures ; there had been, at last, a little rain. The steers went peacefully, pushing the damp air ahead of them with their quiet brows. On the outside rode the men, with Aracea farther out still. No one spoke. The men carried their varas. They and their horses seemed like one.

They encircled the cows' enclosures ; all of them by now, she thought with satisfaction, in calf. Each was recorded, with the bull that served it and the date of the mounting. Down a lane, to left and right, were the youngsters who would later be coming up for their tientas.

Then they moved slowly out, into the deep pastures fenced in by tall, narrow trees. There was the mulchy sound of the trotting steers. The horses went delicately, with only the dry creak of the leathers to betray them. She felt her heart quicken ; it was the first time she had been out here, in the sacred preserves that held the glory of Parral.

Pepe was giving her a sign ; she moved obediently out, out to the left. He wanted her to get away, over by the trees, close to a gap with two bars across it and a man waiting to drop them at the signal. She went quietly on, turned the horse, and felt it freeze under her. A deep breath caught in her throat.

Over there, surprisingly close, were the majestic heads, the great, steel-coloured bodies, with all the weight shot forward, of the bulls of Parral. Qué gloria. She continued to hold her breath, as the steers wandered on. All the horses, save one, stood like statues ; the one advanced, circling the bulls as softly as a shadow ; keeping always at a distance from them ; checking, then moving on under the invisible compulsion of its rider's thighs. Suddenly a bull threw up its head, pawed the earth and backed a few paces. A restlessness spread through the herd, but no kind of panic ; it scattered leisurely. The steers moved on, and then the other horses, urged into almost imperceptible movement by their riders.

A few drops of rain pattered on the brim of Aracea's felt hat, and she wondered if they could be granted the inconceivable good luck—at that time of year—of a downpour. Coolness and rain, and the difficulties of cutting out the marked bulls from the herd would be reduced to a minimum. As she sat there, relaxed, resting her feet in the big wooden stirrups to which she was not accustomed—for Bandera's fine saddle would not fit the tall, raw-boned beast ridden, usually, by one of the men—and gazing between the twitching ears of the horse (the only sign it gave of life) towards the slowly moving herd, she felt her sight blurring. Knowing that she must not lift her hand to clear her eyes —for the faintest movement, now, might catch the eye of a sensitive bull—she blinked as hard as she could, and, to her delight, felt moisture on her lashes. As though in answer to her thought, a low cloud was letting down its burden over the pastures, and, for a moment, the trees, and the herd, and the men on the horses melted into a silvery haze. The steers, driven round between the trees and the bulls, prevented the latter from making for shelter, and the vaqueros were working in close, closer than would have been wise, but for the protection of the rain.

The clouds were now rolling low across the land, and breaking on the sierra. As the downpour quickened, Aracea's leather chaps and her horse's coat blackened with it. Four bulls stood peaceably, headed towards the rails, that went down noiselessly behind her. Obeying her signal, she sent her horse through and turned it into the trees. One of the men followed her. Then a steer nosed through, and another. Enclosed in the loose cage of the steers' bodies came the bulls, their heads lowered to the rain, their feet plugging in the sodden grass.

" That's a big one ! " she whispered to Pepe, the last to come through.

" Sí, big, isn't he ? "

Big indeed ; the great, steel-covered shoulders rode at least a couple of inches above the others ; it moved with a raking stride that forced the steers into a trot. It would have made trouble, but for the rain. But the rain is a mysterious reducer of the combative instinct.

"May be too big," Pepe was saying. "May be when they get him on the scales the vet won't pass him."

"Ca—they can't afford to be fussy about a few kilos at Sanpedro."

"May be Chiquito won't fancy him.—You heard about Ildefonso?"—As she shook her head, Pepe continued in a discreet undertone, "He got the ears last Sunday; they've booked him for Sanpedro instead of Zarcillo. Ildefonso's going to be something to watch out for, next season."

"You know what that bull reminds me of?"—She was watching the formidable head. "He's like Capanegra; he's got the same expression in his horns."

The mayoral smothered a laugh.

"He's a half-brother to Capanegra. God knows what's wrong with that cow; she always drops monsters."

"Capanegra was a bravo!"

"That's not a bravo"—Pepe pulled a face. "That one's a bicho, a real son of the Devil. He'll make trouble for them at Sanpedro—if we get him there."

The conversation, which had been carried on in whispers ended as they closed in on the end of the cavalcade. The lane which, when they came up it was dry, was now filled with runnels and slippery with red mud. The haunches of the beasts rocked down it, the wet brought up the deep cattle-smell and pushed it back in their faces. Aracea sniffed it up rapturously. This was the nearest she had ever been to grown and unenlisted bulls.

The walls broke away into a flat piece of land scrubbed with cactus and wild aloe. The men rode out as the herd spread slightly. "Cuidado," muttered Pepe, "and keep clear of the prickles." Of course; this was where Tonio got himself horned. But on a day of thunder. It certainly would not be nice, to get bumped into one of those prickly pears.

The rain had ceased, and a livid strip broke along the western horizon. The cattle were restless, the even rhythm of their movement altered as they found themselves in an open space. Originally the track had been boundaried by a double row of cactus, but a sharp winter had killed off most of the plants, and the remaining stumps offered little resistance to an animal disposed to break from the herd. The steers were behaving stupidly, bunching and hesitating, confusing the bulls and each other.

The big bull stood still: lifting its great head to look at the light in the sky. It contemplated it dubiously, with manifest distrust, and, suddenly, shouldering a steer out of the way, trotted out into the scrub. There it stood, outlined against the sulphur sky, fine, free and dangerous; blowing quietly down its nostrils; scraping the earth; seeking—but not, as yet, ill-temperedly—something to charge.

As she wheeled her horse into the lee of a patch of aloe, a horseman flashed round on her right, swinging his pic to draw the bull's attention. Josú: if it charged now—if it got its head down—it would go plumb into the deadly spikes and blind itself. A serious loss, for which, in her father's absence, she must hold herself responsible. Without pausing to reflect, she rose in her stirrups. She sent her voice shrilling across the space between her and the bull.

" Huy, toro ! "

Its head half lowered, the bull checked. Its head swung slowly, right, left and right again. Slowly its head came up. The immense swelling of the neck, sinister against the livid background, lent it majesty. It was, for the moment, more puzzled than irritated, its curiosity roused. The feminine voice—of which, in its deep sexual consciousness, it was aware—baffled it momentarily.

Aracea's mind worked quickly. She had them all placed: in the tail of her eye was Pepe, working in like a shadow from her right—Pepe who, as her father said, knew bull-talk, and could read the thoughts in a bull's mind as well as he could read his own. Pepe knew as well as she did the menace of that maze of spiked leaves in the middle of which the big bull was standing, and knew it must be drawn out—but quietly, quietly, as though it had thought of it for itself. Pepe, she thought, is on my right, not more than twenty paces away; if what I am going to do goes wrong, there's room for me to get through that gap on my left and back down the lane—and Pepe, with the others, can manage.

She took firm hold of the reins and, still standing, called again, "Huy, toro!" Then, by the pressure of her calves, she made the horse take two slow steps out, so that she was in the bull's full sight.

Its suspicion was roused, but it was still unwilling to commit itself.

"Ya viene," muttered Aracea, as she let herself down imperceptibly into the saddle and gripped the reins. She knew she could trust a horse trained to carry herdsmen, and to move among the bulls and cows. Now, really, it depended on Pepe—and on how much saltpetre the bull had lately had in its feed. And on the steers, who were mooning up on her left. Ya viene : it strode out suspiciously—ya—ya—until it was clear of the spikes. Now, whatever it does it can't hurt itself. I'll have to hold it a little longer, and then it depends on Pepe . . .

Sitting like a rock in the line of the bull's advance, she listened to her heart marking off the seconds. Then it happened : the thing she had anticipated. Wheeling his horse, Pepe brought it back, circling to within a couple of yards of the bull's nose. The bull charged, and the horn laid open a steer. It fell, and the bull charged it again, while its foolish companions closed in, confusing the bull with the inane ding-dong of their bells. Its prestige left it ; it suffered itself to be collected and conducted beyond the danger-zone of the cactuses.

Aracea rubbed the sweat out of her eyes with the back of her hand. She had saved a Parral bull. There was not much farther to go—thank God, for she was surprisingly tired. Now the bulls had to be turned into the feeding lots, for ten days of conditioning. They would need at least three or four days to recover, after the two days' journey by road to Sanpedro. So the feeding must be good. Her eyelids heavy with responsibility,

Aracea watched the four bulls into the corral. Would Papá ring up from Alicante? Would she be able to speak to him—before, somebody else got in with their version of the story?

III

The return of Don Luis coincided with a more pleasurable incident, for Mary. She was sitting on the terrassa, with a veil round her head, to take care of the flies, when a servant came to her. The girl, a clumsy wench, as yet untrained to the observances of the household, blurted out:

"There's some English here—they asked if the señorita is in the house! I said, Yes, the señorita is in the house!"

Running through the patio she found, as she expected, Grosvenor and Adela Hallatt, laughing at the foot of the stairs. "Come up," she cried, when she extracted herself from their embraces. "I'm sorry, on your first visit, you should meet that little idiot; we're not really savages, in the house of Parral!"

"We couldn't resist coming," said Adela. "Gro's been given a holiday, and we thought we'd spend it seeing some of the places we've had no time to visit since we came to Spain.— What a *marvellous* house! It's like something out of a fairy tale. Gro, for the love of mike, look at that ceiling; have you ever seen such colours, and such gold?"

"I think I must present you to my señora!—Then we'll go to my room and have tea——"

"Mary"—Adela caught her by the arm—"I suppose you've heard?—The war will be over at any minute."

She stood very still.

"Yes?"

"We've come really"—Adela threw a laughing glance at her husband—"to talk about your future. Cheek, isn't it?—I only mention it, because we've not got much time, and we don't want to waste it in being polite to your señora!"

"Don't worry; she's an invalid—she may not even be equal to seeing us: but Aracea would be very disappointed to miss you."—What, she wondered, could her future have to do with these kind people—who followed her along the gallery to the door of the sala.

The brief interview with Leandra was, on both sides, a success. Aracea, who rushed in, on hearing of the visitors, behaved with unwonted tact and propriety.

" I'm sure Miss Mary would like to talk to her friends by herself, Mamá ; shall I tell them to send up some wine—— ? "

Mary laughed.

" I'll make tea, myself, in the schoolroom." She had her spirit-stove, and a jealously-hoarded small supply of the almost unobtainable tea. Fortunately, her taste had so adapted itself to her environment that she drank almost nothing, now, but coffee and chocolate. When they returned to the schoolroom, the Hallatts produced a parcel.

" Here's tea ; we guessed you wouldn't have any.—Have you heard from Elizabeth ? " asked Adela.

" Not recently ; and the books she promised me never came through. I expect they were held up by the censorship."

" Well, I had a letter from her just before we left Madrid. She's got a proposition to lay before you. She wants to know if you'd consider—for a year at least—teaching Spanish and French at St. Margaret's."

" Is the war really going to be over this year ? " asked Mary, after a silence. Grosvenor Hallatt answered her ; she liked his tall, drooping figure and serious, pasty face.

" It's over now—as far as Europe is concerned. We've gotten our problems, in the East, but the fighting here will stop, I reckon, within the next week or two."

" Gro can get you on a plane as soon as peace is declared," broke in Adela. Mary smiled stiffly.

" There isn't all that hurry ! "

" Perhaps I'm wrong—but I've got the impression, the sooner you get back the better."

" For fear I decide to stay ? "

The slow, pleasant drawl of Grosvenor Hallatt filled the silence that followed her words.

" You can't get away from your own country. If you do, you're kind of lost. Europe, before the war, was full of Americans who thought this was their spiritual home. Now—they belong nowhere. It's a matter of belonging ; if you don't have that— you're like a piece of seaweed, just drifting."

" That's not so in America ! Look at the nationalities you've assimilated ! The innumerable Europeans who, to-day, are proud to call themselves American ! "

" It's a different thing ; we're young, and plastic. We're open to any new thought, any inspiration, that comes our way. Here, it's a matter of conforming to a pattern ; and the pattern is set, through centuries of tradition. Each patch of earth has its own pattern—and the patterns don't match. That's the tragedy of Europe. That's why any European must get back to his own plot of earth, or get right out . . ."

While this was going on, another scene was taking place in the sala. Leandra had gone to her bedroom ; Aracea stood, looking on the neglected garden of Parral. Over everything crawled the raging blue of morning glory ; a scent of pomegranate blossom filled the air ; the weeds rose triumphant over stonework on which the lizards basked. She heard a step behind her.

" Wouldn't it be nice, Papá, if we cleared the garden, some time ? "

Leaning against the rejas, she wondered why everything seemed suddenly so lovely ; why she felt restless, and sad, in an exquisite kind of way, with nothing to be sad about.

Paco had sent her, in a formal letter, the list—so far as it went—of his engagements. Málaga—si Dios quiere !—but mainly little towns where the afición was strong enough to put up the money. Castellón de la Plana, for the fiesta of the Magdalena, and, with luck Bilbao. Not a bad card for someone breaking in after the opening of the season, but several of the places she had never even heard of. Under the name Maderas he had drawn a thick, black line. Maderas, for the first time in its history, was putting up a corrida, and Paco, as its son, was starred. That would be late in October, and one could only hope for good weather and tolerable bulls. Aracea sighed. She reached out behind her back, to take her father's hand—and started as though she had been bitten, when a thinner, harder palm touched her own.

" What are you doing ?—I thought it was Papá."

" I was thinking—how lovely you are, against the window," said Carlos calmly.

" You want something ?—I'll call Mamá——"

He was blocking her way ; his teeth glittered in the narrow wedge of his face.

" Prima mía ; don't you think it's time we stopped quarrelling ? "

" I'm not quarrelling. What do you want, Carlos ?—Papá is down at the yard, watching the building——"

" You must have been taking lessons in flirtation, Aracita ! I'm surprised at Miss Carpenter." His voice was the purr of a thin cat. " I thought English ladies did not go in for that kind of thing. But it's quite attractive—and you've grown very pretty, little cousin. Tell me : am I the first person to tell you so ? "

He had recaptured her hand, as though by accident, and was spreading its fingers gently, just by the muscular pressure of his palm. He smiled at it, as though it gave him pleasure. " What a pretty hand—like the petals of a rose ! "—He laid his lips to it.

Up to this moment, Aracea had stood frozen with astonishment. The new and curious sensation of male lips in contact with her flesh was vaguely agreeable : then—*Carlos !* with his one eye and his one leg. Tearing her hand away, she thrust it into the pocket of her skirt and clasped the other over it, for protection. The look on her face was a look of sheer physical loathing ; if she had been aware that her feeling was there, written in her eyes, she could not have controlled it.

" Don't ! Don't ever do that again ! "

No woman had ever looked at Carlos de la Cerna in that way.

It had never occurred to him, so far, to turn the battery of his charms on his little cousin. He had not doubted that, from the moment he let down the barrier of cousinly chaff, she would come to his hand as easily as the others had done. He had not meant it to be quite yet, but there was something so delicately attractive about her young body, silhouetted against the rejas, something so tender and tempting about the slight curves of her waist and hips, that he could not restrain himself.

Her revulsion went down inside him like the twisted blade of a sword. Almost he flinched; then stiffening, unconsciously holding his breath, he waited for the sword to be drawn out; waited, smiling, while she stalked past him with her head in the air, and out on the gallery. He spoke one word of obscenity.

IV

" Tell me about your friend," Leandra was saying. To Mary's surprise, she had come out to say good-bye to the Hallatts as they drove away.

" Adela ?—Well, she married the American just before the war ; he's in the diplomatic service. She and I were at school together. After that, she and her cousin started a little private school, which has turned out a great success——"

" She is muy distinguida."

Mary smiled.

" She happens to be a niece of the Duke of Basingstoke."

" I thought you said she kept a school ? " said Leandra, naïvely.

" The two aren't incompatible ! Her father was an impoverished younger son, with three boys to educate——"

" She's muy simpática, isn't she, Mamá ? "—Aracea had joined them. " And she's asked us to stay with her after the war ; hasn't she, Miss Mary ?—That would be fun, to go to England."

" Washington," corrected Mary. " I expect, when Grosvenor's Madrid assignment comes to an end, they'll go back to America."

When, later in the evening, she was summoned to the office, she thought, This is *it*.

" I think, miss, my daughter does not require a governess any longer."

" It is for you to say, señor." She felt that her calmness affronted him.

" So our contract will finish at the end of the month."

" I am, naturally, prepared to leave at your convenience." Her lips felt dry, she moistened them. " May I make a request ? "

" It is already granted," said Don Luis, with the urbanity of the victor.

" I would take it as a great favour, señor, if I might be allowed to tell Aracea, myself, that I am leaving."

He gave her a suspicious stare

" You have a reason ? "

She forced a smile.

" Only that—she has grown fond of me. I think it is fair I should be allowed to prepare her for the change."

" There is no need to say anything for the present," mumbled Don Luis. She gave him a shrewd glance. So you are no more anxious than I, to provoke a scene.

" I take it you will be appointing someone else in my place."

" We—my wife and I—have come to the conclusion that it is time our daughter had the companionship of a Spanish lady, to introduce her into society."

" I fully understand. If you will be so kind as to tell me when your arrangements are complete, I will have a talk with her. It will certainly be pleasanter all round, if Aracea is prepared to take a friendly view of her new dueña."

" I think it is not necessary to say anything at all," repeated Don Luis.

She looked at him—and grasped his incredible meaning. Did he really suppose that, after all these years, she was going to walk out of the house of Parral without a word to Aracea ?

" It is, perhaps, not necessary to carry the discussion any farther, for the present. I will, with your permission, choose my moment for speaking to Aracea." You know what I am thinking, and I know what you are thinking. Don Luis's eyes lowered themselves. He made a grudging gesture of assent.

She went straight to Leandra, whom she found alone.

" I am sorry, Miss Mary. I am very sorry. We shall both miss you very much. My husband has not spoken to me yet—I suppose he will say something this evening. Have you any idea what made him act so suddenly ? "

" Not the least. But, señora, I shall certainly not go without bidding good-bye to Aracea. It would be a sort of treachery ! "

" You are right," said Leandra, absently.

" And you will tell me when the new companion is appointed ? "—She pressed her advantage.

" I do not know at all who my husband has in mind. It may be one of the Segovia relations ; there is a young cousin who was widowed last year, and has very good social connections. I think you need not say anything for the present, Miss Mary, for it takes much time to arrange a matter like this, and there are several people to be consulted."

" Couldn't you "—burst from Mary—" couldn't you take care of her yourself, for a little while ? I think, at that age, the love and interest of a mother stand for far more than the care of a stranger—however devoted."

" You think," said Leandra slowly, " that I do not care about my child."

" I would not presume to say such a thing," said Mary, colouring, " even if I believed it to be true. But it is not true. I feel—I don't quite know how to say it—that it is difficult for someone who has not watched over Aracea, as we have done, during the last few years, to take charge of her now. Her character is very strong, and she is very quickly antagonised." She hesitated for a moment, then resolved to speak out. " This matter of her marriage to Don Carlos——"

Leandra said quickly :

" That is my husband's idea. I do not wish her to marry Carlos. I do not think she would be happy."

" Surely, in any case, it is too early to speak of marriage—to a girl of fifteen ? "

" We take a different view of these things from yours, Miss Mary. Naturally, she would not be married for two or three years. But it is better for a girl to know her future is arranged—especially a girl in Aracea's position. She is what I believe you call an heiress, and it is necessary to protect her future interests. That is the only reason for her marrying Carlos."

" But supposing she were to fall in love with someone else ? "

" Is there anyone—— ? "

" She is very fond of Paco Ribera," said Mary, wondering if this was treachery to Aracea.

" But she cannot marry a torero."

" I think that is one reason for her refusal to have anything to do with Don Carlos. It is probably only a passing fancy ; but isn't it natural for youth to turn towards youth ? It really is not fair to expect a child of that age to take an interest in someone old enough to be her father."

" I will try to do something," said Leandra, after a pause. " I do not see, at present, what. Evidently, she must marry someone who is capable of looking after the business——"

" Is Don Carlos ? " Mary could not refrain from asking.

" My husband finds him simpático, and when one of my uncles dies, Carlos will have a good deal of money ; that is important. But there may be others," ended Leandra vaguely. " Claro, she must not marry a torero ! "

" Not even—if she loves him ? "

" Miss Mary. You have lived in Spain a long time. Have you known many people—people of our class—who marry for love ? "

The deadly rejoinder, with its implied acceptance of an unalterable rule, froze the words on Mary's lips. Not through her mother would Aracea find escape from the fate that hung over her.

Chapter Twelve

I

THE CLATTERING of hooves in the patio roused Mary from the doze into which she had fallen after a restless night. She heard Aracea's strong, joyous voice call across the gallery, " Olá, Papa ! " and she heard the clack of their heels as they went down the stone stairs. What was it that took them out so early ?—it was barely dawn. Then she remembered : the loading of the bulls for Sanpedro. Aracea would stand on top of the broad stone walls, watching the bulls being driven into the trap whose end was blocked by the great, steel-reinforced truck. It was a manœuvre that had to be performed with the greatest quietude ; none but those directly concerned was allowed to be present ; Mary herself had never seen it, but Aracea had described it to her : the urging of the bulls up the chute, the securing of each in its compartment, the lowering of the shutter, and the pause, to allow them to adjust to their dark and narrow quarters, before setting off slowly on their portentous journey.

She got up and took a cold bath to freshen herself. Concepción brought her a bowl of strong, steaming coffee, laced with fresh goats' milk. She drank it standing on the gallery, watching the sky in flames. How she would miss this life—this narrow and in some ways savage life ; with what ache of nostalgia would she look back to it, from a school-teacher's cell in the Cotswolds, or, during vacation, from some little box in a London suburb ! Now the cows will be dropping their calves, and, in another month, there'll be the brandings. Now is the time for the tientas, and the first lot of Parral bulls will be growing sleek in the lots, and the first troup of ragged little boys will be arriving, petitioning to be allowed to work the cows. Now the fights will be starting—si Dios quiere !—in Barcelona and Valencia. Then Easter. Then Corpus Cristi. The calendar of the Church had become, for her, the calendar of the bulls ; kneeling in some English chapel, preparing to make her confession, she would see, behind her closed lids, the yellow sand and the endless ring of dark bodies and pale faces ; through the ringing of the bell she would hear the note of the clarín . . . What should take the place of all this, under the cold, English sky ?

The pink light dyed the horse and her hands and the folds of her skirt as she rode out towards San Miguel. The ranch was stirring into life ; horsemen and labourers on foot, going about their various duties, seemed all to be under the spell of the fantastic light, all hushed and purified in the innocence of a new day. Mist rose in coloured bands, like flattened rainbows, and hung in frail, multi-coloured veils before the sunrise.

As she rode through the village, she saw the wooden rollers chocked into the rings, barring the lane up which the loading was taking place ; the dueño took no risks, and the casual horseback rider or motorist would have no access to that lane until the loading was completed.

The chapel was as cold as a morgue, but the red light lent a grim animation to its dusty effigies. She said her prayers mechanically. Riding back along the cobbled street, little boys shouted to her :

" Olá, la inglesa. Olá, la señorita. No quiere ver á los toros ? "

There would be no toros to see, but the slow passage of the trucks down the street was always watched with awe by the children. In those wheeled houses that trembled with the onslaught of their occupants was enclosed the pride of Parral ; there might be a glimpse of a horn or a muzzle at one of the small, high gratings that ventilated the boxes ; there might be the sound of a muffled bellow. It was a mark of bravery to throw a stone and then run away—for anyone caught in the act of blasphemy was sure of a beating.

On the steps of the mayoral's house sat his brood of children, chewing crusts of bread. With traditional courtesy, they invited her to partake of their meal, and Mary made the traditional reply. As she went on, a wild hand waved from a window above Mary's head. "Olá, Conchita," she observed. "Is the niño better?"

"No, señorita; muy malo, muy malo. Mucho fiebre; no come!" came in a mournful whine. It was the wife of one of the herdsmen, a feckless girl with children who were always sick or ailing. Mary hesitated for a moment, then tied up the horse and mounted the stairs; she knew what she would find—a filthy room, a swarm of half-naked children, a wailing infant, its stomach swollen with unsuitable food.

"Have you given him milk, as I told you?"

"No quiere, señorita," the mother whined.

"Nonsense; if the milk is fresh, he will take it." She picked up a jug, smelt its contents and poured them out of the window. "What's the use of giving a child of that age sour milk? You know there is plenty of fresh"—unlimited milk was one of the privileges of the Parral families, but, in the hot weather, they were supposed to scald it—which few took the trouble to do. "Go down to the dairy and get some"—she thrust a few coins into the girl's hand. "Be quick, and I'll wait until you come back"—to make sure the pennies were spent on milk, not on sausage, or dried fish, or the garbage these people put into their children's stomachs! Probably the wretched infant had been stuffed with salchicha for days, and garbanzos—a nice diet for a child of a few months. The room stank of dirty bedding and the unclean habits of its occupants. There was one tiny window open on the street, that let in heat, but no air. Mary crossed the room and broke open the shutters on the farthest side. The sunrise remained only in scattered pink clouds, the normal light of morning lay over the fields and the lanes. She drank in the freshness. The children, crowding round her, thrust between her and the window. "Ya viene!" screamed one. "Ya—ya!" —They were all yelling and pointing. "Lo' toro'!"

A puff of dust rose above the boundary walls of the lane that led to the corrales—and as she saw it, Mary realised it was not such a cloud as was raised by the vans : it moved too fast. It could only be somebody on horseback, riding like a maniac. Her view blocked by buildings, she rushed to the other window, but that only gave her a narrow angle of the street. She ran down the stairs. Round the wooden barriers people were shouting and pointing ; running up behind them, Mary caught a glimpse of a horse and rider : the rider lying low on the horse's neck. At the next moment she was nearly flung on her back by the backward surge of the crowd. A woman shrieked, " Madre mia—e' Aracita ! " and someone tried, too late, to knock down the rollers.

Paralysed, Mary watched the girl lift the horse clear of the two wooden bars ; it staggered in landing, and lost its footing on the cobbles. As it plunged on its knees, Aracea shot over its head. As Mary ran forward to pick her up, she staggered to her feet, with blood running down her brow.

" It's Papá. Ring the hospital and tell them to send the ambulance."

" Yes." Some lobe of her brain registered the fact that there was a telephone in the mayoral's house. " What's happened ? " she stammered.

" The big bull—give me your horse ; I'm going to tell Mamá —and send the car."

" How bad is it ? "

" Malo—muy malo. Right through the side." She wheeled the horse and clattered up the street, scattering the frightened children.

The ambulance arrived, filled with reporters, who crowded into the office, where they had laid Don Luis, on the floor. Elbowing the vaqueros and the women of the household out of the way, they set off their flashes, photographing the groaning man from every possible angle. While the hospital orderlies carried Don Luis into the ambulance, some of them photographed Leandra and Aracea. Mary tried to intervene—" Por favor, señores ! " and was pushed aside. Aracea took one look at the pool of her father's blood on the floor of the office, and, for the first and last time in her life, fainted dead away.

The Sevilla radio carried the news at noon :

" Loading the bulls for the fight at Sanpedro on the eighteenth, Don Luis Parral was gravely injured. His condition is serious. Further particulars are not available, but will be given on the next news emission. The sympathy of all followers of the brave bulls will go to the family of this valiant and impeccable breeder, together with hopes for his recovery."

II

Along a short stretch of the boundary of the corral rose a high wall—at some time of the past the frontón of an old pelota court. Pelota is not a popular game in the South, but after watching an exhibition match, the Parral boys had been infected with a brief enthusiasm, and had petitioned their father for a court. Disused since Don Luis's boyhood, the court itself had long gone back to rubble and weed, but the frontón remained, overgrown with morning glory and wisteria. Someone had kicked a series of footholds in one end, and, holding on by the wisteria trunks, it was possible for an active person to climb on to the top, which afforded an excellent vantage-point, for anyone with a steady head, over the surrounding scene. It was high enough—some six or seven métros—for the bulls below not to be aware of anyone watching them, unless he cast a shadow, and, this morning, with the sun full in their faces, there was no shadow at all on the side of the bulls. From that dizzy height you could see, not only the corral, but the trap, and the loading ramp and the boxes themselves ; you could see the men on the stirrup behind the walls of the trap and the boys waiting to pull the gate up ; you could see, far down, immediately at your feet, the burlador, and the man hidden behind it, his bald head shining like a dark yellow football, as he crouched, hat in hand, out of the bulls' sight.

As a child, Aracea had stood up there, holding her father's hand ; now she stood, with feet apart, arms crossed, scowling down at the bull which had resisted from the first all efforts to coax it into the trap. From up there, it looked small, but she knew it was enormous—the one that had given trouble on the way down from the pastures. Trotting round the big corral, it skilfully avoided the efforts of the steers to collect it. Twice the boys had raised the gate of the trap, twice they let it down again, as the bull tossed off its escort and trotted on. A bold youth, who leapt down from the top of the wall into the opening, and hastily scrambled back again, it treated as non-existent. Looking for trouble, it broke into a gallop, and suddenly, having caught a glimpse of the man hiding behind the burlador, launched itself across his head against the blank face of the frontón; fell back clumsily, half-way across the burlador, as the man ducked; scrambled itself off and, as it trotted away, let loose a bellow.

"Pepe was right," muttered Aracea, "he is a son of the Devil." For all its weight, the bull leapt like an antelope. "He'll jump the barrera when he gets to Sanpedro—no, Papá?"

Don Luis swore under his breath. The hangover he had brought back with him from Alicante had passed off, but his stomach was still queasy. He would have preferred not to be standing on the top of the frontón, but his vanity would not allow him to refuse his daughter's unconscious challenge. She had taken for granted that they would watch the loading from up there, as usual, and he followed her up the wistaria trunks. From there, he could control the proceedings by signals to his men, who kept a watchful eye on the dueño.

He had never hated any of his bulls, but he came close to hating this one. For all its handsomeness, there was something evil about it. He silently debated whether to withdraw it; it might, in any case, be rejected, when they got it on the scales. Why had his mayoral picked this brute, of all others, to send to Sanpedro, where the afición was strong, and, though not an important ring, they paid good money? For all its size, it was not a bravo. A tricky braggart, it would probably turn manso in the first suerte—if not, at the first prick of the darts. And they were not using the horses at Sanpedro. Gloomily he watched it ignoring all the gambits to which a brave bull reacts in classic fashion : knowing that this one would not do credit to the name of Parral—if they ever got it in the ring.

The bull went on trotting round, ignoring the steers, who, bunched foolishly together, seemed by the melancholy ding-dong of their bells to express a sense of their own futility. Again and again, urged by Pepe the mayoral on his tall horse, they approached and tried to encircle the bull, which, horning them off, would have none of them. Pepe kept well behind the oxen ; he had no wish to draw the attention of that spawn-of-the-devil to himself, or to his animal. He was keenly aware of the sour looks of the padrón, up there on the wall, and he knew he was in for trouble. He had acted, as he thought, for the best, in unloading this bicho on Sanpedro : an unimportant little ring that could count itself lucky to have Parral bulls on its bills. He watched it, growing at every moment more dangerous, more imponderable, less manageable.

Aracea was thinking—" That Paco doesn't have to take this bull ! "

Late on the night they brought them down, the telephone rang in the house of Parral. Kneeling beside the table in the sala, she said crisply, " Casa de Parral."

" Olá," said Paco's voice.

" *Paco*."—A shock of delight went through her. " Where are you speaking from ? "

" From home, of course. Oiga : I'm fighting at Sanpedro on the eighteenth."

" Who with ?—I mean, whose cuadrilla ? " she breathed.

" Nobody's—I mean, my own. Me, Bastábeles, and—who do you think ? Ildefonso ! That's a joke, isn't it ?—So mind you send us some decent animals ! "

" All our animals are impeccable !—But I thought Chiquito——"

" Chiquito's gone sick in Valladolid. It's the only way I ever get a job "—she heard him laugh—" if somebody goes sick or misses a train ! They've just rung us up : they'd booked Zarcillo, and they'd tried to get Moratín."

" What happened about Moratín ? "

" That brindis they gave him at Málaga's gone to his head—he's asking the earth. They haven't got all that much money at Sanpedro, and Papá's a friend of Don Cristóbal's. So we fixed it up. It will be fun, to fight with Ildefonso ! "

That Paco doesn't have to fight this bicho . . .

The sun was gathering strength. It beat hard into their faces, and, with a slow, cautious movement, Aracea tilted her hat forward. Don Luis felt the heat, and wondered whether they would still be there at noon. The sweat gathered inside the band of his hat, and collected in his eyebrows. Pepe made another slow circle of the corral, urging the steers before him. They went patiently, to the sad notes of their bells. The bull swung round and made an aimless charge back on its own tracks ; the steers scattered, and Pepe wheeled his horse sedately into a slow canter, parallel with, but at a safe distance from, the bull. Behind the walls, the men lay sweating ; the entrance to the trap was at right angles, and close to, the frontón ; the boys on the gate looked up, for direction, to the dueño. As the steers closed hopefully in again, a hat flashed up from behind the burlador, and the bull charged. The crack of the horn, as it struck the wood, made a dull vibration in the heavy air.

Don Luis took an involuntary step forward, to see that the bull had not damaged itself. The sun was in his eyes and his head was swimming. A lump of decayed plaster gave under his foot.

If he had fallen directly to the ground, he would probably have been killed outright, but he dropped on one of the steers. The alarmed animal ducked and backed, shuffling Don Luis on to the earth. And the bull, withdrawing itself from the burlador, went for something more worth while.

. . . Leandra and Aracea went to stay with the de Gaulas, so as to be close to the hospital. Mary dealt as best she could with a household that had abandoned itself prematurely to a wake. On the afternoon of the fight at Sanpedro, the news went out that Don Luis Parral was dying. Standing in the archway of the patio de los caballos, Paco and Ildefonso looked at each other. Paco felt cold, and Ildefonso's face of a gipsy was bright green.

He muttered, "For me, it was my father"—and went out to meet the first bull. For the first time in his short career as a bull-fighter, he earned the bronca—and got it. Paco reaped all the glory of the afternoon. When it was over, he went up to Ildefonso and held out his hand. "Hombre, I'm sorry. You deserved better luck than that."

Fortified by the rites of the Church, Don Luis Parral died shortly before five o'clock, and was buried at midnight in one of the niches of the Parral graveyard.

Mary sat up that night with Aracea, who lay clutching her hand until sleep overcame her. But not restful sleep. She tossed about and ground her teeth ; towards dawn, she awoke, screaming. Mary caught her in her arms ; the girl was trembling and sweating. "I was falling!" she cried, clinging to Mary and sobbing.

Lawyers, executors, creditors and representatives of the houses of Parral and de la Cerna swarmed upon them. From overheard scraps of conversation, Mary gathered that the affairs of Don Luis were in great confusion. She was not happy to learn that Carlos was one of the executors.

There were the uncles from Segovia, at odds with the Andalucían end of the family ; they were there, of course, to protect the interests of the widow and child. There was the neat, short, hard-faced brother of Don Luis—a fruit-grower in Almería—backed by his solicitor ; they had no intention, if they could prevent it, of allowing the control of the estate to pass into the hands of the de la Cernas. Don Federico Parral had with him his two sons, señoritos in their twenties, who, when not involved in the discussions, roved aimlessly about the house— to be snubbed by Aracea.

"What are *they* here for?—Papá had no use for them. They're footballers and they're heretics !"

" They don't look much like footballers ! "—Mary suppressed a smile ; the description certainly did not fit the languid youths, with fainéant written all over them, who seemed totally preoccupied with the set of their new black suits and their broad black satin ties.

" Of course they don't play !—but they are like the people who scream rude things at the toreros, for doing what they daren't do themselves."—Aracea's voice was slow and lifeless ; Mary gave her an uneasy look. The colour drained from her lips, and the bones rising through the ashen skin, her sudden air of anaemia and debility produced in her a startling likeness to her mother ; had the effete blood of de la Cerna at last taken charge ? She said nothing of her father's death, and, except for the evening meal, when she changed, wore no mourning. She showed a sullen indifference to all around her, and, as she ate virtually nothing, the flesh shredded itself off her face and limbs with alarming rapidity. The little vitality she evinced went into morbid antagonism to anyone who tried to be pleasant to her— and there were many who tried. A great deal of importance attached to the young dueña ; much deference was shown to her, and she shied from it, with open suspicion.

" When are all these people going ?—What do they talk about ?—Why doesn't Mamá tell them to get out ? She must be as sick as I am, of having them in the house."

Mary's days were so fully occupied with her charge that she rarely looked at a paper. Since the death of Don Luis, no one switched on the radio in the office, to listen to the news. One of the Segovia uncles turned to her, during lunch, and observed, " I suppose you know, señorita, that the war is over ? "

The room filled with cloud and the blood drummed in her ears.

" The señorita will, without doubt, be returning to England."

She caught the eye of Aracea, filled with a nameless fear. At the first opportunity of being alone with the girl, she said :

" You know I will not go, so long as you have need of me."

Aracea made no reply ; she seemed as indifferent to that as she was to everything.

That night, at supper, there was an open breach in the camp. Parrales were not speaking to de la Cernas, or de la Cernas to Parrales. De la Cernas, clumped round Carlos, and Parrales, with Don Federico as their leader, were separated by an awkward little clump of lawyers and accountants. Leandra sat between the two Segovian gentlemen, who looked like handsome death's-heads, and Aracea's place had been moved, together with Mary's, to their end of the table. It was a most uncomfortable meal: de la Cernas grandly silent, Parrales animatedly conversational among themselves. Only Carlos attempted to relieve the silence at his end of the table, with a flow of his customary levity, to which no one paid attention. After the meal, the whole of the company, with the exception of Aracea, the boys and Mary, retired to the sala, of which the doors were locked.

" Miss Mary."

It was close upon midnight; Mary had taken off her dress, and was trying to write a few letters. She stood up quickly.

" Señora—— ? "

Leandra crossed the room in her long, black dress and sank into a chair. Her face was white as bone, and almost plain, but there was a strength and obstinacy in its thin, well-bred lines that Mary had never seen there before.

" Are you going back to England ? "

" When it is convenient, for you and Aracea."

" I wish you will take Aracea with you."

Her heart gave a leap.

" You know—I think you know—that I would like nothing better."

" At her age it is ridiculous she get married. Girls do not get married at fifteen, in these days. It is more ridiculous she get engaged to one of the Parral boys. My cuñado—Federico—he wants that, because of course he wants to keep the estate in the Parral family. And of course my uncles want she marry Carlos, because that mean the money and everything come to my people." She spoke haltingly, her English failing under the stress of her emotion. She made a sudden gesture of flinging away the unfamiliar language, and continued in Spanish. " Miss Mary, you, as an Englishwoman, understand what I feel about this. I do not wish my daughter of fifteen to be sacrificed to a dynastic marriage. I have told you my feeling about Carlos. I do not like the Parral boys, they are ill-bred, and their father is not a good Catholic. Neither of them will make Aracea a good

201

husband; she needs something more masculine. And I certainly do not wish her to marry Paco Ribera. It is a great mistake, and leads to much unhappiness, to marry out of one's class.

"My Uncle Rodrigo, who has many of my father's ideas, is partly on my side. He agrees with me that it is not right to oblige her to make up her mind, while she is too young to understand the meaning of marriage; he wishes, with my other uncle, Rodolfo, that she should marry Carlos, but he realises, as I do, that her education has not prepared her to accept such a marriage purely on grounds of convenience, or even in accordance with her father's wish."

"I am afraid I am partly to blame for that."

"My father said, always, that only the English and the Germans know how to bring up children; that is why I insisted on English governesses for Aracea. At fifteen, her education is not complete. At fifteen, she thinks she is in love with a boy who fights bulls, and whose father keeps a dry goods store."

"I would not like to guarantee that a visit to England would eradicate that."

"I do not mean a visit to England. I want her to have a year, at least, in an English school. I want to give her an environment as different as possible from her present one, so that she may be able to get her life here in perspective. For the present, Carlos will remain in control of the business; that is arranged for, in my husband's will; he will have, I hope, the advice of my brother-in-law, who is an admirable man of affairs, if careless about his religious duties! That arrangement will stand until Aracea comes of age. She will by then, I hope, have learned to take a soberer view of the act of marriage, and she will perhaps have met people who will appeal to her sense of what is right and fitting, for the daughter of Parral."

Is this, thought Mary, the weak and spineless being whom I have known all these years?

"Who are her guardians?" she asked.

"Myself, of course; Carlos, as manager of the estate; and my two uncles."

"And do they agree to her going to England?"

" Carlos—no ; my uncles, they are not exactly willing, but I shall be able to persuade them it is the most desirable thing."

" And Aracea herself ? " asked Mary.

" I have not spoken to her about it. But what you say carries much weight with her. And—she was devoted to her father ; I think she will be glad to get away from here, for a little while."

" Won't you be very lonely, by yourself, señora ? " Mary was constrained to ask. Leandra smiled faintly.

" I am accustomed to loneliness. In any case, I shall go to my relatives in Segovia, for a time. I have always hated this place," she said, in a low, passionate voice, " and I shall be thankful to get away from it.—Your friend—the señora who called on you the other day : she has a school, has she not ? "

" She had one, in partnership with a friend, before she got married. I believe she still has what they call ' an interest.' I should perhaps have told you, señora : I have been offered a post there, when I return to England."

" But—it is a miracle ! "—Leandra's face blazed into beauty, into youth, and hope. and interest. " You are taking the post, Miss Mary ?—But you *must* ! And Aracea will go with you. She would perhaps have resisted being sent to a strange, English school—separated from everything with which she is familiar ; but if she knows she is going with you—— ? "

Interlude

I

My Darling Mummy,

. . . the new gov, Miss Carpenter, is not bad. There is also a new girl called Aracea (pronounced *Arathaya*, Spanish). It is the first time she has been to school in England. She has beaten the swimming record for the class and Pamela Napier the Tennis captain this year has chosen her as a reserve for the Interschool tournament in July. She is also terribly good at riding, though she won't do anything Foxy tells her. It seems they have different ideas in Spain, i.e. long stirrup, etc., and she won't have anything to do with side saddle. There was a terrific row the other day, we were all jogging round the tan and I suppose she got bored anyhow she put her horse at the rail round the cricket pitch. Well you know those old skins of Foxys that horse had never seen a hurdle in its life so it gave a terrific peck and she came off over its head a real cracker. Foxy absolutely fomed at the mouth and Aracea acted like a bombe glacee and said it was Foxy's fault for putting her up on a thing like that so what *do* you think? She is going to be allowed to have a horse of her own. Only two of the girls have got their own horses so her people must be frightfully rich.

. . . N.B. Can I have some castanets, I mean proper ones. If you ask at the Spanish restaurant I expect Mr. Martinez will tell you where to go for them . . .

Dearest Fiddy,

Everything is the usual ghastly bore but I expect we shall survive until the half term. Now you have had two whole months as free as a bird I am dying to know what it feels like to have left school and be taken seriously by eligible young men and regarded with suspicion by their mothers. Remember you're *on your honour* not to be taken seriously by Tony Parris ; have you seen him lately, and was I mentioned ?

When you come for the half, please bring some langues de chat—Barbellion's are the best—and a large box of Elizabeth Arden, the yellowy not the pinky : I think it's called " Banana." It's not for me, it's a present. Also a book called *Fiesta*. Viola Bruce was reading it in the holidays and got into the most frightful row at home, she's dying to finish it. Its about Spain and people who are drunk all the time and a girl called Lady Brett Ashley who goes to bed with a Jew and an American and a Spanish bullfighter. We all want to read it because of a new girl called Aracea Parral who lives in Seville and her people breed fighting bulls as we breed race horses. She is in love with a bullfighter. He looks a little " com " in the photograph but it may be the clothes. Though Tony wouldn't. I can imagine him looking fabulous in thóse embroidered things with the cape over his shoulder.

Do you think Papa would take us to Spain next summer ? As you are his favourite you might put in a little work on it, but don't say too much in front of Mamma, you know what she is about the R.S.P.C.A. . . .

DEAR CHARLES,

Thanks for the congrats. It's jolly good luck for me, of course, as Captain of the Tennis *and* my last term. St Mag's has never got into the finals before and we never even thought of the Shield ! ! ! Frightfully hard lines on poor old Stella, spraining her wrist on the very morning, but luckily the reserve came up to scratch. Actually it was a pure fluke. She's a Spanish girl, new this term, and she's not all that good except by fits and starts, but we'd lost two of our best so I had to take the chance. I gave her some extra coaching and *a good jaw* about not poaching her partner's ball and not sulking when she was faulted, but I really panicked the whole time she was on the court in case she let the school down in some way. However she happened to be in one of her good moods and I must say she put up a grand show in the singles. St Mag's of course went mad when she beat the Corrie girl who's held the junior and senior championships for the last five years and that actually was what gave us the Shield. . . .

SCHOOL REPORT

Name : Aracea Parral.
Class : Vb   *No. in class :* 11

Subject	Comment	Position in Class
Eng. Literature	Fair	8
Eng. Composition	Shows some improvement	9
History	Lacks concentration	10
Geography	Very fair	7
Arithmetic	Very good	2
Algebra	Very weak	11
Geometry	Pays insufficient attention	10
French	Fair	7
Latin	Good	3
Physical Science	Some interest shown, but importance of accuracy not sufficiently appreciated	9
Domestic Science	Shows some ability	6
Gymnastics	Excellent	1
Dancing	Very good	2
Speech Training	Has made marked progress	5
Drawing & Painting	Very little talent shown	10

(*Musical subjects not taken*)

Conduct in Class : Inattentive unless interest is roused and seldom makes effort of which she is capable.

Conduct in House : Satisfactory.

General Remarks : Appears to be adjusting satisfactorily to the pattern of school life, but requires to cultivate team spirit.

Extracted from

THE RECORD
St Margaret's School Magazine
Summer Term

We are glad to welcome Nadia Fleming, Griselda Napier, Aracea Parral and Serena Pitt-Winters to St. Margaret's, and wish them many happy terms.

. . . *Sports.*

Tennis : The event of the term was, of course, the " glorious victory " in the Interscholastic Tournament, when for the first time St. Margaret's captured the Shield and the proud position of champion of the schools. For a detailed report of the play, see pp 6-7 . . . Aracea Parral, playing as a reserve made a fine contribution to the success of the St. Margaret's team . . .

Cricket : It is disappointing to have to record a bad season. In spite of indefatigable coaching by Miss Gaylor and the Captain, Viola Bruce, the school was heavily beaten in three matches at home and one away. There seems to be a general waning of interest, which is much regretted, and which has undoubtedly weakened our credit with rival teams. Let us hope for better things next year.

Swimming : The usual competitions were held on the last Saturday of the term and included, in addition to speed trials, interesting exhibitions of Life Saving and High Diving. The winners were as follows :

. . . *Seniors :*   Breast stroke   Aracea Parral
                   Crawl   Aracea Parral
                   Relay   A. Parral (leader)

Much amusement was caused in the Life Saving demonstration by Aracea Parral's realistic performance as the " drowning " person. After giving her would-be rescuers the maximum amount of trouble, they were obliged to own themselves defeated, while the " victim " swam calmly away and " rescued " herself ! This (unrehearsed) item, which was received by the onlookers with rapturous applause, was, however, repeated with a more cooperative "victim," who allowed the life-savers to recover their credit.

Sports Day

... The Riding Class, as usual, acquitted itself well, and Miss Fox is to be congratulated on a general improvement in both style and confidence. A very agreeable show, that included Dressage, was given by the whole class, and followed by competitions, in which Joyce Houston-Bell, on her own pony, Feste, won the First Prize for Junior Jumping, etc., etc.

The entertainment was concluded by a most interesting demonstration by Aracea Parral, on her new mare, Mariposa. Riding cross-saddle, Aracea showed herself mistress of the arts of equestrianism, and her jumping, across the bar, hurdle and brick wall, provided school and visitors with a sensation and contributed a much-appreciated touch of novelty to the occasion. We hope, for Miss Fox's sake, that the Riding Class will not be too headlong in its efforts to emulate these feats of horsemanship !

Social Diary

... On grounds of humanitarianism, the Staff Common Room begs to remind Those Whom It Concerns that its usually open windows are within earshot of Junior Recreation, and requests that the Sevillana should not be played more than twenty-five times in the course of one half-hour recess.

... We are asked to remind Certain Persons that Long Field is not the place to practise the castanets.

... Loth as we are to discourage the practice of the Arts, the next person who recites *Lepanto*, or any part of same, at the Social Evenings will be fined a week's pocket money, to be given to the R.S.P.C.C. Note, payment by instalment not allowed.

... A proposition which we understand is on foot, to remove the school, lock stock and barrel to Andalusia (*sic*) is strongly deprecated by the First and Second Elevens, Senior Netball, Hunt members and all who prefer the English to the foreign cuisine. It is hoped that this rumour is without foundation other than the announced intention of Messrs. Cook to lay on additional staff to cope with the unprecedented rush to the South of Spain which is expected in the near future.

. . . The announcement of a lecture on Spanish Architecture by Doctor Thorold Hagenson, on the first Thursday of next term, has been received with unusual enthusiasm. Dr. Hagenson's promoters may be assured that St. Margaret's will muster in full strength. (D.V.)

Complaints have been received of the misappropriation and misuse of the red bedcovers in the Junior House. Some sharp detective work has established the felony as an " outside job," and those concerned are warned that a repetition of the offence will be attended by unpleasant consequences.

II

" I do not wish to go out in a muddy field. I do not like to have my legs broken in pieces with sticks and my nails spoiled with catching a dirty ball and throwing it into a stupid little net. I do not think those things are suitable for a girl of my age. No, I am sorry, I must really refuse."

" It's not a matter of your opinions, or of ' refusing ' ! Go and get your boots on—we're all waiting."

" I regret." Shrugging her shoulders politely, Aracea turned back to the schoolroom fire.

Affronted and baffled, the Games Mistress sought her colleague, Mary Carpenter.

" *Now* what does one do ?—There's the match on Saturday——"

" Don't tell me you've put Aracea in the First Eleven ! "

" Oh, don't be silly, Carpenter ! She's never been out, since the first practice ; first it was ' a cold,' then it was the curse. I don't believe either. But I'm supposed to be coaching the Eleven, and Viola Bruce is taking shooting practice with the seniors. None of the little slackers wants to go out, and they don't see why Aracea should get away with it, if they can't."

" It's certainly not a tempting day," murmured Mary. She glanced from the window at the wind-lashed trees, the scatter of yellow leaves and the clouds, heavy with rain. It had rained most of the week; she could imagine the mud-bath of the hockey field.

" She's had all the usual punishments; she's had her riding docked on Saturday morning——"

" She'll certainly hate that," agreed Mary.

" Well, where's it got us ?—This is just becoming a joke, at our expense," scowled the other.

" Oh, I don't think so. After all, Harriet Sherlock and Ernestine Chapman don't play games."

" They've got doctors' certificates !—It wouldn't matter if the little idiots hadn't adopted her as a heroine. Even the seniors rather admire her, for ' sticking it out,' and the middle school is thrilled to bits. It's an awfully bad influence," she complained.

Mary regarded her thoughtfully; wondering, not for the first time, why proficiency in games was so often accompanied by arrested development. For all her years—she was close on forty—and her diploma, Joan Gaylor was not quite equal, mentally, to the average St. Margaret's pupil of sixteen. The honour of the hockey, the cricket, the netball, the tennis—she herself would say, of the school—governed her every thought and action. She was incapable of respecting a view alien to her own.

" She ruined the cricket, last term ! She let everybody know she thought it was a bore, and they all thought it was ' grand ' to imitate her. Now she'll do the same with the hockey, unless somebody puts a stop to it. Viola's awfully upset ! She says most of the Eleven are loyal, but there's a very nasty feeling among the rest. You practically have to *drag* them out for practice, unless it's a lovely day, and there's no excitement about the matches—like there used to be, last year. It's as though they didn't *care* about St. Margaret's——! " To Mary's astonishment, the big, adolescent eyes filled with tears. " And we *know* it all goes back to Aracea. She's been telling them all it doesn't improve their education, to get chilblains and red noses, by going out in cold weather——"

" Well, does it ? " murmured Mary. Fortunately, the other did not hear her.

" It wouldn't do a bit of harm, if she hadn't made herself so popular, last term. But her tennis and her swimming got her in with people like Pamela and Viola, and of course Foxy never ought to have let her do that show-off at the Sports ! So now they're all—except Viola and a few of the seniors—eating out of her hand. I'm surprised Reverend Mother doesn't put her foot down ! I don't think she's very keen on games, but she does mind about St. Margaret's."

" Reverend Mother has more sense. What, actually, could she do, but expel Aracea ? Think of the drama *that* would create : Aracea's departure, undefeated, in a blaze of glory ; tears in the dormitories ; Aracea permanently sanctified as a martyr to the cause of hockey—believe me, Gaylor, it wouldn't do you or St. Mag's any good. Let it alone for the present ; I'll see if I can do anything," promised Mary.

As usual, she took her problem to Mother Mary Joseph : a wise woman, with a sense of humour, and, privately, as little sympathy as Mary with the games faction, which she discreetly left to her co-Principal, Adela Hallatt's friend.

" She has been so good, on the whole, up to the present, that there must be some way of getting round the present impasse without unpleasantness. You see, Reverend Mother, I know when it is useless, to argue with Aracea. The main thing seems to be, to save Miss Gaylor's face."

" Then you see no point in obedience for its own sake ? "

" I have never seen any point in an *unreasonable* obedience," admitted Mary.

" A curious observation, for a Catholic ! "

" I suppose so," said Mary hurriedly. " All the same, this doesn't concern Catholic rule, and I don't see what use hockey and netball are likely to be, to Aracea, in the future. She will certainly have no opportunities of playing either, at home."

" Team spirit ? "—But the other was smiling. " That, I am

given to understand, is why we lay so much emphasis upon games at St. Margaret's ; and, according to her report, she was deficient in that."

" I don't see that, either, fitting into the pattern of life at Parral, or," added Mary, " into marriage. It is not the kind of thing a Spaniard would expect, or appreciate, in his wife."

" You are better informed than I, and I accept your judgment. But what about physical exercise ? All young people require that."

" She's surprisingly keen on gymnastics ; she enjoys dancing —and, of course, she'd be desperate, if her riding were stopped : the only outdoor exercise she enjoys in the week. I was wondering," suggested Mary, " if she could ride sometimes while the others are at hockey practice."

" Now you are proposing a general mutiny ! " smiled the Reverend Mother. " All the girls who take riding would expect to do the same ; you know they are always complaining about having only one ride a week."

" But—if it were by medical advice ? "

The smile vanished in a frown.

" Continue, Miss Carpenter."

" Let us admit that the winter climate is very trying, for a girl brought up in the South of Spain. She is likely to be more liable to colds and chest complaints than our hardened young people. If you would allow me to suggest that to the doctor, next time he is here, I think we might get over the difficulty. At least, it would put a stop to the dissatisfaction of the other girls, and absolve Miss Gaylor, in their eyes, of weakness, and the rest of us of favouritism."

" And give Aracea a very pretty victory ! "—The speaker shook her head.

" If I may say so, I think you misunderstand her, Reverend Mother," persisted Mary. " In some ways, she's very adult. I've never found her—petty. She is more likely to admire us, for seeing her point of view, and to appreciate our tact in arranging matters to her satisfaction, without disturbing the general organisation."

" You are an ingenious advocate," smiled the other ; nodded acceptance, and let Mary see the interview was over.

So she saw the doctor, who was amused and amenable. In possession of a certificate which immunized her from winter games, Aracea justified it by putting on no airs of triumph or superiority ; to Mary's gratification, she even made a point of discouraging a few immature partisans, who chose to interpret the concession as " a snub for the govs ! "

" It is nothing of the kind. As soon as it was properly explained, they saw I was right," she told them ; increasing, incidentally, her prestige with those who were already prepared to believe that whatever Aracea did was " right," and spiking the guns of her critics who, after her successes of the summer, considered she was " letting down the side " by refusing to play games in the winter term. So she rode when it was fine, and on foggy or icy days gained the envy of her companions by curling up beside the fire to write long letters to Leandra and to Paco. Sometimes she joined Mary, in the latter's bedroom, and over the little electric stove they comforted each other with talk of the pastures of Parral and the prospects of the coming season. She was not yet homesick to the point of longing to return ; the dread of crossing the threshold of Parral without the welcome of the beloved face and voice was still sharp within her. Don Luis was never mentioned in their conversations.

At Mary's suggestion, all the books and photographs, the treasures and trophies Aracea had brought with her were kept in her room ; she had succeeded in persuading Aracea that ears, banderillas, bullfighting posters, and close-ups of the more gory moments of the fight were unsuitable decorations for a cubicle. Over Aracea's bed, above the crucifix that was a regulation feature of all the cubicles, hung, therefore, only the devisa of Parral and a discreet enlargement of a snapshot of grazing bulls ; on the dresser, in the place usually dedicated to family photographs, was the coloured postcard of Paco, in a leather frame. It got by, as the photographs of Laurence Olivier, Gordon Richards and James Mason got by in other cubicles : because no one took them seriously. Anyhow, they changed every few

weeks. But not the photograph of Paco. Mary wondered sometimes, whether she ought to begin to take that seriously : and,
if she did, what to do about it.

Half-term week-end, when the school was inundated by
visiting parents, bearing their rejoicing offspring away to " feeds "
at hotels or home for a couple of nights, coincided with a meet
of the local foxhounds, and Aracea, to her joy, was allowed, with
Mary, to accept the invitation of one of the girls whose parents
had witnessed Aracea's display in the summer, and to sample,
for the first time, the delights of the English hunt. Mary, who
had never hunted, and had had little riding since her return to
England, thought it wiser not to follow, herself, and had some
misgivings about letting Aracea set forth with strangers ; but on
receiving a promise that she would be escorted home before
dusk, gave in to the girl's entreaty, and was glad she had done
so, when a radiant Aracea returned with the brush, and a smear
of blood on her glowing cheek. On Sunday, after mass, a car
arrived, to take them to lunch with their hosts of the previous
day, and Aracea (whose summer holidays had been spent with
Mary in Cornwall and, for a few days, in London) received her
initiation into country house society, and professed herself
entranced with " The dear little rooms, so hot, and so full of
things ! And carpets on all the floors—even on the stairs ! And
in the w.c.s ! And the bedrooms—simply stuffed with chairs and
tables and sofas, as if people sat in them, and looking-glasses
everywhere."

Mary agreed that the standard of comfort of the Manor was
high, as English homes go, and that the carpets made it " cosier."

" Do English people always lay tables like that ?—with all
that silver and four or five glasses for each person and the little
towels with bordaduras and crests worked in the corner for us
to wipe our hands ? " she pursued with interest.

" Well, they used to, before the war ; but I don't think many
people are able to keep it up now. Perhaps it will come back in
a few years' time."

" It's awfully pretty ! I loved the green glasses, and the
little querubínes with shells on their heads for the bombónes.

But why do they have all those knives and forks and spoons ?—
I didn't use half of mine," declared Aracea. Mary smiled, having
noticed her pupil wiping her knife and fork carefully with a
piece of bread, and laying them on her side plate, Parral-fashion ;
Aracea must have some lessons in the usages of polite society
before accepting any more invitations. " That's what's so odd ;
they seem to have dozens of everything—just lying about anywhere ; I don't know how they keep count. And another thing :
did you notice how everybody got up and carried things away,
or handed things round ? Don't they have servants ? "

" Not since the war, I expect ! "

" But who keeps the house clean ? " gaped Aracea.

" They probably have a couple—a cook and a housemaid—
and a lot of daily women. I should think in a house like that,
there would be a dozen or more servants, before the war, but
people now have to manage with what they can get, and do half
the work themselves."

" Qué barbaridad. We have had a war. It is not like home."

" No, not in the Southern country districts," agreed Mary,
thinking how little Aracea had so far seen of this deprived and
demoralised post-war England, and how much she might have
been shown in days before travelling and sight-seeing were
limited by petrol rationing and by the manifold restrictions that
still closed many places of historic interest to the public. They
had done an awe-stricken tour of the ravaged East End, mainly
because she felt it was her duty ; but Mary's conscience so
tortured her that, each time she came on one of those patches of
ruin overgrown with the purple of willow herb, she grew faint
and sick with compunction, and could hardly endure the lively
sensationalism of her companion. " Oh Miss Mary ! Look
there ! You can see the bath sticking out—and there's a towel
still hanging on the rail—and look ! There's a picture hanging
on the wall ! Aren't they *ever* going to clean this mess up ? "

She had decided there should be no more visits to London
for the present, and had written to an old school friend in
Cheltenham, to ask her advice about some place where she and
Aracea could spend at least part of the holiday ; but shortly

after half term, at least half a dozen parents, prompted by their daughters, wrote to ask if Aracea could come to them for Christmas. Faced by an *embarras de choix*, a delighted Aracea, well-primed in the social ·observances—including table manners —which she promised faithfully to observe, set off for a round of visits. Mary had written to Leandra, asking if the latter wished her to accompany Aracea as chaperone, but, receiving no reply, and the assurances both of the Reverend Mother and Miss Morgan that the Catholic families whose invitations had been accepted on Aracea's behalf would take care of her in the fullest sense, she took Elizabeth's advice and let the girl go alone.

" And for goodness' sake, Mary, take yourself somewhere for a rest ; you look as though you needed one."

She did. About a fortnight before the end of the term, an upheaval had taken place which, because Aracea was concerned in it, Mary had taken badly to heart.

First, there had been the discovery, in one of the seniors' pigeonholes in the cloakroom of a novel which was not only on the Index, like a number of blameless works, but proved on examination to be totally unfit for the consumption of excitable adolescents. Among the girls who confessed to having read it, Aracea put up her hand.

" *You* read it ? "—The mistress who had made the discovery looked astonished, as well she might : Aracea never having been known to open a book, apart from those forced upon her by the curriculum. " Do you mean, you read it all ? " gasped Miss Stewart.

Aracea nodded, with more pride than veracity. She had, in fact, skimmed it from about half-way through to the end, mainly because it was supposed to be about Spain, but she had found the characters—who were all English, or American—very boring and their conversations unintelligible ; they were always " very drunk," or they " felt like hell," and one of the women kept saying she was " a bitch "—though on what grounds Aracea could not gather. The only good bit was the bullfight, although the thing about the colour " catching the bull's eye " was rubbish, as everyone knows bulls don't see colour at all.

Fortunately the mistress guessed something of that; among the pallid or crimson faces that answered the summons to the parlour, Aracea's was normal and unperturbed. Cross-questioned by the Reverend Mother, she said, No, it had not struck her that the book was immodest; perhaps she had unintentionally skipped those parts. Improper language?—Well, they said "Damn" and "hell" a few times; but Shakespeare uses both, doesn't he? "Out, damned spot" and "Hell is empty and all the devils are here"? "I don't think there's anything else; 'wench' isn't bad, is it?—or 'sadist'—I don't know what that means at all."

"You know the rule: that all books brought into the school must be approved by the Librarian and carry the stamp inside the cover."

"I didn't look."

"Don't prevaricate. You knew this book had been brought in against the rules and that it was being read secretly by other girls in your form. You therefore knew you were doing wrong in reading it."

A look out of the corner of her eye warned Aracea that she had better admit it. Given her punishment for disobedience and deceitfulness, she was dismissed, while her fellow culprits continued to writhe under the Reverend Mother's reprobation.

But the second incident was graver, and, involving the same group, very nearly put an end to her Christmas plans.

A meeting of the Sports Committee left Aracea and two of her classmates in undisturbed possession of "Senior Sitter," an agreeable room overlooking the yew hedges that enclosed the Head's private garden. "Senior Sitter" was effectively a club, and age alone did not qualify you for membership; you had to be proposed, seconded by one of the teaching staff and have your name submitted to a secret ballot. Election meant that you were, theoretically at any rate, a person of discretion, good manners, good influence and, it goes without saying, popularity; to sum up, an important character in the world of St. Margaret's. You might tell the people whose names were "up" for Senior Sitter by their anxious, harried and haunted look—one Clarissa Ormsby-

Smith was said to have had hysterics on the day of the ballot, thereby setting back her own election by a term.

But of latter years the constitution had somewhat slackened, and it was not unusual for visiting Smogs (i.e members of St. Margaret's Old Girls' Society) to remark, " *She* wouldn't have got into Senior Sitter in *our* day ! " Corruption and favouritism were freely alleged by unsuccessful candidates, and for some time, High Authority, aware of disaffection, had been considering the abolition of the titles and privileges of Senior Sitter. The upshot came in the following conversation, overheard from the adjoining stationery closet. It was not Stationery Day, and Miss Holmes had no business to be there ; it was unanimously agreed that it was a piece of deliberate snooping. The closet, which had a separate door on to the landing, had originally been part of the room itself ; cut off only by a piece of thin boarding, whose starkness was concealed by bookshelves, every word spoken in either compartment, every sound, from the rustle of a sheet of paper to a cough, was clearly audible in the adjoining one. Miss Holmes must just have sneaked in and stood there in the dark, for when the light in the closet was switched on it was visible through a crack near the door and acted as a useful danger signal to the occupants of Senior Sitter.

This was the conversation Miss Homes overheard, and— crowning infamy—actually *took down on paper*, using the very pencil the Lower Fifth had given her for her birthday ; one of the kind that has a little electric bulb inside the point.

" I often wonder how fat men manage "—this was the fluting treble of Mirry Scott : still nominally in a state of penance for her responsibility in the matter of the novel.

" How do you mean, manage ? "—Rachel Coke, with a titter that gave her away.

" ' Prinny has let loose his belly, which now reaches his knees ' "—

" Caramba," with calmness, in the unmistakable voice of Aracea, and renewed giggles from Rachel.

" Well," said Mirry, in her high-pitched, over-innocent voice, " it must have been awfully awkward for the ladies."

" Worse than bulls and cows ? "—from Rachel doubtfully.

" But it is not at all awkward for the cow; why should it be ? "

" Oh, Aracea, do tell : have you ever seen a bull and a cow making love ? "

" Of course; plenty of times."

" But isn't it awful for the poor cow ? "—Rachel, who had exaggerated sentiments in regard to animals, sounded almost tearful, and Aracea much amused in her reply.

" But why ? I think it is as much fun for the cow as the bull."

" Oh, it *can't* be ! " moaned Rachel. " Just think what you'd feel like, with all those tons and tons of bull on top of you."

" Well, what did Lady Conyngham feel like, with tons and tons of Prinny ? I mean, she must have liked it, or she wouldn't——"

" I suppose she was asked ; but nobody asks the poor little cow."

" Now, let's get this straight," said Mirry in a business like way. "How does the bull manage ? Does the cow lie down and hold its tail up, or what ? "

It was Aracea's turn to giggle.

" Don't be so silly ! They do it like dogs."

" That's what I thought. But I still can't see how the bull does it. I mean, just *think* of a bull; to start with, its chest's practically on the ground ; its legs are only a few inches long——"

" Ay—entendido ! But our bulls are not like yours," explained Aracea. " Their legs are long, with much strength, especially the back ones. They can jump like galgos—what is it you say—greyhounds ! They look very fine, when they make love."

" Like Spaniards, I suppose. Do tell : are Spaniards as passionate as people say they are ? "

" All men are passionate—no ?—when they are in love."

" Well, I can't imagine my Pa ever being passionate—in that way," declared Mirry. " Fiddy and I can never imagine how we came to be born, because we're quite certain Pa would think it awfully caddish and Ma would be furious."

" What about artificial insemination ? " suggested Rachel.

" I don't think it had been invented. Gracious, fancy missing all that fun !—Now, Rachel, don't start being gloomy about cows again.—Oh, Aracea, you are lucky ; fancy being engaged. Do tell what it's like when Paco kisses you."

" Like—like being kissed, I suppose," said Aracea, evidently taken aback.

" Tony's only kissed me once, and he made an awful muck of it," admitted Mirry. " He missed my mouth and landed smack in my left eye ; it watered for hours."

" I don't think kissing's much ! "—Rachel sounded superior. " The other's more exciting."

" What do you mean by ' the other ' ? " asked Aracea, interestedly.

" Doesn't Paco do anything besides kissing you ? " giggled Rachel.

" What—what sort of anything ? "

" Oh, fiddling about with the top of your dress and stroking ; things like that."

This was the point at which Miss Holmes entered.

" Did you tell the girls you were engaged to Paco ? "—An hour later, she was in Mary's room.

" It was just a joke," muttered Aracea.

" It may have been a joke ; it was certainly a lie."

Aracea's lips closed in a sullen line.

" Has he ever kissed you ? "

" No." One lie led naturally to another.

" Have you ever taken part in that kind of—dirty talk before ? "

" I don't understand what you mean by ' dirty talk.' All girls are interested in love. And, actually, we were talking about the bulls," Aracea defied her.

" Have I not told you that you were not to talk about bulls here ?—Even if you were brought up on a ranch, you must realise it's not a subject for ordinary conversation. You don't talk about it to the de Gaula girls——"

" They would not be in the least interested," was the lofty rejoinder.

" And neither are Rachel and Mirry, in a proper way."

" Oh yes they are ! They wanted to know how bulls make love, and they had such stupid ideas, I thought they had better know the truth."

Mary looked at her in silence. What was the use of putting the idea of indecency into Aracea's mind, in connection with an occupation that involved her own future, and about which she had as little sense of guilt or embarrassment as one of the vaqueros ?

" Well, the only thing I can say is—we shall have to alter our plans for Christmas."

Aracea's eyes widened, her face crimsoned with apprehension.

" What do you mean, Miss Mary ? "

" I simply can't take the risk of your talking in other people's houses as you have been talking this afternoon," sighed Mary. Aracea's hands clenched themselves in the folds of her skirt ; the defiance dropped from her like a discarded veil.

" Oh, but I won't ! I promise I will not ! I didn't begin it ; truthfully I didn't. If you don't believe me, ask Miss Holmes ! "

" You didn't attempt to check it either, did you ? "

" But there wasn't anything to check, Miss Mary. It was just a matter of English bulls being a different shape from ours —and Mirry didn't see—— "

" Oh, leave the bulls alone. Why did you talk in that foolish way about Paco ? "

" I didn't see any harm in it. Mirry is enamorada with a boy called Tony, and Rachel had an affair in Scotland with a—what do you call the men who lead the ponies—I must say," observed Aracea, on a note of righteous surprise, " English girls have a great deal more liberty than we do. I think it is surprising that they get married. Our men would not at all like to marry a girl who had had affairs. But nobody seems to think anything of it over here."

" Don't you make any mistake about that ; it is just as much disapproved—by decent people—here as it is in Spain."—It would be Mirry Scott and Rachel Coke that Aracea had chosen as her particular cronies : the only two in the Senior school who were regarded with faint—and, up to the time of the novel incident, unfounded suspicion by the staff. Rachel's parents had figured in a divorce that shook Catholic society to its foundations (and, incidentally, rendered Rachel illegitimate in the eyes of the Church), and Mirry's were fashionable, frivolous and neglectful of their duties. But at St. Margaret's the sins of the parents were not visited on the children, and it was hoped that its influences would sterilize, if not exterminate, the germs heredity had inflicted on the pair.

It was natural that Aracea should gravitate towards them because, under their veneer of childish levity, both Mirry and Rachel had a hard core of adult sophistication that made them more acceptable than the average people of their age to one who was, in many respects, already a grown-up person. All the " Up the School ! " and " St. Margaret's for ever ! ", that Aracea found profoundly silly, was jeered to the echoes by those two. The three hearts beat as one over such matters as making effort " for the School's sake," winning the Form Trophy for the best class in work and conduct, " backing the side," and " playing the game." Individualists in thought and action, they simply had no time for such puerilities. Both Mirry and Rachel played, when they chose, an elegant game of tennis, whacked a neat hockey ball and swam a pretty length, without the least interest in winning (differing in this from Aracea, who could not endure being beaten), and were therefore quite useless to the School when it came to inter-school rivalries. They got away with it because they were amusing, quick-witted, generous and pretty ; their popularity (which had got them into Senior Sitter) was equal to Aracea's, when once the gilt of novelty had worn off the latter.

They were, in many respects, the most suitable companions, from point of view of compatibility, she could have chosen, and Mary had condoned, if not approved, the choice, in the face of the deprecation of the Staff Common Room.

" You'll not make Aracea into a loyal little schoolgirl in twelve months ! " she warned them. " First, because the Spanish nature doesn't lend itself to attaching importance to trivialities——"

"Oh, come, Carpenter; trivialities?"—throatily, from Joan Gaylor.

"Even I," said Mary, "can't feel it's a matter of life or death, if we win or lose the match against Branksom.—Second, her character is already formed, and her adult interests make it difficult for her to appreciate the more childish enthusiasms of English girls of her own age. It's a pity, in some ways, that she has chummed up with Rachel and Mirry, but for all their silliness, they seem to me pretty harmless, and Aracea may do them good."

She now realised that she had been unduly optimistic, regarding the last possibility.

"If that tale about Rachel is true, she has acted disgracefully, and to talk about it is unpardonable." Realising belatedly that a red herring had been drawn across the trail, she reverted to the subject of Paco. "And there *is* harm in talking about Paco; apart from its being vulgar and untruthful—what on earth possessed you, to make up such a silly tale?"

"I told you, it was just a joke!—Please, Miss Mary, you won't stop me going to Harriet's and Paula's, will you?"

Reflecting that instinct must have prompted her to refuse on Aracea's behalf, the invitation from Mirry, Mary answered:

"I don't expect it will be for me to say. The Reverend Mother and Miss Morgan will decide."

"Oh, *do* ask them to let me. Say I promise faithfully— palabra inglesa—not to do anything wrong. I'll make a good confession—Father Jacoby is hearing them all that week, and I'll ask him to hear mine on the very last night, so I'll have my penance to think about all the time at Harriet's!"

. . . So Aracea spent three weeks, learning the routine of great English houses; the etiquette of the ballroom, the butts, the hunting field; never having met anything like it before, she was vastly impressed by such traces of pomp and circumstance as had survived five years of war. Observing the relationships between men and women—superficially so much less formal than in her own country—she was shrewd enough to suspect subtleties that she was not in a position to appreciate. Taken to the ballet, a pantomime and a Nativity play, she was enraptured by the first, hopelessly confused by the second, and impressed by the third. With the rest of the house party, she attended Midnight mass in a private chapel, whose fifteenth century gilding burnished by the candlelight and solemn music afflicted her for an hour with the worst homesickness she had known since leaving Spain. She took part in charades, dressed up as " La Maja " for a young people's *bal masqué* on New Year's Eve, tried roller skating and abandoned it after a couple of falls—more on account of injured dignity than of physical grief; had a few demure and vaguely disappointing flirtations with young men, learned to play squash —and returned to St. Margaret's a few days before the beginning of the term, breathless with pleasure and boastful, to Mary, about her successes.

" I wore my red, the first night at Paula's ! It was much the nicest—the other women looked so bare : like raw meat."

" I got such a lot of partners at the baile de máscaras, I had to split up every dance ! And I'd taught Paula and her sisters and four of the boys the Sevillana and we danced it at the baile and everybody watched us and clapped and our photographs were in *The Tatler* : did you see it ?—never mind, I've brought back a copy, to send to Paco."

" We went up to the gallops one morning and schooled the horses over bars and I beat them all ! One of the men said he would like to buy Mariposa when I go back to Spain ; I think it is a good idea, no ?—because I don't want another horse just now."

The effervescence continued into the first week of term, then went suddenly flat. For another week, Aracea's moods alternated between lethargy and a bored restlessness. The novelty of school had worn off, routine had become distasteful ; at the end of the first month's tests, Aracea slid ungracefully from seventh to the bottom of her class of eleven. Admonitions were received sullenly and led to no improvement. She had had too much excitement in the Christmas holidays, was the general verdict of the staff. Mary thought differently ; the year was slowly moving towards spring; soon the cows would be dropping their calves in the sweet grass of Parral; the ranch was rousing from its winter sleep; in less than a month, the novilladas would start in Barcelona . . .

She was a little puzzled, that Aracea seemed to avoid her. She was prepared for excited conjectures on the prospects of the season, plans for the return—promised at Easter—and grave discussion on the form of young novilleros, of whom, at the end of the past year, reports were good.

But the girl held herself away; looked sulky and unhappy, and had evidently something on her mind.

The separation between them ended when Aracea came to her room, and showed her a letter from Leandra.

III

" Did you ever expect this ? " asked Mary, after reading the letter.

" That Mamá would go into a convent ? "—Aracea shrugged her shoulders. " It never entered my head. But it is not a bad idea. She's quite unfit to lead an ordinary life, and she wouldn't be happy for long, in Segovia."

And Aracea herself ? It hardly seemed credible that Leandra would abandon the daughter who had no one else to depend upon. A pang of compassion made Mary lay her arm round the girl's shoulders; Aracea suffered the caress woodenly, her eyes on her folded hands. Surely someone would write to her—Mary —and explain the plans for Aracea's future ? It was cruel and unjust, to leave the child like this, in the dark. Again she referred to the letter.

" It says she hopes to be received at Easter."

" Yes. I must go home now."

" I think we had better wait until we hear something more about it. I expect you will be having a letter from your uncles."

" It won't make the least difference," said Aracea, coldly.

" Nothing in the world will persuade me to live with the de la Cernas in Segovia."

" What do you want to do ? " asked Mary, after a pause. No other future seemed imaginable, unless Aracea stayed in England.

" I shall get married, of course," was the calm reply, " and go back to Parral."

" Do you mean, you will marry—Carlos ? " breathed Mary.

" Carlos ? I've said I'll never marry Carlos. I shall marry Paco, as I always intended."

" Let's talk sensibly," said Mary, after a pause. " Now, to begin with : you know your uncles will never consent to your marrying Paco."

" They won't be asked." Her jaw set, she was the picture, thought Mary, of Don Luis.

" I'm afraid they will." She spoke gently. " You are not of age, and they are your trustees. No priest would marry you, without their consent."

" Mamá is also my trustee, and her consent is enough."

" Even if it were—which I very much doubt—you will find her as much against the marriage as Don Rodrigo." Again she paused. " And Paco's parents ?—You know they would have to be consulted ; their consent would be necessary as well."

" Don Amadeo will be on our side." Aracea gave a sharp, positive nod.

Obviously he would !—as would any other parent whose son had an opportunity of marrying the heiress to Parral. Mary sighed.

" You are both very young, to know your own minds."

" We've known them a long time.—I will tell you something now, Miss Mary." She looked up into Mary's face with a perfect assurance. " You accused me of telling a lie, about Paco being my novio. It wasn't a lie. We have been novios since last Easter, in Sevilla."

" That night—— ? "

Aracea confirmed it by a bend of the head.

" We have been enamorados since we were children. We won't marry anyone but each other, so it's no use arguing."

226

" Chica, I'm not arguing. I simply can't imagine how you are going to do it."

" That is why I am going home. I must see Mamá. I must tell her that she has got to arrange this before she goes into her convent. She can, if she pleases ; and, after all, it will make no difference to her ! "

" It will involve her in a great deal of trouble with her family," pointed out Mary.

" And she escapes from all that the minute she joins the community. The de la Cernas can't torment her when she's in there."

" Well, it is putting a great strain on her," said Mary gravely. " She is delicate and inexperienced ; all her life has been planned and governed by other people——"

" Qué disparate ! " retorted Aracea impolitely. " If Mamá has not always had her own way, it was because it was too much trouble. She is lazy, like me——"

" That is not fair ! Her ill-health has sapped all her vitality ; she can't make the efforts of people like ourselves——"

" Oiga, Miss Mary : whatever Mamá has really wanted," said Aracea with emphasis, " she has got. The first thing she wanted was old Tía Carmela, from Segovia. If you ask Concepción, she will tell you how mi Papá raved about that. And the second thing was an English governess for me. Papá was very much against that, too ; but because my grandfather de la Cerna had insisted on all his children learning English and having English nursemaids and tutors, I had to have the same. What Grandpapa Ramiro said, to Mamá, was the tablets of stone ! "

" I know ; but, however strong may have been his disagreement, I think it was over-ruled, in Don Luis's case, by the wish to please his delicate wife."

" Vaya ! "—Aracea was grinning broadly. " Now you are being English and sentimental ! Papá wasn't like that ; he never cared much about pleasing me—let alone Mamá. What he hated was arguing with people who refused to alter their opinions. He would far rather give in—sometimes against his own judgment —than have the annoyance of feeling them all the time—what

is the word?—gritting up against him. And, don't forget, Mis
Mary: when he gave in, he always made them pay for it."

Yes, that was true. Doña Leandra had surely paid a heavy
price.

" Still," put in Mary, " there is some difference in winning
an argument with your husband and winning against a large and
powerful family."

" Caramba, that will make no difference to Mamá," said
Aracea mildly. " What about my coming here?—They were al
against her over that, to begin with, but she just went calmly
on her own way, and even Carlos stopped arguing, when he saw
her mind was made up. People like Mamá are always the
strongest in the end, because they seem to be so weak and
indifferent that no one quite believes it when they make up
their minds about something, and by the time the others know
where they are, the thing is done ! "

Mary was obliged to admit the truth of this.

" All the same, this is a more complicated matter, and I very
much doubt that Doña Leandra can handle it."

" I shall tell her she *must*. It is the very last thing in her
life that she can ever do for me. And, don't forget: Mamá i
very rich—though I suppose she'll take all her money into the
convent. People who are rich can do a lot of things," nodded
Aracea wisely. " I shall tell Mamá that all the things she ha
done so far were for herself——"

" They were for your benefit ! "

" I dare say ; but she wanted them, I didn't. So now she
must do this one thing for me.—So now," she concluded, " you
had better tell Reverend Mother and Miss Morgan that I am
going home, to be married ! " Her voice swelled with satisfaction

For the next twenty-four hours, telegrams flew between St
Margaret's and Segovia. The first from Leandra categorically
forbade Aracea to leave school before the end of the term, " a
arrangements for your future are not yet complete." Without
submitting it to Mary, Aracea sent off a two-page cable, protesting
her desire to spend some time with her mother before the latter
removed herself for all time from her sight ; demanding post

ponement of all " arrangements " until she was there, to con-
ribute to them ; complaining that she was " utterly miserable "
t St. Margaret's and would rather be anywhere else on earth—
" even in prison "—than spend two more months there ; and
nding with the classic threat to " run away " unless she was
llowed immediately to join her mother in Segovia. Mary wired
nore moderately, that Aracea was most anxious to see her
nother on a matter of grave importance, and that, although her
luties would prevent her from accompanying the girl herself, an
scort could be arranged, subject to the señora's instructions.

By the time Leandra's laconic message arrived—" Come if
ou please but understand I cannot alter my own plans "—
Aracea was in a state of frenzy ; she refused to hear of waiting
or her belongings to be packed, she was going by air, not by
rain, and her baggage could be sent after her. Air reservations
vere still difficult ; the lines were still monopolised by V.I.P.'s
nd the pundits of the War Office—and it was nearly a week
before places could be booked to Paris for Aracea and the two
nuns who were escorting her. The journey on to Madrid might
have to be taken by train ; the airline could give no assurances,
promised to " do its best " in the event of cancellations.

" Let's not be uncharitable ; but—laus deo ! " was the joint
opinion of the Staff Common room, as the car rolled down the
drive from a St. Margaret's which, for the last ten days, had
nore nearly resembled a cage of hysterical young female apes
han a Convent School for young ladies.

Her nose pressed against the window of the plane, Aracea
watched, without regret, the English beaches falling behind ;
he minute, V-shaped wakes of ships, and hailed with a deep-
drawn breath of relief the European mainland. Not Spain, yet :
but before the sun went down she would be, with luck, over the
Pyrenees !

Luck, needless to say in 1945, did not hold. Cold, nervous,
and chafing with impatience, they sat on the bleak airport until
dusk, arguing as to whether it would be better to continue the
trip by train. But Sister Mary Ursula, a seasoned traveller, had
confidence in the assurance of an official that there would be

room for them on one of the Madrid planes in the morning.
They trundled wearily into Paris on an airlines bus ; were told
to be at the terminal at 5.30 in the morning, and, after consuming
petits pains and bowls of *soupe à l'oignon*, crept into the beds of
an economical hotel recommended by the reception clerk,
where Sister Mary Ursula and Aracea promptly fell asleep, while
Sister Monica dithered her way through the dark hours, in
mortal dread of oversleeping.

IV

The means taken by Leandra Parral—soon to be Sister María
Dolores de la Santa Merced—to fulfil her daughter's last request
hardly matter. Within a few steps of the cloister, she recognised
and apparently sympathised with Aracea's horror at the prospect
of being left in the charge of her Segovian relatives. She herself,
during the short period of her widowhood, may have suffered
something in that cold house, among those cold people whose
every thought and action was dictated by narrow tradition. She
must have realised that the home she had loved as a young girl
was a home lit and warmed by the personality of her father, that
bird of bright plumage among his sable companions. Her mind
already fixed on her own marriage to the Divine Bridegroom,
some small, sharp part detached itself to deal with Aracea's needs.

She said nothing to the family, and bound Aracea to silence.
Paco was sent for, and, to his alarm, cross-questioned by Doña
Leandra, her confessor and two attendant priests—deliberately
chosen for their inacceptability to the de la Cernas. Having
proved himself a suitable husband for the daughter of Parral and
grandchild of the muy distinguido señor Don Ramiro de la
Cerna, the consent of Don Amadeo was obtained by telegram,
together with the assurance of his presence at the ceremony.

On the Saturday following Good Friday, at six in the morning,
Paco and Aracea received the Holy Communion. Immediately
afterwards, in the presence of Leandra, Don Amadeo and his
wife, the nuns of the convent and several lay witnesses, María

Aracea Parral y de la Cerna, soltera, was joined in Holy Matrimony to Francisco Pardo Ribera, soltero. Having signed the register, they remained, rather nervously, in the side chapel, while Don Amadeo left for a momentous interview with the lawyers. Sitting there, shivering a little, clutching each other's hands, they heard in the great chapel beyond, the sounds of its preparation for the awful ceremony to come.

Presently they were summoned to a closet, through whose grille they could see, across the breadth of the sanctuary, the other grille behind which were silently gathered the nuns of the Order in which Leandra was presently to be received. There was no sound except the shuffling, beyond the screen of the chancel, of de la Cernas, their relatives and friends, come to look for the last time on a de la Cerna daughter before she was claimed by the cloister.

As Aracea began quietly to cry, Paco put his arm tenderly round her shoulder. For the first time in his heedless life, he was deeply awed. His brain felt clouded. He was afraid. · Jesus Cristo, what a wedding for a matador.

PART TWO

PART TWO

Chapter One

PACO GOT the horn on the second day of the feria of Pilár at Zaragosa, but it healed up well enough for them to fly out in November to Mexico City, where the Niño de Maderas had an excellent reception which he confirmed in Lima. It had been a rugged season in Spain, and he owed his Mexican début to a series of disasters that put one matador on the mortuary slab, another permanently out of business and afforded the surgeons a lot of interesting experience.

He was then offered Caracas and Maracaibo; but this meant cancelling Casablanca and filling in with odd dates at Torreón, León and San Luis de Potosi: not a very alluring prospect for a young matador with a growing reputation at home. That year the local phenomena were having it all their own way, and there was no great demand for foreign talent to supplement the home-grown variety.

"I believe I ought to take those two dates in Venezuela."

"Why?—You've got plenty of éxito now, and next year you'll come out with everything fixed in advance."

"Papá will be mad I didn't fight Caracas."

"Qué disparate. It means stopping on into February, and you know we can't spare the time."

"You could go back . . ."

"Of course, there is that." Her eye, avoiding his, went slowly down his naked back. The last cornada was in a nasty place, rather high, curving from under the shoulder-blade towards the right armpit. It had broken open a bit in the

Mexico City fight, and again in Lima, but now it was healing
and there was no more inflammation. He is absolutely clean and
healthy, she thought, and I mean to keep him so. So I don't
leave him by himself for a couple of months at the top of the
season. " And the important thing, amigito, is to build up your
name in Madrid and Barcelona."

" My name is already established," he said coldly.

" Por cierto. And I want to see New York."

They flew to New York, and inside of four days spent a
large part of his earnings. Paco did not like New York. No
one had heard of him and the January climate was execrable.
They saw shows he did not understand and ate in restaurants
where he was treated as an ordinary customer, instead of as an
honoured and valued patron. Sweating in the Waldorf or shivering out of doors, he felt himself nobody, and this was bad for
his character. Aracea—blissfully content in the shops on Fifth
Avenue—bought him an overcoat lined and collared with beaver ;
he accepted it glumly. There was no point in wearing a fur-lined
coat unless the Press photographers got on to it, and there seemed
to be no Press photographers in New York. He was affronted
when Aracea's picture appeared in one of the papers, without
so much as a mention of his name.

" We go home to-morrow."—They were in the lobby, and
Aracea was reading a letter she had just been handed. She replied
absently.

" Yes. But you have heard of my friends the Hallatts. They
want us to visit them in Washington."

Paco was surly. He now wanted to get home as fast as
possible. He was spiritually chilled by the icy scene of Manhattan,
and teased by memories of the heat and light of Mexico—where
Ildefonso, unchallenged, was reaping all the kudos he might at
least have shared. They argued, and, as usual, Aracea won. She
compromised by allowing him to make the air reservations ; they
would fly to Washington, spend a night, fly back and be on the
French plane for Paris ; then Madrid, then Sevilla—and home.

The flight to Washington was as bad as that flight can be.
Too ill, on arrival, even to be civil to their host and hostess,

they retired to separate rooms. Aracea, the first to recover, lurched wanly in to where Paco lay groaning.

" Aren't you going to get up for dinner ? "

" No, no. Let me alone."

" All right. You'll be better in the morning."

" I shall probably be dead," groaned Paco.

" Hombre, we've got to be on the ten o'clock plane."

" Nunca ; nunca de mi vida," said Paco violently. " I would rather face eight bichos on a day of wind than get into another aeroplane ! "

" But we must get home ! " gaped Aracea.

" I will go back to Mexico, I will leave my home and family for ever, but I will not travel by air ! "

" It's a nasty flight at this time of year," said Grosvenor Hallatt, when she took her problem to him, " but we'll give him something that will see him over."

" You'd better get train reservations for them, Gro," Adela suggested.

" Then we'd miss the Paris plane ! " said Aracea despairingly.

In the morning they quarrelled furiously. Paco would not consider taking the plane back to New York, would not hear of dramamine.

" Then we waste all that money ? "

" What money ? "

" Por dios, you've bought our passages to Paris ! "

" Mujer ! "—A wan smile broke through Paco's jaundiced mask. " If they won't refund the money, I can make it in one little afternoon. What are the fares to Paris, beside what we have spent in New York ? "--He took pleasure in rubbing that in, because it was not he who had wished to come to New York. He adored her, and was passionately in love with her, and he was lucky to have married a beautiful, rich girl, whose whole life was devoted to himself and his career, but there are times when a man must exert his authority. To please Aracea, he had learned to wear a dinner jacket, to carry himself with confidence in exalted company, and to play host to people of whom, in the old days, he would have been shy ; and it had all been very amusing, very expensive, and had contributed to his self-importance. But it had its disadvantages; and it was the recollection of these disadvantages which, occasionally, piqued him into a stubbornness she might resent, but knew better than to challenge.

"Bueno; we will go back on a boat." She spoke with philosophic mildness. "And you will probably be sicker than you were on the plane. But if you want it that way, it is all the same to me."

In the train to New York they sat separately, enclosed in their thoughts. Presently Aracea's head dropped into the collar of her mink coat, the magazines slid from her knee; she slept like a child. Paco, his face peaked into a yellow mask, watched the black and grey landscape of winter flash past the windows.

Apart from two fights in Morocco, eight empty weeks lay ahead. Papá might, by now, have fixed him a novillada in March, but there was nothing of importance until Easter. How much better to have stayed in the sun, picking up such fights as came in his way, being stimulated by the public contacts from which the soul of the artist derives its inspiration. It was good, perhaps, not to be dependent on work for a living, but it was also bad. It cheated one of something. Something to do with *pundonor*.

Ildefonso was out there now—somewhere in Colombia. He was booked right through to the fiesta of the Magdalena, at Castellón de la Plana, in March. Always sure of the big money, always penniless, he went on trailing his destroyed body from ring to ring. He had married a peasant girl from Sanjorje, and, by her, had a brood of children. He had been the lover of a famous dancer and of one of the duquesas. He had taken the horn more often, in the last two seasons, than any other bull-fighter, and dragged himself back to the ring, tubed, plugged and plastered, but always "the maestro," always the exponent of "the impossible," always surrounded by the celestial aura he had inherited—according to the fans—from Manolete.

They were saying that, apart from the hazards of the profession, Ildefonso could last only three or four more years; that he led a life of stupendous indiscretion, even for a matador ; that he was burnt-out, like a piece of charred wood. Yet—to change places with Ildefonso, if only for a season ! To carry—with the pain and torment of an abused body—all that tragic glory ! The black and grey landscape blurred in a gush of tears.

A few of the smaller papers, in order to work up a sensation, had named them as rivals : a suggestion which would have been gratifying if it had emanated from one of the pundits of the Press. But even the thick layers of his vanity could not protect Paco from the knowledge that there was no truth in it ; that Ildefonso worked on a plane to which, at present, he had no means of access.

He once overheard an abominable conversation. The speakers were not aware he was sitting behind then, when they liberated their opinions in tones sufficiently resonant to override the babel in which it took place.

" The Niño put on a show last Sunday at Málaga."

" Ya lo dije. A show like a plate of cold tripe."

" Hombre ! "—The first speaker chuckled. " Tripe's good enough, if you know how to cook it."

" Or else it's manure. Oiga. The Niño is good. Very good. Pero—es aficionado."

The word stabbed Paco like the sting of a wasp, and inflamed. They called Ildefonso many things, on his bad days—but they never called him an amateur.

II

" *Darling !* I've been sleuthing you for hours. My dear, this *jungle*——! "

" Darling." " Honey." " Sweetness."

" Señora de Ribera, you must meet Leo Mond ! "

" Encantado."

A pair of snake-cold lips descended on the back of her hand, and Aracea looked up, with faint, distasteful surprise, into a face of pseudo-youth, carefully embalmed in yellow wax, framed in studied waves of white and gunmetal; into a calculated smile and long-lashed, empty eyes.

"I'm *such* an admirer of your husband!—'O, blanco mura de España; O, toro negro de pena; O, sangre dura'—" A fluting voice, a silvery flake of hair swept back from a temple. The Englishwoman with silver eyes, silver-blonde hair in a ruffle over her distinguished little head and big solitaire diamonds in her ears batted one eyelid gently at Aracea.

"You know who he is, of course."

"Excuse me; I don't think so."

Sylvia Brett Pawl laughed indulgently.

"Look; he's talking to Bianca de Aranda, finding out exactly how a matador grades, socially! It will be terribly funny, to see if you make it."

"If I make—what?"

"The lens of Leo's camera. It's easier to go through the eye of a needle than through that little black hole, into our best glossies!—I'm sorry; your English is so good, I take it for granted you understand the jargon. Leo's what they call a 'society photographer.'"

"That is interesting," said Aracea politely.

"Only royalty, and the more sumptuous debs, and absolutely gilt-edged celebrity. You should give him a sitting, if he asks you; 'il connait bien le métier,' and you're both madly photogenic."

"Paco likes very much to have his photograph taken," said Aracea with simplicity.

The matador and his pretty, English-speaking wife had been instantly adopted by the smart English and American crowd of the first class. Paco loved it; he loved the foreign titles, the privileged society, the flattery, the lavish spending, the smell of luxury and of elegant women. It restored his amour propre, which had been damaged in New York. All were at pains to demonstrate their bad Spanish and their familiarity with the vocabulary of the bullfight.

"When in doubt, quote Hemingway."

"'Oo is it," inquired Paco, "zis Emminggué?"

" We met a guy in New York, said he used to fight bulls in Spain. Said Hemingway put him in a book. Say, Paco, did you ever hear of a guy called Franklin ? "

" Don't be dumb. Sidney Franklin was washed up when this one was in his cradle," drawled one of the women, as Paco shook his head.

" Do you think it's possible for a foreigner—I mean, anybody who isn't a Spaniard—to make a really first-class bullfighter ? "

He understood the question, but his English was not equal to answering it.

" My wife speak English very good. She is at school in England two year." His brilliant smile claimed a share in Aracea's accomplishment. She tapped the ash off her cigarette before replying.

" It is not very possible. The English—and, of course the Americans—are very brave. Very sporting. But the bullfight is not a sport."

" Explain," cried someone. She shrugged her smooth shoulders in their sheath of white satin.

" I am sorry. It is something we take for granted, and it is difficult to talk about. I have read the book by your writer Hemingway ; it is not bad at all, but a little old-fashioned. Perhaps it is still useful for people who want to learn something about the bulls."

" We're going to Spain. We want to see some fights." It was the tall, blond Englishman—the husband of the silver eyed woman—with a tuft of faded yellow hair overhanging his face of haggard and hopeless innocence ; he had been drinking steadily, since they left Hoboken. He was not drunk, only serious and sad.

" January is not good time," Paco answered him. " There is nada—nothing. Sometimes there is fight in febrero, if it is good tiempo."

" That's too bad." He lapsed deeper into gloom. " But we could see some bulls ? "

" You must come to my ranch," Aracea smiled at him.

" You mean, your husband's a breeder, as well——? "

" It is I," said Aracea with authority, " who breed bulls. It is in my family four generations. I shall have much pleasure in showing you bulls. We have many visitors ; the Duque of Albacobaca—he and the duquesa stayed with us last year——"

" That's done it," murmured Sylvia Brett Pawl ; she inclined her head slightly towards the adjoining group. " Leo's there—all ears. You're on the front page of *London and Paris* already.—Don't you "—she raised her voice—" don't you go through hell when your husband's fighting ? "

" Not specially." Her eyes widened. " I am in panic, a little, for the bulls—for my bulls—that they behave properly—that they are Parrales——"

In the gust of laughter that covered the end of her sentence, she saw Brett Pawl bend towards Paco and say something. Paco's face was flushed, a little confused ; he was surfeited with compliments, and had had plenty to drink. As he rose, she looked up at him quickly. The band was playing *Begin the béguine*.

" Aren't we going to dance ? "

" Más tarde."

She bit her lip. The American boy who knew Sidney Franklin was bending over her.

" Come on, Mrs. Ribera ; let's go."

Paco and Brett Pawl were swallowed in the crowd round the bar. The American swept her out on the floor. He danced well. It was a long time since she had danced with anyone but Paco.

The American was paying her compliments in a sultry drawl, his eyes fixed on her mouth. This was her favourite dance number, and she wanted to think about that and nothing else. The hot, scent-laden, smoke-laden air made her drowsy ; she would have liked to go out on the deck, to walk round a few times before going to bed.

" Excuse me, you are holding me too tight, it is uncomfortable," she was driven, presently, to protest.

" Sorry—but you've got me kind of mad about you. I've been wanting to dance with you all night." His breath was hot and a current of sex ran from his limbs into hers. He wanted, of course, to sleep with her. She felt very cool, amused and immune. Then Paco was there, with his hand on her arm.

" Excuse, señor ; my wife only dance with me."

" Then why the hell don't you dance with her when she asks you ? "

Paco dealt the American a stinging slap on the cheek which took him off his already uncertain balance. Before he could retaliate, a couple of stewards closed in.

Back in the stateroom, Paco sullenly poured out some gin and laced it with tonic. Aracea dragged off her bracelets and tossed them furiously on the dresser.

" I wish you wouldn't behave like the foreigner's idea of a Spaniard ! "

" You have no business to dance with foreigners."

" I wonder what you'd say, if I objected to your dancing with other girls ? "

" I do not dance with other girls, when you are there. And if I did," said Paco savagely, " it would be better for my reputation ! " ·

" Ay-ay ; Don Juan of the palcos ! "—She slid her arms round his neck. " Don't be angry, Paco mio ; but please don't make scenes in front of these people. They will only laugh behind our backs."

" You say the English laugh, when their women flirt with strangers ? "

" Sí-sí ; of course." Her fingers were twisting his hair. He jerked his head away, though his body continued to press against hers.

" They are not jealous ? " he persisted, with scornful incredulity.

" Of course they are ; but they think it makes them look ridiculous, so they make jokes——"

" And the women—they are the same ? "

" Naturalmente," she yawned.

" Por dios ; do you tell me the English haven't got—— ? "
She laughed and bit his ear.

" Yes, darling, they have, but they keep it in their bedrooms like their vasos de noche ! "

" Por qué—— ? " gaped Paco.

" I don't know "—she was beginning to be bored. " It i something to do with somebody called Oliver Cromwell——"

" Qué barbaridad de nombre !—What is he, this——"

" He's been dead about three hundred years.—Querido,' murmured Aracea, " I'm sleepy. I want to go to bed."

Suspecting that she was laughing at him, Paco gave her look of furious resentment, dragged himself loose and refillec his glass.

" I'm sick of all this. I want to be home. I want to be a work."

" Hombre, there's no work, until Casablanca."

" This season, I'm going to take every damn' fight tha comes my way. I'm not going to have folks say I'm a fancy bull fighter who sits back on his wife's money ; who's held up as pattern in the schools ; who only mixes with the aristocracy and fights when it pleases him."

A shock ran through her ; was this really the way he felt ?

" Belmonte took a hundred and nine corridas in 1919. The say the kid from Huelva's booked for a hundred already. Ilde fonso fought a hundred and three corridas before he went t Mexico. And I took forty, because I didn't have to earn th money."

" Your papá——" she began.

Paco swore one of the unclean oaths he seldom used befor Aracea, and gulped again.

" You'll have to cut down on that, hombre," she murmured " if you're going to fight a full season."

He glared at her, slammed the glass through the open doo into the bathroom, where it shattered on the tiles, and crossed th floor to the mirror. He passed his hands anxiously over his body —round the ribs and across the diaphragm. There was nothin much, to worry about, but, arching his ribs and hollowing hi spine, he looked anxiously at the profile.

" You're right. I'll cut it out, when I get home."

In the morning, they went up to the gymnasium. The heat was full on and Aracea wore a bikini. He got on the rowing machine, she timed him : Uno !—dos !—tres ! The sweat ran off him. All this was Aracea's idea ; she submitted him to it, even at home.

" I bet Ildefonso doesn't go in for these antics."

" Ildefonso's a milagro, and it's very fine, being a milagro. But it's not so fine to take the horn and know it's your own fault."

" What's penicillin for ? " growled Paco.

" Penicillin is very good, and so are the clinics ; and the sensible person has no need of either."

" What an Englishwoman ! " he mocked her.

Brett Pawl walked into the gymnasium, and Aracea, obeying a look from Paco, huddled her shoulders modestly into a cardigan. Brett Pawl wished them good morning, took a crack or two at the punch-ball, lit a cigarette and sat down to watch Paco. He was in bad shape. His legs were long, pale and hairless, but they were, or had been, the legs of an athlete. The pattern of scars on Paco's back appeared to fascinate him. He waited until Paco had stopped rowing and Aracea threw him a towel.

" How many times has the bull hit you ? "

" Mierda—I don't know."

" You mean, you've stopped counting ? "

" Eso e'," agreed Paco.

" I'd like to try it some time."

" What—being hit by the bull ? "—Aracea smilingly waved the cigarette he offered aside. " It's really very easy ! "

" I bet it is. I'd like to try being missed by the bull. I used to be quite a sprinter." His smile avoided his brow and his eyes —eyes of cold, English grey, deep-set, worried, separated by two chiselled lines that drew his eyebrows into a rough, pale fringe. His eyes seemed to be trying to see beyond what was actually there, beyond some curtain of disillusionment which had descended between him and his soul.

" What is it—' sprinter ' ? "—When Aracea explained, Paco laughed. " Hombre, the bullfight is not to sprint, it is to stand still "—he set his feet together and sketched the movement of the cape; the fluorescent lighting changed the play of muscle into liquid copper.

" May be I could stand still, if it came to the point." From the look of the long, stubborn jaw, it seemed likely.

" You can try with some little calves, when you come to the ranch."

" Is that a date ? "

Paco's nod and smile meant nothing at all, but the Englishman would not understand that.

Paco said, " Vamos," and, pulling on their coats, he and Aracea went out on the deck, where the stalwarts were pacing their morning rounds. Paco swore at the wind and wanted to duck in again, but she seized his arm, and with set teeth and lowered heads they drove against the icy drizzle.

" Por dios—that's enough ! "

Shaking off her hand, he dived in through a door and she followed him laughing ; the rain had bedewed her splendid hair, and stung colour into her soft olive face ; standing there, looking up at him, she looked beautiful, and triumphant and in love.

" Now we'll go to bed."

" No, we won't, amigo ! Now you'll take a shower and get. some clothes on, and you can smoke and drink all you like for the rest of the day, because we've worked all of yesterday's poison out of you," she told him, with proud satisfaction.

It was true ; he had felt like hell, and been disgracefully sick in the night. Now he was fighting fit—and wanted to make love to his wife. As she passed before him into the stateroom, he turned and locked the door.

. . . At the end of an hour, she yawned, and hitched the peignoir up across her hips. She felt sweet and lazy. She was glad they had not gone by air ; that they had had these five days, in which to relax and love each other. She knotted her fingers into his hair, scattered across her naked shoulder.

" Qué quieres ? " he murmured.

" Nada. Te quiero."

He was almost asleep. She waited a little, then slid off the bed. He lay face down, his head in the curve of his arm. She did not have to be quiet, while she took her shower, and dressed, and did her hair.

In twenty-four hours, or a little more, they would be in the house of Parral. There would be the lawyers, still, nearly five years after Papá's death, wrangling over the estate.

In the empty months before Easter, when their only journey of importance was to Casablanca, she would get a grip on the business. Carlos should no longer have it all his own way. " Seis toros estupendos de la ganadería de la Señora de Ribera, hija de Parral " should carry the authority of the dueña. And, with all that behind him, Paco should have the greatest cartel of any bullfighter in the Peninsular.

That night she wore the dress of ice-blue slipper satin they bought in New York ; the satin and the broad bangles of diamonds and paste Paco gave her after the fight in Mexico City embellished her warm, toast-coloured skin and gave her the advantage of all other women—to Paco's delight.

He was a matador, and he had the best woman, and he'd been to Mexico and had two big fights and come back without a scratch, with nearly two hundred and fifty thousand pesetas in his pocket—well, that was before they went to New York, but he would make four times as much this year, probably more.

The smart foreign crowd had stuffed him with compliments and were coming from New York, London and Paris to see him fight ; that was good publicity, and Aracea would see that the Madrid papers got the names right. There was the London pansy who wanted to photograph him for the smart magazines, and a Spanish-speaking American who was going to do his biography.' All this would look good, when they got it in the papers back home. It would be fun, to see the Life of Paco Ribera, Niño de Maderas, running in instalments through one of the illustrateds, with lots of photographs. And he was going home, to live like a caballero on his own ranch, until the season opened.

His sidelong glance caught his own reflection in a mirror ; he made an imperceptible gesture with his glass. Mucha suerte, Niño.

Chapter Two

I

" I'M GOING to spend a few days with Papá. I want to talk business and see if there's any chance of fixing up a couple of good fights before Easter."

" You oughtn't to take anything between Casablanca and Barcelona—unless it's Madrid."

" We'll see what Papá says."

" You've got to get in your sulphur baths and your massage —and don't forget we're going to ride and play lots of tennis and diet ourselves. Mamá mia ! " groaned Aracea, smoothing her hips. " Look what I've got to get off ! "

" I like you fat," said Paco complacently.

" And if I have a week of Mamá Amalia's cooking, I shan't be able to fasten anything. Oye : let's ring them and say we're coming over early to-morrow. Then you can talk all night if you like, with Papá Amadeo, and we can start back after breakfast. I don't want to be away more than a night ; I must go over the accounts with Carlos."

" Tanto mejor. I'll go by myself."

" No, no——"

" I'll go by myself," repeated Paco. " It was what I intended to begin with."

" But," gaped Aracea, " that will surprise them very much ! They will think we have quarrelled."

He laughed and kissed her.

" And we have not quarrelled, no ? "

" We've never spent a night apart since we got married."— She was surprised to find that the prospect disturbed her.

Paco said gravely :

" We've had mucha suerte. I don't like to leave you alone, but—shall I tell you something ? It will please Mamá and my sisters very much if I go home, for once, by myself."

" Ya lo creo." From the day of the marriage, the Ribera women had held themselves pointedly and mistrustfully away from Paco's wife. " They're jealous like cats."

" Mujer, it is not that," he told her easily. " They think I do not care so much for my home, since I married a beautiful, rich woman—the dueña of Parral ! "

" Parral has always made them welcome."

" Ay—they don't understand our way of living, and it makes them shy, to meet our friends. Oye : it is happier for everybody that I go by myself. We make jokes you do not understand, and people you don't like come in and talk to me, because we were at school together. I want to see Ruiz, and find out if he'll pic for me this season ; I'm fed up with Curro, and so's the public. He's never got out of the bad habits he learned with Zarcillo, and he's too frightened to do as I tell him. Even when you put him up on a decent animal, he's just a great, cowardly bag of jelly."

Aracea was not, however, to be cheated of her grievance.

" I do all I can, to make it agreeable when your Mamá come here—and let me tell you, it is not easy ! She does not like me, and I can't think why ; I've always been very polite to her. And to the rest of your family. I don't see why I should be blamed——"

" Madre mia, I was not blaming you."

" You criticise me, and that is the same thing."

" You're loca," said Paco shortly. " It is reasonable Mamá does not understand you. She comes to stay, and you walk about everywhere in your calzones——"

"Everybody wears slacks nowadays ! "

" Not in Maderas, and not Mamá's friends. And you contradict Papá——"

" Am I not supposed to have opinions of my own ? "

" Mamá has her own opinions, on cooking, and the house,

and what the servants steal, but she doesn't interrupt the men, and talk about things that are not women's business anyhow."

" Vaya : all that's old-fashioned."

" If you hadn't been to school in England, you would see Mamá's point of view."

" But surely, now we've both been abroad, and you've met so many foreigners, you can't think hers is the right one ? Look at Sylvia Brett Pawl and Lady Stanways ; they aren't only pretty, they're witty and amusing, and they're so well-informed——"

" Hell, women are not for information."

" And that applies to me ? "

" You are my wife, and I have to put up with you," he grinned.

" Míl gracias. Then your mother can do the same."

" None the less "—he was beginning to lose his temper— " there's no need for you to push all that English stuff down her throat."

" And there's no need for you to get mad with me, because I happen to have more intelligence than your people."

" Callate ! I am Niño de Maderas ! I am fond of my Mamá and my sisters ; I belong to them."

" And not to me ? " she gasped.

His nostrils were flaring and his teeth set.

" You are my woman and I am your man. Nothing can alter that. So why do you try to alter the other part of me, that belongs to Maderas ? "

" I don't try to alter it," she replied, with sudden meekness. " But I want to share that, as well. Everywhere else we go I am received with honour, as the wife of Paco Ribera ; but in Maderas I am made to feel like a stranger. I wouldn't care—but it's your *home*. It ought to be mine as well."

He let her see he was tired, bored and confused.

" Why do you trouble yourself about Maderas ? When we were children you made mock of it. ' Plaza de toros de Maderas,' you remember ? Pues, it is a very little town, but I happened to be born there. I go back where I was born ; e' sencillo— no ? "

That did not answer her question, but she was wise enough to let it go.

"Then Concepción had better pack some things for you."

"Mujer!"—Recovering his temper, he turned to laugh at her. "What do you think I want at Maderas? My smoking?—The silk pyjamas you bought me on Madison? All I want's a couple of shirts——"

"Oh, you're only going to stop overnight," she said with relief.

"Mamá will wash my shirts for me." He evaded specification, glancing at the watch on his wrist. "I'll go and tell Martín to fill up with gas and see if he's remembered to change the wheels."

"Don't be too late in getting back; I'll want Martín in the morning."

"I shan't take him; I'm going to drive myself."

"What—the Ford?"

He arched his brows at her offendedly.

"No—the other."

"The Alvis?—And what am I supposed to use, if I want to go out?"

"Pues, the wagon," he mumbled.

"Many thanks, amigo. I happen to prefer the Alvis—and you will find the wagon much more convenient, for riding your friends about."

The old Ford wagon used by the cuadrilla would lend no prestige to his arrival in Maderas, but she had no intention of giving way. The car—*their* car, of the honeymoon and all their journeys together—should not be used for trips into the mountains, with parties of youths and girls, and the wine-skins, and, a gipsy or two. But his disappointed face melted her to the point of saying:

"Oye, Paquito: let Martín take you over in the Alvis and get back as soon as he can to-morrow morning. Then we will both come and fetch you when you've finished your business with my father-in-law.—And if you try to keep him," she added inwardly, "Martín knows too well on which side his bread is buttered to disregard *my* orders!"

Paco left at dusk, in the big car, driven by Martín, the fur-
lined coat bought in New York draped round his shoulders.
They would drive all round the town, before going to the Casa
Cigarrón; he would have gran éxito at least on his arrival in
Maderas.

II

It was good to be home: to sit at a table covered with a
pure white flaxen cloth, over which if you splashed your soup
or wine, nobody minded; loaded with rich food—the chicken
in the pot for which Mamá was famous, the endless varieties of
sausage and strong salt fish; casually scattered with the bare
necessities of eating—a few knives, forks and spoons you used
as you pleased, or abandoned, at your pleasure, for fingers. The
strong, unshaded lights, the men without collars or ties, the
amiable red faces of the women, the ease and informality brought
a sense of warm well-being absent from most of the convivialities
to which, since his marriage, Paco had accustomed himself. You
sweated, so you pulled off your coat and dropped it on the floor
for one of the women to pick up. You swelled with good food,
so you unbuttoned without embarrassment. You contributed
your share to the roar and bellow, to the sly allusions and jokes
in the rich local dialect.

"But where's your wife, Paco?" he was asked, when the
excitement of his personal welcome died down.

"She sends her recuerdos; there's a lot of business to be
seen to since we got back."

There were cries of delight and triumph from the women,
his sisters threw their arms round his neck and kissed him
soundly, one of the sisters-in-law shouted to her hubsband:

"You heard, hombre?—The wife of Paco—at last!"

"How long has she been that way?"

"Is she being sick?"

"Does she have cravings?"

It was taken for granted that the only possible reason for a wife's not accompanying her husband on a visit to his family was pregnancy. Paco grinned sheepishly, knowing the news would be round in half an hour—that he was an expectant father. He put up a show of sly self-satisfaction, to conceal his irritation. It was not considered creditable, in Maderas, for a husband not to have put his wife in the family way, after three and a half years of marriage, and he wondered how to get out of it.

Word had gone through the town that the Niño was at home ; his friends came running from all quarters, to beat him on the back, to hear about Mexico, to go out and boast they had been talking to the matador. Customers who knew him only by name contrived to insinuate themselves behind the counters of the shop and into the private apartments. He shook the hands of innumerable strangers. Presently he went out, to distribute handfuls of coppers and bombónes among small, grimy paws, to push larger coins into the hands of the blind and halt and to receive their murmured blessings : " May God repay you, may God keep you."

After supper a party arrived, to sweep him out on a round of the taverns ; it was a fine thing, to be seen with the boy from Maderas ! Brushing aside his mother's laments—" You have just arrived, and already you're leaving us ! " " Anda, Mamá, there are plenty of to-morrows "—he slicked his hair and went out into the little cobbled town, with its dim street lighting, which he had known as long as he had known anything. No sparkle of foreign cities could hold, for him, the intimate thrill of this his home town.

They were drunk by the time they arrived at the house of Teresita—still regarded by the majority of his companions as the very apex of luxury. All the boys graduated to manhood by way of Teresita's ; he remembered how, after the sober domesticity of his home, it had seemed to him the wildest of adventures.

The room stank of scent and the fumes of braseros and Turkish cigarettes. Two or three of the boys had brought their guitars ; they played " Barca lenta " and " Una noche encantada." He bought drinks for everybody and thought of nights in Mexico

City, of the endless glitter, of girls with bodies like diamond-encrusted snakes, of dancing to music emanating from ruffled sleeves of orange and scarlet, of a thin mestiza with a mouth like a burst pomegranate writhing behind the mike, of places he took Aracea to dance the tango and the samba, of hotels where they made love.

He remembered places in Madrid and Barcelona, where the girls had nothing on under their fringed Gibraltese shawls ; they drank pink champagne with the customers and afterwards did sex dances on a velvet-covered stage no bigger than a café table. It was in one of those places he got his first (and only) dose . .

He had an overwhelming desire to be at home, in his own bed. The house of Teresita was boring, and, in some way, sad ; the girls were too old, too jaded and brutalised, and he knew too much of their individual histories. One of the boys in the party was a doctor. The law obliged them to go to him for their check-ups. Sometimes he let them off with graft.

Under his loaded eyelids the room blurred into a ring of sand, sparsely scattered with petals of giant geranium. The trotting, steel-coloured death-emblem, ignoring the capes, encircled the ring with its head lifted like a question-mark. Have a good look at death, hombre : at its shape, its size, its movement, before going in to engage it. Have a good look, Paco, from the safety of the callejón. . . . How many bulls have I gone in to by now ?—Enough to get the feeling : the momentary loss of control, the big leak, followed by the slow, cold urge that takes you through the gap in the barrier, out on the flat sand. The sand is under your feet, that curve down and grip on it, as your hands curl down and grip on the folds of the cape, as you wait for the bull—the perfect bull that exists somewhere : that carries your honour between its horns and over its broad brow and in the lift of its morillo . . .

With an immense effort, he lifted his head, which had fallen on his chest. It was a long time since he had been drunk like this, so that his wrists were gone, and his knees, and there was no power in his thigh muscles to lever him up out of the chair. His half-open eyes slowly followed a sinuous upward curve that

broke into breasts, and arrived finally at a nut-shaped face and
a big dark crimson mouth.

" Olá."

The girl brought a pair of long, doe-like eyes to bear on his.
Her lips hardly moving, she murmured :

" Olá, matador."

Her immature body was a blur of cheap red silk, split to the
knee. She hung one bare knee over the other and hooked the
foot round the ankle. Her elbows, planted on the table, brought
her hands to his eye-level, and the hands themselves, with
abnormally long, thin fingers and nails filed into crimson talons,
reminded him unpleasantly of spiders. He fumbled the wheel
of his lighter towards the cigarette she had taken out of a cheap
jewelled case. Her high-heeled slippers were cracked across the
straps, but there was luxury in her movements. He watched her
spread her hand and stare at it, as though there were nothing
more fascinating in the world ; turning the wrist slowly, curling
the fingers, one after another, into the palm, then spreading them
and repeating the manœuvre so that the varnished nails, catching
the light, were like drops of blood on the petals of a revolving
flower.

" Bailarina—no ? Anda, niña ; dance for me."

She scowled, twitched up her skirt, and exhibited, on her
naked thigh, an outrageous scar, healed, but surrounded by an
angry aura of inflammation.

" What did that ? " asked Paco, without interest.

" A knife."

" Como ? It is as dangerous to be a dancer as a bullfighter ?
Where did you get it ? "

" Morocco," she said indifferently.

" Where they smoke the kif." He recognised the sickly sweet
scent of the cigarette.

" And they fight bulls."

" I fight there next month."

" Casablanca."

" Sure."

" Matador ? "—Someone laughed. " Claro. Ordinary bullfighters don't wear things like that." She touched the flexible band of gold round his left wrist with the tip of her nail.

" A gold watch doesn't make a matador," he mumbled.

" I have a friend who is matador."

" Does he have a gold watch ? "

" They call him Aguilucho."

Ildefonso ; he might have known.

" That is a great one with the bulls. And with the women."

She moved closer, and presently made him a proposition. He shook his head.

" No. I'm tired."

" You go soon to Casablanca ? "—She seemed in no way offended by his refusal.

" I told you. Next month."

" You will take me ? "

He laughed.

" Why do you want to go to Casablanca ? "

" I live there. I came to Cádiz with a friend. I want to go back but I have no money."

He made an effort and pushed himself to his feet. Standing there, swaying, he felt in his pockets, and threw the few notes and coins they contained on the table between them. Some of the coins rolled on the floor. Two girls at adjoining tables swooped simultaneously on them, there was a chatter of outraged parrakeets. Teresita was there, her fat straining against stained black satin, her teeth, crusted with lipstick, glittering in a mask of melting wax.

" You are not going, Paquito ? "

" Sí, me voy," he muttered.

" But what have we done to displease you ? " she whined.

" Nada—nada. I am tired. I have been travelling for months."

" Hombre ! A bottle of champagne, quietly, in the other room, and the little Mariquita to keep you company—— ! "

" Hasta luego—another time."

He reeled out under the crackling stars. Bed was all he wanted. As he stumbled over the cobbles, he tried to remember nights when the whole pleasure of his young manhood seemed to be summed up in one of Teresita's dingy couches, impregnate with the scent of innumerable copulations ; in one of those big-bellied women in whom, with a shock, he had recognised the houris of his youth ; in the sense of bold participation in those sins of the flesh against which the priest specifically warned one—when the prospect of confession added no more than a dash of paprika to a prohibited dish ! It was true, he was too tired and too drunk, at the moment, to want a woman, but on the fresh linen and cool, hard mattress of his own bed his drowsy hand, seeking the sweet, familiar flesh, drew back discomfited.

" . . . Where's Paco ? They said he was here."

" Hombre ! He went home, more than an hour ago."

" Pues——" The newcomer looked at his watch. " *Home ?* —But it's early ; not yet three o'clock."

" 'stà mucho cambiado," was the mournful verdict of the house of Teresita. And—" If that's what marriage does for a torero, it's bad for the bulls ! "

III

Don Amadeo Ribera—El Cigarrón—was a sick man. For years his health had been failing, and it had become a painful effort to get about on his crutches. He had at last been obliged —reluctantly and with suspicion—to hand over the management of the business to his eldest son. An even more bitter day came, when his conscience forced him to resign his directorship of the bullring. A superannuated ghost, all that remained to him was the guidance of Paco's career, and about that he was uneasy.

Paco went in sleepily in his bathrobe and kissed his father. It was one of the afternoon ; he had just wakened up.

" Buen' día', Papá ; 'sta vien ? "

Don Amadeo put down the receiver which—and the radio— alone stood between him and a growing sense of uselessness and inoccupation. He looked under his tired eyelids at his handsome, careless boy, with whom, so far, he had had no conversation, because the women had swallowed him.

I

" Pues—how was it, in Mexico ? "

" Muy vien. Mucho éxito," smiled Paco.

" And the bulls ? "

" Regular.—Papá : I want a lot of work this year. What have we fixed, up to now ? "

Don Amadeo fumbled among his documents and extracted a sheet of paper, which he passed to Paco.

" Good. Very good." (All the same, not so good as it might have been. Half a dozen ferias—Sevilla was not among them—and on the same bill twice, Madrid and Córdoba, with Ildefonso.) " And now we've got to push ahead with a lot more dates. The first thing we've got to do is put it around that I'm not doing a limited season ; that will bring them in —falling over each other ! How many bullrings have we got in Spain ?—About four hundred, isn't it ? About a hundred of those can, if they choose, put up the money, and only a dozen have seen Niño de Maderas !—You saw to it that my Mexican notices got into the Press, didn't you ? " he concluded anxiously.

" It's early, yet, for the smaller bookings." Don Amadeo ignored the question. " You should have stayed out in Mexico, if you are in a hurry to make money."

" I'd got to be back for Casablanca," mumbled Paco, " and it's not so easy, when you don't know the ropes ; I didn't fancy putting myself in the hands of those crooks out there. But I've promised to go back in November and do a big season.—Now, Papá, you'd better start selling me ! How about the Magdalena festival ? Ildefonso's coming back for Castellón. And Valencia." He ran off a string of smaller towns, all of which might put on a corrida before Easter, with the bait of a distinguished name.

" Are the bulls not doing so well ? " asked his father dryly.

" What are you getting at ? "—Paco bridled. " What should be the matter with the bulls ? They are magnificent."

" I am glad to hear it, my son. It is well they should be, when you get bills like that." He pushed one across the table. Paco glanced at it, and pulled a face.

" Hell, Papá, I had to have plenty of clothes for Mexico, and they'd have cost twice as much out there. Silvestre gets all his suits from Manfredi—they're the only people who can cut the taleguillas."

"Agreed; at the same time, another dress cape would not seem to be a necessity."

"You've got to put on a show with those mejicanos," muttered Paco, snatching up the bill, and stuffing it in the pocket of his dressing gown. "You don't pay the bills; I don't see what you have to complain about. All I'm asking you for is some work."

"I have been thinking," said Don Amadeo heavily. "I have been thinking, hijo mio, that it is time for you to find another manager."

"Papá——!" He was aghast; yet, through the shock, ran an almost imperceptible current of relief.

"I am not young and I am not well. I can't get about. You talk of a Mexican season; I can't handle that for you. I'm out of touch; my old friends in the business are dying or retiring, and I can't make new contacts. And—though I can manage a bullfighter, I cannot manage a bullfighter's wife."

The blood ran up his cheeks.

"What has my wife got to do with my work?"

"Oye. You have married very well, with a woman who has money, and is the daughter of my friend Luis, and knows something about the business."

"Pues——?"

"I have said enough."

Paco scowled and bit a hangnail on his thumb.

"I know what you mean. But it's all right. It's going to be different." He changed the subject hurriedly. "What's that you were reading, when I came in?—oh, those old notices of mine." The smile of easy satisfaction broke on his healthy young face. "Nice, aren't they. You'll see: I'll get better ones this year. Somebody's going to write a book about me; I didn't tell you that, did I?"

"What is there to write a book about?" inquired Don Amadeo with such candid astonishment that Paco roared with laughter.

" You wait, Papá ; you'll get a surprise. There'll be lots about you, of course—and we're going to butter up the critics until every one of them thinks he's the Voice of God Himself ! It will give them such a shock, I'll be in their good books ever after."

" You will make yourself a laughing stock ! " roared Don Amadeo. " You have had the alternativa only two years and you have fought in fewer corridas than any other matador. You were brought up on a feather cushion——"

" And who provided the feather cushion ? " retorted Paco, with reason. " You wouldn't let me fight the novillos until that malete of a Zarcillo got himself knocked out. Then you picked and chose my fights, and bought me the Press through the whole of my first novillero season."

" Is that what you are going to put in the book ? "

Paco took refuge in injured dignity.

" Books about the bulls are very popular now, in England and America. There was a writer called "—he remembered the name with an effort—" Emminggué. He made a pile out of writing about bullfighters. And Bombita and Belmonte had books written about them——"

" Sweet Mother of Jesus, has it come to this—that you compare yourself with Juan Belmonte ? " exploded his father. " What have Belmonte and Torres made out of books ? "

" It's helped to make them famous outside of Spain," sulked Paco.

" To be famous outside of Spain, hijo, you must first be famous within it."

" Mierda ! " yelled Paco. " You talk as if I was a kid, farting about with the becerros ! You know as well as I do, they don't give you the alternativa for nothing ! You may have bought me write-ups from the Press boys, but you didn't buy me the sword from Bienvenida in the Monumental ! I've been heading the bills for two years ; I've got more cartel than Ildefonso in Málaga—and Valladolid—and Valencia——"

Don Amadeo heard him in patience to the end.

" You told me to find out if Ruiz had got himself a job. He's gone to Moratín."

It was a slap in the face. Paco took it, and shrugged his shoulders.

" That's too bad. You ought to have been sharper off the mark. I wrote to you about it from Lima."

" He turned it down."

" So I'll have to carry on with Curro. That's a nuisance. He's a bloody awful pic. I wanted Ruiz. He's the best pic in the business."

Don Amadeo's silence gave consent.

" You should have gone after him. I bet you could have bought him—even if he'd signed on with Moratín. He was probably trying it on, to get more money." It was incredible, that a Maderas boy should not leap at the chance of being with him, the Niño.

" There are things," said Don Amadeo, " more important than money." He said it on a note of surprise, as though it had just occurred to him.

" Claro. But you can't pretend Moratín's got more cartel than I have ! "

" There are two sorts of cartel : the kind you have with the public, and the kind you have with the people who work for you."

Paco's jaw dropped.

" When we worked for Zarcillo, we never knew if we'd get our money or not. The boys know they'll get paid off, on the tick, after every fight. If they're in a jam, they can draw on their wages. I can assure you, they're owing me plenty ! "— He laughed.

Don Amadeo closed his eyes. Like the majority of bull-fighters, he had not a vocabulary. He could not say to his son, in plain terms, All right ; they'll take your money and stick their tongues in their cheeks about you. He could not say, Until you are a hero to your cuadrilla, you cannot become a national hero. He could not even, distinctly, formulate these thoughts. He only knew that, owing to circumstances he was unable to control, his son was in grave danger of not fulfilling the bright promise of his beginnings. And this, to Don Amadeo, was a pain—worse than the pains in his stomach, the pains in his heart and in his crippled limbs.

The boy was a brave, elegant and intelligent fighter, of impeccable technique and unquestionable valour. So far, the well-oiled Press did him no more than justice. But Don Amadeo was skilled in reading between the lines; through all those laudatory paragraphs ran a vein of irony, which Paco was too conceited to recognise. They might tear strips off Ildefonso; they might load him with the abuse for which bullfighting journalism is infamous; but somewhere, among the murderous lines would appear the brief statement that proclaimed Ildefonso for ever " the maestro." Paco smiled at it, but it cut into his father; Don Amadeo remembered the thin, shy, gipsy-like boy he had seen for the first time on the Parral ranch, caping the bull-calf for Paco. His son had had all the advantages a boy like that could never command, had come into the ring with a ready-made reputation, and yet . . .

It is not a good sign, when a matador does not manage to hold on to a first-class cuadrilla. Paco had started well; plenty of fighters, not good or lucky enough to make the grade, were prepared to enlist with the son of El Cigarrón. But, even in his first season as a novillero, they had begun to drift away. The reason they gave—that there was not enough work to earn a living—was fair; the payment of the cuadrilla depends on the number of fights in a season, and there was no need for Paco to work the flesh off his bones. But there are hundreds of out of work bullfighters from whom an espada can take his pick, from whom he can build up the permanent support that con-tributes in no small degree to his success in the ring, as they learn by experience to interpret his thoughts, and provide a solid background to his performance.

There is a saying: You cannot buy a good cuadrilla. As a matador, you stand primarily for the pay-packet; as a great matador, you stand for something that is not to be computed in terms of cash—which is not to say that, if you fail to produce the cash, your team will be loyal to you: they cannot afford it. But it means that each time you go into the ring, if you get the bronca, the hatred of the team will be kindled, not against you, but against the crowd. It means that the belief of the team will hold out, for a long time, against public opinion. It means, you may give a bad show, and the team will know it, but they will curse anyone who says so behind your back. This quality of loyalty is rare, and few command it; but Don Amadeo had known it for himself, and it was what he coveted for his son.

" You've still got the bunch you took to Mexico ? "

" I've got Gusano and Caldos and Campillo—and that bastard Curro, because he knows he'll never get another job !—and El Sastre says he'll come to Casablanca if he isn't fixed by then, but he wants more money——"

" Is he worth it ? "

" Who's worth it ? " sneered Paco. " These damned unions have got us fixed. I've got my eye on a kid who may do for a fill-in, but I'm fed up with the lot. After Casablanca I shall look out for a real crack crowd—I'm not scared, like some people, of being cut out by my own banderilleros ! " He laughed as he reached for one of his father's cigars. " I'm going to shoot the moon this season, Papá !—and Ildefonso can watch out."

" Buena suerte," said Don Amadeo.

" You don't believe in me ! " Paco accused him.

" Have I said so ? "

A growing sense of injury held Paco silent. He had had, for months, nothing but adulation. He had done credit to his name and his home town in a foreign country, and, before that, had worked through an admirable season. He was regarded as one of the two white hopes of the ring. Ildefonso, of course, was the other. He was not going to start being jealous of Ildefonso ; their methods were too different, they worked, as it were, on different levels. Papá did not seem to understand that.

" So you're going to do a big season."

" Ojalá." He shrugged his shoulders. " I suppose—if you mean what you said, Papá," he stuttered, " I've got to look for a new manager."

Don Amadeo inclined his head. The room had grown chilly ; he wished someone would come and attend to the brasero, whose glowing heart was choked with ash. His cold palms slid over his knuckles ; he looked at his boy.

" It is true, what the women say—that your wife is embarazada ? "

" Not to my knowledge."

" Is she sterile ? "

" Por dios—there can be accidents ! "

" Ya lo creo. It is a good thing to be in love with one's wife, my son, but it is better to keep her at home."

He was on the point of saying, " Hell, you don't think I *want* to take her around with me ? " but rejected the lack of authority it implied.

" You'd sooner I went to brothels and caught the clap ? "

Don Amadeo lifted his shoulders. It was futile to observe that the bulls do not offer the only danger to matadores, and that if you can avoid the horns, you can avoid the other.

" You should be seeing more of the boys."

" I know, Papá." He tried to speak good-temperedly. " I don't have much time—it will be better, when we start work again. Not joking—I want to get at least a hundred fights before I go back to Mexico."

" Fighting every day of the week ?—You're loco."

" Ildefonso does it ; why shouldn't I ? "

" Because he is Ildefonso, and you are the Niño of Maderas."

Paco whitened. His father continued gently :

" Don't be foolish, my son. You will make no impression, if you ruin yourself in a couple of years, instead of lasting— si Dios quiere—ten."

" Ruin myself ?—Por dios, I'm as sound as a bell ! Unless I catch the horn in a nasty place, I've got years before me. You know what they say about Ildefonso ?—that he'll be washed up by the end of the season. At Córdoba, he looked like a walking graveyard ; on top of everything, he'd got a dose of malaria. The bull didn't get him, for once, but, when they carried him into the hotel, everybody was saying it was a milagro he'd got the sword in ! "

" You have said it. Ildefonso is a milagro."

" Well, I've been called a ' milagro,' once or twice "—by the smaller, less reputable papers, that are paid to call every promising novillero a " milagro." Seeing this in his father's eye, he hurried on. " Ildefonso's been built up into a legend ; his manager's seen to that ! There are scores of towns where they haven't seen me, though my name's as well known as his. You say, it won't make ' an impression,' if I ruin myself in a couple of years ; well, let me tell you something, Papá. This business of only fighting a limited season has made ' an impression '—of the wrong sort. There are some dirty tales around ; one is, that I won't take a bull unless its horns are doctored——"

" That is a pernicious lie ! " Don Amadeo thundered.

" Of course it is ; but when people are jealous they say anything. And, you know, there's some hot competition coming along : Camará's got a couple of kids, and they say Lalanda has something up his sleeve that will burn up the afición when the season gets going. A matador's run isn't what it was in your day, Papá ; the crowd keeps changing its mind—and there's only room for a few at the top."

" The crowd can't change its mind about something it doesn't have pushed down its throat."

" There's something in that ; but if I'm going to step into Ildefonso's shoes next year——"

" My son, they would not fit you."

" Hell ! What's Ildefonso got that I don't have ? "

Don Amadeo's face had gone the colour of purplish lead. He pressed his hand over his left breast and spoke with difficulty.

" I do not write books, and I am not a critic. The difference between the good and the great can perhaps be said," he gasped, " with the sword or the cape. Or a poet might say it. It is something that only the heart can feel—or the soul."

" So it comes to this," said Paco, after a pause. " You, my Papá, do not believe in me." Deaf to the laboured breathing, the evident discomfort of the elder man, he fixed his eyes on his locked hands. " Perhaps it is a good thing, to be managed by someone who thinks you are ' un milagro '—even if you aren't ! " —He gave a bitter little laugh, recovered himself and looked up.

" You've not been well lately, Papá ; it means a lot of work—and a lot of bother," he stammered, trying to make excuse for himself.

Don Amadeo could have said many things, but his heart and his stomach were hurting him too much. My son, he could have said, although I no longer see in you " un milagro," I believe in you. I am proud of you. I honour you for the fine things you do in the ring, and my heart cherishes you when you have your failures. Belief and pride and honour cannot be bought—although you may buy their simulacra. The manager who will fawn on you and bilk for you and sweat for you in your hour of triumph will sell you to the enemy from the moment you begin to waver. He'll strip you until there's nothing left, then he'll jeer at you, and scrape the gilt off the image you've left behind you, to daub it over some newcomer.

You're right ; I'm too old and too sick to go on handling you. You'll have a tremendous season, and I'll have no share in it, except as your shadow. And I wonder how the new manager will handle the woman you've married.

" Where's Papá ? " asked someone, when they sat down to eat, at two in the afternoon.

" He does not wish to come down. Mamá has taken him an egg in soup."

Paco sat, guiltily silent. There was no reason to feel guilty ; it was Papá's suggestion. But he would ring up Don Pasquale Basilio in Sevilla, and fix up a talk on the way back ; it was better to get on with these things without delay.

Don Pasquale was " fuera " ; four separate calls tracked him down in one of the casinos. It was a big thing, to be offered the management of Niño de Maderas—the rival of Aguilucho, Ildefonso García. Don Pasquale was polite and business-like. As he replaced the receiver, it occurred to Paco that his expenses were going to be notably increased. But he was sure of a big season.

The afternoon wore on. He sat about, enduring the fondness of his family. When dusk fell, he yawned, and went to bath and shave. He looked in the glass at his lathered face, dipped the

razor in hot water and applied it to his jaw. A sudden shriek
drove it in a zig-zag under his chin. Watching the blood dye
the lather pink, he swore. The door burst open; his brother
stumbled in.

"Papá! He has had a stroke. You had better come to
Mamá. They've gone for the doctor."

Innumerable relatives arrived from all parts of the country
for the memorial mass: countrymen, with black bands round
the sleeves of their light suits, smothered in Andalucían capes
with facings of brown or green plush; countrywomen, with
velos tucked into the collars of their thin black coats, pulled on
over woollen shawls and cotton dresses. Representatives of the
ayuntamiento, the police, the local hospital. All the magistrates.
The entire personnel of the bullring, and, naturally, of the Casa
de Ribera; with representatives of neighbouring bullrings, and
a little group of Don Amadeo's contemporaries and colleagues of
his active days. The ragged hordes who gathered in the patio
on Saturday mornings, to receive the alms of the house of
Ribera, and the nuns from the convent to whose funds Don
Amadeo had been a generous contributor.

All these were packed into the church, when a slim girl,
with a mink coat over her black tailor-made, with a little hat with
black wings and a heavy veil, descended from a big car and made
her way through the crowd to Paco's side. In that rustic gathering, her appearance was sensational. As she slid her hand into
his, Paco muttered:

"I thought you weren't coming."

"A tyre burst, up in the sierra; I had to wait for Martín
to change the wheel."

The scent of her clothes penetrated him, penetrated his grief,
and made him want her. They knelt with bowed heads on the
stone flags. The mass took a long time. He felt himself wanting
her more and more, and was ashamed, for he should have been
weeping for his father, whom he deeply loved.

When it was over, and the people started to stream out,
everyone stared at Paco's wife. The women stared at her clothes
—particularly her hat, for hats were not worn in Maderas. She

sensed their enmity, and shrugged it aside, guessing its reason. Which of the big-bosomed, sullenly handsome girls had expected to marry Paco?

They went back to the house of Ribera, where she did her best with the weeping women, knowing that her composed but correct behaviour was creating a bad impression.

"You must come and stay with us, Mamá Amalia; Paco would like it very much. It will do you good, to go away for a little while."

The black-currant eyes, drowned in water, of Doña Amalia stared at her with shallow resentment; she clutched her favourite son to her, hunching her shoulder on her daughter-in-law. Aracea found herself face to face with a hatchet-faced woman she recognised as the wife of one of the sons: Inés, the daughter of a local agriculturalist, who had brought a big dowry to the house of Ribera. She looked half-witted, and spoke in a dialect so thick that Aracea had to ask her to repeat her words.

"Do you want to eat things like dog's dirt, and the bits you clip off your nails?"

Recoiling, she stammered:

"I don't know what you mean"—and turned, to clutch Paco's arm.

"Come; let's go home."

"Already?—I don't think Mamá would like it——"

"She's got all the rest of them. Darling, please! I want you to myself for a while."

He looked at her eyes, her lips and the soft curve of her bosom, and followed her into the car. Presently she repeated Inés's remarks to him:

"Is she mad?"

Paco gave her a look out of the corner of his eye. He laughed, a little self-consciously.

"Perhaps—just a little."

"But she is absolutely disgusting!"

"Oh—you know what women are like—at those times."

"At those times——?" Light dawned on her. "She's going to have another child! Qué desgracia—that's the seventh:

or is it the eighth ? And all of them half-witted. She should be ashamed of herself."

" No," said Paco, bluntly. " She's not embarazada ; but she thinks you are."

" I ?—Who ever heard of such a thing ! "

" Mujer," said Paco, in the voice he rarely employed, which almost stopped her heart—" when are you going to give me a son ? "

Chapter Three

I

As a great impresario, Don Pasquale Basilio had prestige to maintain. He was therefore something less than gratified to receive what amounted to a command from Paco Ribera, to come out to the ranch and talk business. The Niño was a smart matador, with more than his share of swelled head, and evidently felt he was conferring a favour on Don Pasquale. He was supposed to have stopped off in Sevilla, on his way home from burying his father in Maderas ; instead, he had swept grandly on, in the swell car his wife had bought for him, and he allowed her to drive. Qué barbaridad ! But for his regard for Amadeo, Don Pasquale would have put the youth in his place ; there were several matadores of as great promise as Niño de Maderas in the ring, and a conscientious manager knows how many he can handle, with profit to himself and his customers.

It meant losing a day in the office—in other words, a couple of hours on the telephone ; after which Don Pasquale was in the habit of retiring to his favourite café, where anything that came in was relayed by his confidential clerk. Don Pasquale liked transacting business in this public manner ; he enjoyed the hush that fell when Alberto hurried to his side and spoke quickly in his ear. Alberto had a very keen sense of theatre; he could make the mere crossing of a room a portentous event. Whether one of Don Pasquale's clients had got himself the horn and was obliged to cancel a contract, or Miguel, Don Pasquale's small son, wanted money for the ciné—Alberto's demeanour was that of the messenger who brings grave news. Don Pasquale inclined his head gravely, excused himself to the company, retired with Alberto to a small room placed at his disposal by the proprietor of the café, and settled the matter with a telegram or a handful of duros or an outburst of spleen—as the occasion demanded.

Don Pasquale had looked after four generations of bull-fighters; he had seen many changes, and found them, on the whole, depressing. It was not to his interest, to admit that the fighters of the present were not equal to those of before the war, but he looked back with regret to days when matadores could not read a contract; when they laughed-off the autograph hunters because they could not sign their own names; when they ate with their fingers, and the only place they were good, apart from the ring, was in bed with a woman.

However, the Parral car was waiting. Don Pasquale got in. He had not been out to the ranch since the days of Don Luis, and he thought the chauffeur was making a mistake, when they swung under an imposing archway, over which, in a semi-circle of iron letters, ran an inscription he had no time to decipher. The rutted road he remembered had been re-metalled, with a sand track for horses at the side. A double row of young elms led to the familiar, yet altered, frontage—in Don Pasquale's memory blind with shutters and leprous rejas. The rejas were now a gay turquoise blue, the shutters ajar, on evidently occupied rooms. When they drove into the patio—formerly austere with its cobbles and stone colonnade—a foam of greenery descended from the galleries, clumps of foliage broke into the stern design of the pillars—and a young woman ran down the curving staircase from the upper floor.

She was dressed for riding; that is to say, she wore a thin muslin shirt under a loose jacket of knitted wool, and foreign breeches, swelling out over the flanks and laced tightly about exquisite calves. She was strikingly lovely, but, if she had been his daughter, Don Pasquale would have preferred her to have been dressed in a way less relevant of her charms. The blouse was transparent. An inner sheathe of satin supported her breasts. The snake-like flexibility of her waist was confined by a broad band of silver-studded leather, which held the jodhpurs up above her hips. It took him a few seconds to recognise the " niña " he vaguely remembered ; Paco's wife, who was reputed to " run " him. He was conventionally shocked that she was not in black, for her father-in-law.

" Olá, Don Pasquale." She thrust out her hand with masculine frankness. " Qué tal, amigo ?—Paco's having his bath ; he's been working all morning. You know my cousin, Carlos de la Cerna ? "—Carlos had appeared from the doorway of the old office ; she indicated him negligently. " Come in and have a cocktail." She led the way under the colonnade into regions previously unknown to Don Pasquale. " You haven't seen the house since we altered it, have you ?—This part was a kind of slum ! " she laughed. " We cleared it out when we got married."

He followed her into a big room with an arched ceiling, a polished floor, a casual scatter of furniture that included a billiard table, a radiogram, and, at the far end a modern bar. Round the walls were the heads of bulls, each with the devisa of Parral on a small shield that bore its record. Don Pasquale looked round with grudging admiration. Muy elegante.

" You'd prefer amontillado ? "

He admitted it ; he had not acquired the modern taste for foreign drinks. At a gesture from the dueña, Carlos de la Cerna went to the bar ; dissipated, withered and nervous, the black eye-patch exaggerating the handsomeness of his ravaged face— Don Pasquale wondered, as well he might, how that one fitted into the household. Aracea pulled a cigarette case out of the pocket of her jodhpurs and offered it to her guest ; she had an air of sparkling assurance and gallantry—more like a handsome boy than a young married woman.

" Y los toros ? " inquired Don Pasquale politely.

" Maravillosos ! " Her teeth glittered. " We brought back

a heifer—Pastejé ; we'll have something to show you next year—won't we, Carlos ? "

" Your judgment is impeccable, prima mia," was the dry response.

" Do go and tell Paco Don Pasquale is here." She added, when they were alone, " His father's death upset him very much ; it will do him good to be at work again." Don Pasquale inclined his head noncommittally. " So now we must fix him up a big season ! "

We ? The impresario stiffened. " He has no doubt made some dates."

" He'll give you his list." She paused to tap the ash off her cigarette, went to the bar and set down her empty glass. " There's Casablanca, and then Barcelona, for Easter. My opinion is he'd be better employed in getting himself in condition than taking a lot of small fights before Easter."

" Mexico, perhaps, did not agree with him ? "—What a woman. No wonder there were funny tales about the Niño, with this in his background.

" On the contrary ! " she came back sharply. " He couldn't be in better shape. The scratch he got at Zaragosa has healed up and we're working every morning. Some of his friends come out, and we spend a couple of hours in the corrales. You should see his verónicas now ; they're as fine as Manolete's ! You know how his cape-work was ? " said Aracea anxiously. " It was very interesting, very varied, but there wasn't enough emotion. Wait till you see him ! You will have a surprise."

Don Pasquale made a restless movement ; it was for him to appraise the work of his new client.

" We ride a lot, and we play tennis. I make him exercise on the wheel and the skipping-rope "—Her eyes turned towards the door, she missed the expression on Don Pasquale's face. " Hallo, darling," she said, in English.

Paco came in. He was wearing flannel slacks and a turtle-necked sweater, monogrammed in crimson on the left breast. A radiant air of health, confidence and general well-being surrounded him ; he looked, thought Don Pasquale, more like

a prosperous young football ace than a bullfighter. He grasped
the visitor's hand and slapped him on the back.

" Olá." He clapped his hands and a manservant appeared
in a white jacket, with cigalas and big green olives and delicate
strips of ham on a silver platter. The man went to the bar and
occupied himself with a cocktail shaker; three tall glasses, ice-
cold, foaming, coloured like absinthe, were set before them.
" Salud ! " said Paco.

" Los toros," offered Don Pasquale—remembering he was in
the house of Parral.

They talked about Mexico, about New York, and, presently,
went through an archway which, cut into the end wall of the
former cellar, led to an interior staircase and up to the dining-
room. The big, bleak room had also undergone transformation;
the smoky panels between the rafters had been repainted and
gilded. An imposing set of upholstered chairs replaced the
leather-slung seats of Don Luis's day, and some fine tapestries
and an eight-fold screen of Cordoban leather dispelled its former
air of a hotel comedor. The table was elaborately laid, with
damask and a glitter of crystal and silver; all very elegant, and
the cooking admirable; all very different from the days when
twenty or thirty people sat down to a big stew, and, at the far
end of the long table, drooped a pale, silent woman, with, on
her left, a talkative little girl, and on her right the English
governess.

When the meal was ended, a large silver tray was placed in
front of Aracea, with a Cona machine and the flame lighted under
it. Paco watched her proudly as she spooned the freshly ground
coffee into the vase of glass; his eyes went to Don Pasquale,
seeking an impression.

" You see, señor, my wife is accustomed to the English style
—según la moda ! " he observed naïvely.

Don Pasqauale cocked a wall eye. He knew what the house
of Ribera was like, and he misdoubted these foreign tricks with
coffee, which he liked thick and tepid, well loaded with coñac.
Aracea gave her husband a frown.

" And now shall we talk business ? "

Paco got up, fetched a box of cigars and offered them to his guest.

"There's plenty of time."

"Certainly." She glanced at her watch. "Don Marcos is coming to look at three-year-olds; they're putting on a novillada, if the weather's all right, immediately after the Magdalena. You'll look after him, won't you, Carlos?"

"I took for granted you'd want to see him yourself. I've got to see a man about some horses."

"What horses?"

Carlos shrugged his shoulders and lowered his eyes to his coffee.

"It's a pity to keep animals that don't pay. We're using a lot of gasolina——"

"Ah——! Well, I'd like to see them, before they go."

"Certainly. It would be a pity to miss a sale."

Her eyes darkened; she bit her lip, but, recalling her manners, turned to the guest.

"This is an old argument——"

"Mujer," put in Paco. "It is not amusing for Don Pasquale —to listen to our arguments."

"Perhaps it will amuse him. Carlos wants to sell off the old horses to the horse-flesh dealers."

"E' práctico," muttered Don Pasquale.

"Yes—they're past their work on the ranch, but they're well-fed and accustomed to good riding."

"She's thinking about the horse suerte," interrupted Paco. Don Pasquale hunched his shoulders; most people had given up thinking about the horse suerte.

"It doesn't pay, to sell to the bullring," he mumbled.

"That's what Carlos says; and I don't agree."

Don Pasquale was silent, inwardly despising a man who could not keep his wife in order. Paco frowned.

"I've told you. If you put the pic up on a real horse, he wouldn't know how to ride it."

"He'd soon learn—if his credit depended on saving the horse, as well as himself."

" If every pic was a Cañero ! " jeered Paco. " We'd be paying our pics more than we earn ourselves."

" You're always cursing your pics ; but you can't blame somebody for looking after his own skin, if he's just sitting there to be hit."

" That's the management's business," snapped Paco.

" You'd soon make it your business, if it was in the contract, that pics had to be properly mounted."

Don Pasquale and Paco exchanged smiles of toleration, for this female intransigence.

" And a lot of people would be out of a job."

" You mean, pics that can't ride ?—So they should be ! Don Pasquale "—she turned to him passionately—" Everybody hates the horse suerte ! Hundreds of people who are fans of the bulls would rather see a novillada than a corrida, because of the horses."

" They'd rather watch the football," sneered Paco.

" You all blame the football, for the decadence of the bullfight."

" Naturally. They go to the football, because it is cheaper."

" Qué disparate ! It is in every Spaniard to follow the bulls, and the football is a foreign disease, which has spread through this country because the people are not satisfied with the bullfight. The horse is the disgrace of the bullfight ! Do I breed brave bulls, to have them ploughed down the spine by a panic-stricken fool on an animal he can't manage ? You've been cursing Curro out, ever since he worked for you——"

" He's a bag of manure ! " roared Paco.

" He's got a family to keep, and you put him up on a thing that bends in the middle when he's in the saddle——"

" It's got nothing to do with me, what he gets up on—and if you put him on a real horse he'd still be a white-bellied, rot-gutted maggot out of a manure-heap ! "

" So you say. And let me tell you something, amigo : the manager who brings credit back to the ring will be the one who puts the pics up on decent horses and makes them ride properly and not use the lance like a shovel ! "

" And are you going to breed special bulls, with chiquitillo horns, to go with your fancy horses ? "

She spat out an expletive which, in the experience of Don Pasquale, was not used by ladies.

" The bulls of our ancestors had not chiquitillo horns, and the horses were real horses ! "

Paco, by now, was white with rage and deeply mortified that such a scene should take place before Don Pasquale, whose unspoken opinions were written in his face. He would retail this in every club along Sierpes. A servant came in, to say that Don Marcos was waiting in the office.

" Make my excuses," Aracea said imperiously to Carlos, who, through the foregoing, had sat, smiling curiously at the tip of his cigar, " and remember : no final arrangements until we have talked it over together.—A thousand excuses, señor ; we have wasted a lot of time with our foolish arguing, but now we are quite ready ! "

Paco's hand on her elbow raised her slowly out of the chair. He spoke quietly, with his eyes on hers.

" When you have finished talking, bring Marcos in for a drink."

She realised, with incredulity, that he was dismissing her. Her cheeks turned crimson, her lips parted, and closed again. Then she made a dignified little bow to Don Pasquale, who returned it with polite irony, and went through the door which Carlos was holding open for her. Paco missed the wink Carlos gave him, because he was pouring out brandy. When he brought the glass to Don Pasquale, his face was still pale and his jaw set, but he had gained control of himself. Don Pasquale began to feel better about the assignment he had been inclined to pass up. Up to the last five minutes, he had been prepared to believe all they said about Niño de Maderas ; but the boy was ultimately the master of his household, and, between the pair of them, thought Don Pasquale, they would soon have this diabla of a wife in her place.

An amicable discussion lasted for over an hour : in which time Paco recovered his good humour—and, incidentally, got over the shock of hearing the percentage of his earnings that would go to his new manager. He had the sense, however, not at this stage to start haggling, and a certain cold intelligence in his companion's eye kept his boasting within bounds. He admitted there were two or three towns where he had not the cartel he hoped for, though they booked him each year and he had always put up a good show; he couldn't make out what that was about.

Don Pasquale decided, for the moment, to reserve the explanation. He knew what it was about. He knew all about the hostile demonstration at Talavera, after Paco had been awarded the ear; how the always incalculable crowd—after handing him the triple Olé—suddenly let rip; how Paco, on his way round the tablas, stood still, looking stunned, looking foolish, while the audience filled the air with their cushions, water bottles and whatever insulting missile they could lay their hands on. Everyone who fights bulls is used to the sudden veering of mass opinion; no one, whatever his degree, is immune from it. But this demonstration of what was unmistakably personal antagonism, unrelated to his work, took Paco aback. He stiffened, looked contemptuously round the ring, and after a pause long enough to show the crowd his indifference to their insolence, lifted the ear above his head and strutted slowly into the callejón. Within a few hours of adulation from his personal supporters, the incident was a grain of dust on the horizon of his memory; but it had been marked by others who remembered. Don Pasquale remembered it, when, his self-confidence restored by the brandy and the simpático attitude of his companion, Paco confided to him his immediate ambition: a mano a mano with Ildefonso— the hand-to-hand contest between two rivals, which is the greatest thrill that the ring offers to its followers. The last and greatest of the mano a manos was Manolete against Arruza, and no one, so far, had challenged Ildefonso to this final test of skill.

Don Pasquale contemplated his new client coldly. In some respects, the Niño was a better fighter than his rival: neat and deadly with the darts—which Ildefonso had long abandoned— very stylish and statuesque with the muleta. Yet he was one of the few matadores who had never built up a permanent support that followed him to every fight. Ildefonso's arrival was like a Semana Santa procession ; a mile of cars, every mantilla in the town on view along the balconies! That little matter, thought Don Pasquale shrewdly, had to be attended to, before they risked the big show-down. A great deal of tact would be called for, and tact was expensive. Don Pasquale began to feel good.

II

" Hombre, you'd better stop in bed to-morrow, and the next day. After that banging you're going to be as stiff as hell. And you want to be in shape for Sunday."

Lying face down on the couch, he made no reply. There was a spreading stain of purple from just above the left buttock to the base of the right shoulderblade ; the stain was netted with the patterns of old scars. There was a big contusion on the back of the left thigh, and strips of plaster held in place the fresh dressing they had put over the old cut in his abdomen that had broken open when he was thrown against the barrera. He had been saved by a smart piece of cape-work—a lucky day. His head was cracking, and he kept his eyes shut tightly against the glaring light overhead. The room hummed and roared with doctors, medical students, friends and Pressman—making a fuss about nothing. He mumbled for a drink, and someone put a glass of mineral in his hand. He cursed, and flung it on the floor ; a *drink*, not something to wash with.

Presently the room was empty, except for himself and the Little Tom-Cat, bent and shrivelled like a dwarf, who was folding the vest and jacket they had pulled off him and rolling them round the montera. His face half-buried in the pillow, he followed with a sour eye the sword boy's occupation.

" What are you doing ? "

" Nothing. Taking these down to the car."

" What am I going home in ? "

" Your cape—and pull your pants up."

" Get me something to eat."

" Sure—but they'll have it ready at the hotel." With the bundle in his arms, Gatito halted on one foot for further orders.

Ildefonso turned over carefully ; his profile beaked itself over the ridges of his chest to stare at his naked limbs. Gatito put down the bundle and made to hoist the taleguilla. Ildefonso told him to get to hell.

" I'm hungry," whined Gatito.

" All right ; go get yourself some food."

" But they'll be waiting at the hotel." He used the impersonal " they " tactfully ; the only " they " who mattered was the diestro's current girl, she who was indirectly responsible for the battering he had taken that afternoon.

" Go and eat. And—oye ; bring me a suit from the hotel."

He closed his eyes and put his hands over them, to shut out the light. The white room became deadly quiet. From afar came the noise of the choppers, dealing with the last of the carcases, and the tremulous clatter of hooves, as the horses were led away. Somebody with a rattle of keys was locking up cupboards. Beyond the dark blue square of the window, light after light went out. In a few minutes the bull ring would be empty, the conserje going on his final round.

It was worse, an afternoon like this, than getting the horn ; the long torment, unrelieved by the letting of blood, left his teeth chattering for hours. The vicious bruising, the wrenching of muscles, afforded no outlet for the tension that began even before they dressed him in the suit of lights. He was not yet thirty, but it was time for him to retire : he knew that, every time he went into the ring. Through all the yelling and the ritualistic adoration of the crowd, he knew he had no business to be there. He grinned sometimes, when he was doing the trick he had copied from Manolete—" mirando al público "—passing the bull with his eyes fixed on the gradas ; he did it only when fear was so far advanced in him that death was of no consequence, and he grinned because he knew they were all holding their breath in the hope of seeing him die. Well, they should have that gratification one day, because he could not afford to retire.

Like a dying god, he would vouchsafe to them their moment of grief and glory !

Sometimes it was as though the spirit broke loose from his body, and, from somewhere overhead, watched the skeleton walk out on the sand ; and he knew the dual rapture, of spectator and of participant in the act. Sometimes, imprisoned in its fleshless cage, his spirit shuddered with awareness of a ruined physique, of limbs that only obeyed the direction of the brain through an act of will, and then doubtfully. No one of the present generation had taken the punishment he had taken ; was that why they called him " the maestro " ? Was that why, after each of his appearances, there were a dozen women avid for his favours ? Was that why he now felt sick at the prospect of going back into a hot room, and the hot body of a girl—— ?

" Here's your suit, Ildefonso "—How long had he been alone ?—" And the señorita says to hurry up ; she is tired of waiting."

He dressed, very slowly. As he limped through the dim archways, hands came out, to clutch his. He emptied his pockets. The conserje told him, " There's a crowd waiting outside for you ! " and Ildefonso swore ; he was not in the mood, or the shape, for crowds. " It's all right ; the police will see you through."

He flung himself into the car.

" Al hotel ? " asked the chauffeur.

" No," said Ildefonso. " To Sanjorje."

A dusty road to a village, a ramshackle house, a woman who —though little more than a shabby vehicle of sex—was the mother of his sons.

III

" Just a little more shoulder—the left one. Oh no, no, dear —you've stiffened up ! You'd better relax a bit. I'm afraid you're tired."

Paco gaped. Apart from after the fight, he had never been

tired in his life. He was prepared to go on posturing for the whole of the morning—although he was disappointed that this English photographer did not apparently want to " take " him in the traje de luces. His valet had laid out all the suits, and Leo had skipped along them, with cries of " Ravishing. Oh, my dear, what a colour. But, my dear, the *weight* ! Can I try this on ? "—Tossing back a silvery wave of hair, he rushed to piroutte in front of the long glass, in one of the chaquetas, dove grey and frogged with gold. " Sylvia. Sylvia, do come here and look. Couldn't one *do* something "—his fingers flickered expressively —" with this ? "

While Paco and the man waited, they went into an animated discussion about the adaptation of the fighting coat to modern evening dress. Even Aracea and Remedios joined in it ; Paco began to feel that he was not holding his own in the picture ; he snatched up another coat, and thrust it towards Leo.

" That is more good. I pay two hundred fifty dollar for that one. I like be photograph in that." There was no need to speak English, but he was feeling a little aggressive, at the spectacle of his chaqueta on the wriggling shoulders of Leo, who, turned quickly, glanced at the lemon-yellow satin and murmured soothingly :

" It's very pretty, darling ; such fun, all that embroidery. Oh, somebody, take this off me ; it's quite weighing me down. Now, are we all ready ? "

" I put zis on ? " asked Paco, indicating the yellow.

" Let's go out," said Leo, twining his arm through Paco's, " and find some backgrounds."

The women, left together, smiled at each other ; Sylvia lit a cigarette and offered her case to the others. The Brett Pawls had arrived the night before, with Leo, who was supposed to be leaving after luncheon. The young Albacobacas had been staying already a week ; Tano Albacobaca, a great amateur of the bulls, was there to practise with some two-year-olds which, not having reached the standard set for Parral bulls, had been reserved for the use of Paco and his friends. He and Brett Pawl and the boys were somewhere, working the capes ; there would be, Aracea calculated, at least eighteen for luncheon, and several of the young men out for the morning would probably be invited by Paco to stay the night. She excused herself to go about her duties as mistress of the household ; she had not yet quite come to take for granted the pride and glow of being the dueña of Parral. How much happiness Mamá might have had out of it ! —if she had not been Mamá. Now, enclosed in her convent in Castile, she had found, presumably, her own kind of happiness. It was strange, to remember one's mother only as a ghost, drifting across one's youth. Yet she must have been more than a ghost ; herself abandoned to tradition, she had preserved her daughter from her own fate.

" Shall we go and watch Leo taking photographs ? " proposed Sylvia. Remedios agreed, a little poutingly ; a very beautiful young woman, it seemed odd that anyone else should be photographed, when she was about. They drifted down to the garden —no longer the wilderness on which the melancholy eyes of the wife of Parral rested from her upper windows, but a formal design of lily ponds, young lemon trees, small rotundas with curved seats of faience and sheltering hedges of box and yew that entrapped the sun. Threading the maze to the high white-washed wall that enclosed the privacy of Parral, they found Paco, looking puzzled, contemplating his own shadow, and Leo rushing from point to point with his camera. Paco was puzzled indeed ; it was not his idea of being photographed—standing with his back to the camera, staring at a wall. And the rejection of the yellow suit still rankled. He had come down to breakfast —it was Aracea's suggestion : " Mira, chico : you must be ' tipico ' for these foreigners "—in his riding clothes, although there had been no suggestion of riding : the short, coffee-brown coat and darker trousers, the crimson waist-band and silver-grey cordobés—very smart, but it was a nuisance to get oneself up like that, and then have to change into the suit of lights. It was not the get-up for an important photograph, and he had become restive, while the little English pansy insisted on taking snap after snap ; Paco had counted at least thirty. Supposing the film gave out before they got on to the real publicity ? He knew exactly how he wanted to be taken : facing the camera, with the cape sheathed round his hips, his head up and smiling. And now he was told he was tired, and had better relax ! He scowled at Leo, as the women came along.

" Now I think I change my clothes."

Leo turned and rushed at Sylvia.

" Darling, he keeps nagging me to do him in that yellow thing ! You know, the *terrible* photographs they do here of bull-fighters—like something out of Madame Tussaud's. Can't you explain I'm *not* that kind of person ? I've got the most marvellous set of studies—do try and make him understand ! "—The big empty eyes were filled with tears.

" Don't be silly, darling ; it won't do you any harm to give him what he wants. Look, why don't you get something now while he's talking to Remedios ?—After all," said Sylvia dryly, " she's the duquesa de Albacobaca." She waited while Leo hurriedly focused his camera ; that was a sure one for *London and Paris.*

" Paco ! "—Aracea was coming down between the box edges. " Guess who's here ! Ildefonso."

" But that's fine ; bring him out." It was a good idea for Ildefonso to see him surrounded by smart foreigners, having his photograph taken ; Paco beamed.

" Not here, tonto—at home, at Sanjorje. We'll ask him to supper, shall we ? I'll send one of the boys over with a note."

" I don't expect anybody can read at Sanjorje ! Send a message—and say we'll send the car for him," said Paco superbly ; his good humour restored, he stalked towards the house. He meant to be photographed in the two hundred and fifty dollar suit. Aracea smiled at Leo.

" They are good, the photographs ? "

" Darling, they're wonderful."

" Paco photographs very well."

" Really ? "—It was annoying, to be told that someone who had given infinite trouble " photographed well." " He's very difficult—I suppose most people are, who are used to the old-fashioned photography. They'll be wonderful for The Book. I'm encantado that Wilbur's going to do The Book; he's such a simpático! But I have to have my copyright!"—he wagged a roguish finger. "You know—'derechos de fotógrafo'; you'll explain that to Paco, won't you, dear?" he added anxiously.

Aracea promised, and suggested that they went down to the corrales, to watch the capework. Leo had the gratification of taking some snapshots of the duque de Albacobaca with a little Parral bull (a nice spread, with suitable letterpress, for *London and Paris*), and a perfunctory photograph of Paco, in the yellow suit.

"But suppose it does not succeed?"

"All my photographs succeed," said Leo petulantly, "and I've finished the film."

Paco was furious; to have spent three-quarters of an hour in getting into the suit of lights, for one photograph! He had no faith in the snapshots; he went away, to get undressed and to sulk.

The dining-room filled itself for luncheon with gay young people; the boys had had showers and changed; Paco came down gloomily, in a sweater and slacks. The bright morning had darkened, but the flames of a great wood fire leapt on the hearth, and all under the long table a line of braseros transformed the chill of the immense room into glowing warmth.

"It's the only cosy house I've been in, so far, in Spain," Leo confided to Aracea. "My dear, some of those Castilian palaces! They've not *started* to cope with winter!"

She smiled at him—"Next winter I hope we will have central heating"—and turned to the servant who was bending over her shoulder.

"Don Ildefonso returns his thanks to the señores. He will come—but he has his own car."

She let out a ripple of laughter.

"You heard, Paco?" she called down the table. "My little maestro—he has his own car.—You know the name of Ildefonso García?" she said to Leo, who gave a high-pitched shriek.

"But who doesn't! I've practically had to bribe the whole

embassy, to get a seat for his corrida next month—there's the most frightful black market——"

She raised her eyebrows; a hush had fallen.

" You know he grew up as a little boy on this ranch ?—So, naturally, we are very proud of him," she concluded royally.

" And is it true he's a gipsy—like Joselito, and El Gallo—and all the famous fighters ? " babbled Leo.

The wife of the Niño de Maderas lifted her head.

" It is not at all necessary to be a gipsy, to be a famous fighter."

" Oh darling, I'm so *silly*," said Leo, in genuine distress. " After all, I'm only a poor little foreigner, you mustn't be angry with me. Of *course* it isn't necessary; there's Belmonte, isn't there, and Manolete——"

" And the Niño de Maderas ! " shouted someone.

" I wish you wouldn't interrupt," said Leo pettishly. " The most important name naturally comes last." He raised his glass and his smile of practised charm to Paco, at the far end of the table; that one raised his non-committally; he had not caught the rest of the conversation, but Aracea looked like a thunder-cloud, and Carlos was smiling. The young man next to Leo said, with malice in his smile :

" What a pity, that you will not be here to-night ! Aguilucho is coming; he and Paco are muy amigos. Aguilucho, you know, is how we call Ildefonso García."

" Let me see—that means ' the little eagle ' ? Oh dear, my Spanish is really dreadful; I thought the word was aguileño," complained Leo.

" That is different," was the serious reply. " He looks like an eagle—a little ; but we called him aguilucho when he was muchacho because he moved like *that* when he planted his darts." Thrusting back his chair, the speaker made the gesture of planting the darts in his neighbour's shoulders, which brought a shriek from Leo and a roar of laughter from the company. Even Paco joined in it ; the tension was broken, and the name of Ildefonso buzzed freely in the conversation. Leo was shrewd enough to subside ; an idea was taking shape behind those big glassy eyes.

Among his other gifts was an almost infallible news sense—not only for the immediate, but for the future. The big hired car—provided by *London and Paris*—in which he had brought the Brett Pawls was waiting in the patio.

Sylvia turned to Aracea, as it purred out through the archway :

" Honey, I'm sorry I've let you in for this."

" For what ?—Paco is very pleased about the photographs."

" Leo's terrible—but he's terribly spoilt. He's so used to being persona grata——"

Aracea laughed politely.

" It was fun having him—for a while."

" You don't suppose you've got rid of him ? "—As Aracea's eyes widened, Sylvia continued, " I bet you—I bet you these ear-rings of mine "—she touched the big diamonds—" you'll see him back before the day is over."

" But why——? He has gone to some friends near Málaga——"

" The friends at Málaga will have a message that Leo is unavoidably detained," said Sylvia dryly. " They have a great deal of money—like all Leo's friends—but they are not ' in the news.' Paco is ' in the news '—and so is Ildefonso."

" Por dios, he has seen enough of Paco, and Paco of him ! And he has no more film for his camera——"

The silver eyes of her companion covered her levelly.

" If I'm wrong, you get these ear-rings ; and if I'm right— I keep them," she ended, with a laugh. " I hope I do, because Tommy'll be mad ; he won them in a bet with a guy in New York ! "

Slowly, as the February dusk closed in, the house of Parral decked itself in lights ; once, at nightfall, a block of darkness, it was now visible for kilómetros across the pastures ; the cattle, clustered under the trees, turned their accustomed heads towards it, no longer rendered uneasy by an unfamiliar brightness. Only the brave bulls, in the remote folds of the hills, were unaware of the changes that had taken place since the days of their fore-fathers. As a car hummed into the patio, Aracea lifted her head from accounts in the office.

" Who do you suppose that is ? " she asked Carlos, who went to open the door. Leo minced in.

" Darling, isn't this too awful of me! Something's gone wrong with the car; I've had to leave it in a garage. Can you possibly find a teeny-weeny corner for me ? "

So Sylvia's diamond ear-rings were safe.

Sylvia, changing for dinner, heard a tap on the door and called to her husband, in his bath.

" Like to bet me a fiver that's Leo ? "

" Hand over the cash. He's in Málaga."

" He's here," she said, opening the door.

Leo skipped in, wearing a silk dressing gown, his silvery waves in a net.

" So you worked it."

" Darling, the car broke down! I'm so lucky, aren't I ! " He tittered. " What a marvellous room; I must get a photograph of this to-night. I've bought acres and acres of film——"

" Sure you have. Leo, you really are terrible; I suppose you know you made yourself thoroughly unpopular at lunch."

" Don't bully me, Sylvia. You don't suppose I'd miss the chance of meeting Ildefonso? Now listen "—he cast himself into an armchair. " I've had an idea; you're so clever—tell me you think it's wonderful. Tommy : come here this minute."

" He's in the bath."

" Is that a bathroom ?—Oh dear, I haven't got one, but there's one just along the passage. They're getting awfully civilised, aren't they—the Spanish ? It's almost a pity—they'll be like any other country in a few years' time. Now, Sylvia : do listen. An *album* !—characters of the bullring. Don't you think they'd love it—at home, and Paris, and New York ? "

" Do people outside of Spain care so much about the bullfight ? "

" Darling, you're so shortsighted. Within the next year or two there's going to be a boom in Spanish travel. The thing is to have your material ready. I know at least three people who are writing books about Spain—and of course there'll be Wilbur's thing about Paco; is he really a first-class matador?" frowned Leo anxiously. "I've spent a frightful lot of time and trouble on him to-day, but it's worth while, if I get Ildefonso. Now listen; I've got to get dozens of pictures of Ildefonso to-night and you and Tommy have got to help me."

"Hell, Leo, you don't make use of the house of one matador to make pictures of another. Paco and Aracea are friends of ours, and we don't want to be involved in any rows," frowned Sylvia. "And, anyhow, Ildefonso and Paco are old friends——'

Leo giggled delightedly.

"My dear, rows are such *fun*! They may be friends, but I'll bet they're madly jealous of each other, underneath! Don't be tiresome, darling; I've given up the most divine party at the Hinojosas', to be in on this, to-night, and I do think I owe myself some fun. And I'm only asking you to coax Ildefonso out of the crowd into one of those great, bare, whitewashed rooms with funny shadows! You know my thing about shadows." Leo turned petulant. "Really, I don't think these people realise what it means—to have their portrait done by Leo Mond! I *did* think that you and Tommy would put me over. After all, I'm used to photographing royalty, and I've never been treated so casually in my life."

"Don't cry about it, old boy." Brett Pawl, draped in a towel, had emerged from the bathroom, and dropped a comforting hand on Leo's shoulder.

"After all, it's my *living*!" whimpered Leo.

"And you can't help having a dreadful, vulgar, little nose for anything that's likely to become fashionable," said Sylvia. "Short of sleeping with him, I'll get Ildefonso for you to-night. I shouldn't—on my limited acquaintance with bullfighters—say it would be difficult; but we don't have to hurt Paco's feelings, or upset Aracea."

"Darling, do I ever upset anybody?" said Leo reproachfully. "Well, I must go and get dressed. My pale grey velvet with the cut steel buttons—don't you think? Oh dear, I'm so thrilled to meet Ildefonso. I hate missing the Hinojosas' party, but there was only going to be a Brazilian millionaire and two or three rather tatty Roman princesses ; no news value whatever," concluded Leo happily, as he pranced out of the room.

. . . At a quarter to ten, Aracea said :

" He can't be coming ; shall I telephone ? "

" If he is coming, he will come. Let's eat," said Paco. He was disappointed ; he would have liked Ildefonso to have seen him against this background of a fine house, a beautiful and elegant wife and distinguished foreign guests. He would have liked, also, to demonstrate their friendship before his own friends, so that they might have grounds for the contradiction of the ridiculous rumour that he was jealous of Ildefonso. He led the way up to the dining-room.

Shortly before midnight, Aracea said, with a glance at the clock, " He won't come now." Even Andalucían indifference to time fell short of arriving three hours late for a formal meal. It was mal educado of Ildefonso, to accept, and then not to appear ; under all the veneer of latter experience and the acquaintance he by now had gained of society, he was still the ragged urchin who had taken a beating because she had broken up a car !

For Leo, it was a miserable evening ; ravenous by the time they sat down to dinner, his squeamish stomach could not digest the strongly flavoured Andalucían dishes, and, for some reason, they all persisted in talking the andaluz, of which he could make out only a scattered phrase or two. Oh for the cosmopolitan household of the Hinojosas ; the gossip of three capitals to which he could have contributed ; the sense of power and prestige that attached to one celebrated in the social annals of London and New York ! It was anguish to be ignored, or have a patronising phrase in the castellano occasionally tossed to one ! —to be aware only of the word " toros " clang, clanging for ever in one's ears : he, who, in Madrid, was quite famous for his recitations of Lorca, his well-displayed (if trivial) acquaintance with Rubén Darío, Jiménez and the Quintero brothers, and his parrot-like little quotations from the classics ! Here, he was a nobody among savages . . .

IV

"Stop here; I will walk the rest of the way," said Ildefonso, to the chauffeur. "And there's no need for you to wait."

"Pues—I come back at what time?"

"I'll walk back."

"Hombre, it's a long way!"

"Por dios, I've walked four times as far, when I was as old as my youngest son!" swore Ildefonso—an exaggeration, for his youngest legitimate son—to whom he was referring—was barely two years old. He stood under the cold stars, watching the red tail-light of the car grow dim along the flat road, and turned his face towards the lit house of Parral. It was about a mile away.

Along this road, which he now trod in custom-built shoes, with a scarf of heavily woven silk tucked into the neck of his expensive overcoat, he had shivered as a little, barefoot boy, with only a rag of a shirt, a pair of tattered trousers and perhaps an old sack between him and the chill of a winter night. He thought himself lucky, because, in comparison with some of the village children, he was well fed, on the rich residues of the house of Parral. On cold nights, he slept on a truss of straw, in one of the stables; in summer heat he lay out naked in one of the patios. He looked after the hens and the geese and the turkeys, and thought and dreamed of the bulls. Several times he took a beating, because he was caught crawling into the pastures, to try his skill against the monsters of Parral. Then, one day, when he was sweating with an old cape at the back of one of the barns, the dueño saw him . . .

His heart seemed to swell, until it was crushed against the cage of his ribs, and it was as though an iron band closed round his throat. How many times, along this very road he had met the dueño, riding his chestnut horse; the pair of them god-like and shining in the morning light. Sometimes the dueño would say, "Olá, chico," and toss him a copper; sometimes, his mind on other things, he would ride past scowling, with no glance for the humble figure standing still for him to pass. And always it was like an encounter with a god.

He crossed himself in the dark; "May God keep thy soul." He jerked out the linen handkerchief to stop the tears that were running down his face. To me, fatherless, you were my father; but for you there would have been no Aguilucho. There would, perhaps, have been a starving young bullfighter, talented, but unable to make the grade for want of support: dependent on chance alone—one could afford, now, to admit it: now that one's inner, inflexible confidence had justified itself. Confidence alone is not enough; there are so many chinks in that armour which can only be filled up with the help of someone who believes as one believes in oneself, and can implement his belief with support of the right kind at the right time. Tu eras de verdad mi padre. The iron band round Ildefonso's throat burst with an audible sob, and he allowed the tears to flow. At that moment, he would have given all that remained to him of his squandered earnings to hear the beat of a horse's feet on the road and to see, hardening against the stars, the high head and broad shoulders of Don Luis Parral; to lay his own weary head against the stirrup leather, to feel the hand which, not seldom, had cuffed him, on his shoulder, and to say, "Master, such as I am, Ildefonso—Aguilucho—you have made me."

He started to find himself outside the great, iron-studded door, with the bell-pull that would summon the porter—who was it to-day?—from his lodge, to switch on the light and usher him into the patio from which, as a little boy, he had so often been driven by the orders of the dueño. He was to walk into that patio, now, as an honoured guest; wearing the kind of clothes the guests of Parral wore, he was to mount the curving stone staircase and be received by the little girl he had taught to use the cape—Aracita. He had seen her several times at the bullfight—grown very beautiful; she would probably be wearing evening dress and smoking a cigarette . . .

His heart gave a suffocating leap. No! It was impossible. How could he, Ildefonso, walk up there, with all those ghosts

behind him ? Everything that had given him assurance to accept
the invitation—his celebrity, his pride to display in the house of
Parral that which he had become—his old affection for Paco—
dissolved ; left him, a thin, ragged boy, cringing at his patron's
door. Only one thing could have restored his confidence : the
face and the voice of the dueño, to welcome him. Those absent,
the house of Parral was a tomb, from which Ildefonso drew back
shuddering, as he would have shrunk from a newly-turned grave.
All of the superstition of his profession surged up in him,
weakening his limbs, breaking the sweat at the roots of his hair.
His hand, raised towards the bell-pull, remained trembling in air.
Gulping back a cry, he lurched away.

He did not know how long he had been stumbling in the
dark, or where he had got to ; there were many changes since
he had known the place—walls had raised themselves in unfamiliar places, fences were drawn across tracks he might have
remembered, an emplacement of new buildings made him wonder
whether, in his absence, a village had grown up on the threshold
of the house of Parral. He could make out the lines of the roofs
against the stars, and the sides gleamed white ; not wishing to
get a night watchman's bullet in his ribs, he kept away from them.
But the bruising he had taken at Jérez was so painful that he
began to have difficulty in walking, and he knew he would not
get back to Sanjorje that night.

He could get a bed in the village, but his appearance would
create a furore, and he was not in a mood to be lionised. Crawling
along in the dark, he knew himself at last on familiar ground.
His outstretched hand touched the mud wall of the big corral
where, sometimes, they tested the young stock, and occasionally
penned a few cows with their calves. His hand, trailing the wall,
came to the gap and finding it was not barred, he knew the
corral was empty. His lips stretched themselves in a smile. Many
a night he and other boys, playing truant from the house, slept
in a cave cut out of the vast thickness of the wall, secure from
wind or rain. Within a few minutes, Ildefonso García, le
Aguilucho, who for years had known the luxury of beds in
first-class hotels, the voluptuous couches of women in Society,

and the state bedrooms of palaces, was stretched out on a thin spread of dirty straw, smelling of human and animal manure, infested with lice. When he had found the least painful position for his sore limbs, he slept like a child.

When he awoke it was daylight, and he wondered where the devil he was, then remembered. As he cautiously moved a leg and an arm, swearing at the stiffness, he grinned through the pain ; whatever his wife at Sanjorje and his mistress in Jérez thought of his disappearance, neither would envisage his present surroundings. Carai, that had been good !—that night of solitude, almost under the stars. Not quite so good, to think of the trudge home—but he could at least crawl down to the village, before anyone was about, knock up the mayoral, get some breakfast and telephone for the car. He was about to put this plan into practice when he was checked by the sound of voices. He drew back into the cave and listened to the click of hooves : Don Carlos, and probably Paco, riding out to the pastures. He would have liked to see Paco, but did not choose to appear in this ridiculous fashion, from a hole in the wall. So he waited for them to go past—and was taken aback when he realised, from the sounds, that the horses had turned into the corral, and that there were many more than two.

Por dios, they had chosen this morning to work-out here ! His watch had stopped, and he had no idea of the time ; but the sun was up and this meant they had breakfasted, and might work for two hours, or even more. He stole a cautious glance round the corner ; they were all talking and laughing, hitching the reins up to the iron hooks in the wall of the corral, pulling off their coats and sweaters, shaking out the practice capes they had brought with them. Paco—olá hombre ; you look fine. And the duque, and a big lanky inglés, and a bunch of the boys from town, and—por dios—three women ! One the duquesa— guapísima—and a rubia, probably the wife of the Englishman— and the third, the third . . .

Ignoring the hands outstretched to help her, the third dropped out of the saddle as lightly as a bird, stripped off the fitted jacket of wool, and stood revealed in a thin pullover of flesh-pink, bound round the throat with a dark silk scarf; the trousers she was wearing moulded her flanks almost as closely as the pale woven stuff did her torso, and her hair, lifted by the morning wind, blew like a heavy black flag behind her head.

" Ai-ee ! Hard work this morning. Give me my cape, Tano ! " he heard her say. " And water, please. Of course I want water ! "—Somebody had protested laughingly. " What's the use of pretending to work the capes in a wind like this unless they're wet ? It is excellent practice," she asserted, with a toss of the head.

He watched her drop her head, seize the collar with her teeth and work her hands along the stuff into the proper grip. He had seen women working with the cape before, had even, when they teased him enough, taught them how to do it; but he had never before felt the emotion that went through him as he watched those two small hands, one with a huge diamond on the middle finger, feel their way along until they bit into the percale. Then the pause, the few short steps forward, and the planting of the feet; the profiling towards the imaginary bull and the slow extension of the left hand . . .

Although she was looking straight towards him, he knew she would not see him, or anyone, or anything except the bull she had in her mind. His body emptied itself of breath while with a cold, professional gravity, she completed that so simple-seeming movement. She performed it four times, so slowly that the pink wing of the cape seemed barely to move before she ended with a half-veronica, and, dropping the cape, rubbed her wrists.

" Olé, la Aracita ! "

" So that's what your wonderful figure comes from ! " called the rubia. " I should think ten minutes of that does more for a girl than a morning in the Turkish bath. Come on; show me. Judas," she cried out, as she picked up the cape Aracea had dropped, " You don't mean you carry that weight with your arms stretched right out like that ? "

" It's wet, because of the wind, and my wrists are aching; I only did four—I'm out of condition. But if you want to improve your figure—not that it needs it at all," said Aracea politely, " you can do the movement just as well without the cape."

She lifted her arms and sketched the swing of the body from the waist; the clear morning light slid down her like water. Ildefonso had no recollection of Concha at Sanjorje or Gildí biting her long pointed nails in bed at Jérez.

Chapter Four

I

AT THE long table in the room that had been Doña Leandra's sala, Aracea finished her letter to Mary Carpenter.

" It is very long since I wrote to you, please forgive me. We are so happy to have your letters, I always read them to Paco. There are so many things I mean to send you, Press notices and pictures and articles from the newspapers, and there is never time but they will all be here for you when you come.

" We are so disappointed you did not come this season. Paco's cartel is now enormous and so far as the public is concerned there are only *two* matadores in all Spain !—Paco and of course Ildefonso who continues to be ' un milagro ' but they say is getting more and more unreliable. I have only seen him twice this year and he was estupendo. It is of course quite a different school from Paco's and it will be a pity when it comes to an end for if he is not killed a great many people think Ildefonso must retire at the end of next season.

" It has been a tremendous season for us and I am a great deal more tired than Paco ! I have seen nothing since Easter but roads and hotels and bullrings. We have had with us a good deal of the time a young American named Wilbur

Savage who is helping Paco to write his book and this has been quite a good thing because when there were a few days between Paco's dates we did sea-bathing or went up to the mountains for Paco to have baths and massage and the book kept him from being bored.

"I am not very sure about the book, but I have so much forgotten English that I think I may be mistaken. Paco of course cannot judge at all and they both laugh when I point out faults in spelling or grammar and say a torero is not supposed to write like a college professor, which no doubt is true. But I have read quite a few books by Americans and I think Wilbur Savage is not as good as he says he is. Cannot you come and stay with us after we come back from Mexico? If you will do that I will make them keep the book until you come. W.S. wants to rush it to the American publishers to be out next spring but it is not necessary I am sure, and in any case the translation will not be finished by then. Wilbur has a friend (Spanish) he wants to do the translation ; we met him (the friend) at Malaga, and he is not at all a person of education, nor does he know the andaluz. Wilbur and I agree that it would be a good thing to have parts of the book serialised in the andaluz and it will help to sell the book when it comes out in the castellano. But it must be very good or else it will not have a good éxito with the critics. It is naturally very important and interesting because no one knows as much about the theory and the practice as Paco but I think it is not at all well expressed and that is Wilbur Savage's fault for he does not seem to put down things the way Paco says them and I think he is trying to imitate other Americans who have written about the bulls.

"Paco asks me to thank you for the copies of *London and Paris* you sent. The pictures are very good, I think, although it is a pity they did not put in the one in the fighting suit, and Paco was a little disappointed that the only big one they used was the one of him with Remedios, instead of by himself. We both wondered why they printed *two* of Tano, with the bulls ; I think one would have been sufficient especially as they did not have any pictures of Paco with the bulls. Some of the pictures of the house are very nice and ought to be in the book, but it was very stupid to take Tano and Remedios on the staircase and all four of us together in the sala. I managed not to translate the article for Paco, it was all about the Albacobacas, was it not, and Paco was only mentioned twice, which would have annoyed him very much.

" We are just at home for a few days before Paco's last fight, at Zaragosa, and then we shall spend two weeks with some friends who have an estate in Morocco, so that he can relax before starting to get ready for the Mexican tour. Then we come back here so that I can put everything in order before we leave at the end of November. We shall be away all December and January.

" You *must* come to us in February for a long visit, for I am longing to show you all the alterations Paco and I have made since we got married! You would hardly know the house itself, and there are many improvements on the estate. Carlos is doing quite well. I had to dismiss the new mayoral when we came back last spring because he had not enough authority and many things were happening I did not like. Now everything seems satisfactory but there is a great deal to do before we go away.

" Queridísima Miss Mary, give us your word you will come : ' palabra inglesa ' !

" Paco sends un fuerte apretón de manos. Un abrazo con todo el cariño de tu amiga,

ARACEA

" Please give my love to Reverend Mother and Miss Morgan, and say I *insist* you come out here for a rest and a change from teaching ! I am sure it is not good always to be with English schoolgirls. You know it is wonderful here in the spring and we will give you a wonderful time. Then there will be the feria, and you will see what a stupendous matador Paco has become ! They've got a new name for him —' El Escudero.' He has only had two little scratches this season——"

She dashed her pen across the last sentence and went over it carefully, so that it was illegible ; better not tempt providence, Paco had one more fight to go, and it was at Zaragosa he got his last bad cogida. Her eyes ran rapidly over the pages ; she bundled them into an envelope and sealed it. Then, suddenly exhausted, she set her elbows on the table and her chin in the palms of her hands ; she looked out through the windows no longer black with ilex, and, without knowing it, her face aged.

That bright picture she had painted for Mary Carpenter ;— or, rather, for herself. Superficially, it was true ; they had gone through the months of March to September from triumph to triumph. Sleek with health, success and vanity, it naturally did not occur to Paco how much he owed to her. No matador at the height of his career had ever led a more sane and healthy life, none, certainly, reached the end of a strenuous season in such prime condition. All the theories of physical training learned at St. Margaret's—where, as in most English schools, " mens sana in corpore sano " was brought to the level of a cult—went into her care of him. His diet, his exercise—even his loving, up to a point, but here, as might be taken for granted, Paco was contumacious, and she would have been affronted if it had not been so !—were regulated by her, and her reward was in his flawless physique, his endless resilience and the hair-trigger perfection of his reactions. He slept like an infant, rose fresh as a lark, and, away from the bulls, appeared never to give them a thought. He could take an occasional binge—she knew better than to draw the reins too tight—without the least effect on his performances, and she had, she believed, after a long struggle and many arguments, managed to establish in his mind the connection between the moderation she had striven to enforce on him and the achievement of his ambitions. El Escudero, they had begun to call him —the armed one—because the fineness of his judgment and the impregnable sheath round himself and his valour, enabled him to take chances, suicidal to others, which, in the case of Paco, were not chances, but dead certainties. People were astonished, and sometimes shocked, by her coolness when Paco was in the ring ; but so long as he could depend on himself, she could depend on him. Through two seasons he had taken the horn only three times, and the wounds, though showy, were superficial; he healed like a healthy young dog. And this he owed to her.

Sometimes he was furious, and accused her of attempting to dominate him; and she was clever and humble and cajoling; and managed in the end to turn it into a jest that ended locked in each other's arms.

For the last few weeks he had been in a mood of smouldering irritability—as well he might be, having packed over seventy fights into six months—and she was disconcerted to find herself both mentally and physically unable to deal with him. And that was no wonder, either; for the endless travelling, coupled with ceaseless tension, had worn her out. Their loving had become, on Paco's side, a kind of fury, as though—the thought flashed into her mind one night when, fearless as she was, she found herself quailing under his savage attack—he were trying to punish her for something. What folly, she told herself, when his weight lay across her, leaden in sleep; I'm tired—too tired; that's all. She shed a few tears of self-pity, and woke him by laughing hysterically at herself, and he made love to her again, but, this time, so tenderly and gently that she felt herself dissolving in ecstasy. They were both a little overwrought with the work and the travelling; all that would smooth itself out when they got to Morocco.

It was a pity, really, that they had taken these few days at Parral, instead of accepting the Albacobacas invitation, but, apart from the fact that Tano's and Remedios's house-parties were apt to be uproarious, and that after fighting five days in succession (that was bad management on the part of Don Pasquale), it would do Paco good to be quiet for a while, she had begun to be uneasy about affairs at home.

Carlos had, inevitably, assumed the full authority of dueño; it could not be otherwise, during their long absences. She had confidence in the new mayoral, but knew Carlos was capable of obstructing him in the performance of his duties—for no reason but that he was her choice, and not Carlos's. She knew all about

Carlos's indolence, and was prepared, on their return, to find the accounts in chaos. And so it had proved. Asked, on the evening of their arrival, to produce the books, Carlos answered easily, " Mañana." She looked him straight in the eye. " Mañana por la mañana—por favor. I'll be down at ten o'clock."

" A sus ordenes, señora." He bowed ironically, and to her rage, she saw a glance pass between him and Paco. She felt the two men in sympathy against her, a woman. Qué perfidia ! She went out of the room. When she returned, having regained her self-control, Paco was alone. She laid her hand gently on his shoulder.

" Amigo. You and Carlos get on very well together, but I am your wife."

" Qué ? " gaped Paco, who seldom saw any point which was not put to him in plain syllables.

" It doesn't matter ; but Parral belongs to me," she emphasised.

" Claro, it belongs to you." He no longer pretended not to understand ; he spoke quite gently. " Mujer, a man does not like being given orders by a woman—especially in front of someone else."

" But don't you realise," she cried " the only way of getting anywhere with Carlos is to *insist*."

Paco shrugged his shoulders.

" When we are away Carlos has all the responsibility."

" Yes—unfortunately ! But the final responsibility, to Papá, to my grandfather and to our customers is mine. *I* am the one who writes the cheques, *my* name is on the bills, *my* credit will suffer if people are not satisfied," she emphasised ; she could have added—" and yours as well," but wished at all costs not to offend him, so that he would league himself with Carlos against her.

" Por cierto," agreed Paco, " but in my opinion you will not improve matters unless you get rid of Carlos."

" And how can I do that ? " she cried. "You know he's on, the consejo, together with my uncles ! I'm only a shareholder the same as they are, and though I've got the controlling number of shares, I'm completely helpless against those men. They say —and I suppose they're right—a woman can't run a ranch; and this is a beautiful job for Carlos, to whose support they might otherwise be obliged to contribute, since he left the Army——"

"I know all that; and if you are dissatisfied with the way Carlos handles the business, there's only one thing to do."

"And what may that be?"

Again he shrugged; his eyes avoided hers.

"Obviously, to stay where you can keep an eye on him."

Her lips opened, then closed and tightened. She changed the subject; but she lay awake that night, wondering whether Paco really meant it; whether he cared so little for her company and her solicitude that he was willing to leave her at Parral, and go on his journeys by himself. Her astonishment for a while dulled the pain of the wound he had dealt her, and, when astonishment began to die down, anger and obstinacy took charge. Por dios, no! Whatever solution was found, it should not be that.

When she went down to the office in the morning, she found, as she expected, that the books were not ready. She set her teeth and sat down to wait—having realised, from a glance at the files and in some of the drawers of the desk, that she could not hope to make sense of the jumble they contained. The room, like the rest of the house, had been redecorated—that is to say, the smoky walls and ceiling were now varnished white and the paintwork pale grey. Littered as it had been in Don Luis's day, the litter was no less, but had altered its character; a number of novels jostled stud books on the shelves; two guitars lay on the top of a cupboard: on the borders of the bullfight posters were pinned various photographs of a young woman with flashing teeth and gipsy curls plastered on her temples—evidently the current charmer. A strong smell of scent made Aracea contract her nostrils; like most of her sex, she detested other women's scent. No woman, in Don Luis's time, had ever crossed this threshold, save on the briefest of business.

Carlos lounged in, looking as though he had not been to bed, and apologised for keeping her waiting.

"It is of no importance. And please leave the door open," she said crisply. "Well—the books?"

"Bueno—presently." He offered her a cigarette and she waved it aside.

"Excuse me. I have many things to do, and we are going to ride round the new buildings before lunch." She threw her cheque book on the table. "When we have been through the accounts, perhaps you will be so good as to make those out and I'll sign them this afternoon."

"There is a small matter that calls for our attention before the accounts," he said dryly. "The men are asking for more wages."

"Absurd. The season's nearly over, there will be less work, and we're paying the union rates already."

"That's all quite true. They want a rise of three pesetas."

"But it's ruinous!" cried Aracea. "Of course you told them so?—What are you hiding?" she added sharply.

He spread out his hands with a grimace.

"It would be difficult to hide the fact that no animals have been carted from this ranch for the last four days."

"The men are on strike?" she gasped. He nodded. She calculated silently. "Do you mean the bulls haven't left for Ubeda on the twenty-eighth?"

Carlos shook his head. She asked more questions, which he answered coolly. She snatched up the pad on which were rcorded the bookings.

"The lot for Antequera should be going out to-day. I suppose we'll have to pay," she muttered. To default on two loads of cattle was impossible, apart from the loss, for the credit of Parral. She pointed to the telephone. "Go on; ring the mayoral and say they'll get their money. And we'll sack every damned one at the end of the month!" she ended viciously.

Carlos looked at the tip of his cigarette.

"The Antequera lot aren't down. They should have been brought in on Tuesday; the men walked out on Monday night," he offered.

She looked at him for a moment without speaking.

"Bueno," she said slowly. "I shall go and see the mayoral myself. And please have the books ready by the time I am back."

"Buena suerte," He rose and bowed ironically.

"Carlos," she paused at the door to ask, "why did you not telephone me that all this was going on?"

"I rang four times and left a message." Although aware of the unreliability of hotel concierges, she knew he was lying; she tipped enough to make sure of getting her messages.

"But—it was extraordinary of you, not to mention it, when we arrived last night!" she said slowly.

"Why spoil your homecoming, prima mia?—There was nothing to be done, by the time you arrived."

She glanced at her watch; there was no time to have a horse round. As the car bowled down the new avenue of elms she thought, There's something very wrong going on here. Paid at full union rates, well-housed and well-fed, Parral workers had always been noted for their loyalty. Never had such a thing as a strike been known in the days of Don Luis. Could she possibly have made a mistake over her appointment of the mayoral?—Her uneasiness on this score was relieved when she looked into a pair of grey Andalucían eyes and saw the evident distress on the man's face. Benito Gálvez, the new mayoral, was a superior type, of old-fashioned stock that saw no shame in deference to its superiors. She was led into a room as empty as the street down which she had just driven; a room out of which a gentle-faced young woman had swept an armful of children on her arrival. The room and the house were as conscious as the street of the arrival of the dueña.

Inside of an hour Aracea had the full story. They were not mala gente; they did not wish to make trouble. But there had been much mischief: this emerged from a labyrinth of Andalucían evasion. The men did not know whom to obey: Don Carlos or himself, Benito Gálvez. Don Carlos had one way, and he another; he was obliged, very often, to act on his own authority, because Don Carlos was not available. The men did not like it when they got into trouble for acting on his, Benito's, instructions, and they decided, finally, to strike. They made the rise in wages a pretext because they did not wish to put him in a bad position with the dueña; Don Carlos was the cousin of the dueña, and it would naturally be difficult for her to take Benito's part.

" But, Benito, couldn't you have persuaded them to load the bulls for Ubeda ?—You know how bad it is for our credit not to keep our contracts."

She gathered, from much circumlocution, that it had been taken for granted that the dueña would be informed, on the day the decision was taken; that her return was expected at any hour, and that several of the men would have gone back to work if they had not been over-persuaded by their companions, who thought it was right that the dueña should find out what went on in her absence.

" And what does go on ? "—It was like drawing a tooth, finally to extract the information that Don Carlos spent the greater part of his time away from the ranch; that he left on the evening the men declared their intention, and only returned a few hours before the dueña's arrival. That he, Benito, had taken the autobus into Sevilla, to search for Don Carlos, and could come on no trace of him. On his return, he had pleaded with the men, and cursed them; they were not to be persuaded—even when he told them that, as the result of this action, he would very likely lose his job.

She sat for a while in silence. Carlos must have known she would find all this out; but, secure in the support of his kinsfolk, he did not care. Was he such a fool—were they all such fools— as to imagine that an estate like Parral could be run with an absentee manager ? One, moreover, who was not satisfied to abide by his absenteeism, but made of his returns an excuse for undermining the authority of one who did his best to carry out the duties he—Carlos—neglected ? Had he the education to deal with correspondence and keep accounts (at which Carlos was proven bad enough), Benito would have made a thousand times better manager than Carlos.

" Can anything be done," she asked, " about Antequera ? "

" Seguro, señora ! "—His face lit up. " We can have the bulls down this afternoon. Although it is late in the season, they are not bad ; a day of readying, instead of three, will be sufficient, and they can leave at midday to-morrow—if——"

" Pues—what's your condition ? "

" Not mine, señora," he reproached her. " But the men will ask for assurance whose orders they are to take ; whether mine or those of Don Carlos."

" Bueno ; I will talk it over with Don Carlos." For the sake of any authority Carlos might have, she would not commit herself further. She rose. " You will tell the men that Antequera is expecting its bulls. You will tell them "—she moistened her lips—" that most of them worked for my father. You will tell them that Parral is a great name, and its honour rests in their hands. You will tell them that, although I married Ribera, I am the daughter of Parral, and I claim their loyalty in the name of my father——"

The words held an echo of the past that carried no message to a modern age. She knew how useless an appeal it would have been to industrial workers, builders, the men who worked on the forges—to a generation reared with the doctrines of communism ringing in its ears ; but these were the aristocracy of labour, bred, like nobles, to attendance on the great royal race of bulls. She saw the light in her own eyes reflected in those of her companion ; suddenly she thrust out her hand, and felt it swallowed in a big hard palm. Benito ; he was to be trusted to find the right things to say. Now to get home, and deal with Carlos.

The interview was conducted with surprising mildness. She took care to flatter him, to emphasise the confidence Don Luis had reposed in him, to assure him of her own support—if things worked out to her satisfaction. (What did he care, so long as he drew his salary and his dividends ?)

" You see, Carlos," she said craftily, " if Benito has his instructions from you, he can save you a great deal of trouble, by dealing directly with the men ; and the more unapproachable you are, to the workers, the more you'll have authority. The whole thing was a misunderstanding, and now it's cleared up. Benito will come up and have a talk with you about future arrangements, and we'll have a discussion, beforehand, so that he knows you and I are in agreement. That will strengthen his position, as well as yours, and you will find that everything will settle down quite peacefully, and you will have much more time to look after the accounts—which, naturally, Benito knows nothing whatever about."

He looked at her ironically, under a lowered eyelid.

" So you're going to Mexico with Paco, after all ? "

She stiffened.

" What do you suppose ? "

II

" Don Pasquale is here, señora."

She swept round from the table.

" Bueno ; have you told Don Paco ? "

" The señor is asleep. I knocked at his door ; there was no answer."

" Ask Don Pasquale to come in."

She was prepared. She crossed the floor and held out her hand as Don Pasquale was ushered through the double doors. They hated each other, so their greeting was more than amiable.

" Encantado, Don Pasquale. I will go and wake Paco up. Una copita ? "—She indicated the glasses on a side table.

" Muchas gracias." He wagged a negatory finger. " Mucho cambiado," he added, glancing round the room.

" I forgot ; you must often have been in here, in my father's time."

" Not often," corrected Don Pasquale ; he had, actually, suffered only one uncomfortable introduction into the realm of the wife of Parral. The room was certainly much more agreeable ; he approved of the light paint, the disappearance of the depressing layers of books, the light modern furniture ; a woman's room, but not too womanish. The chair which his hostess indicated, although austere in outline, was surprisingly comfortable. It was a stylish background for a matador.

" I'll go and fetch Paco."

" Let him sleep for the present." He stiffened, looking up at the elegant girl who, by misfortune, was the wife of Ribera. " Will the señora accept a cigarette ? "—He produced his case.

" No, thanks ; I don't smoke much.—Of course," she returned, to his " Con su permiso ? " She sat, smiling slightly, while he spun the wheel of his lighter. What was this visit about ? Paco was not expecting it, or he would have told her. She decided suddenly to carry the fire into the enemy's camp. " Well, Don Pasquale ; I think you are pleased at the results of our first season ? "

" Qué—O, muy bien, muy bien," he grunted, through the smoke of the cigarette.

" Paco has advanced very much," she stated. He looked down his nose at her ; who was she, a woman and a wife, to offer her opinion ? " I think it would have been better, not to give him those five fights in succession——"

" Oiga," said Don Pasquale. " I think, señora, it is time we had a talk, and, with Paco asleep, this is a good opportunity."

" Con mucho gusto," she answered politely. She smiled at him, got up, lit one of her own cigarettes and returned to her chair. Don Pasquale said :

" I am not at all satisfied with Paco."

" Como ? "—He had startled her. " But I don't understand."

" Naturally," said Don Pasquale dryly.

She bit back her anger. So this was going to be another show-down. What a home-coming ! But perhaps it would clear the air between her and the enemy. So she moistened her lips and spoke mildly.

" We are both agreed on one point ; that we're devoted to Paco's interests. If you will tell me what is disturbing you, I will see what can be done about it."

" Don't molest yourself ; what is to be done I will do, if——" Don Pasquale checked himself ; he was used to being courteous with women, but the wife of Paco put a great strain on his politeness. She said, after a pause :

" But you *must* be gratified ! Paco is now at the head of his profession ; he's one of the three best-paid matadores in Spain. He has a long career ahead of him——"

" Perhaps too long." She stared at him. " A dish that is served at every meal loses its savour."

" But that is exactly my opinion ! " she cried triumphantly. " That is why I have never wanted Paco to work these long seasons—taking four or five fights a week ! No one can last against the strain of that. Look at Ildefonso—he's only a few years older than my husband, but he's already an old man. Why should a torero be finished by the time he's thirty—as many of them are ? If Paco continues to follow his regime——"

Don Pasquale wagged his head slowly.

" It is, perhaps, that a matador cannot be bred in the way you breed a fighting bull. Oiga : from the day it is born, the brave bull is surrounded with care, it is isolated, its feeding is regulated, its virginity is preserved, for the sake of that one hour in the ring when, by its manner of dying, it justifies the seed. The matador must live through many hours, señora ; he must look upon death often and closely, he must be familiar with death as with his brother ; and, like his brother, he must never forget him. And the more often he looks upon that Face, the greater he becomes——"

" Don Pasquale, you are telling me things I know already. The brave bull is born to die, and so, perhaps, in the end, is the matador ; but the bull's glory is in rushing upon death, and the matador's in defending himself. The better form he is in, the stronger are his defences. If the bull is in perfect condition, why not the torero ?—I know what is in your mind, and I know that a great many people agree with you: but surely no particular credit attaches to taking into the ring a ruined body—to adding that much hazard to the lawful ones of the fight ? "

" The ruined body was once the means of changing the whole art of fighting," said Don Pasquale meaningly.

"Come, there was only one Belmonte. Let us speak in general; let us talk, if you like, in the abstract." Her rancour forgotten for the moment, Aracea leaned earnestly on the edge of the table. Don Pasquale shifted uneasily; women who talked were the devil, especially educated women—like this one. At all costs he would put a stop to a matter that was being discussed in the family: the entrance of one of his granddaughters to a university.

"To present the bull with an effete adversary is to dishonour it in some way—no?" (This was one of Mary Carpenter's theories.) "It is like watching a man knock down a cripple. If the bull were human, it would reject its enemy for the sake of its own dignity——"

"Bulls are not human," muttered Don Pasquale disgustedly. "What would Luis have said to all this? How had Amadeo put up with it? What in God's name was the matter with the Niño, not to put a stop to it?—" And cripples, as you call them, have killed many bulls."

"Conforme. But let us imagine, for a moment, the perfect torero!—the athlete, trained as the Greeks trained their young warriors——"

Don Pasquale sulked; he knew nothing about Greek athletes and cared less. He wished he had never embarked on this interview and his temper was rising.

"Or, if it comes to that—the way the young men at English universities go into training for the boat-race——"

"Mother of Jesus!" shouted Don Pasquale. "Do you, the daughter of Parral, the wife of the Niño de Maderas, compare the bullfight to the boat-race?"

"Don't be foolish, amigo." She flashed her teeth at him. "You have just said that the ruined body once changed the whole art of fighting; I say that the perfect body might change it again; that things might become possible which can never be attempted unless the one who attempts them is as sure of himself as—as an angel," she concluded with a laugh.

He looked at her from under his lowered lids with an illimitable contempt.

"*You* think that the great matador is made out of bone and muscle and flesh?"

"That is ridiculous; it is deliberately perverting my meaning!"—She had begun to be angry again. "You know very well what I mean: that valour and honour and will come before everything, but why should those have to carry a body that is rotten with abuse? I will tell you what would be the great matador: a combination of Paco and Ildefonso—with Ildefonso's genius and Paco's physical strength and courage."

"And where, do you suppose, Ildefonso gets his genius?"

"Do you mean, he gets it out of his drinking and his women?" she said scornfully. "That is a very old-fashioned idea, Don Pasquale! Ildefonso has been ' forced,' because he has had much more experience than Paco, although they started about the same time. Wait a year or two!—and you will see."

Don Pasquale reached for his hat. There was nothing to be gained by further argument, but he had not reached the point towards which he was travelling.

"You are going to Mexico with Paco?" he said abruptly.

"But naturally."

Her smiling assurance burst something inside his brain. Don Pasquale Basilio was not merely a man of business; he was a dedicated spirit. He had not much power of expressing himself —that he left to the writers, the artists, the intellectuals of his wide acquaintance. Among the bullfighters he handled were many with not a third of the cartel of the Niño de Maderas, but much more flair than he seemed likely to possess. Yet Paco was a first-class espada, with an established public; it might not have been so, thought Don Pasquale grimly, in the old days, when the afición was greater and more discriminating, when the detestable and degrading game of football had not undermined the rising generation and the depleted ranks of the faithful were not so ready to accept competence in the place of genius. The name of Ildefonso, it was true, embodied a superstition, even among those lost souls who watched, and played, the ball game, and there were two or three others to whom Don Pasquale and his kind pinned their faith; he wanted Paco to be one of them.

He liked the boy, he gave him full credit for his technical perfection—but he could not forgive the emptiness of his performances. He came out on the sand like a charming robot, with an air of invulnerability ; given a good bull, he put on a show of dazzling variety, the crowd yelled, gaped, Paco collected the ear—almost as a matter of routine—and only the old hands along the barrera were conscious of not having had their money's worth. It was a curious and baffling sensation, not easily put into words. It infuriated Don Pasquale. It infuriated him even more, when other professionals, at the mention of Paco's name, hoisted a shoulder and smiled in a certain way ; it might be jealousy, but ribaldry, when it reflects jealousy, is dangerous, and soon spreads. The hawk-eye of Don Pasquale had watched it spreading and, as the Niño's manager, it stung his dignity.

That smiling certainty of Aracea's broke down the last resources of the politeness he owed to Paco's wife.

" They call him El Escudero," he said.

" Yes; it is a good name," agreed Aracea. "Very appropriate."

The eyelids of Don Pasquale narrowed.

" The other name they give him is not so good."

Her lip curled amusedly.

" And what is that ? " she challenged him.

Don Pasquale's nostrils expanded as he drew a deep breath through them. He had gone so far ; let it be the whole way. He hissed :

" El Impotente ! "—and had the satisfaction of seeing her face blanch as though he had struck it. " You will excuse me, señora ; muy buenas tardes."

III

During the last six months, Aracea had taken advantage of her married status and her position as the dueña of Parral to claim a seat on the barrera. Paco, to begin with, had objected ; ladies—except for a few foreign women, and the wives of elderly aficionados—did not sit on the barrera; the palcos were for them.

"I know, chico," she coaxed him, "but if I sit in the palco I have to be with a lot of silly women who don't know anything about the bulls and spend half their time trying to catch the piropo! I don't go to the fight to chatter about Dior and Schiaparelli and hear the local scandal.—Of course," she added, artfully, "I won't come down to the front if it makes you nervous."

This drew, as she expected, a shout of laughter from Paco.

"Mujer! What do you imagine you are—a bull?"

She had, of course, to find a companion, for the prejudices of sex and class did not permit a beautiful young woman to sit alone on the barrera, even if she were the wife of a matador, so, unless she were going with English or American friends, she took a servant; she preferred this because she was not obliged to talk, and could deliver herself completely to the action beyond the rail. She was annoyed to hear that Wilbur Savage was joining them at Zaragosa, because he would take it for granted they should sit together, and his drawling assumption of special knowledge in regard to everything that went on in the ring irritated her—although she was obliged to admit that most of his judgments were right. When they met, however, at the hotel, Wilbur had collected a party of his own, an American girl and a French boy who, it appeared, had no word either of Spanish or English. Rapidly deciding to pretend that she knew no French at all, Aracea arranged that he should sit next to her, insulating her from the other couple, and thus securing for her the mental isolation she preferred while watching the fight.

It was the last fight of the Zaragosa season, and the names of Ildefonso, Niño de Maderas and a young, very promising novillero they called Dinamo packed the tiers. There was not a bed to be had in the town, to which the fans had flocked from all parts of the country, and fights kept breaking out between customers who found themselves crowded out of their seats; the Civil Guard, there to deal with such incidents, abandoned themselves to a majestic aloofness and confined themselves to a few languid gestures directing the crowds that poured up the steps.

It was not a good day; overcast and chilly, with some wind. Aracea pressed down the skull-cap of dark green velvet and turned up the collar of her loose woollen coat. The French boy took shy refuge in a paper-backed edition of Pierre Mac Orlan, and the Americans were self-absorbed. Paco's sword boy, Tonio, came along the callejón, nodded up at her and began to spread out the fighting capes, fold them and lay them over the inner barrier; then he bent down and laid open the case of swords on the top of a basket, just below her feet. The beautiful Toledo swords looked cold and lifeless in the grey light.

Where they were sitting, they were almost opposite the Puerto de Cuadrillas; she could see the men collecting; the bad light stole the colour from their suits and reduced them to chalky patches of pink, green or orange. She lifted her field-glasses; there was Paco, well in the foreground, light-heartedly smoking a cigarette and apparently cracking a joke with the new boy, whose mouth wrenched itself into a smile, while his eyes were blank with terror. Paco was wearing one of the new suits they had ordered for Mexico; he looked superb. It would be a pity if the rain spoiled it; he had insisted on putting it on— she guessed, because of Ildefonso. Where was Ildefonso?—Ah, there he came, under the archway: his head poked forward between his shoulders, his eyes shifting to left and right, as though seeking a means of escape. It looked as if it might be one of his bad days. Poor devil; what a waste of all that glory. Yet—you could not look at Ildefonso without feeling something—something———

Paco invaded her line of vision. Through the glasses she saw him toss away the cigarette, walk up to Ildefonso and clap his arm round his shoulders. And then—she strained her eyes incredulously. Ildefonso switched his head away, flung off Paco's friendly arm, and, pushing through the cuadrillas, went to lean on the partition, with his back to his companions.

It could have been a nervous reaction; few people were as cool as Paco before going into the ring. But the look on Paco's face, his schoolboyish look of surprise and discomfiture, told her it was something more. What had happened between these two, long comrades and friends? Why should Ildefonso put an affront like that on Paco, just as they were going out to take equal risks, and lend colour to the malicious legends about their enmity? If she had observed it, many others must have done so as well. She lowered the glasses resentfully. Down in the callejón, under a white hat, she recognised the broken profile of Don Pasquale; he raised the hat, she bowed coldly. She would never forgive him; suddenly she began to wonder whether he, also, was one of Paco's enemies, to plan ways of persuading Paco to get rid of someone who, while taking his money, traduced him behind his back. If Don Pasquale would say such things to her, what would he say to others?

They had not sent Parral bulls to Zaragosa, so she was at liberty to concentrate on the men. As the paseo broke up, and the passage below her filled itself with the matadores and their cuadrillas, Tonio handed up Paco's cape; spreading it mechanically on the rail in front of her, her eyes anxiously sought her husband's. Paco looked up and grinned; he had already forgotten about Ildefonso—who, a little farther along the barrera, was propping himself against the wooden blocks and retching, in a vain attempt to expel some of the bile that these moments of anticipation brought up in his throat. Thinner than a drain-pipe, bent at knees and shoulders, he seemed hardly to have the strength to support the cape his man handed him. But when he rested his elbows on the top of the barrier, to watch the preliminary caping of the first bull, Aracea found herself unable to take her eyes away from that beaked profile with its line of unconscious doom. She had never observed it closely before; apart from her attention being given to Paco, it was the man's work and not his appearance that roused her interest. As Paco's rival, she had long had a secret antagonism to Ildefonso, which she knew Paco did not share. Paco's self-confidence did not leave him time to trouble about rivals, and, when Ildefonso was gone, there would only be one Niño de Maderas! She had often reminded herself of this, and told herself that the Ildefonso

Legend would die as quickly as it had arisen; that only a few names had survived the disappearance of those who bore them, and that no one had ever claimed for Ildefonso that he was a Joselito or a Manolete. He was—just Ildefonso; the ragged boy who had taught her, as a child, to use the cape in the cellars of Parral, who, thanks to her father, had had the chance denied to many no less talented, and who had made good.

She reminded herself of all this: and yet—it was as though the grisly light, like twilight of the gods, brought up something she had never noticed on the many occasions she had watched Ildefonso in the full burn of the sun: something that hypnotised, puzzled and evaded her; something to which she could not put a name—but she found herself thinking of one of the El Grecos Mary Carpenter had made her look at, in the Prado. The way the starved, deteriorated body hung on the barrier, with drooping head and bent knees, was almost the attitude of the Crucifixion.

She caught herself up, scandalised by the licence of her own imagination: shocked to discover that Paco was in the ring and that she had not even noticed his entrance. The figure on the barrier slowly straightened, almost as though the effort gave it pain. Cautiously it drove its heels down on the earth, and waited; and those who were watching—because, to them, the stillness of Ildefonso was more significant than the action of the Niño de Maderas—saw, as it were the sap rising, strength flow up into the limbs and along the spine. With his movement of a leopard, El Aguilucho padded along the callejón below Aracea, who, although she did not look down, was as aware as though he had touched her.

She must be going crazy. She fixed her eyes in desperation on Paco, winding the bull round him like a kitten after a ball of string—and seemingly as carelessly. He was getting the Olés all right; with his usual neat timing, he left the bull fixed, and swaggered coolly away just as the trumpet sounded. As though he could hear her, Aracea muttered to Ildefonso, " You can't beat that ! " and the French boy, looking round startled, inquired:

" Vous dites, madame——? "

" Rien," muttered Aracea, forgetting she was not supposed

to speak French. She forced all her attention on the ring—ay, Paco was right, for cursing Curro. The luckless picador suffered the customary abuse, and allowed himself philosophically to be plucked off the barrier, as the horse went down. She heard the American girl exclaim :

" Say, Wilbur, this is disgusting ! "

The bull was badly damaged, and no particular credit attached to Paco for planting his three sets of darts with his usual flourish, but the crowd in the sombra gave him his Olés and the crowd in the sun yelled its head off; he had done it once with his back to the barrier and once sitting on the stirrup—circus tricks that invariably get the cheaper parts of the house, showy, and admittedly dangerous, the older fans do not hold with them, but Paco's public had learned to expect them. (" And you can't do that anyhow." Why had she got to be aware of the figure in orange and gold, a little to her left, which had not moved from beginning to end of the suerte ?)

There was no point in prolonging the muleta act, because the bull had evidently had enough—which was a pity, because it showed Paco to his best advantage. He managed to make it take a few passes, to an increasingly impatient house, but there was no time for adornos, and, after the kill, no question of an ear. Aracea's heart ached for him as he came sullenly back into the callejón ; he had done the best he could. The young Dinamo went up to him and obviously said " Bad luck, chum ! " but Paco acted as though he was not there. His back turned to Ildefonso, he was chatting with one of the Civil Guard.

Dinamo had drawn what turned out to be the best bull of the day, and in spite of the wind that had risen, and the hampering necessity of working with a wet cape, justified his sobriquet. Getting into trouble in the suerte of the muleta, both Paco and Ildefonso went in to help him. He killed with much style, and got an ear, because he was still a novillero, and Zaragosa believes in encouraging promising young toreros.

When Ildefonso went in, for the third bull, the whole atmosphere of the ring changed. Aracea felt it, resentfully. So this was what came of a legend. Accustomed as she had become, to the sensation surrounding Ildefonso's appearances, she had never before been conscious, in quite this way, of his hold on the public. Certainly she had never felt it herself! Ildefonso was " un milagro," and did certain things in a way that had not been done before, and the contacts he established with his bulls was something like brujería, but she had never abandoned herself to his genius, in the way most of the fans did! Why should she? She was the wife of a famous matador, who could do things Ildefonso, on account of his physical shortcomings, could not attempt. She decided coldly to analyse the spell Ildefonso cast upon his audiences; to destroy, if possible, for her own satisfaction, the great illusion which, apparently, blinded fifty per cent of his admirers to the weak spots in his performances, and excused them to the rest. He had been known to come out of the ring in a rain of bottles and cushions; the critics had torn his reputation in shreds—and one of them had been forced, by so august an authority that it was not to be gainsaid, to recant in public of his opinions. The name of Ildefonso was defended with knives, and, however vile a show he put up, he was received on his return like a king.

. . . Half an hour later, Aracea awoke, as one awakes after a crack on the head, or from a long, exhausting dream. They were shackling up the horses, to drag out the dead bull. Trotting towards her from the medios came a figure, with a lump of fur clutched in its hands. The air still crackled with shouts, the cuadrilla was picking up flowers, cigars and cigarette cases, and slinging hats back into the audience. But the figure came on. It was like being in a cinema, watching a train rushing towards one : at any moment it would break out of the screen, over their heads. The headlights of the train were a pair of eyes sunk in the caverns of a face carved out of yellow wood. They remained fixed on hers, as Ildefonso came into the callejón. They carried a message—or a threat? She was incapable of thinking; everything inside her was draining out, towards those voracious eyes . . .

Paco did better with his second bull, and got an ear. She drew a breath of relief; the disaster of last year had not been repeated. And young Dinamo rode on the horn and was carried to the infirmary with a punctured intestine.

She drew a difficult breath as the last bull came in. Ildefonso did not even glance at her as he stepped through the barrier and unfurled his cape for the first of his fabled verónicas. She found her eyes were misting as the famous series of passes followed their routine of cold, pure dignity. Ay, no one could use the cape like Ildefonso. His relationship to the bull, no less than his movements, lifted the whole act on to a sacramental plane ; when he drew the bull round him, standing straight, so close that the horn brushed his stomach in passing, it was an act of love ; when, having fixed it, he laid his hand for a moment on its lowered brow, it was a blessing. The crowd was already hysterical when the suerte ended ; it was one of Ildefonso's " great days," that set the seal upon the name of El Aguilucho.

In the act of the horse Paco took the first quite, which he finished with a showy revolera, and Ildefonso signalled to him to take the second, which would have been Dinamo's. Charmed to do so, Paco went into a spectacular farola, ending with the serpentina, which earned him a shower of Olés, and sent him swaggering towards the fence, very pleased with himself. Ildefonso took the third, in which the matador is expected to outclass his rivals in style and variety.

Stepping quietly forward, he drew the cape across the bull's nose while its head was still buried in the horse, and, as though the cape were a magnet and the nose made of steel, it came out, following the backward movement of the man. As it broke into a rush, Ildefonso drew it into the cape softly, like a caress. There were a dozen passes he might have chosen ; as master of the cape, he was master of them all. He chose to butterfly it very gently and slowly across the ring, and those old enough to remember Lalanda had tears in their eyes when he ended the faena with a series of verónicas so close that the front of the orange suit was smeared with red when he lifted his head and walked smilelessly out towards the yelling crowd.

While his banderilleros placed the darts, Aracea saw him walk up to Paco. She could not hear what they were saying but she

saw a look of astonishment come over Paco's face; he seemed
to hesitate, then he nodded his head—" Sí-sí "—she thought
doubtfully.

She saw Gatito pass the folded muleta across the barrier to
Ildefonso, and the latter, montera in hand, walk out opposite
the box of the presidente. She realised that he was coming back,
that he was standing opposite her. Impossible; he could not be
dedicating his bull to her. In her confusion, she did not catch
the words; but, as he wheeled towards the ring and the montera
flew over his shoulder, Paco, with a leap like a footballer, caught
it and handed it up to her with a wink.

Paco was rather distant and offhand when they got back to
the hotel. She decided not to duck it, but to tackle him right-
away.

" It was nice of Ildefonso, to dedicate his last bull to me. It
was nice of you, to allow him."

" I wasn't too pleased," grunted Paco.

" Amigo, it meant nothing; really, it was a tribute to Papá,
who made Ildefonso what he is."

She knew he was looking at her out of the corners of his
eyes. She busied herself at the dressing table. Above all—for
the present—she must not *think*! There was time enough—too
much time—to face the truth: that Ildefonso was, for ever, the
maestro, and that Paco was—a very, very good bullfighter. *And
we love each other*, she told herself; as though that stood for
anything, against the claim of a pair of voracious eyes.

Next day, the critics went to town with a full column on
Ildefonso; they gave Paco an adulatory, but slightly patronising
paragraph, and Dinamo a line or two, which was less than he
deserved, but the boy was short of money.

" The Mexican public is indeed to be congratulated in receiving the greatest matador of our day——"

Paco swore, bunched the paper and flung it across the room.

" And what about me ?—The sons of whores ! As if I haven't
greased their dirty palms from the hour I went into the ring."

For once she was silent. She, who once would have shared
in his virulence, wondered if, after all, bullfighting journalism

was not as corrupt as it was made out to be. But Paco should
be *made* as great as Ildefonso ! He'd got everything—got it all—
except that unnameable something, which (she told herself) was
just the outcome of hard experience. Perhaps she had been
wrong, in persuading him to limit the number of his fights ;
perhaps Don Pasquale was right. . . . In any case, in that matter
she would interfere no more.

Chapter Five

I

" MANFREDI WANTS another fitting," said Paco laconically.

" Right." She had heard the telephone, but she was talking
to Concepción, now, next to the dueña, the most responsible
figure in the house of Parral ; but Concepción was growing
very old, and it was a worry, sometimes, to know how to replace
her. Only to Concepción could be entrusted the keys of the
stores, in the dueña's absence, and, to look after Concepción,
there was her great-nephew, a handsome, humble-mannered boy
who had grown up on the estate, and was now employed in the
house. Honest, reliable, very serious and religious, he, Antolín,
stood respectfully behind his aunt's chair ; he was her body-
guard, helping her up and down the worn staircases, fetching
and carrying for her, interpreting for her the written instructions
of the dueña, which she could not read. " You'll be in for
lunch ? " Aracea called after Paco, who stood hesitating in the
door.

" I don't expect so. I think I'll go over and see Mamá."

" Then you won't be back to-night ? "—She turned round,
surprised.

" There's nothing for me to do here."

" So long as Tonio knows about the packing." She got up

and followed him on to the gallery. "Nothing's the matter, is it ? "

"What should be the matter ?—I must see Mamá before we go away."

"Claro." Down in the patio, evidently by Paco's orders, was the big convertible he had recently bought from Tano Albacobaca. Tano let him have it at a bargain (according to Paco). It was ruinous in gasolina, but he was delighted with it— especially as no one was allowed to drive it but himself. The old car was finished at the end of the season, only fit for hacking about the estate, or short runs into town. When they got back from Mexico, there would have to be a new van for the cuadrilla. But she hated Paco's new buy, its flamboyance, its roar, the hood that let in rain and the want of the comforts to which she was accustomed. It was a man's car, and a sheer extravagance, for when he was working Paco obviously could not drive, and it lay up in the garage, dropping value with every month. However, when they came back there should be enough in hand to pick up a good English saloon at one of the dealer's.

They kissed, and, very dapper in a new grey suit with a light overcoat by a Madrid tailor, Paco ran down the stairs, and, a moment later, shot under the archway with a wave of the hand, a roar and a spurt of gasolina. As he burned up the road to town, he had a lightsome feeling ; a feeling—of which he was slightly ashamed—of escape.

He had a pleasurable session at Manfredi's, and a gratifying reception in the clubs. Caught up in a ring of admirers, he was persuaded to stay on. Shortly after dawn, he left a flamenco party in Triana, and set out for Maderas. Sleep overcame him in the cork forests, and it was dusk when he reached the Casa Cigarrón—his first visit home since his father died.

He had not announced his arrival. When the outcry of astonishment and greeting died down, he had a curious feeling of being a stranger. They seemed to be looking at him from a distance, with awe—because he was a famous matador—and with something like fear. Josú, what had they to be afraid about ?

He spent the evening trying to get on terms with his elder

brothers. He asked about the business, and their replies, though not unfriendly, seemed to him both grudging and evasive. He felt puzzled. The house was evidently flourishing; there were two new assistants, the shop was crowded at all hours with customers. It dawned on him that they were afraid he would ask them for money!—a good joke, that.

But the worst was Mamá. Loaded with black, she had taken to sitting under Papá's enlarged and coloured photograph— usually in tears. Her heavy cheeks sodden, the corners of her mouth pulled down in a perpetual grimace, as though she were about to let out a wail—her great black eyes pouched in leaden circles, held an endless accusation. He had deserted her, and his home, for a woman who set him against his family and his class; who ignored her existence and had given her no grandchildren. He, the sun of her soul, the favourite of all her children, no longer belonged to her; he belonged to a world in which she had no share, and from which she was excluded by his wife.

He felt the injustice of it; they had begged her, repeatedly, to come to Parral. Even when Papá was alive, apart from one grudging visit, she had refused their invitations. It was, perhaps, the fault of Aracea; brought up in a different manner, she did not understand Mamá, she did not know how to talk to her. She could not picture—as he could—Mamá's discomfiture in unfamiliar surroundings, cut off from the kitchen, the comfortable household occupations in which she had authority; set down in a room full of books, to talk to a young woman who wore slacks and smoked a petillo. He felt a sudden gush of resentment against Aracea; if he could adapt himself to her family's way of living, why could she not adapt herself to his?

The boys came round and wanted him to go out with them, but he excused himself; mañana. He wanted a good night's rest, and, before midnight, was stretched out on the hard mattress which he had shared, as a boy, with one of his brothers, in a bare, marble-flagged room with one glaring light in the middle of the ceiling. When the light was put out, the street-light, shining through the uncurtained window, barred the floor with the shadows of the reja. A bat flew in and flopped about the ceiling. He pulled the sheet over his head and went to sleep. It was noon before he woke, shaved, rubbed himself over with the agua de colonia he had left behind on his last visit, pulled on his shirt and trousers, and, without troubling about collar or tie, lounged out in the town. His royal progress through the taverns lasted until twilight. He recaptured the sweet sense of the son of Maderas, the sophistication of his life beyond its walls peeled off him, leaving him with a sense of purification. He was a little drunk when he returned to the Casa Cigarrón for the evening meal.

But he found himself, as the night wore on, being critical of his people : of the ignorance, opinionatedness and self-satisfaction of his brothers, their persuasion that Maderas was the centre of the earth, and its views the only ones that carried weight with people of commonsense ; of the shrieking voices of his sisters-in-law, their peasant way of dressing, their indifference to any-thing but local gossip and the care of the children. When Papá was alive, none of these things had struck him, because, in some way, Papá dominated the household ; his big, rich voice, the roar with which he quelled the women's chatter, the mere tap of his sticks on the stone floors stood for home. Queer, how one never realised it. Paco had opened, for a moment, the door into the room that was Don Amadeo's office, and closed it again quickly. His eldest brother, of course, had taken it over ; in place of the posters, the clippings of Paco as a boy, in his first suit from Manfredi, as a banderillero, as a novillero, receiving the alternativa in Madrid and in his first long cape of a matador, there were account books, piles of samples, bales of goods waiting to be unpacked—all the truck Papá kept in a wide passage behind the shop. The head of a Miura bull was used as a hat-rack ; all the proud trophies of the career of El Cigarrón were cleared away. Strange, that the sons of a matador should care so little about that brave past ; but, from their boyhood, neither Juan nor Marco had had a more than casual interest in the bulls ; their principle preoccupation was the shrewd amassing of money, they hated spending, as they hated anything that carried the risk of loss. And they mistrusted him, Paco, as a matador, because

the extravagance of matadores is proverbial, and they meant him
to know that if he lost his career and his money he need not turn
to them to support him, but to the rich woman he had married,
who was fool enough to stake him.

To hell with them, for sons of bitches ! They were too smug
and too mean to pay a round in a tavern ; too anxious to preserve
their standing in the community—they were both santurrónes,
and Juan a mayordomo in the church of San Bartolommeo—to
risk the slightest departure from local convention ; in little more
than six months they had cleared out the cheerful, bullfighting
crowd that swarmed over the house in the day of Don Amadeo,
and drawn in the long-faced confraternity of the local government and civil services, who, of course, could be useful to an
important house of business.

He had learned, to his fury, that the bullring was in a bad
way ; that the new manager had no pull with the agents, and
that all summer they had had only two indifferent novilladas and
booked another which was abandoned at the last moment because
Maderas would not pay the money demanded by the novillero
who, since the opening of negotiations, had had a big success
and mounted his charges. It cut Paco deeply, that all his father's
work should thus be brought to nothing ; that the name of
Ribera no longer attached to the ring. And his rage burst its
bounds when he was told that his brothers, when asked for a
contribution to the funds, had both refused.

"Jesus and Mary ! " he exploded. " Why didn't you ask
me ? "

" Hombre," said his informant with a wry smile. " Matadores
aren't expected to contribute to an organisation that furnishes
them with their living ! "

Paco swore, ripped out his cheque book and filled in a sum
out of keeping with the state of his account, then, on the point
of signing his name, halted. What was the point—even for the
sake of making a grandiose gesture—of paying money into a
concern that was being mishandled ? He tore up the cheque,
pushed the book back in his pocket and said he would speak
to his brothers.

" But, for the love of Christ, can't you see that keeping up the ring is a way of bringing business to the town ? " he accused them.

Juan retorted—probably with truth—that for all the trade that came in on the day of a bullfight, they might as well close the shop. In any case, that men weren't purchasers of groceries and dry goods, and, apart from a few boxes of cigars, they were likely to sell nothing to visitors who came in only for the fight.

" A decent fight would pack the Duquesa for a couple of nights ; they get all their stuff from us—and we used to have the monopoly of supplying the mineral waters and beers for the ring ; what's become of that ? " persisted Paco.

It amounted to nothing, he was told, it was not worth considering. It was suggested he should get on with his bull-fighting and leave the management of the Casa Cigarrón to those who knew the business. He subsided into a sullen silence, and when the meal was ended, flung himself out of the room, dressed himself and went out again.

It was good to be with the boys, to be wrapped in the warmth of old friendships—enhanced by his status as the Niño of Maderas; to revive old jokes, and to enter places where he was treated like a prince. There was nothing new in the last, but the adulation of Maderas held a special quality for its son, who was not only El Escudero, but Paquito of the Casa Cigarrón, son of the lamented Don Amadeo.

" Ay, Paco, the bulls are in a bad way since your father died ! "

" Shut up about the bulls ; I'm sick of the buggers." He scowled at the reminder. Someone suggested going to the house of Teresita.

" It's too early," he was reminded. " How about Las Parras? " —A shout of agreement went up from the company. " Come on ; let's find Cristóbal, and see if that rattletrap of his has fallen to pieces yet. It'll get us put there in a couple of hours."

" Hey, what's wrong with my car ? " said Paco, as he shoved the money for another round across the counter.

There were guitars to be collected, and someone suggested taking girls. When they set out, the car, at the most generous computation a six-seater, was loaded with eleven; two of the boys sat beside Paco, one with a girl on his knee; five were crushed into the seat behind, and two crouched on the folded hood—reducing, to Paco's regret, the speed; he would have preferred to show off the power of the engine and his prowess as a driver. But it was fine, setting off like this on a romería; he had got out of the way of them, since his marriage—though there had been, unknown to Aracea, a few outbreaks. Or perhaps she had known about them, and found it better to say nothing. He and Carlos had had a number of nocturnal jaunts, at Parral, and Aracea had sleepily made nothing of his return, at four o'clock in the morning. She was good—esa niña! and by Christ, he loved her. If only she would have a baby, there would not be a cloud on their horizon; a baby, which would tie her down at home, and leave him to get on with his work in his own way.

The sky was crisp with stars, and it was very cold when they started to climb into the mountains. He had forgotten the way, and they yelled directions at him; they all sang and shouted, and he sang and shouted with them, and he remembered Las Parras, when they reached it: the white wall hung with shrivelled vines, and the patio that was partly scooped out of the rock at the back, and the rooms that went deep back into the rock, lit all day as well as all night with little electric bulbs—because, fortunately, the cable that supplied the valley came past Las Parras and they were able to avail themselves of it. Admirably placed to catch the tourist trade, Las Parras, the resort of the gay blades of Maderas and two or three neighbouring villages, had not got too good a name for itself before the war; nominally a tavern, kept by a gipsy couple who originated from Granada, it had a reputation for rooking strangers. It also offered to its regular customers the amenities of the house of Teresita, in a more beguiling setting.

" Olé el matador! Olé plaloró! "—They were greeted with a rattle of castanets; the hostess came out to welcome them, her movements had all the grace and sinuosity of the gipsy, in spite of her bulk and weight, her face still bore the traces of a remarkable, venal beauty. " Come inside, it's too cold to sit out of doors. What did I tell you?" she turned to her companions to inquire. "That good luck was on its way!"

Paco grinned; this was going to cost him something. One could guess La Faraóna's interpretation of good luck. But his eyes were on the girl who, on the way up, had been sitting on Ramón's knee; Luz, her name was—Light. One of Teresita's girls, but a newcomer, not more than fourteen or fifteen years old. Her bronze hair freshly washed, she had a delicate air of cleanliness that distinguished her from the other two, with their faces caked with powder and their crumpled dresses of cheap silk —probably from the Casa Cigarrón. She looked back at him and smiled; she was rubbing her bare wrists and hands.

"You're cold?" asked Paco.

"I'll be warm presently"—she nodded towards the olive-wood fire whose smoke blackened the surrounding wall and the arched ceiling. Paco whispered:

"I promise you that!" and she nodded again, slightly as though accepting the purpose for which she had been brought.

Through the smoke and the wine and the conversation, the singing and the dancing of a beautiful girl, La Faraóna's daughter and therefore untouchable, he kept his awareness of the little Luz. Solely on her account he did not mean to get too drunk, he meant to keep enough about him to enjoy what was coming. Since his marriage he had had very few girls; it just happened, quickly, accidentally, almost, and as thoughtlessly as one drinks a glass of water to quench one's thirst. He wondered if Aracea really believed he had never touched a girl since they got married. It seemed as though she did, for she would certainly have made him a formidable scene if she had suspected anything. Considering the assiduity of his attention, most women might have taken his fidelity for granted; but in Aracea—knowing all she knew about the life—it seemed a little stupid. She knew all about the nervous stress of a matador's calling, and not even she could pretend to be with him at every hour of the day and night— although he suspected she would like to be! But she must realise that among all the women of fashion and society who were her friends, as well as in lower walks of life, there were plenty prepared to gratify the taste of a matador; plenty with the aplomb—or shamelessness—to go straight from his arms to slip their own round Aracea's waist, and call her "Darling!"

For some reason, he felt always a distaste for this form of feminine treachery—though it was no worse than his own; it disposed him to a greater tenderness towards her. Her trust in him—although foolish—was so complete! Or perhaps it would be more accurate to say, her trust in herself. He had often felt her watching him, when he was in the company of other women; had sensed her suspicion. But, by good fortune, the women in whom, for the moment, he was interested had been, invariably, the kind as sophisticated as himself, in giving nothing away. And there had been no clutching; they appeared to feel, as he did, that that was *that*, a very pleasant experience, but not to be prolonged or complicated by useless efforts to establish a permanence.

As, trained unconsciously by Aracea, he had developed a habit of fastidiousness in regard to the other sex, he was rarely tempted by vulgar encounters; it had meant nothing, on his last visit before Papá died, to resist the offer of the girl at Teresita's—and had he seen Luz against that sordid background, he would have hesitated long before having to do with her. But something—the drive through the starlit air, Ramón—a rare singer of the flamenco—singing the coplas of Cádiz, the height and remoteness of the mountains, and the immaculacy of her skin and hair sharpened his desire, so that to embrace her became the logical climax of a night of wine and music among intimate friends.

When he got up and went deeper into the caves, La Faraóna, knowing what he sought, followed him.

" Here ? "

He looked in at a broad bed, spread with spotless linen deeply edged with lace.

" Here," he said. " Later."

II

The engines brummed beneath them. She became aware of Paco, looking at her in surprise.

" Do you feel ill ? " he shouted at her, above the roar of the plane.

" A little," faltered Aracea. She felt humiliated ; it was she who, after long argument, had persuaded Paco to come out by plane. The sea journey was long and, at this time of year, doubtful ; they had had to delay their passage as late as possible, on account of clearing affairs at Parral, but she now thought wistfully of the cuadrilla, bumping across the Atlantic. Paco would have been with them, but for the impossibility of leaving her to travel by herself ; he had not forgotten the horrors of that Washington flight. She reminded him of their first flight across the Atlantic, and of the comfort of the flight to New York. He allowed himself, reluctantly, to be persuaded. They were travelling through the air as smoothly as along a road, Paco, having eaten a large meal, was enjoying himself, and it was she who, after struggling for an hour against sensations she hardly knew how to describe, felt suddenly as though she were going to faint. She had a wild desire to break the window, to fling herself out, to die, rather than continue in this echoing box on a journey that would never end.

She had barely let out her first scream of hysteria before the stewardess, summoned by Paco, was bending over her. Paco, much flustered, was banished from his seat, and the separating arm removed ; Aracea was laid along the two seats, and was made to swallow a glass of cloudy liquid. She was crying now, and her heart was beating to suffocation, but the stewardess assured her she was " All right." She closed her eyes, trying to believe it. Paco returned and looked at her apprehensively.

" Estás mejor ? "

" Yes," she answered faintly. " Do you want to sit down ? " —She tried to move her feet. A voice said, in Spanish, with an American accent :

" Take my seat for a while, señor ; I'll look after your wife."

She opened her eyes ; a middle-aged woman was settling on the edge of the seat, looking down at her, and Paco, with an air of relief, was moving along the plane. Aracea said in English :

" Thank you very much. I'm all right—I just thought—I was going to be suffocated."

" Claustrophobia," smiled the woman. " I've had it myself, on these long flights. I find it helps to shut my eyes and imagine I'm on top of a mountain. Not too high a mountain, just a kind of hill, but you can see for miles and miles—rivers and trees and roads with little cars running along them. You can sit there and push your hands in the grass and hear birds singing——" The voice was slow and almost drowsy ; Aracea felt herself smiling, felt her eyes closing.

" Go on, please."

" There's rather a lot of wind : it blows your hair back and makes your skin feel cool——"

She did not know how long her eyes had been closed ; when she opened them, the woman was still sitting there, in an uncomfortable position, turned sideways on the seat, but she did not appear to be troubled. She smiled at Aracea.

" There ; that's better, isn't it ? "

" How long have I been asleep ? "

" Nearly an hour. I'll ask the stewardess for some fruit juice ; it will freshen you up." She bent towards Aracea and added in a low voice, " You're going to have a baby, aren't you ? "

She almost fainted. When she could speak :

" Oh, no, no," she whispered.

The woman looked surprised.

" Pardon me. I very seldom make a mistake like that. I'm a nurse, you know.—Well, I expect you'd like your husband to come back now. I'll send the stewardess with the orange juice."

She powdered her face hastily, and Paco came back, and put his arm round her and kissed her a great many times, and wanted her to put her head down on his shoulder.

" No, chico, I'm quite all right." The hand that held her lipstick was trembling ; all of her was quivering. The stewardess arrived with a long, frosted glass; she drank thirstily, holding the glass in her left hand while Paco held the right jealously. She spilled a little of the juice on the front of her suit, and Paco took out his handkerchief and wiped it away, and wiped her mouth, as though she were a child. A sob broke from her, but she controlled herself quickly. Whatever happened, she must not cry.

Paco went to sleep, still holding her hand, and she sat staring at the blue blank of the window.

Not really. Not at this time, of all others. She had had several scares, which she had never confided to anyone, but they all proved groundless. She supposed it was the constant travelling, the restlessness of their way of life. What a mercy. There simply could not be a baby, while she had Paco to look after. She had taken every precaution within the rule of the Church, but contraceptive methods were forbidden and Paco would never hear of them. What if she were to start to be ill, while they were in Mexico?—if Paco were obliged to trail about an ailing wife, unable to share in his work or his pleasures? It was so much harder to keep him fit out there, than at home : to look after his diet, to regulate his social life, to arrange for his exercise and head him away from the destructive kind of company that, in every city, gathers about a matador. Last time, she had worked incessantly on her job of companionship; riding, swimming, dancing, gambling—until, for all her youth and health, she had been ready to drop with fatigue. This time it would, perhaps, not be quite so hard, for he had a fuller card ; much of their time would be spent in planes and cars, and the immediate urgency of keeping fit would to some degree relieve her of an endless watchfulness. Paco, by now, had learned to accept her constant preaching of sane and healthy living, on which his quick recovery from his wounds had set the seal. But, left to himself, he was an easy mark for all the roistering crowd who would swarm upon him. Why, even when he came back from Maderas, he looked as though he had been drunk for days !

It must be imagination, now, she thought, that made her feel so terrible : the idea of the baby that had put her in a panic— and suppose it were not true? She wished she dared withdraw her hand from Paco's, to open her bag and look at her diary. Those weeks since Zaragosa had been so crammed, the final weeks at Parral so filled with innumerable cares that she had not had time to notice ; she had thought she was a little overdue, but there was no time to worry even over that. She was frequently irregular and seldom paid attention to it—but she now began straining her memory to the time of her last period, while an increasing pain developed in the lower part of her body and caught her breath two or three times with a stab like a knife.

Suddenly she knew what it was ! Her heart gave a great leap of relief as, cautiously loosening her hand, she stepped across Paco's knees and went down the gangway to the toilette.

In her joy and excitement, she could not help waking him when she returned. She had washed, combed her hair and freshened herself with Cologne water ; she had re-made her mouth and changed her blouse. Paco yawned, rubbed his eyes and opened them wide suddenly.

" Mother of Jesus, I thought the sun was shining in my face ! Chica, qué pasa ? You look as though there was an electric bulb of a million volts inside you ! "

" I'm better ! And I want you to take me down to the bar and give me a drink."

III

The first appearance of Niño de Maderas in Mexico City on the last Sunday in November was, if not a sensation, something to talk about ; something to sell out the ring for his second appearance, at the end of January, when he shared the bills with Ildefonso and a Mexican boy who was fighting his first season as a matador. Ildefonso had always had bad luck in Mexico City ; it was said he was not worth a block in the sun to the promotion. His big towns were Lima, Carácas, Tampico—a dozen others as well, but just not Mexico City. It was as though it jinxed him ; he had taken the horn there once and given, each time, a bad show. If his agent had let him, he would have cut it out ; but, as the agent pointed out, there were just enough people in Mexico City who went on hoping, with faith and prayer, that Ildefonso would justify the reputation he had in other parts of the country to make it worth while to go on until the jinx was beaten.

For his first show, the Niño brought out all the adornos—the stunts—that would have earned him the bronca from a discriminating public on the Peninsular. Blessed with good bulls, he gave a cold, dazzling performance and collected two ears and the tail; good for a foreigner. The whole set-up made him feel good; the agent to whom Don Pasquale had passed him on had done an excellent job of publicity, the day after their arrival the papers carried pictures of him and Aracea arriving at the airport; there was an interview with " El Gran Diestro y su bellísima esposa, hija de Parral " and some members of the " big " afición put up a dinner for them both, at which, to Paco's gratification, Aracea outshone the local women with her beauty, her dress and her jewellery. Most of the diamonds were fake, but her manner of wearing them lent them authenticity; her gown of tulle, layered in orange and red, was scattered with crystal spangles; she sparkled from head to foot. They were photographed at the table, photographed while dancing, photographed getting into the car and getting out of the car; as Paco remarked, with a gratified chuckle, when they were back in their bedroom, the amount of film used, since their arrival, on the señores Ribera would have stretched across the bullring, and back again. He took pleasure in the big posters outside the ring, and in the balloons with his head on that the children flew in the streets. He took pleasure in everything. That was the mood in which to give a good show.

She sat, of course, in a palco, with the wives of some of the city high-ups. She was unusually nervous. Several times, when he took a particularly spectacular risk, she felt her mouth go dry, sweat break at the roots of her hair and her throat felt as though an iron band was closing on it. Only afterwards did it occur to her how extraordinary, how unlike her, this was. She had very seldom been afraid for Paco in the ring; she knew his work so well, had so much confidence in his judgment that her only disturbance on his behalf was a bad bull, some dishonest beast that broke the unwritten rules between man and bull, and might take him at a disadvantage.

On the two or three occasions, since their marriage, when she had not been there to watch the fight—once because she was sent for by the nuns who were looking after Doña Leandra, who was seriously ill, and once because the car broke down on the road, and in the one that picked up Paco and swept him on, only just in time for the fight, there was no room for her— she waited calmly, with no particular perturbation, to hear the news.

But for some reason she had started being nervous while she was having breakfast in the parlour adjoining their bedroom, where Paco still slept as sweetly as an angel. She had hard work to control it, so that he should have no idea how she was feeling. While they were dressing him, she fell on her knees and prayed for it to be over; and, now it was over, she could not imagine how she came to make such a fool of herself. But the clothes she took off were wet through—wetter than the matador's shirt and pants, after his session in the sun. And the following morning, to her dismay, she found she had a temperature and a chill —whose onset accounted, no doubt, for her strange behaviour the previous day.

By lunch time, her throat was so sore and the aching in her eyes so bad that she woke Paco and asked him to get a doctor. He did so—and was no less dismayed than she when, having examined her, the doctor said she must spend at least a couple of days in bed.

" But it's impossible! We're flying to Monterey in the morning! My husband's fighting there," she croaked at him.

He shook his head; for her there was no question of a flight. He took a swab of her throat, said he would have it analysed, and for the present she had better move into hospital; it was not easy for a sick person to get the attention she required in a hotel. He gave her some capsules to bring down the temperature which, owing to her agitation, had by now shot sky high, and went with Paco into the other room.

"My wife's pretty sick?"—Like all people unaccustomed to illness, Paco was terrified.

The doctor, like the rest of his kind, was noncommittal.

"What's this about putting her in hospital?"

"It's a matter of convenience. If you've got to go to Monterey, you don't want to worry about how she's being looked after." Strangers in Mexico City frequently developed septic throat, with the change of climate, the wind and the dust : it was common to run a very high temperature for twenty-four hours, and after that, of course, there was a relapse. It was out of the question for Señora Ribera to travel before the end of the week, and he would ring the hospital and find out what time they could send the ambulance. Meanwhile, he would give her an injection and that would make her sleep ; it was just as well she should be spared the excitement of the journey in the ambulance.

Weakly crying, she suffered the needle in her arm. When she awoke, she was in a high, narrow bed in a white room ; Paco, his hands in his pockets, his legs stretched out before him, was staring at her dejectedly. She frowned, trying to remember— then, as it all flashed back, thrust herself up in bed. Her throat was giving her so much pain that she could hardly get out the words.

"You're not going to let them keep me here?"

He flung himself on his knees to clutch her with his arms.

"You're sick, alma mia : awfully sick ! Suppose you were to get worse in the plane ? I wouldn't know what to do," he stammered.

Again she was crying, pulling helpless faces, like a child ; the crying hurt her throat, but she could not stop. Distracted, he flung himself on the bed, dragged her to him and tried to comfort her. She whispered, "Don't leave me ! " and they clung together, each knowing it was inevitable, until a nurse came in. A buxom girl in her late twenties, she grinned at Paco as he crawled off the bed.

"Olá, matador ! We'll look after your wife, until you fetch her back the ears from Monterey ! If you're going to be on the early morning plane it's time you were getting some sleep."

She was dizzy with pain by now. As he bent over her for the last kiss, her dry lips whispered against his :

" *Be good.*"

" Sure ; and I'll telephone you immediately after the fight."

For forty-eight hours pain had its way with her ; she who had never known illness in her life was reduced to a helpless, whimpering object at the mercy of people who talked in loud, cheerful voices across her bed, clattered objects and clicked their high heels across the floor ; slammed doors, sometimes whistled or sang. In a room across the corridor someone had the radio on almost all day ; in the room next to hers, a woman kept groaning, " Ay, dios, ay, dios ! " Sometimes it rose to a shriek.

She who had never been sensitive to noise felt each little sound like a hammer tap on her unprotected brain. From the street below rose an endless blare of car horns, clanging of bells, screel of street cars, yelling of street vendors. (When she began to get better, she asked if she could have a quieter room, and they looked at her in astonishment. " Why, señora, this is one of the quietest rooms in the hospital ! Look how high up you are : nearly at the top of the building." " Then for God's sake keep the door and the windows closed," she muttered.)

She lay there, burning with heat, thinking of Paco in the plane, imagining every kind of disaster ; looking at her watch every few minutes, wondering how near he was to Monterey. When the doctor came, she was given another injection, and gained a few hours of oblivion. It did not occur to her, before or after, that the " septic throat " had very little to do with her condition ; that she was paying the price of two years of stress and strain that would long ago have reduced a less healthy woman to invalidism.

On the day after the fight she was nearly demented, but refused flatly to have the injection, fearing her sleep might last until the corrida was over. She started at three to say the rosary ; her hands shook so much that the beads slipped out of them and rattled on the floor. She thrust at the bell, and no one came, so she crawled out of bed, over-balanced and, in falling, hit her head against the iron frame. Someone must have heard, for the door burst open, she was thrust back in bed with an accompaniment of shrill chatter, ordered to keep quiet and the beads put back in her hands. They were no use, anyway ; she let them drop again.

" Paco, Paco ! "—She began to scream and toss. " Paco ! " —Seizing the thin linen sheet the nurse had just drawn over her, she tore it in half. The noise of the tearing stuff checked her for a moment ; as she stared at it, the wail came from next door— " Ay, dios ! " No doubt she could be heard, as well. She set all her will into an act of self-control ; was she not behaving in the way for which she despised Mamá Amalia ?

When the nurse came back, she was lying on her side, with her eyes shut, her face crimson with fever, and the pillow was speckled with blood from her bitten lips. If they didn't take care, this was going to be a tiresome case ; however, it was a piece of luck, to have charge of a matador's wife ! It ought to be worth a thousand pesos, at least.

" Now, señora, the time's getting on ; we'll soon be having some news."

" Oh, please take me to the telephone ; let me be at the telephone when my husband calls through ! " she prayed in a whisper. The nurse laughed merrily.

" Come now, do you want to get me in trouble with the authorities ? "

IV

Waiting for them to roll the steps up to the open door of the plane, Paco, staring in black glasses across the sun-blasted tarmac, spoke across his shoulder to Tonio.

" There's Chano—and that nickel-plated cow-jumper Curro— all the boys are here ! "

" Somebody must have phoned them," said Tonio, who had put through a call to Monterey while Paco was at the hospital.

" What a funeral ! It's a pity they forgot the black bands on their arms," muttered Paco, as he went down the steps. But it

was decent of the boys to meet him ; he had not been that close
to his cuadrilla. They kept their eyes away from him as each
gripped his hand, and on Tonio, to see whether it was permissible
to crack a joke. Paco's nervous depression lightened a little as
they all got together into somebody's car, and Chano started
telling him about the bulls, and the state of the afición, and the
publicity.

" You like to ring back to the hospital ? "—They were at the
hotel ; Tonio was unpacking. Paco scowled and bit his thumb
nail.

" There's no sense in it. I can't talk to her."

" That's true."

The truth was, he dared not ring up. Whatever happened to
her, by Christ, he must not know, before to-morrow evening !

He spent most of the night in a café with the boys, had more
to drink than he should, and was called just in time to start
dressing. For once, Tonio let everybody in ; the room was
filled with people, shouting and smoking and asking for his
autograph ; their noise set up a screen between him and his
thoughts. He felt pretty good, only just a little more nervous
than usual, when they set out on the drive to the ring.

The papers next morning gave four-fifths of their space to
the two Mexican fighters, Paco's photograph did not appear,
except in a shot of the paseo, and one of the critics wrote:

" It is unfortunate that so accomplished an espada as Niño
de Maderas does not give his audiences more for their
money——"

" Jesus and Mary, what do they want me to do ? " said Paco,
when he had read so far. " Take my tripes out and make a plait
of them round the bull's horns ? "

" He demonstrates the whole art of the fight as though he
were reading from a book, but his performance as a whole is
more surgical than artistic."

Back in Mexico City, Paco's agent held the receiver away

from a sensitive ear-drum, nodded a few times, spoke when he had the chance, and replaced the receiver calmly.

" That was the Niño."

" Telling you off for the plastering he got at Monterey? What slipped up—the money? "

The agent stuck out his lip.

" You can never trust the sons of whores. The money was all right, but I suppose they just felt like telling the truth—for once. It's a pity they chose the time when his wife's dying in hospital."

Chapter Six

I

THEY WENT from dry heat into sweaty heat, from chill to burn ; always in planes, or cars. When not in the air or on the roads they were in hotels, switching electric fans on or off, listening to other fights on the radio, too tired, and sometimes too bored, to make conversation.

Aracea had—to the annoyance of nurses cheated of their perquisites—willed herself into recovery by the end of the week, but will alone was not enough to support her against the pace, the changes of climate and of habitation. There were certain assignations for which she was obliged to save herself : visits, as the dueña of Parral, to ranches, for conferences with other breeders, and a few social occasions for which they were let in by introductions it would not have been politic to ignore.

Paco was working so hard there was no need to trouble about exercise ; that was one good thing. They managed to snatch a few languid days on beaches, but she was too tired to swim. They got a few rides—when they were staying on the ranches—and Paco was seeing more of the cuadrilla ; that also was good. He continued to merit, in the ring, his title of " The Armoured One "—although he got the horn once. It was a fiesta fight, on a Wednesday, and he was fighting the following Sunday, but he could not take the darts because the horn had torn a muscle in his thigh. The wound was superficial, but he was in great pain and swearing blue murder by the end of the afternoon. Of course, an accident like that had to happen in a bug-hole of a village, and prevent his doing himself justice in front of an important audience. On the advice of the doctors, he cancelled a not very important fight, and they went off for ten days' rest at one of the ranches.

Aracea was thankful for it. Although she was now well, she seemed unable to shake off the fear that overcame her, each time he went into the ring. She was ashamed of it, and terrified that Paco would find out. She thought it must be because she was still tired. It started with nausea on the morning of a fight, and by midday had developed into a racking headache. Behind the coloured glasses, she flinched like any amateur each time the bull went near him. She was as scandalised as she was ashamed ; she felt she was being a disgrace to her own casta. She no longer accepted invitations or asked people back to the hotel after the fight ; her one idea was to get back as fast as possible, stretch out on her bed and relax, so as to be all right when Paco came in. But, for all her efforts to deceive him, he noticed at last ; was at first incredulous, then angry, although he tried to disguise the latter by laughing at her. She knew he had right on his side ; a torero has enough to do in controlling his own nerves, without being hampered by those of his wife. He had sometimes said that her coolness helped to steady him, and that was the only reason he allowed her to come with him when he was fighting !

And the result was a growing irritability between them, for which the only remedy was to keep away from each other as much as possible. She knew he was drinking, and that under his swagger, which he had begun to exaggerate, even with her, there was a creeping dissatisfaction with his receptions by the audiences he had been so confident of conquering. Jealousy of a foreigner ! he sneered. Put up any sort of a flea-bitten beginner in the ring with him, and the crowds would bawl their heads off; if the bull had four ears and two tails, they would demand all of them for the Mexican! So they called his work "surgical." Better ask one of those white-coated bastards in the infirmary to change places with him. He was worrying about the muscle in his leg, whether it would heal up in time for the January fight with Ildefonso. His work with the banderillas was the one thing that would give him a bit of advantage with a public which, apparently incapable of making up its mind for itself, had decided to accept the Ildefonso Legend from the Peninsula!

She allowed him to use her as an outlet for his spleen, but it did not smooth their relationship. Although her loyalty made her reject it, her cold brain, full of knowledge, had given her the answer. Paco's unpopularity with the afición, their reluctance to award him his very great dues, was not based on critical depreciation of his work, or even on jealousy—though the latter might enter into it; There was something wanting; something for which there is no name; something that slides down into the heart like the sword and tears at the entrails. They call it emotion, but the word is too loosely and generally applied; it is no longer adequate for the holocaust that a matador like Ildefonso can conduct with an audience, his power to tear them apart from their corporeal selves and for an unbreathing moment, reincarnate each man in the pattern of his own nobility.

Like everyone else, she recognised this power in Ildefonso, she had been swept by it, she knew what it was that made men and women regard him as a god. She envied it for Paco; why should he not have it—who could do so many things Ildefonso could not attempt? She, who had dedicated her life to giving him everything, why could she not command this for Paco? What was missing, in all her offerings—that the mystic flame did not ignite? She had waited, confident that, one day, it would happen. Now—to her horror—she had begun to doubt. She must not doubt; sweet Virgin Mary, she must not doubt. It was bad enough to see Paco puzzled, furious, resentful—as, fight after fight, he delivered the goods impeccably, and never received the reward he hoped for; developing a grudge that soured his blithe nature and threatened their mutual happiness. He had been arrogant and aggressive. He demanded that people should fawn on him—and they laughed at him behind his back. He flung money around like a maniac—but would meanly question the expenditure of Tonio, who dealt with all the travelling expenses, and the payment of the cuadrilla; who had known him since boyhood, and whose sour and stubborn faithfulness had, on several occasions she learned of by chance, alone held the restive cuadrilla together.

But, up at the ranch, in the thin, cool air, things seemed better. Don Emmanuel was an old friend of Parral; he and his sons ran the ranch with only a few peónes, and his fatherly kindness was no less grateful than his advice. Paco accepted without question his orders to lie up for a few days, and she was free to ride out with the wives of the boys, young women like herself, dedicated to the life of the ranch, but eager to hear all she could tell them of the life of the Peninsular. The housekeeping, it appeared, was left in the hands of the wife of Don Emmanuel and his eldest daughter-in-law; there was a clutter of children. The little boys clustered about Paco—she had not realised before how fond he was of children, and how he got on with them.

In the evenings the talk was all of breeding; Paco was interested and deferential to the dueño. His manner, it amused Aracea to observe, was that of the proprietor of Parral. She made no demur—although it occurred to her once or twice that the rest of the company accepted a little too readily this claim of authority on the part of one who, so far, had avoided responsibilities. To Don Emmanuel it was, naturally, incredible that she should be the ruler of Parral; no estate would accept the authority of a girl in her twenties, even with the great name of Parral behind her.

In those few days they seemed to recapture the lightsomeness of their early days of marriage; Paco was again her lover, and there was no bliss in the world like being in his arms. The nights in a big, primitive room with no furniture but the bed, a wardrobe and a chair were nights of rapture for them both, and the simple, homely life, so similar to his own in Maderas, cleared away the accretions of the past months. Best of all, for Aracea, it had so steadied her nerves that she could contemplate without dread his next appearance in the ring.

The following day—a Sunday—they all gathered to listen to the fight at Mexico City. As she settled in the leather-slung chair and lit her cigarette, Aracea had a sense of calm disassociation, as though bulls and bullrings were no concern of hers. They had spent the morning looking through the stud books; she wondered uneasily whether her own were in such good order. They had been, in the days of Don Luis, but she had lately had her suspicions. The vaquero who was supposed to be on watch during the mounting season had proved to be a lazy, drunken fellow, amenable to bribery. A tale had come to her ears—too outrageous to be believed, but not wholly to be dismissed—of a cow from another herd being brought at dead of night to a Parral bull. Carlos, when she told him of it, was as incredulous as she, but agreed that the man must be dismissed. That was all very well; but in the time of Don Luis such an act of treachery was unthinkable. The worry of this revived in her mind as she sat there, blurring her attention to the voice of the speaker on the radio. The dark, attentive faces of Don Emmanuel and his sons were riveted on the wooden cabinet, as though seeing through its panel the bulls who carried their credit that afternoon into the ring. How admirably Don Emmanuel ran his ranch— although they had few of the modern amenities of Parral, and only half the number of peónes. There was no need of all those workers, when each member of the family carried his share of the responsibility, and each his own clearly defined duty to perform in the charge of the beasts. What would they make of Carlos—sitting in the office, having a few casual words with the mayoral, riding round the estate, perhaps, in a lordly fashion to cast a superficial eye over the workings, and spending half his time in town?

" The crowd is giving Silvestre the bronca for a barbarous thrust with the sword——"

A faint smile of gratification spread over Paco's face; he

liked to hear of somebody else, one of their own lot, getting the bronca.

" A fiasco," commented Don Emmanuel, as he got up to switch off the instrument after the dispatch of the last bull. " Mother of God, it makes one sick, to be breeding brave bulls for excrement like that to handle ! "

Paco, that night, was so loving that Aracea made up her mind to open a subject which had been in her mind ever since their arrival at the ranch. She waited until the men had gone out, until they were alone on the broad gallery where Paco had spent most of his mornings ; having taken one of the girls into her confidence, the children were kept out of the way. There was only another day before Paco returned to work.

" Chico, it's been a lovely time," she sighed ; her hand sought his. He gripped it as he smiled at her.

" Ya lo creo. A lovely time."

" It makes me think of our first year at home, when we spent nearly all the time planning the house and watching the new buildings going up, and you rode out with me every morning— the way Papá and I used to do."

" Yes, that was good," agreed Paco.

" I wish there were someone really to depend on, when we are away. Benito, of course ; he's to be trusted like the tablets of stone. But it is difficult for him, with Carlos. I sometimes wonder how much damage Carlos is doing to our credit."

" Pues—he knows plenty about the bulls ; your father taught him."

" It's not much use being taught, unless you put your teaching into practice," she pointed out. " Our people are lazy enough, without having an example of idleness set them by the padrón— as I suppose he calls himself ! " She laughed shortly. " The last thing I told him was to be sure to send me regular reports of what was going on, and, as you know, I've had one letter : a few lines of gossip—he might have saved the paper ! "

" You won't alter Carlos," shrugged Paco.

" Claro ; but, darling, don't you understand why I am anxious ? Some day, you will be the master of Parral. It will be a fine thing, if I hand over to you a business in ruins, a great name that has lost its authority ! "

He shifted uneasily.

" Carlos won't let it come to that; he knows too well on which side his bread is buttered."

" He's not as dependent on it as all that. He could go back to his vine-growing family."

" So far as it goes, he need not have left them."

She smiled shortly.

" Oh yes, being Carlos, he need ! That side of the family is very practical, and as greedy for money as my uncles in Segovia. Carlos would have been obliged to work hard ; he would have been buried in the depths of the country and not had nearly as much liberty as he had with my father," she said shrewdly.

" Or he could have done nothing," pointed out Paco.

" That would not have suited him either, with his extravagant habits. His army pension would not have kept him in the style he likes, or bought him his car, or paid his bills at the Casino ! " was the scornful reply. " I know ; we shall never get rid of Carlos. But someone else must be there, to keep an eye on things, or we shall be in trouble by the end of another year."

" Is that not what I have said ? "—He sat up ; the triumph in his eyes sent a pang through her. Was he really prepared— no, more : eager—to sacrifice her ?

" Amigo," she murmured, " let us be sensible. We know it is true, what my father said ; what Don Emmanuel has shown us he believes—that a woman of my age cannot run a ranch. We have made a great deal of money on this trip "—she might have added, and spent it—" and if we are careful, we can live for a year. Will you not "—though she tried to speak calmly, her voice trembled—" come home for a year, and help me to put things in order at Parral ? It is, after all, to your own interests to do it," she concluded.

He looked at her as though she were mad.

" And my work ? " he gaped at her.

" Plenty of toreros have left the ring for a year, and gone back with enormous éxito," she reminded him.

He looked away from her and scowled.

" No. No."

Although she knew she was defeated, she appealed again.

" It might not take so long. If you were there to support me, I dare say I could get everything under control by the end of the season. We could build up Benito's authority, and I could master all the office-work while you made yourself familiar with the workers."

He was obdurate. He did not believe that Carlos was as bad as she made out ; knowing her, and her love of authority, he suspected her of a little jealousy of one who carried the responsibilities from which she was debarred by her sex. He allowed her to see his resentment of the suggestion that he should abandon his career at the very moment when he stood to become the first matador in Spain. No one, now, stood between himself and his ambition but Ildefonso—and Ildefonso's days were numbered. But, to retire, even temporarily, before he had vanquished his rival was to leave a ghost unlaid. To return to the ring, once more to face the Ildefonso Legend—that was not to be borne !

" You're loca," he stammered. " This year Pasquale's fixing me my mano a mano with Ildefonso."

Her eyes covered him with darkness. He stared resentfully into their unfathomable dark ; angry, and uneasy, and for some reason afraid, because he could not read what lay behind it. She thought, Pasquale will not arrange that mano a mano unless he wants to ruin Paco. She thought, Why can't I save him, while there's yet time ?

All of her fears revived, as she realised that, in his determination to outsoar Ildefonso, he was capable, from now on, of indulging any folly, any indiscretion that might deliver him into her hands, a piece of human wreckage, and close his career in ignominy.

II

They were back on the game. Counting the days to their departure in the middle of February, Aracea abandoned herself to conditions she had not the physical energy to control. She tried not to imagine what he was doing, during the lonely hours she spent in hotels, having her hair washed, her nails manicured—anything to kill time. One day she started a letter to Mary Carpenter, but gave it up after a few lines. She found herself unable to write on her usual high note of triumph and assurance, and her pride rebelled at the thought of betraying her unhappiness. For the first time since her marriage she started to read voraciously; Paco scoffed at the books which piled themselves up in their room. What did he expect her to do? He would have been resentful enough, if she had gone out and amused herself. She was sick of the company of rich women, who had nothing to talk about but clothes and Hollywood stars. One day she found herself wondering whether she would have been happier if she had never known Mary Carpenter; never spent the time in England that had helped to condition her away from her own people.

She got a little comfort out of the discovery that Paco, also, was looking forward to being back on the Peninsular; he wanted to get on with his book and enjoy the importance of its publication—and out of a boy who came in one morning, to paint Paco's portrait. The inept daub did not interest her, but it was nice to to talk to somebody who dreamed of going to Madrid, and who was excited by her description of the Prado—until she realised that Paco was bored and resentful of any conversation that did not centre in himself. (Yet he had allowed her to coax him into the Prado, and seemed to be as thrilled as she in the Goya rotunda. The reproductions of the Scenes of Tauromaquía she had given him hung in the sala at home, and were often proudly pointed out to visitors by Paco, as proof of his own culture.)

He continued to neglect her for a great part of the days, and two or three times, imagining she smelt a woman's scent, she felt almost murderous, but decided to restrain herself for the present.

There came a day when her suspicions were confirmed : when Paco dedicated his bull to a very pretty young woman seated some way along the gradas to her right. Aracea knew who she was, the daughter of the presidente, married to a wealthy aficionado who had invited them to his table in the hotel. She had seen the way Paco looked at the girl, and the girl at Paco. It was a fiesta ; Paco was appearing twice and they were spending three nights in the town.

To the onlookers it must have appeared a commonplace compliment, that included the presidente and the husband ; but on Paco's face, uplifted from the sand, was the look it had worn the night before, the look unmistakable to any wife. Leaning forward, as the girl laughed and caught the montera, Aracea continued to stare at her until, uneasily, the other turned to look over her shoulder. Their eyes met ; the girl batted her lashes, smiled falsely and said something to her husband, as though invoking his protection. They both bowed to Aracea.

When Tonio had finished with him, and they were alone, she flung accusations at Paco. His overdone look of astonishment, some secret satisfaction in his relaxed limbs in the silk dressing gown, told her she was right. For a little while he tried to laugh it off, then, suddenly, he flamed. Ripping off the dressing gown, he faced her, naked, with the patch of dressing on his thigh ; pointing at her, yelling at her—incredible things. Half-stunned, she felt as though she were his mistress, not his wife. Then he flung on some clothes and left her alone.

He walked into the room next morning while she was dressing and pushed an envelope at her.

" There's your ticket for the plane."

" But——"

" I'm going with the boys. Tonio'll look after you, I've given him my ticket. I'm tired of flying."

" Do you realise," she said, when she could speak, " that I'll have two nights by myself, before you get there ? "

" You've got plenty to read, haven't you ? " he sneered.

So this, she thought, when they were above the clouds, was what came of her proud descriptions of the independence of foreign women ; her raillery at Spanish customs and her earnest insistence upon his confidence in her. " Don't you see I'm different from other girls ? Isn't that, perhaps, part of the reason you love me ? Whatever I learned from Miss Mary, she gave me a sense of honour, and I can assure you I know how to look after myself," she told him, to his amusement. " Bueno, but I don't happen to like you to look after yourself," he told her good humouredly. " When we go to England I'll watch you looking after yourself ! But in Spain I'll do the looking after."

He was right, for, in Spain, a pretty young woman, travelling alone is still conspicuous, and, when Paco could not be with her, she had always managed to find a woman companion. When she went shopping in the Mexican towns, she paid one of the hotel servants to accompany her.

She thought, with bitter, irrational resentment, that he would never have allowed his mother or his sisters to take a journey by plane alone. The plane was not much more than half full, and Tonio, having tipped the steward to keep the seat next to Aracea's empty, had taken himself somewhere up in front. When they were on the airport, he had said, guessing her distress, " It's all right, señora—Chano will look after him." The slow tears gathered on her lashes and overflowed when she found herself alone.

Paco, when he turned up, had the grace to look ashamed of himself. After two nights in the train he looked damaged. She guessed he had been drinking all the way. He embraced her sheepishly and stumbled into bed. She lay awake and wondered what would become of them. He was very good to her for several days.

The time wore on ; each town they came to was branded with the Ildefonso Legend. Always the fabulous shadow seemed to move ahead of them. He had had the cornada four times ; once so badly that nothing but a monster could have appeared the following Sunday in the ring! It was a scarecrow, animated by the divine fire. No boy in any town or village he had visited but would die for Ildefonso.

Her heart ached for Paco, moving ever more sourly in the wake of this monstrous legend; carrying always the weight of a comparison as cruel as it was unjust. Some unhappy things occurred; in one town, by some carelessness on the part of the publicity, every tavern and café was still plastered with Ildefonso's posters on their arrival, and, in response to a furious gesture on the part of the conserje, the big coloured spread behind the reception was dragged down only as they walked up to it. Paco's posters went up an hour or two before the fight. The management excused itself by saying there had been a strike of printers; why should there be a strike of printers before the arrival of Niño de Maderas, and not in time to catch Ildefonso? It was a conspiracy! Aracea had the hardest job of her life, calming him in time to receive the reporters, to whom he blurted out a mouthful of indiscretions that they had to pay to keep out of print.

And so, at last, they came back to Mexico City; to what the clubs were openly calling a " show-down " between the two fighters from Europe.

The billing was equal; that, in itself, was something of an affront to the Niño, who carried more cartel in that ring than his mighty rival. But the royal progress of Ildefonso through other cities had influenced the management; at last—si Dios quiere—they would be shown the revelation for which they had patiently waited. The third on the card was a popular young Mexican fighter, Silvestre, whose fans would certainly see he got his deserts.

A party of their friends insisted that Aracea should join them, on the barrera. She accepted, for the sake of being close to the fight, although she felt so ill that she would have given much to be alone, or with a paid companion. The ring was sold out—all the good places had been gone for months. A sensation of claustrophobia added itself to her discomfort, for, of all places, there is no escape from the barrera, when once you are there.

Human bodies formed an impenetrable wall between her and the concrete steps—themselves packed—leading to the exits, and, whatever came, she was here to the end. The figures in the callejón, the vast empty circle of the sand, swam before her eyes. At the base of her throat she felt her heart beating in slow, hard bumps.

She managed to draw a breath when the paseo was over : Paco in the suit of pure, shining gold he had kept for this occasion ; the Mexican boy in a bright blue that reminded her of Paco's first uniform ; and, apart—a little too far apart from the others to preserve the symmetry of the group, something in pale bronze, encrusted with a gold darker than Paco's. While the others walked in sunlight, that seemed to be surrounded by an occult light of its own. Amid the roars of the crowd, she could not distinguish which was for the Niño and which for Ildefonso. Paco looked pale, and unusually serious ; the flashing smile that rewarded the fans for once was absent. But there was determination in every pace he took ; ojalá, that the determination did not turn into madness.

Her eyes dragged, against her will, to Ildefonso, she looked hurriedly away. There was nothing there, except a long sheathe of crumpled satin, dragged seemingly over a set of bones ! What locura took a wreck like that into the ring ? With short, jerky paces, like a disjointed doll, it reached the callejón, and she found herself drowning in horror and pity. Why, she thought, controlling herself, should she feel those things, when all that she felt belonged by right to Paco ? It was so evidently true, what they said of Ildefonso, that he could not last through another season ; and she should be glad, for Paco's sake. But—it was perhaps better that he should suffer eclipse in a foreign ring, by a younger rival, than yield up the legend before a madrileño or sevillano audience. And, even as the thought passed through her mind, its heresy made her reject it. Ildefonso might die, but none could take from him that which he would carry with him into the shades.

Although he knew where she was sitting, and had sent Tonio with his cape, Paco kept his back to her, and she managed to swallow the lump in her throat as the gate of the toril swung open and the first bull ploughed out on the sand.

There were only two things which, later, she remembered; her shock, on finding that Ildefonso was dedicating his first bull to her. She supposed he had Paco's permission, although she had not seen them speaking to each other. She felt the same grip of the eyes that she had felt at the Jérez fight; the eyes of a damned soul that drove right down into her and took possession. Someone caught the montera and put it in her trembling hands. Her hands shaking, she held it, unconsciously, upside down, like a chalice—a chalice containing the blood of its owner. She held it as though she were holding the life of the man about to perform the final, sacramental act out there on the burning sand. The noise of the crowd made great waves of sound that echoed inside her skull. Blinded, she saw nothing of the great act of preparation, or of the tender killing. Nothing. She too was slain, by a pair of eyes. She, like the bull, was lying there on the sand, delivered into an eternal peace. When she came back, the man on her left was standing up, the tears running down his face, shouting, " No hay qué uno ! No hay qué uno ! " and the tiers were a snowstorm of waving handkerchiefs.

And the second thing she remembered, in the second half of the fight, was Paco's bull; the suerte of the horse, when Paco, and Ildefonso, and the Mexican boy were all in the ring.

Paco took the first quite, and dealt with it admirably, leaving the bull in position for the second horse. The next quite should have been Ildefonso's, but he ceded it to the Mexican, who, after a creditable show with the cape, in some way lost control of the bull, which trotted away into the distant part of the tercios. Chano went after it and turned it, and then happened one of the unaccountable things that can happen in the ring.

Presented to the third horse, the bull suddenly changed its mind and its angle, and charged straight at Paco, who, with his back turned to it, was making way for Ildefonso, nearest to him on the sand. Ildefonso stood still. At the last split second, the slap of a banderillero's cape across the bull's nose saved Paco— and that was where Aracea fainted.

She had no recollection of being lifted by the ambulance people over the barrier and lowered into the callejón; she came to on a stretcher behind the stands. Her instant wish was to get back to her place before Paco had realised her absence, which might gravely disturb him, but she was told there was not the least chance of getting back to the barrera, every inch of space was jammed, and even if she succeeded in forcing her way up the steps before the fight was over, she would then very likely be caught by the outpouring crowds and might even be injured in the rush.

"My husband's all right?" she managed to gasp. "You know who I am—the wife of the Niño!"

"Ah, señora, the Niño's all right—muy bien, muy bien!" she was told, with tolerant amusement. Her heart sank; it was plain that Paco had lost his éxito with the Mexican audience, but at least he was alive and sound.

She lay in the green light from the persianas, wondering if she could have imagined the whole thing: the silence, the bull's rush, Paco's helplessness and Ildefonso's immobility. He could, of course, have judged that the peón, although farther away, was better placed to intercept the bull than he. That must have been how it appeared to the onlookers. But her instinct told her that it was deliberate; that it was—if only for a fraction of time—Ildefonso's intention that Paco should get killed. Her head swam with the horror of it. He must have gone mad.

She lay in the fading light, waiting for Paco's return. Presently she heard his and Tonio's voices in the adjoining room. Perhaps he would come in to her. They might have told him about her mishap. But when, after a while, he gave no signs of coming, she got up, brushed her hair and straightened her gown crumpled by lying on the bed. Tonio seemed to take a long while in undressing him. She went out on the balcony, and watched for a while the traffic moving under the trees luminous with the street lamps. Suddenly she became aware of silence in the next room.

She opened the connecting door and looked in. Everything was tidy; on a string across the window swung on hangers the chaqueta, vest and taleguilla. She went to touch them, still hot and wet from his body. Tonio came out of the bathroom with a handful of lint and cottonwool.

" Pues—where's Paco ? "

" He's gone out; he didn't know you were here," he stammered.

" Didn't anyone tell him——? " She felt the blood rising in her face.

" Yes, they said you were with friends—I guess Paco thought you'd gone home with them. I'll find him, if you like."

" Don't give yourself the trouble." She slammed the door.

She waited until nearly ten o'clock, then, as she was very hungry, rang for the menu. The boy who brought it was not the usual waiter; he excused himself by saying there was a ball in the hotel.

" The señora has been to los toros ? "

" Seguro." She realised, to her amusement, that he did not know who she was. " You were there too, chico ? "

" I was given a ticket. And if I die to-morrow, I can say I have seen Ildefonso ! "

" He was good ? "

" Hay muchos toreros; Ildefonso—no hay qué uno," he spoke as though they were reciting a creed.

" Is that what they're all saying ? "

" Sí, señora." He nodded with confidence.

" And—Niño de Maderas ? " she faltered.

" Muy fino. A smart boy ! " He grinned at her. " The señora is from Europe ? "

" Yes—and so is Niño de Maderas. And so," she added, " is Ildefonso."

He shook his head.

" Ildefonso is from heaven. Es santo de los toros."

It was after midnight, when Paco returned. He greeted her with a casual " Olá," and told the waiter who followed him with gin and iced water on a tray to leave the bottle. He poured himself a drink. Infuriated by his indifference, she burst out :

" So it comes to this : you leave me to eat by myself after a fight."

" I didn't know you were in."

" You didn't take much trouble to find out, did you ? "

He gave her an odd look.

" You're all right now, are you ? "

" No thanks to you."

He drained the glass, keeping his eyes on her, and set it down. He came towards her slowly.

" So Ildefonso dedicates his bulls to you."

" So you dedicate yours to Señora Martínez."

" No es iguál."

She laughed shrilly.

" I'm glad you admit it. And I hope you've had a pleasant evening."

" Bueno, I have."

" And which of your girl friends contributed to it ? "

He had her by the shoulders and was forcing her back towards the bed. At first she tried to make a joke of it.

" I'm not one of your women and even if you're drunk you needn't start rough play with me. Other people may like it, I don't."

Yet, for all her defiance, she was frightened when he pinned her down.

" Are you my wife ? "

" What is this nonsense ? "

With a movement of shocking brutality, he tore her bedgown from throat to hem.

" That is enough," he muttered. " You shall have a child, if I kill you for it ! "

Chapter Seven

I

" Holy Week in Sevilla. It is a great privilege."

" Yes, Reverend Mother ; I'll try to be worthy of it."

The wise eyes twinkled ; a deep chuckle came from behind the snowy wimple.

" And of the brave bulls ? "

They both laughed. As she closed the parlour door behind her, Mary tried to realise that each step she took was a step towards Spain.

" Please, Miss Mary, begin saving up at once, so that you can come and stay with us as soon as we are married ! "—Those had been Aracea's last words, in parting. They quickened the pang of separation. Go back to Spain she dared not, for, once there, she could never bring herself to leave it again. When I'm an old woman, I shall go back, and die in Spain. She smiled now, remembering the thought at the back of her mind when they said Good-bye, for, as time wore on, and the work of the school lost its novelty, the longing again to see Spain over-rode the dread of returning. She had been " saving " now, for more than twelve months, for the journey—rejecting the cheaper sea passage, which would have cut all of a week out of her too-brief holiday. Her heart was set on being there for the Santa Semana. If only one could add a fortnight of the summer vacation on to the Easter month ! But perhaps it was as well not to allow too much time for the old spell to re-establish itself.

The beat of her heart quickened as the plane, partnered by its small, faithful shadow, flew over the green and brown and ochre velvet of the Spanish landscape : almost ceased as they wheeled over the Guadalquivír marshes, as the Giralda came in sight, and—oh heaven !—the Maestranza and the Torre de Oro.

. . . The first day passed in " showing her everything." There was so much to see—though much was incomplete. The distaste of the Spanish labourer for carrying any one task to its completion brought a smile to her lips ; who cared ? In the bedroom she was given, beautifully and even lavishly furnished, one wall was yet unpainted. Aracea apologised ; the new bathroom was still as much of a showpiece as when its fittings occupied a Madrid shop-window. " They haven't connected up the water supply, but the drainage is quite in order, and they will fill the bath whenever you choose."

" But where did all these beautiful things come from ? "

" The furniture ?—Oh, it was pushed away somewhere, and we found the damasks in some old chests in the cellar. They must have been locked up for a hundred years."

" What fun it must have been."

" Indeed it was. We spent a whole week, breaking into rooms that had never been opened in Papá's time. There was even a travelling coach, that must have belonged to great grand-papá, piled up inside with deed-boxes and documents ; and piles of old-fashioned harness, and—oh yes : an old picador's suit, of, I imagine, the early eighteenth century."

" That must have interested Paco."

" Oh yes. He was very interested, in everything," said Aracea flatly.

Mary gave her a quick look. The girl was even more beautiful than formerly, but had aged in a way that struck Mary to the heart. It was less a physical than a spiritual ageing, that conferred on her the tragic aura that surrounds so many young Spanish women of the educated classes to-day. Andalucían volatility played like cold lightning over an impenetrable reserve. What, wondered Mary, has education done for them, so far, but open a gateway into an empty world ?—To make the triumph of the modern Spanish girl over tradition complete, one needs also to alter the man !

Paco, who happened, on her arrival, to be at home, greeted

her with immense warmth and assurance ; did the honours with
a flourish, and before she had time even to remove the clothes
she had travelled in, insisted upon conducting her into his special
domain—the great, vaulted room that she remembered as a
cellar, where Aracea and the boys practised their capes. A group
of young men grinned, muttered " Qué tal ? " or " Olá ! " and
gripped her hand, as Paco presented her. She dutifully admired
the new bar, the billiard table, the collection of trophies and a
shocking life-size daub of Paco, specially lighted, in a frame of
glaring gilt, taking inward note of Paco himself. Paco the
matador, physically superb in a sharp-cut, American-style suit,
a hand-painted tie. He looked like a handsome young spiv, and
his manner towards Aracea was more overbearing than the
husband-wife relationship justifies, even in a country of male
supremacy. No flicker betrayed Aracea's reactions. He could
probably make himself irresistible to a beautiful or worth-while
woman, but to the ex-governess his manner, although not
actually bad, was somewhat too free and jovial for a young man
towards an elder lady.

He departed before dinner, with his flock of friends.

" You must come and see me fight before you go back to
England," he told her.

" Yes, indeed," said Mary politely. " Where are you booked
for Easter ? "—hoping it would be in the north, if not at the
Maestranza. When he told her Málaga, a pang of disappointment
shot through her ; it was to be taken for granted they would
go to Málaga, and she had been living in the thought of the
white and gold of the Sevillan ring.

" You should have come last month, when I asked you to,"
Aracea reproached her. " There was no reason you should not
ask a favour, for once, I am sure ! Don't you remember when
Miss Bellamy took nearly a month away, in the middle of the
School Certificate term ? "

" She got leave, poor thing, to nurse her mother, who was
dying."

" Well "—Aracea shrugged her shoulders—" it's a pity, for
after Good Friday we shan't have much time to ourselves. We

are putting up a lot of business people for the feria; it is a nuisance, but it was Carlos's suggestion, and, for once, I think, a good one. Most of them were old acquaintances of Papá's, and it's a good idea to keep in touch with them. You'll have to help me to play hostess to the women," she grimaced. "The men will spend most of their time looking at the bulls, or in town, and we'll all have to go to the feria in the evenings, I suppose."

"And the fights?" Mary could not resist putting in.

"I've got seats for you. I thought you would want to see Ildefonso."

"How very kind. You will be going to Málaga, I expect?"

"Possibly."

She was introduced to a stout, handsome, young woman, with a castilian accent, who smilingly recalled their meeting in Segovia, and left them by themselves.

"With Paco away so much, I had to engage a companion, and I decided it was better not to have one of the family."

"That must have taken some decision!" She knew how every Spanish family has its hangers-on, who live in the hope of such a post as the one Aracea offered.

"She is family, in a way," admitted Aracea. "She married one of my cousins, who went off with someone else, leaving Olalla quite penniless. The de la Cernas were very angry with her because she insisted on earning her own living, but she has a boy to educate, and she did not wish him to be turned into a professor or a priest by the Segovian lot! I always liked Olalla; she's not bad company, and she's very tactful. She looks after the housekeeping and writes most of my letters."

"I imagined from your letters you went everywhere with Paco."

"Oh—didn't I mention it? I'm supposed to be having a baby."

The casual announcement brought home to Mary the rupture in their old relationship. She had felt it from the moment of meeting, despite the warmth of her reception: the touch—wholly unconscious—of patronage from the married to the unmarried woman; the hint of a veil she was not supposed to penetrate. She should have expected it; one of her sisters, who had married in the Christmas vacation, was the same. But there had never been between them the close relationship that existed between her and Aracea. She felt it strangely, that Aracea should be the one to bring home to her the dedicated solitude of her life of an old maid, seeking in vicarious emotions some relief of its emptiness. She had long realised that the career of a schoolteacher was no solution, for her, and felt foolish and a little guilty that this girl should stand for so much in it: reassuring herself with the thought that what Aracea stood for, really, was a symbol of Spain, her one remaining contact with the country of her love.

Her first encounter with Carlos was singularly unemotional on both sides. As his dry lips touched the back of her hand, and she looked curiously down on the back of the dark, polished head, with the strap of the eye-shade running round it, she had not, to her surprise, the faintest sense of embarrassment, resentment or even distaste. If she felt anything, it was a trace of pity for so much " come to dust," the Don Juan bereft by time of his magic. Not that there was any awareness of that in his deportment. But she felt nothing but a dry amusement when his eye brushed her with the perception that she also had aged.

Ay, there were many changes in the house of Parral; but, when she slipped down into the patio of the horses, to lay her head for a moment against the snowy neck of Bandera, when she felt on her cheek the soft muzzle and the sweet breath, the joy of return revived.

II

From the Easter week-end onward, the house was, in effect, a hotel, crowded with strangers, the only ones of whom offered prospect, to Mary, of entertainment were an English couple, the Brett Pawls. Cars were continually rushing in and out of town with the men of the party, while the elderly wives sat about, gossiping, gaping at the transformation of the house of Parral, endlessly drinking coffee and chocolate and nibbling sweetmeats, sufficient—to the relief of Mary and Olalla—to themselves and suspicious of the foreigners. The whole caravanserai went in for the Easter High mass, and those who were going to the fight lunched at the Andalucía Palace. Aracea took most of the women back to the house, and, to Mary's surprise, Carlos offered her his escort to the ring.

"I thought Aracea would be going to Málaga; I suppose she will join us, later on."

"I doubt it. Since they came back, my cousin has not been much to los toros," she was told, significantly. Aracea was probably taking care of the baby; was that by Paco's wish, or her own? More likely the former, for Mary had often been surprised at the number of young women, embarrassingly pregnant, who went to the fight, it appeared, almost to the day of their delivery. She murmured something about its being sensible, and Carlos observed:

"No doubt. But it is a pity she reserved her discretion to this late hour of the day."

"Why?—The child isn't due for six or seven months, is it?"
Carlos laughed.

"I must admit I wasn't thinking of the future of Parral! It just occurred to me that it would be better for Aracea, if she had conducted her marriage along less original lines."

"No doubt she is quite satisfied with the way things are."

"Caramba, you have not lost the art of the snub!"

"I'm sorry. But I'd rather discuss Aracea's affairs with her, than behind her back," said Mary icily.

"Has she shown any inclination to discuss them?" he said, with patent curiosity. "I think not! It is not very pleasant for a wife, to admit that she has lost her husband's interest before she has even borne him a child."

"It would distress me very much, if such a thing were true," she answered, after a pause.

"But why? You should be gratified, as you are a good deal responsible for it."

" What a disgraceful thing to say ! " burst from her indignantly.

" Not at all," was the cool rejoinder. " If you believe in your own principles, you must allow that Aracea has reacted admirably to your training. For me—let me say that my sympathies are wholly with Paco, who, since his marriage, has put up with a great deal more than the average husband would have borne."

" If he has, it is because he has chosen to bear it, and he has certainly got a great deal out of it," she retorted.

He gave her a curious look.

" Paco has done very well, considering his unpopularity with the afición, and the way he has been made a laughing stock in the profession. It is bad enough, to be called an amateur, with nothing to do if he gets a bad deal in the ring but retire in comfort to his wife's ranch——"

" Why should they blame him for a piece of good fortune that comes to him only by the chance of his marriage ? It is merely jealousy ; everyone knows that any matador, if he gets the opportunity, marries money. And it so happens they were very much in love."

" Jealousy is a little weapon that can cause a big wound. A bullfighter whose wife travels around with him, instead of stopping at home to look after the children, invites much malice. If there are no children, he is a target for some very rude remarks. Especially," concluded Carlos, as he took her elbow to guide her through the crowds streaming towards the ring, " if he is not a ' milagro.' "

The slow river shining on their left, the familiar sights and sounds, the vibration that fills the air on the day of a fight—above all, of the fight on Resurrection Sunday—so moved her that her reply was perfunctory.

" Last time I was here, they were calling Ildefonso a ' milagro'; I suppose they still do."

" Sometimes," he told her laconically.

. . . It was better, she told herself, at the end of the afternoon, to have seen a mediocre fight than none at all. The day was chill, with some wind ; spring had been long delayed, and the bulls had not come into their own. Christ was risen—and was recrucified a dozen times in the Maestranza on that dreary afternoon. She found herself sickening with disgust of the whole human race, when, after four abortive attempts, Ildefonso killed his first bull, and took in his face of death a barbarity of abuse.

It was some hours before she recovered from her disgust. The next day was a little better, but not much. Later, under the garlands of the feria, in the Parral casita, its walls a solid mass of crimson carnations, its seats covered with the gold and violet of the Parral devisa ; with the guitars and the girls' swirling flounces and the click of castañuelas and the flamenco singing— she still felt unable to enter into the lightheartedness of these people, many of whom, but a few hours ago, had assisted at the Immortal Tragedy.

III

It was Sylvia Brett Pawl's suggestion, that they should go on at midnight to the Casino.

" But the dancing won't be nearly as good there, as here. It's very ordinary cabaret, and the band isn't much."

" Candidly, honey, I'm a bit worn down with all this un-diluted Spanish."

Aracea laughed ; she, too, had had enough of performing her duties as dueña of Parral ; of shaking hands with strangers, exchanging jokes and introductions, drinking sherry and receiving the piropo from the multitudes drifting past the garlanded balcony. It had been amusing, when Papá was alive—to be free to dance and flirt, to visit from booth to booth, to be toasted in the important clubs as daughter of Parral and dance the sevillana with a group of young accredited friends. She had had enough of answering inquiries about Paco, and diplomatic congratulations on the show he had given in Málaga. Paco should, and could well have been, there, to lend his importance to the reception. He had given a half-promise, which, of course, he had conveniently forgotten, some more alluring prospect having opened up. He was not likely to have stayed over in Málaga, and the probability that he was somewhere here, in Sevilla, and that the people who shook hands with and congratulated her knew about it, was humiliating.

They were a party of six—the Brett Pawls, two American boys and a girl—when they settled at a large round table, having left Carlos and Mary to deputize. Mary was not to be drawn from the feria, and Aracea did not try to persuade her. The tourist stuff held no attraction for Mary, and Aracea found herself envying her as the longueurs of the night developed, with cabaret girls pretending to be gipsies and a band massacring the American dance rhythms.

A wave of excitement among the groups near the curtains which cut off the foyer from the dancing floor drew her eyes across the room to an arriving party.

" Olé, La Carmelita ! Olé, matador ! "

It was Ildefonso, entering with the star of the Casino bill ; he lost in a tuxedo, she in ruffled white, with three yards of train following her like a serpent across the polished floor. Her arms loaded from wrist to elbow with sparkling paste, immense pendants swinging from her ears to the brown flesh of her shoulders, she made insolent acknowledgment of her reception. A brown, shining brow, long Moorish eyes and delicate nose redeemed the sensuality of mouth, jaw and chin. She sat down with her back to the Brett Pawls' table, and Aracea found herself looking across the floor into the eyes of Ildefonso.

It was like being in a trap, with no means of escape. She felt herself shrivelling, as she wondered if the night would ever end. She refused an invitation to dance. In the intervals between the turns, the others were dancing ; all the women trying to attract Ildefonso's attention—so fatally, even when she was not looking, riveted on her ! " Por dios," she felt like shrieking, " don't be such a fool ! " It might easily, if his companion noticed, provoke a scene.

" Can't we ask them over here ? "

" Do as you please," she shrugged.

"But, honey, you *know* him! Don't be a heel, and keep that gorgeous piece of male to yourself!"

She looked at Brett Pawl.

"Do you want to send a message?"

"How about sending over a bottle of pop?"

"That, perhaps, would be best."

She watched the waiter carry over the ice-bucket; watched him fill the glasses; watched Ildefonso rise, glass in hand, and La Carmelita turn, to flash acknowledgment across a lovely shoulder. They all drank; as she expected, he drank with his eyes on her.

"Well, don't we ask them over now?"

"She's going to dress for her first number. And—you see—he's going with her."

Neither, to the disappointment of the party, appeared at the table again. La Carmelita presented half a dozen glittering numbers; it was getting on for four in the morning, and Aracea dizzied with the smoke, the heat and the wine, was grateful when her guests suggested departure.

While they waited for the car in the great, pale foyer, she, in her mantón, envying the other women their fur coats, a Casino attendant came up to her.

"Co su permiso: there is one who wishes to speak to the señora."

"Who is it?"

She gathered from the boy's sly smile that he had been paid not to give a name, and knew at once it was Ildefonso.

"I am engaged, with my friends."

"Es una persona muy distinguida!"—Fearing to lose credit, the boy's face was anxious and crestfallen. The others had drawn tactfully aside.

"What distinguished person does not give this name?" she was about to say. She had not realised how close she stood to the curtains which cut off the artistes' quarters from the public rooms of the Casino. Something like a wing swept over her, and she was facing Ildefonso.

Looking at everything but her companion, the vast, bare

space reminded her of the bullring ; a blood-coloured frieze, shoulder-high, was like the fence round the callejón, and the pale walls above it might be the gradas. And she stood there, on the sand, with not even a cape for her defence.

He stood back from her, a smile jagging his face which was like a slice of lemon.

" You don't have to look like I was one of your bulls ! I just wanted to give you a message."

" A message——— ? " she faltered.

" A message for Paco. Say, he doesn't have to get himself killed, to beat me. Living or dead, no one can beat Ildefonso. It's silly to try." He said it wearily, with an indifference that robbed the words of their vainglory. She remembered a phrase current at St. Margaret's ; " I couldn't care less ! " It was usually a bluff on the part of the speaker, but, in this case, it was no bluff. She moistened her lips, to answer.

" I will tell him."

He said :

" I've dedicated two of my bulls to you. Some day, I'll dedicate another."

" Please don't ! " she cried. " You've got no right—and—and it only upsets Paco."

He moved forward. He swept the curtain aside, inviting her departure. And, as she went through, he said :

" By that time, Paco won't count ; because you'll belong to me."

Paco, to her surprise, turned up the following morning.

" They gave me a formidable reception, at Málaga ! "

" Naturally." She had not meant irony to echo in her voice ; she was appalled to realise that Paco had heard it. Paco had always been conveniently deaf to anything but adulation.

" Muy bien ; in time, you will hear." The words came as cold as flint.

" Hombre, it is enough that you should tell me." She spoke with compunction. " I wish I had been there. I've seen the notices——— "

" The notices are cow-shit, and those who write them are

the sons of whores and I spit in their milk." He seldom used the language of the cuadrilla in front of her. "They took the tripes out of Ildefonso after Sunday, didn't they? Well, perhaps it's my turn to be 'un milagro'!" He laughed and patted her stomach. "Y el niño? You are making me a fine little torero, to carry on the blood of El Cigarrón?"

She was surprised, a few days later, to receive confirmation by word of mouth of his success at Malaga, and from an unexpected source. It was Benito who, with a shining face, gave her the news.

"Paco was like Jesus, Mary and Joseph at Málaga! My brother-in-law, who was there, says it was an annunciation."

She stared at him. It was unlike Benito to bestow praise save where it was merited. She wondered why she was not more glad. Was this not what she had worked and prayed for?

The house had settled into its normal quiet, with the departure of the guests. There were now only herself, Mary, Olalla and Carlos, and occasional people who came, selling machinery, or cattle food; or young toreros, asking leave to work the cows, or parties invited by Carlos to watch the tientas. She left most of them to Carlos. It was surprising, what her continual presence on the ranch had achieved, so far as the work went. She seemed to do very little, but every morning she rode out with Mary, round the smithy, and the stables and the building that housed the electric plant, and the dairy and the matadero and the yards where they kept the turkeys and pigs and geese and hens that supplied the household, she received some fresh proof of renewed devotion to the interests of Parral. She should have been very happy . . .

The last Sunday before Mary's departure, Paco was fighting at Antequera. He had had fights at Bilbao, Vista Alegre—an unimportant one—Lucena and one good one at the Monumental. The reports varied; at Bilbao he had given, it appeared, one of his cast-iron, copper-riveted shows with as much emotion as a plate of meat. At the minor ring of Vista Alegre he put on a show that sold out the Monumental on the day the booking opened: and, having collected the ears at Lucena, gave in

Madrid a performance of such consummate dullness that he got the bronca on a scale rarely given to a top-flight matador at the supposed height of his career. All this, however, in some ways heightened his reputation with the afición. In place of buying a certified exposition of the complete art of tauromachy, in which many of them were, or considered themselves, as well informed as the exponent, they might be buying a surprise. The critics were reputedly annoyed because, instead of writing the Niño's notices on the eve of a fight, they were obliged to get down to it and give their readers a picture of what actually happened. And the fans were bewildered, because their faith was being let down. The aggregate of opinion was, however, that for some reason unknown, the Niño de Maderas, regarded heretofore as a bull-killing machine, was going through a sea-change it was interesting to watch. If it resulted in his death or disappearance from the ring was a matter of small import. But a number of people who had been frivolous about the Niño packed up their frivolity.

A very little of this filtered through to the house of Parral ; just enough for Aracea to say, when Mary suggested their going to Antequera——

" I wish you could have seen him last season ; you could have been sure of—something."

" But isn't it much nicer, not to be ' sure ' ? Do you realise I've never seen Paco since he took the alternativa ?—that I've never seen one of the most important toreros in Spain ? " smiled Mary. " Let's not tell him we are going, and give him a surprise ! "

IV

She knew instantly that Paco was terrified. It struck chill into her blood. She had never before seen him anything but cool—at least, on the surface. None but an idiot can go out on the sand without fear, but he had always had the power to control his fear, to cover it with that shining veneer of confidence that the fans expected of him. His seeming carelessness was part of the picture that was completed by his skill.

She found herself realising, for the first time, how much of Paco's success he owed to sheer luck. Other fighters were skilful and courageous, and it did not save them from the horns. Strength and judgment and impeccable reactions contribute, but it takes more than these to preserve the one who goes out to meet fifteen-arroba Death with no protection but a pink rag and a little sword that could bend double if it went in in the wrong place !

Although they were immediately behind him, Paco was unconscious of their presence. His brown skin looked dusty and he kept asking Tonio for water. As he spat it out, she was near enough to see the muscle working under his jaw. The vanity scared out of him, he was frightened, and he did not care who knew it.

As though he felt something, Tonio looked up suddenly and saw her. She made a slight negatory movement of the head— " Don't tell Paco "—and saw him understand. He looked sick and worried.

The two peónes had run themselves nearly to a standstill by the time Paco went out, and the crowd had started to get rude, but it gave the Niño a cheer as he went out, with a curious, jerking reluctance, as though at each step someone was giving him a slight push in the buttocks. The bull, an enormous nevado, with horns like hat racks, stood and stared. For a moment Paco stood too and stared back at it. It was the bad one of his pair and he had chosen to take it first, to get it over. I would draw a bull like this to-day. He had a feeling of not being there, that all this was taking place in his sleep, and that his body had turned to fluff. The bull would rush straight through his body and on, with a mass of fluff on its horns ! There was an absolute silence, while his body hung there, between the sand and the air, wondering what he was supposed to do.

When the rush came, he automatically spun out the cape and stepped back. The shaking of the earth as the spotted thing went by—like a snowstorm shot from the heart of a thundercloud—

restored solidity to him, and fear. Preparing his veronica, those horns seemed to span the horizon, they made a grey bar that touched the fence both sides of the ring. From the waist down he became incarnate fear. His arms were still, apparently, capable of performing their function; as the bull came back, they sailed the cape out, low, and as the horns came through, level with his shins, his irresponsible legs went back again.

The crowd was silent, because it was Niño de Maderas, whose cartel was strong in Antequera. The ancient wooden ring simmered in silence, then, as the ignoble manœuvre repeated itself, twice, thrice—burst into rebellion.

Mary's eyes met Aracea's. Their two mouths stretched in the muscular rictus of a smile. Each knew too much to speak, neither would condescend to false palliatives. Aracea's heart beat steadily, a rhythm of acceptance, but Mary's was heavy with self-reproach. They were here by her suggestion, and it was a bad afternoon for Paco. Ojalá, that nothing would happen—she would never forgive herself.

Paco recovered some credit in the act of the horse by a fine quite. He did not know how he brought it off. It was as though clouds were passing across his brain; inside the cloud he seemed to become part of it, a floating intangibility. When it passed, he felt himself abandoned to his own body that waited to betray him, to clusters of jumping nerves, to the horns which, as though made of elastic, at one minute stretched across the whole width of the sand and at the next seemed to shrink to thimbles on either side of the great square head. When the trumpet went, he was in a staring clarity of blue and yellow and the horns were horns, one of them a slimy red. The wet red caught the light and winked at him. One of the boys was working the bull away from a dead horse and they were picking Curro up and carrying him along the callejón. The bag of manure! By Jesus and Mary, he was out, this time. In his usual blind funk, he had practically missed with the iron; sweet Mother of Christ, was it possible? It went in at a glancing angle, in spite of the guard, as the bull got its head under and the horse went up and Curro, uttering a shrill scream, cracked backwards on the fence. When the third man drew the bull out, it had received, in effect, only half of its punishment, and was hardly out of its levantado stage. Oh, those bastards of pics.

" You and Mundo take the sticks," he muttered to Chano. That torn muscle, though it was supposed to have healed up, was not to be trusted; the ache in his thigh was probably imaginary, but a bicho like this one left no margin for chance. He listened sourly to Chano, garnering the cheers. There were no supporting clouds when he stepped out of the burladero and took the sword and muleta from Tonio. Everything was brutally clear when he went through the routine below the president's box. Tonio had run round behind the fence to take the montera after the salutation. As he turned to face the bull, wondering how to open his faena, a feeling of absolute solitude descended upon him. It was like being left on a mountain, in the track of an avalanche.

While he hesitated, a derisive whistle burst out behind him and the crowd accepted its signal and started booing. He turned his head sharply, to glare at the tiers behind him—and, in the very act of turning, felt himself again caught up into the cloud.

As the bull came through, he unfolded the first of his estatu-arios. As though a plug had been driven into the throat of the crowd, there was silence, that broke in a shout as, having given them their money's worth of the two-handed pass, he took the muleta and sword into his right hand and lifted the bull with the pase por alto. It was a folly, with a bull so little reduced, but it came off. He tried it again, and as it went through, one of the banderillas caught him hard on the cheekbone.

The trivial blow, taking him by surprise, broke his trance. Fear flowed back in him, as, after that deceptively meek begin-ning, the bull started to show him and the audience how far it was from accepting its fate. The sweat poured into the palms of his hands, and he felt the stick slipping, while his wrist sagged with the endless chopping from horn to horn. His heart was pumping and time was going on. He saved himself with an ignoble sideways skip from a lunge with the horn, which grazed his right thigh and a strip of lavender-coloured silk dropped down over the pink stocking, leaving a panel of white—like the slashed breeches in old-fashioned pictures. The crowd by now had abandoned itself to abuse ; this was not bullfighting. Some people were standing up, yelling their disapprobation of the management, which had prudently removed itself from the callejón, and cushions were sailing through the air. And that immortal bastard of a nevado bull still had its head up, still came after the rag ; with its elastic horns lengthening and shortening, so that one could never judge their distance from one's defence-less flesh and had to concentrate on keeping out of their way ; refusing to accept a pass, as though determined to reduce its enemy to the last extremity of ridicule . . .

The plaza was in an uproar and the police had been called to deal with a section of the crowd that had started to break up anything it could lay its hands on. Chano, his face tormented, his eyes glazed with tears, was muttering, " You'll have to give it them, Paco."

The bull was facing him, heaving, its head down for the first time, but its feet, as though by instinct, wide apart. He slid the sword out of the rag and shook the red, taking two short steps towards the bull. Somebody laughed. He felt something inside him burst, like an abscess. " Ah-ha, Toro. Ah-ha ! " His voice came out in a dry crackle. The bull pulled its feet out of the sand and started towards him. He heard Chano yell, " Not now, Paco ! " as he aimed along the blade, but by that time he was on his way.

He felt the bull's nose hit him at the precise moment the crack of the brow lifted him in the air. He seemed to take an infinite time over coming down, as though someone had slipped a sling under him and was lowering him gently—oh, with indescribable gentleness ! Before this illusion was dispelled by the crack on the sand, he heard himself murmuring, " The horns, the beautiful, bloody horns ! "—whose branching alone had saved his life.

" Don't move." Mary's hand gripped Aracea's ; the girl had risen, and Mary with her ; the latter's knees were trembling. " Tonio will come and tell us."

It was not Tonio, who had followed the men carrying Paco to the infirmary, but Chano who came running, and lifted his face that looked as though it had been dipped in water towards the two women.

" Not a scratch—grace to God ! Tonio's mending his pants —and the next bull is a good one."

" Does he know we are here ? "

" I guess Tonio will tell him, when he's done his needlework!"

" Do you know if he's coming home to-night ? "

" I couldn't say, señora."

" Do you want to wait for the second bull ? Wouldn't you rather we went home ? " asked Mary. Apprehensive of the effects of the shock on Aracea, she thought of the long drive, the late arrival and the nervous reaction that must follow an afternoon like this. Aracea was smiling ; her face was grey, and she added to its greyness by powdering it, but the hand that applied the powder appeared to be steady.

" Oh no. I want to see something good—after *that* exhibition ! "

" The bull was an abomination ! "

" And so was Paco's performance." She spoke with a light defiance that covered, guessed Mary, deep mortification. " He'll be better after this. Ai-ee, Mary ! You can't go back to England with that impression of my husband ! "

" I'd hate you to stay on my account. It can't be good for you," faltered Mary.

" Qué disparate ! It would take more than that to upset a little torero ! "—She laughed and patted her belt.

Paco came straight along the callejón and stood below them.

" Olá ! " he grinned, with a mixture of surprise, sheepishness and toleration on his face. His eyelids were heavy and there was —not surprisingly—a battered look about him, which Aracea decided to attribute to the mishap. " I hope you enjoyed the circus act I put on for you ! " he laughed at Mary.

" Well—once is enough," she smiled back at him. " Are you all right ? "

" I'll show you I'm all right with the next one."

" Hombre, you'd better come home to-morrow. There's a letter from Wilbur ; he wants to know what's happening about the book."

" What's he want to know ?—It's finished, isn't it ? "

" We've just finished going through it—endless mistakes—and the translation's a disaster. Wait till you read it ! I shouldn't think Wilbur's friend has been near a bullring in his life."

" Bueno," scowled Paco. " I'll be home."

He turned towards the ring. Thank God, the cloudiness had gone, and most of the fear. By the time came for his next bull, he would be all right. Machado's men were running his bull—another Devil's son, by the look of it. Somebody ought to shoot up the management, for the bunch of butcher's meat they'd laid on this afternoon ; un escándalo. The crowd was making rude remarks. Well, let's see what they give Machado.

Paco's second bull turned out to be the only good one of the day, and he managed to give something like one of his old performances—although his act with the cape was nearly ruined by the intrusion of an espontáneo, who, before he was chased from the ring and captured by the police, had managed to break up the line of connection between man and bull that Paco was labouring to establish. He stood, swearing a steady stream of filth, feeling like an actor who has lost the atmosphere of a tragic scene to a snigger in the audience. His anger stayed with him for the rest of the fight, unbalancing his performance : but at least it nailed his feet to the sand, and the crowd, veering in the easy fashion of bullfight crowds, yelled its applause as, formerly, it had yelled its derision. He found himself despising it for its facile enthusiasm and equally facile condemnation—its assumption of omnipotence : up there, safe on the stands, condescending to one who risked his life for its entertainment. Stripped by contempt of the last traces of fear, he killed, at last, with such cold perfection, such apparent ease, such absence of emotion that there was a perceptible pause before the applause broke out. Niño de Maderas walked back to the callejón with a sneer on his face. They were disappointed, weren't they ! He had given them none of the fun of the near-death on which they were

374

counting! Thanks to a brave bull, which had contributed its full share of honour to the honour of the matador, they felt cheated! The sneer was still on his face, at the back of the bright mechanism of his smile, when he went the round with the ear they belatedly conceded him. Surely they must realise that, with a bull like that, anyone could be good?—and that Ildefonso himself could have made nothing of a bicho like the first?

" He's terribly good! " Mary was crying to Aracea.

" Yes," said Aracea flatly.

" It's marvellous, after all these years, to watch someone you believed in from the beginning, and have your judgment confirmed."

" Yes," said Aracea. As Paco came up, she bent forward and smiled at him—a heart-rending smile. He was still in his anger and contempt; he glowered up at her. " Bravo, hombre."

He muttered something and turned away. She resigned herself to watching the remainder of the fight.

In the car she closed her eyes, too tired to speak. Mary, no less exhausted, settled back in her corner; sleepily remembering the many times they had driven back like this, through the darkening country, watching the striped olive-groves being swallowed into the dusk, and lights shining out on precipitous streets as they passed through villages crusted on the steep hillside, and at last nothing but the fan of the lamps penetrating the long darkness of the highway. . . .

Something of silk brushed her lips, settled on her shoulder. " Te quiero mucho." As she slid her arm round the slender body, she thought of the child she had loved and cherished; the child, now woman, who in sleep delivered herself back to the keeping of one she had loved in the past. " Te quiero mucho." How could she bring back happiness to this child, for whom her love had never wavered? She sat stiffly in the dark, holding Aracea; wondering whether she would ever be received back into a confidence which had been withdrawn from her.

Chapter Eight

I

"Don Pasquale?—This is an unexpected pleasure." The three women were playing cards. Aracea performed the introductions. "The señorita Carpenter—inglesa—muy amiga mia. Mi prima —Doña Olalla de la Cerna."

"Tanto gusto," muttered Don Pasquale, over the extended hands. "So Paco is not here." He had learned as much, downstairs ; he had debated the interview with Paco's wife—for whom, however, his resentment had died down. And he was bursting with news. So he had carried his weight up the curving staircase, in the wake of a servant, and allowed himself to be ushered into the sala.

"No. You haven't heard from him lately ? "

"Not since Antequera. That was bad—no ? "

"We were there. He did very well with the second bull. Won't you sit down, Don Pasquale ?—Una copita ?—Prima mia, do me the favour to pour a glass for our visitor."

Olalla went to the cabinet with the manzanilla and the glasses, brought Don Pasquale his copita, and modestly retired.

"I drink by myself ? Pues—salud ! " He drank, and set down the glass. "So Paco is not at home."

"I'm sorry you molested yourself to come out."

"Nada, nada. I could have used the telephone. But I had business at Sanjorje and this was in my way," explained Don Pasquale, reaching, as he spoke, into his breast pocket and producing some sheets of paper covered with typescript. "This is from my friend, Pedro Santillana."

The critic ?—Aracea turned quickly and Mary pricked her ears.

" He proposes to publish it in his paper. He did me the favour of sending me a copy in advance. With your permission, señoras ? "

With an actor's air, Don Pasquale proceeded to deliver himself of the opening phrases.

" ' Niño de Maderas gave an infamous performance at Antequera with his first bull '—naturally," put in Don Pasquale, " Don Pedro must prove his good faith to his readers. It is generally known, Antequera was very bad."

" And the bulls were scandalous."

" There is no question. The señora must pardon my friend Don Pedro, whose responsibility to the public obliges him to be exact."

" Undoubtedly," said Aracea, with a thin smile.

Don Pasquale hurried on :

" ' After a display of cowardice that offended the audience and an ill-judged attempt with the sword, he took a toss with no ill effects. The bull was killed by the valiant sobresaliente, José Gandarillas—— ' "

" Won't we read all this in the papers ? " yawned Aracea.

" Un momento." Don Pasquale lifted his hand. " ' The Niño improved with his second bull and was awarded the ear and a considerable ovation.' "

" It would be difficult to say less ! " She laughed shortly. " It seems a pity, taking all things into consideration, that Don Pedro did not find space to mention the three molinetes ; the naturales and the pase de pecho that gave him the ear ! "

He looked at her heavily.

" Perhaps there were matters of more importance."

" There is more to come ? "

" You don't suppose Don Pedro would trouble to send me that routine stuff ? "—His courtesy broke down, as, with an imperious gesture, he resumed his recital.

" ' This matador is at present confusing the public which formerly rated him in the highest category by a series of performances that have gone far to reduce his established reputation. He is capable, however—as at Bilbao and Vista Alegre—of confounding his critics by a display for which, in the present ring, it would be difficult to discover a prototype.

" ' Long known as an exceptionally brave and accomplished exponent of the art—which makes more remarkable his ignoble performance at Antequera—he has failed to make an impression on a certain group of traditionalists, whose opinion carries much weight, and who profess to find his work mechanical. He had, nevertheless, a considerable following among devotees of the pure art of tauromaquía. This he is in danger of forfeiting by performances like the one at Antequera. It is also known that he made no overwhelming impression in Mexico, from which he has recently returned.

" ' It would, however, be indiscreet to dismiss Niño de Maderas on the score of half a dozen indifferent performances such as he has given since the opening of the season. He had a great reception at Málaga, on Resurrection Sunday, and has added to his laurels on at least two other occasions.

" ' A cold and impeccable artist with the cape, a brilliant bandillero and a master of the sword, Niño de Maderas has a reputation for filling the plazas. But, in his innumerable and excellent performances, which have been accepted as a model by the rising generation of bullfighters, there has been, up to now, no flash of genius. In his recent failures, one may detect possibilities to arouse new hopes in the devotees of the fiesta brava. Niño de Maderas, who so far has presented himself as a machine-made killer of bulls, may yet cross the borderline between efficiency and inspiration.' "

Don Pasquale ended triumphantly. There was a silence. Aracea said :

" That is very interesting.—You're very pleased, aren't you ? " she flung suddenly at Don Pasquale—who gaped.

" But naturally !—Let me be candid : I was not happy, at taking on the management of a bull-killing machine. I did it only for the sake of my friend Amadeo. I have been in the business too long to put money before credit ! I've made plenty out of the business, and now I can choose. Mire, señora : I booked Paco through the season—that was in our contract. But when the contract ended, I had made up my mind to tell him to look for another manager."

" Why ? "

He stuck out his lower lip and spread his hands.

" That's the way I am."

" But, surely—he's been well worth your trouble ? "

He shrugged, and dropped his head towards the left shoulder.

" He's been a good boy, Paco, and there are plenty of good boys who'd like to be managed by Pasquale Basilio."

" I'll tell him," said Aracea slowly.

" Tell him," said Don Pasquale, pushing himself up out of the chair, " that's to say, if I don't see him first—that I, Pasquale Basilio, devote myself to his interests from now on ! He'd better drop in at the office, and renew the contract—that expires at the end of next month. I want to start booking him through the winter season ; and, if things go on the way they are at present, I want to fix up that mano a mano with Ildefonso," said Don Pasquale heavily. " It'll have to be at the end of the season, when we've worked up the publicity, and it'll have to be Madrid. Tell Paco to ring me up——"

" That," said Mary, when Aracea returned from conducting Don Pasquale to the head of the stairs, " is a wonderful notice—from Santillana ! "

Aracea lit a cigarette, stuck it between her lips, slid towards the window and leant against the rejas.

" Yes—wonderful." Her voice shook. Whirling round, she dropped into a chair ; she buried her head in her arms on the table.

" Darling—— ! "

" You know—you've seen the notices—the way they've always written about Paco. You know, as well as I do, the formula they've got for the ones who have the money. You know how Papá Amadeo bought the Press for Paco, when he started, and how it's as much part of a matador's expenses as paying the cuadrilla—and we could pay more than most," she ended bitterly.

"I know all that, and I know Paco earned all the praise they gave him," said Mary stoutly. "And it is hard, to have to pay for the truth."

"Truth? Who cares for it? Paco paid, so they gave him all their stereotyped phrases of commendation. They never gave him credit—at any rate, in print—for the qualities that made him what he is. They wrote down their parrot-phrases, in praise of his ' valour,' and now and again they described a faena, or wrote him up as the maestro of the sword ! They acted like paid publicity agents. Never, never once did they give him—even the best of them—a line of serious criticism, a sentence that people of intelligence could get hold of. They were satisfied to take his money and make him ridiculous in the eyes of everybody who knows how bullfighting journalism works !"

"But his accomplishments saved him from ridicule—at any rate with anyone who saw his work," persisted Mary.

"That is true ; but many who would have admired him—I mean, the people whose opinion counts, who influence the afición—were put off by the Press. And the mob that accepts the papers as the word of God was offended, because he made it all look so easy !—because the bull didn't hit him often enough ! They'd rather watch Ildefonso being slammed against the barrera, than Niño de Maderas dominating a brave bull !"

There seemed to be no answer, for one so long out of touch with the world of the bulls.

"And the critics are the same. They will spend a column on demolishing a whole performance of Ildefonso's, and go back on all they have said in a last paragraph that makes him out to be the Messiah of the bulls. And it takes a wretched show at Antequera and a ride through the air to make Pedro Santillana indicate that Paco is, perhaps, after all, a torero to be taken seriously !"

"Isn't it something, that a critic of that calibre and influence should admit it at last ?"

Aracea beat her hands on the table.

"That is not it at all. For years they've hidden their knowledge that Paco is truly important behind their sentences of

adulation that every torero can buy, while he is making money.
They wouldn't forfeit the cash, so they put their tongues in their
cheeks and wrote down all the old things that every journalist
of the bulls learns at the beginning of his career. Even Paco,
easily as he accepts flattery, had begun to notice it. He wanted
to attack one of the critics—I think it was in Barcelona—for
practically repeating one of his earlier notices ; it turned out the
man had not even been in the plaza ! But I persuaded him not
to ; it would go all over the country and increase their malice
and hostility——"

"But there is nothing malicious or hostile in this."

"Santillana is one of the better people," she admitted. "He
is an intellectual—but even intellectuals are fond of money ! He
has been, at least, a little honest."

"And others may take their tone from him. But I don't
understand," said Mary, knitting her brows. "Paco is, as this
notice says, in the first category. What is this hostility you speak
about ?—on what is it based ? "

"I will tell you. Since we were married, Paco has made my
friends his own. He does not spend his time in clubs and bars,
making friends with disreputable people. He likes, as I do,
respectable society ; it meant a great deal to him, at first, to meet
people like the Albacobacas and the Bradomíns, and the rich
foreign set. Of course, he was flattered. It gratified him, to be
invited to famous houses and see how people of that class spent
their money—instead of squandering it in foolish ways. That
was, perhaps, superficial, and he might have got bored ; but
Tano and the elder Bradomín boy were genuine aficiónados and
both had appeared in the ring as amateurs ; so that, you see,
made friendships. It also made a great deal of jealousy."

"But why ?—All the great matadores have been honoured
in that way."

"Claro ; and were friends of the artists and intellectuals. I
don't know why, Paco's work has never appealed to the intellectuals. All the poets, the writers and painters clustered round
Ildefonso. And naturally," concluded Aracea bitterly, "the
Press followed their lead."

Mary sat silent, looking through the smoke of her cigarette at the blue sky which had not yet hardened into summer. Only a few more days. But at least, before her departure, the barrier had broken down.

" Ildefonso—always penniless, for all the money he earned ; always sick, or in trouble of some sort, or tied up with women— was their idol. Paco was despicable, because he was dedicated to the work ; because he kept himself in perfect condition, because he strove endlessly to improve himself ; because he had a sense of responsibility to himself and to the public ! He didn't disappear for days on end, with wild parties, or flaunt himself publicly as the lover of a Society woman, or a cabaret singer ! He loved *me*—and I and the work were close together ; we were enough. Ay, that's what they couldn't forgive him ! A matador's wife should have money, and stop at home, and breed like a sow. She shouldn't go around with him, and prevent him from getting into bad company, and look after his health and his pocket !— And, in the end, their sneers and their jeers began to influence Paco. He started to resent the life we planned out together——" She caught her breath. " So you see, he is not here now," she concluded, with a gesture of futility. " You heard him promise he would come home, after Antequera. He's fighting on Sunday, at Andujar, and then there's nothing until the feria starts at Jérez. He will have had more than a fortnight of drinking and racketing, and he'll come into the ring at Jérez like you saw him last Sunday ! He'll come in, to Parral bulls, and take a ride on the horn, and then—perhaps then—Pedro Santillana will write of him as ' un milagro.'

" In the name of Jesus and Mary ! "—again she smote the table—" Has a torero got to be dissolute ?—has he got to become a cripple, before writers like Santillana give him the credit he deserves ?—before he can command the support of someone like Pasquale Basilio ?—Pasquale—with his ' dedication ' to Paco's career !—his fine disclaimers of financial interest ! Vaya ! Paco's career is already assured, and it was I who assured it ; and that was what curdled the milk of our friend Don Pasquale. I was to be the—what is the word ?—the backer, and keep out of the picture ; I know, I know ! As I know that, from the time Paco gave him his business, Pasquale has been intriguing against me. And, now he has succeeded, he is, of course, very satisfied."

Mary said, after a pause :

" Tell me how it was between you and Paco, before these things happened."

A curious softness gathered about the girl, as she folded her arms and leaned on them ; her lips curved into gentleness.

" Ay, it was so happy. All the time he was not working Paco spent out here, with me. We were in love. But we were not at all lazy ! We worked with the cows, and Paco was always in training. I would not let him waste himself on small fights, and when he went into the ring—ay dios ; it was as though Apollón himself walked out on the sand ! If you could have seen him," she sighed. " And everything he did was good. On my word, it was good ! "

Why, to the quick ear of Mary, was there a ring of defiance in the words ?

. . . Aracea's preoccupation with the estate left her with much time to herself. She wandered through the house of Parral, conscious of its changed atmosphere. The old, haphazard ways of running the household had given place to a regime ; not, perhaps, very efficiently enforced, but its traces were evident. She smiled, sometimes, to see how Aracea had tried to impose an English training on an obstinately Spanish background ; but Mary regretted it—and, because of her regret, accused herself of romanticism. She, who had always prided herself on the fact that her approach to Spain was wholly realistic, should not deplore a state of affairs for which, as Carlos had pointed out, she was largely responsible. Yet . . . the house of Parral, in accepting its transformation, had surrendered something. She tried to imagine the effect of the surrender on a youth reared in a remote Andalucían town, untouched by cosmopolitan influences, swung suddenly, and with little preparation, into a way of living as remote from his home conditions as that of an English manor would be from an Eskimo's.

It must have been fun, at first : the relative grandeur, the formality, the importance that attached to the husband of the dueña of Parral! Playing host to important people, riding out on shining mornings, to cape the calves, and coming carelessly back, to take the head of a table laid as for a banquet! Departing in state for the fight—with never a care about anything except the bulls themselves. His own glory enhanced by the glory of Parral.

And was not the reaction inevitable?—The growing sense of incompleteness, mounting gradually to frustration? The slow, indistinct perception that this life of ease and luxury and healthy living was not the life of a matador; separated him from the essentials of his work; deprived him of something for which there was no name, but on which his future depended.

Why should she—Mary—be able to see this, and not Aracea? Because—the answer was too plain—like all converts, Aracea was the victim of an obsession; because she had swallowed, hook, line and sinker, the training of her English year. Because she confused athleticism with art, and believed that, by building up the first, she could arrive at the second. The perfect man, the perfect bull, and, therefore, the perfect act. It came to Mary, with a sense of shock, that she knew more of the qualities that go to the making of the fiesta brava than the daughter of Parral.

" Promise me you will come back at the end of the summer." They were driving to the airport; each kilómetro they covered was, for Mary, a station of farewell.

" I can't promise, chica." She tried to speak coolly. " It's a question of pennies, you know!—and I've used up most of my travel allowance."

She saw Aracea's hands tighten on the driving wheel.

" The baby will be born in October—si Dios quiere. You *must* be here."

A car sneaked up behind them, let off a blare under their back wheels and shot past on their left, its driver and his companion grinning back across their shoulders—one of the lovesome tricks to which Aracea, as a woman driver, was hardened, and which had long ceased to disturb her. This morning, to her annoyance, it made her start and brought a faint dew out on her temples. Mary, who had felt the start, looked at her, and thought it was time Aracea stopped driving, for the present.

The usual river-mist lay thick on the port when they arrived there, and they learned here was a long delay. They sat in the waiting room, with the fog packed in round them like cotton-wool, drinking coffee and coñac, watching the passengers gather for other planes, listening to the Tannoy announcements, making little laconic comments. Mary laughed at last.

" There's something about waiting on an airport that's worse, even, than a railway station. It's perhaps the sense of having already parted with one's normal element and occupations, and being suspended in a kind of limbo before launching into the next. You don't get that feeling before a train journey, when you set out straight from the heart of a town.—I wish you wouldn't wait any longer. I am sure you have a lot to do. Do me a favour." She took Aracea's gloved hand. " Let Martín drive you back."

" Look, the fog is clearing. Look, here's the Madrid plane coming in," Aracea interrupted her. They sprang up, collecting Mary's magazines, her travelling case and handbag. " Pasajeros para Madrid——" After the long torpor a fluster and a surge ; people thrusting towards the door to secure for themselves the best seats on the plane, escaping with relief from their relatives, sweethearts, friends. It's always like this on airports, thought Mary, as she took Aracea in her arms ; you sit for hours, in an increasing coma, trying to think of the important things you meant to say, and the end comes like a shot.

" Dearest Mary, go with God ! "

" God keep you. And you'll let Martín drive—— ? "

" Sí-sí—ah, don't let all these savages push in front of you, or you'll not get a place by the window."

She stood, driving her hands into her pockets, as Mary hurried across the tarmac ; her eyes misted. To her own astonishment, she found herself wanting to cry. A feeling of loneliness she never remembered experiencing before suddenly descended on her. There—there went the only person who really cared

about her. The only true and loyal one. The one who understood. These things seemed only just to occur to her as the
wings swung slowly round and the silver insect started down
the runway. She ran out, her heart crying, " Stop, stop—or take
me with you ! " and, far in the distance, saw it rise and vanish
in a flash of blinding silver as it was struck by the sun.

Martín was asleep in the car. She pressed the self-starter and
let off the brake, glancing at the clock on the dashboard. Martín
roused with a grunt.

" Se hace tarde. That's what one gets for travelling by air.
You think you get there sooner and you spend the day waiting
to start ! "

She remembered the commissions she was supposed to do in
town, and the people who were coming out for lunch. Carlos
could well entertain them, but the prospect did not please her.
One was an old friend of Don Luis, the proprietor of one of the
small northern rings, who had always taken Parral bulls. She
knew why he was coming, although Carlos had not seen fit to
enlighten her. The last batch of Parrales had not done credit
to their name. Carlos, in spite of the hints she had given him,
had a habit of high-handedness with the little rings, of using
them as an outlet for the less impeccable products of the famous
stock. There was, of course, no such thing as a " bad " Parral !
That was seen to, in the tientas. But if, among the glorious
survivors of the tests, there should develop one with some
minor flaw, a damaged horn, vision impaired by a fight up in
the pastures—Carlos would see to it that it was included in a
batch for some small town that might think itself lucky to present
Parral bulls.

Papá never did that ; he had a soft spot for the little rings
that put all they had into one grand fight for the fiesta of their
patron saint. One grand fight that would light up the afición
for twelve months, and show the younger generation that the
great art was still alive. " If they can only afford to buy our
bulls once a year, let them have the best," said Don Luis. So he
had built up the credit of Parral—that needed no building in
Madrid, and Sevilla, and Barcelona ; so he had secured not only

the honour of the name, but the personal respect of innumerable people whose livelihood was linked into the ring.

This she had striven to explain to Carlos, who was polite, deferential—up to a point—and amused.

" No doubt you are right ; the principle is admirable."

" Then observe it," she told him shortly.

But of course he did not. And she could not interfere without reducing his authority. And, because he was the manager, and she a woman, she could not afford to reduce his authority. There were plenty, still, who ridiculed her status, as dueña of Parral : " ella es la que lleva los pantalones "—and who accepted Carlos as the ruler ; and she was shrewd enough to realise that he lost no opportunity of encouraging this impression. If Paco had but accepted the position that would eventually be his . . .

Don Pablo Villaruega, from his remote northern province, should receive assurance, from the dueña, and not from her substitute, that there would be no repetition of that unfortunate affair. Her right hand on the wheel, she passed a page torn from her notebook across her shoulder to Martín.

"I shan't have time to see to these things. I'll put you down on San Salvador and you can go to the shops and come out on the autobus."

II

She found herself behind one of the Parral camions, in a smother of dust, and slowed at the Sanjorje crossroads, to see which way it was turning. By the roadside stood a miserable little group, a woman with a clutch of children, and one in her arms, waiting evidently for the midday autobus. The woman was heavy with pregnancy. She did not belong to the estate. A fellow-feeling made Aracea wind down the near window and call :

" Where do you want to go ? "

" Sanjorje, señora." A look of surprise, and presently of recognition, lit the woman's face. Her dress of dark cotton was powdered with dust and her swollen feet thrust into alpargatas, but she did not look like a peasant. The four little boys and the little girl were in American-style clothes, one of the boys in a Disney-patterned shirt over his cotton cowboy trousers. They looked like people who could afford to hire a coche, but she pushed open the door and invited them in; the détour by Sanjorje would add little to her journey and would get her out of the traffic of the highroad.

"Muchísimas gracias!—The señora doesn't know who I am?"

Puzzled, she looked into a face which might once have been pretty; the face of a woman probably not much older than herself, but, with its lines, its missing teeth, the bags of discoloured flesh under the eyes and the pouch under the jaw, the face of one twice her age. Suddenly memory awoke.

"It's Concha—the wife of Ildefonso."

"Sí, sí."

"Me alegro mucho," she muttered, as she took her foot off the brake. Two wives of two matadores, riding together. "Have you seen your husband lately?" she presently inquired.

"No, señora, not since he gave me this"—she touched her body proudly. "And the señora too"—she smiled wistfully— "has a regalo! That God may send her many more blessings."

"You haven't been to any of his fights lately."

"Ay! Dios no lo quiera! I have never seen a bullfight in my life; I would die of it. It is bad enough to listen to the radio."

"And the boys——?"

"Ay, dios, they listen every Sunday, as though to the word of God. Pepillo—the shameless one!—already announces that he is going to be a torero when he grows up. As though one gives sons to the light for a purpose like that. Every Sunday my life runs from me in blood and water—the señora knows how it is for the wives of bullfighters. It is we who die, as well as the bull. The bull dies once, but we have to go on dying, year after year. Dying and giving birth to little animals who will make us die again!"

" Claro ; but it is what we accept, when we marry bullfighters. It is much, to be the wife of a matador."

" Claro," was the submissive reply. A few more remarks revealed that the wife of Ildefonso was more ignorant than any child of her husband's career. When they drew up at a big, flat-faced house on the main street of Sanjorje, and the children piled screaming with excitement out of the car, Aracea resisted invitations to enter.

" You must excuse me, I am in a great hurry."

" But how shall I tell Ildefonso that the señora has refused to enter his house ? " was the reproachful answer. " What shall I say to the neighbours, when they ask me why the wife of Niño de Maderas refuses the hospitality of Ildefonso ? A minute— only a minute—to silence these malas lenguas who are all watching to see what happens, and to honour the house ! "

Guessing that the true motive of the invitation was to display the resources of the house to a rival, Aracea switched off the engine, locked the car and left it under the proud protection of Pepillo and his brothers. She remembered that Concha, before her marriage, was a peasant girl who had known only conditions as primitive as those of a farm beast, as she followed her from room to big empty room. " We have eleven rooms, señora ; think of that ! " Some were not furnished at all ; but their existence evidently filled Concha with pride. In some was little but a litter of children's expensive toys—mainly broken ; railways with the tin coaches scattered over bits of bent or broken track ; miniature motor cars, with most of the paint kicked off the coachwork—" Look, señora ! These stand for a fortune. There is nothing he will not buy for the children—he would give Pepillo a horse of gold, if he asked for it."

For the first time, she was glad of the child in her womb. It occurred to her, for the first time, that she might find—as Concha had done—in motherhood something, not to replace, for some things are irreplaceable, but to fill up the emptiness that lay before her. At the same time, she had a sharp stab of envy for someone so simply satisfied as Concha, as she followed, admiring, congratulating, praising all she was shown ; marking, at the back of her mind, the absence of indoor sanitation (what should a boy reared in the cellars of Parral care for bathrooms or toilets?) the lack of anything that, by civilised beings, could be described as comfort.

The pièce de résistance, Concha's pride, was reserved to the last: a locked chamber, which opened to a key the length of Aracea's forearm, stuffed with furniture, with cabinets loaded with pottery collected on fairgrounds—" Donald Ducks," and " Plutos," and flattened-out heads of girls with Rita Hayworth mouths and hair, intended as wall decorations, but propped behind the smaller pieces; with paper flowers in china vases, with plaster saints·encased in glass. A multi-branched chandelier with ruby and white moulded glass shades descended over the centre table spread with a Gibraltese shawl, which set off a tortured centrepiece of twisted glass stuffed with paper carnations. Across one corner stood an immense radio-gramophone, and their progress was impeded by a series of spitoons as Concha led the way into the room. " It has to be kept locked because of the children. They are only allowed to come in on Sundays, to listen to the wireless—they are very good, but they cannot be allowed to do as they like among all these valuable things. This is where Ildefonso receives his friends when he is at home, señora."

She looked up at the big coloured photograph that dominated the room; one of the typical " waxwork " studio portraits that bullfighters like because the lines are taken out of their faces and they are given nice pink cheeks and red lips and the suit of lights looks good, and if you like to pay a bit more the whole thing is picked out with tinsel and it looks like a film star.

She sought, wondering, behind the coloured mask the living original; a little fan of half-derisive anger beat up in her. How could *you* let them make such a fool of you, such a painted dolly? She found herself wanting to smash the glass, to slash the cardboard from side to side.

" E' bonito—no? Cuesta mucho dinero. Un retrato muy fino, muy artístico."

Would Paco, she wondered, as she left Sanjorje behind, have been satisfied with all that? Was it so very much different from the home at Maderas? Was that what he would have liked—rather than the air into which she had lifted him? the air in which, finally, he found it difficult to breathe? Someone to go to bed with, a couple of old women over a carbon stove, to hand him a plate of gazpacho or soup when he felt like it, a hideous room he could fill with smoke and the loud voices of his friends, a litter of children to be carelessly left, until the time came to increase their number, a house he could walk into and out of as carelessly as a hotel, but of which he was the unquestioned master?

A descent, for the son of Don Amadeo and Doña Amalia Ribera; but a descent, perhaps, into freedom. Did he, sometimes, feel it that way, and feel he had paid, perhaps, too heavily for the sumptuous background his marriage had brought to him? Did he feel that Parral and its dignity stood between him and development as an artist?

Ay, dios, what a foolish way of thinking; foolish, and ungrateful. But people like Paco don't think; they are only swept by their feelings. Disappointed, he must find someone or something to blame for his disappointment, and the someone must, of course, be her. Gorged with the fare she provided for him, he reacted suddenly and violently—as an artist reacts—towards raw meat. Well, she defied herself, this went surely to prove that the artistry was there; that she need not accuse herself of stifling it. And a few months of libertinage—they could not undo all she had built since they were married.

Aided and abetted by Don Pasquale, he was now running his life in his own way. The results had yet to be proved. She was not a crying wife, staying at home, like Concha; she was a woman with a business to be looked after. With a child to be given to the light. Why—oh why, cried her heart, could she not accept Concha's easy satisfactions—she who had so much more? Because, came the quick answer, she was not an animal! Because she was not, like women of Concha's class, conditioned to humility. If jealousy of Ildefonso's women entered Concha's mind—as it must, into the mind of any daughter of Andalucía—she had accepted its hopelessness. So long as Ildefonso continued to give her children, and pay for the maintenance of the household, she was content. Such content was not within the reach of the daughter of Parral !

Dios—here were the gates ! She braked, and, without thinking, her left foot went down on the clutch. The big car, travelling at sixty, skidded, and, with a crash that resounded in the outbuildings, piled up on the brick post. There were shouts and people came running.

The bumper, the bonnet, a couple of lamps and the near-side running-board were scrumbled ; but the dueña, crawling out from under the wheel, professed to be unhurt. The walk up the avenue of elms seemed endless ; sweat blinded her ; the final effort of mounting the stairs nearly defeated her, but she managed to get to her room.

" Señora—— ! " One of the girls came running ; of course, the news had reached the house already, nothing could be kept secret for a moment, that affected the dueña. And Olalla hurried into the room. She screamed at them to get out, and when, at last, she achieved solitude, bent her head and clasped her hands over her still trembling body.

" Forgive me, heart ; I won't be so careless again."

Ten minutes later, composed, though white as chalk, she held out her hand to Don Pablo Villaruega.

" Bien venido, amigo mio ! It is good to see your face after so long a time."

" La señora was not hurt in the accident ? "

" Not in the least. But "—she turned to laugh at Carlos— " the car's in a devil of a mess ! "

" Cars can be replaced, but not the dueña of Parral."

It came to her in a flash that if she died before the child was born, and before the deed was executed that made Paco a partner in the business, Carlos would be the master of Parral. Whatever happened—whatever opposition she had to encounter from the de la Cernas, and from her uncle Federico, that deed must be made effectual. She had fought for it on her marriage, and so, naturally, had Don Amadio, on his son's behalf ; but the opposition was too strong, and the provisions of Don Luis's will, unfortunately, too nebulous, except in so far as her personal inheritance was concerned. The combined wits of de la Cerna and Don Federico Parral proved too much for Don Amadeo, who had no inclination to waste money on lawyers. Was it not an axiom that the richer party invariably wins ? The inheritance was at least secured to Aracea's son, and with that the Ribera side had to be content.

But supposing, thought Aracea, under cover of the conversation ; under her quick retorts, and her diplomatic handling of Don Pablo Villaruega—supposing I were never to have a child ? Please God this little torero is safe ! But just supposing ? And Parral goes to Carlos, and, after him, God knows to whom. She could leave her shares to Paco, giving him nominal control, but the combination of de la Cernas, Tío Federico and a clever lawyer could easily result in an endless lawsuit, during the course of which Paco would figure as " a man of straw," a mere puppet in the administration of the estate. Dios, there were enough of those lawsuits, prolonged through generations, that left the protagonists, finally, fighting over a skeleton.

When the meal was over, she ordered the horses. Carlos offered his car, but she turned with a smile to Don Pablo.

" We never used cars in the old days, did we ? Do you remember last time you were here, just after the war, when you and Papá rode up to the pastures, and brought down the bulls for the Easter fights ? "

" Are we going up to the pastures ? " asked Don Pablo, his square, handsome face lighting.

" Not, perhaps, quite so far. We have three lots down I would like to show you, and some little calves. I've been trying a cross with a Mexican strain ; I would be grateful for your opinion."

She felt heavy in the saddle, and for a moment the landscape swung before her eyes. The calzones nipped her waist, and she tried to pull herself up out of them. Carlos had remained behind.

They sat quietly on horseback, looking over the walls into the lots where the brave bulls of Parral were preparing for their great day.

" Muy fino. Muy Parral.'.'

" Your next fight is on Sunday week ? "

" A novillada. We can only run to the horses twice in the year," admitted Don Pablo.

" Bueno ; and who have you got on your bills ? "

He named them; Aracea inclined her head gravely. One was a boy who had been consistently disappointing since taking the alternativa, and was rapidly descending the precarious ladder that leads to success ; the other two were promising youngsters, one of whom was marked for graduation in the course of the season.

" Very good. The bulls are your own, Don Pablo ; whatever you choose shall be reserved and delivered in time for your novillada."

It was a gesture of Don Luis Parral. Don Pablo was taken aback. He knew he had not the money to buy Parrales. He had already entered into negotiations with another breeder, who supplied most of his animals for the novillo fights. Business unconnected with the bulls had brought him south, and he had taken the opportunity to visit the ranch of his old friend, not to buy bulls, but to add a few words to his written disapprobation of the last consignment. In Luis's day, he, though a humble patron, had received invariably the best. For the dignity of his small ring, he felt obliged to protest about the delivery he had had for the Easter Sunday fight. His town was small, but the afición was strong ; Luis would never have let him down to the tune of three bulls out of six—knowing how they counted on their two corridas of the year !

He fenced, looking greedily at the animals across the wall.

" One doesn't put animals like that in a novillada."

" Listen, Don Pablo. Your ring lost credit on the Easter fight. I'm offering you a chance of recovering it. Any of these is yours ; all, if you please," said Aracea, exaggerating the gesture, as she was inclined to do.

" You are very generous," mumbled Don Pablo, and wondered if she meant to bring the price down.

" We also have our credit to consider," she replied smoothly, knowing what was in his mind, and not for a moment intending to do anything of the sort. They smiled at each other guardedly. Presently Don Pablo gave a regretful shake of the head.

"I feel it much; it is a misadventure, that I have already contracted with Carbonell." The contract was not yet signed, but he was not going to spend that money. Aracea, who had banked on this excuse, lowered her head with grave acceptance of the decision.

"And I feel it much also. But there is the September fight, and I give you my word, señor, I will personally choose the bulls for Tierraplata. There shall be no repetition of the Easter fiasco."

So that was fixed, with satisfaction on both sides. Don Pablo, much pleased and flattered, would return to the north with the assurance that his standing with Parral was no less secure than it had been in the old days. She made a mental note that, for the future, all the small buyers must be referred directly to her; Carlos could deal with the top-line.

Olalla met her on the gallery. Her comely, matronly face reflected disquiet.

"You have the bad face, Aracita; qué pasa?"

She found herself crawling into bed: a thing she had never done in her life during the day time. She found herself curling between the sheets over her little torero; comforting it, telling it she was sorry, and she would never frighten it again.

Chapter Nine

I

THE STATION wagon, driven by Chano, bounced over pot-holes, whirled through villages, scattered flocks of rust-coloured goats that glared through mad amber eyes and flung its occupants about the leather seats. Chano, his jaw set, his eyes dark with pleasure, bent over the wheel and blasted on the horn. The new van was good and it was good to be the driver.

" Where are we ? " muttered Paco, jerked out of sleep.

" Salas de los Infantes."

" Where the women bear seven children at one birth ! " shouted Campillo from the back. " Think of that now ! A cuadrilla and a couple of reserves for the price of a night's lodging ! When I start out on my own, this is where I shall come, to cut my expenses."

" They'll be old enough to carry the coffin," sneered Curro, through his broken teeth. Tonio's high tenor soared behind Chano's shoulder :

> *Yo tenía una mujer*
> *Que era más blanca que el sol*
> *y ahora tengo una gitana*
> *Que es más negra que el carbon !*

Paco yawned and stretched himself. They were all in good form—like going to a verbena. A matador and his cuadrilla—the way they ought to be : a group of people controlled and welded together by a single thought, a single interest. Even that bastard Curro. Even that bag of manure he had been trying to get rid of for the last three years—there he was, still hanging on—and the big, pasty, aggrieved face and long, shapeless body stood for something, if it was no more than pigheaded devotion to self-interest. Fired half a dozen times in every season, he managed always to whine himself back. Curro was the oldest member of the team, in age and in years of service; its deadweight, its Achilles heel. He was a disgrace and he smelt and he was the worst pic in the business—and if he went one would miss something : something to hang abuse on, a butt for one's witticisms. Paco stretched, smiled, and allowed himself to feel magnanimous, because magnanimity is a facet of power. Chano, Gusano, Camillo, Tonio, Peral and Curro ; it was—with the exception of Curro—a good bunch. And it was different, now they were so much together. It *felt* different ; more solid.

To-morrow afternoon—Talavera. A bad town for him. Why couldn't he ever manage to put on a decent show anywhere near Madrid? Talavera—where they killed Joselito. A cold drop ran down his spine and he hitched himself round in the seat.

" Where's the wine? I'm thirsty."

Somebody passed over the skin, and Chano slowed to allow him to drink without splashing his clothes. He lit a cigarette; his fingers were bright yellow to the first knuckle and his hand twitched as he spun the lighter. He swore, pushed it back in his pocket and glanced at the watch on his wrist. This time to-morrow afternoon he would be going in for his first bull. Chano pushed his foot down on the accelerator and the car leapt forward —every damned kilómetro it covered a kilómetro nearer to-morrow, every kilómetro registering with a tick inside him as though he had a clock under his ribs. He stared at the empty plain with its evil shadows; why, even in afternoon sun, did this stretch of the country look like the frontiers of infernal regions? The singing voice of Tonio, the conversation among the boys grated on his nerves. He slumped back sullenly. Half an hour more, and then . . .

" Let's stop here."

He spoke so suddenly that the brakes squealed; they skidded to a standstill, scattering some mongrels, catching their fleas in the dust. The cuadrilla gaped out at a ramshackle square, empty as the afternoon.

" Where's this, Paco? "

He got out; they followed him, jerking down their clothes that were creased with heat. The earth burned through the soles of their shoes and a dry, vicious heat settled on their heads and the backs of their necks. Chano locked the wagon. They stepped past tethered asses and old men asleep into an icy patio. A boy brought a porrón of red wine and his face lit up with delighted recognition. " Olé, matador! " They settled into the grateful coolness. Two middle-aged countrymen were playing dominoes in a corner, and Paco went to watch. Neither of them knew him, and each was more interested in his game than in the strangers. He got bored, and went through the patio to a little walled garden at the back, where there were grass and fruit trees; as quiet as Parral. He stood for a moment, under the trees, staring through their foliage at the hard blue sky; then the silence was too much. He gave a shudder and went back and ordered more wine. Some more people came in; they all started to shout and argue.

"It's time we were getting on," said Tonio. It was his business to get his matador settled into the lodging and quiet for the night.

Paco said, "You'd better take on some more gas and have that front wheel changed"—and Chano got up obediently. "The gas station's round the corner. We'll come on and meet you there."

Chano went out on the square, keeping in the shade, and saw the garage sign pointing down an alley on his left. The alley broadened into a plazuela opposite the pumps, and drawn up on the right, out of the sun, was a big black saloon. Chano swore.

The black saloon had turned up several times in their recent travels, and stood for trouble. It was evidently there by appointment. The blinds were drawn, not completely, but low enough to conceal its occupant. There was a chauffeur in uniform, wall-faced, at the wheel. While they jacked up the wagon, Chano continued, inwardly, to swear.

Paco came along the street with the boys, taking his time. Paying no attention to the saloon—of which the others were as much aware as Chano—he put on an act of examining the wheel. Tonio, with a sick face, paid the boy at the pump. They all avoided each other's eyes. Paco lit a cigarette. He said, behind the flame of the lighter, "You'd better be off. Take it easy. I've paid plenty for this van, I don't want a bill for repairs when we get to town."

Chano got silently behind the wheel and the others, except Tonio, piled in behind.

"It's the Celeste, isn't it?" said Paco carelessly. "Put my stuff in. See you in the morning."

Tonio climbed in. Chano pushed the starter.

Half-smiling, Paco watched the wagon disappear. He pitched

away his cigarette, brushed his hands over his hair, pulled down his jacket and walked smartly to the black saloon. He jerked the door open and got in. The car started immediately.

" Ay—you've kept me waiting a fine time ! "

" Is that . . . and that . . . worth waiting for ? "

" That's good news for to-morrow," grunted Camillo, and spat. The ebullience had departed from the cuadrilla. In his depression Chano allowed several coches to overtake them before a whine came from Gusano, the youngest of the party, whose sense of personal dignity was affected by Chano's lapse.

" Cow droppings—what's this we're in ? A bullock cart ? "

A silence fell. Then Campillo muttered :

" That's the fourth time he's done it on us. I'll start dreaming about that big black bug one of these nights There was a tale in our village about a vampire——"

" Had it got four wheels ? "

" And a number plate ? " sniggered young Gusano, who specialised in number plates.

" Tell you where that black bug better stay away from," growled the picador. " That black bug better stay away from Málaga. That black bug better stay away from the Caverna. Something might happen to its paintwork."

" Something might happen to Paco. That gachí of his in Málaga may be doesn't like bugs on four wheels with Madrid number plates."

" One of these days," whimpered Curro from the back, " we'll all be out of jobs because Paco's been working black bugs instead of bulls."

" Cow droppings. Paco's got a good line in faenas with the sheets," put in Gusado—merely because Curro had spoken, and he, like the others, despised Curro.

On the front seat Chano and Tonio sat silently side by side. Those two, the confidential banderillero and the sword handler on whom most depended, withdrew into their own silence from the ribaldries of their companions ; Chano because, to his own surprise, he had, during the last few months, discovered in himself an attachment to Paco as a person ; Tonio because he was resigning himself to spending the night in Paco's room at the Celeste, instead of getting himself a rest in bed, on the thin chance that Paco's commonsense would conquer his pleasure. It had been known to happen. Paco might turn up, drink a pot full of tea and roll into bed, and Tonio would have to remain on guard, seeing he was not disturbed until it was time to dress.

He sat there, his immensely wide shoulders curled over his thin stomach, his short legs barely reaching to the floor; his lower lip stuck out so far that it nearly met his down-drooping nose, his sour eyes fixed on the road—trying to persuade himself that was how it would be. Paco had been as jumpy as a flea all the way down from the north and had not been sleeping. After the Talavera fight they had ten days free. Tonio wondered if they would go back to Parral—and thought the chances were poor. Times had changed—in some ways, for the better. But, so far as he, Tonio, was personally concerned, for the worse; for his duties had trebled, and, because he was " Un hombre de bien," his responsibilities with them. If only in order to keep his job, it was his business to produce Paco in decent condition for each fight; it was for him to worry about women, about drinking, and, up to a point, about expenditure.

There was nothing the matter with Paco; the season, so far, had been a successful one, though he had given a few poor shows and had had some strokes of fantastic luck. He had taken to celebrating after the fight with a tremendous batter, that went on sometimes for forty-eight hours, but that was normal, and his excellent stamina, assisted by Tonio's care, had him steadied up in plenty of time for his next appearance. He had been, up to recently, too ambitious to risk prejudicing his reputation by indulgence on the eve of a fight, and the black saloon, which appeared at intervals of their journeys, at first occasioned no unease among the team. Paco disappeared—perhaps for half a day; occasionally overnight. That was in the pattern of the matador's life. And reappeared, in some café or bar where the boys were drinking, to sit yawning for an hour, and then take himself to bed.

But the black saloon had taken to following them and the periods of Paco's absences had lengthened, and, twice already, Tonio had had the misery of pushing a jerking body into the suit of lights and passing the sword into an uncertain hand. It made no difference that, on each of these occasions, Paco had put up a great performance and had the afición at his feet. Tonio had, each time, the benefit of the reaction, and he was old and wise enough to know that luck could not hold for ever.

He knew—as did the rest of the cuadrilla—the owner of the black saloon ; Gusano's memory for car numbers and Chano's wide acquaintance with the proprietors of garages had given them that. One day, the information—which was a subject of common gossip—would reach Parral, and Tonio was uneasy about that, as about other matters. Like the rest of the cuadrilla, he respected Paco's wife ; they respected while they disliked her. They all agreed that Paco had done the right thing, in fixing her ; he should have done it before. But the daughter of Parral would not take this business easily, though she might consider the Málaga affair beneath her notice. It was a nuisance, for a bull-fighter, to be tied up with a woman, not only of money, but with influence and social position ; it was foolish of Paco, to engage in a serious affair with a friend of his wife, and start up a scandal that might have serious repercussions on his career.

For the dueña of Parral was not the kind to be bound by tradition, convention or any of the considerations that keep a wife in her place. Her unfortunate, foreign upbringing had emancipated her from many of the dignities and discretions that govern her sex and give the male his authority. She could easily, if she chose, make things very bad for Paco—and she would have the support of her family, who had been against the marriage from the beginning, and who would exercise all their ingenuity to prevent Paco's claim on the property of his wife.

They pulled in, at nightfall, to the Hotel Celeste, and unloaded the baggage, and the boys went off to their lodgings, leaving Tonio to wait. The reception carried one of the big bills, with Niño de Maderas pulling a bull the size of a cathedral round him ; the printers had gone to town with red and yellow and bright

blue shadows. Tonio unpacked and went out to get some food.
Chano, who joined him, had been to see the bulls.

" Four of them are bichos ; two are fairly decent."

" Did you have the draw ? "

" No ; the others weren't along. I stopped in for a talk with
the porter." He cracked his nail against the rim of the glass.
" He says the tickets aren't selling too good. Ildefonso's got all
the cartel ; the fans are saving up for him, Sunday week."

" Sure ; they don't want to miss the finish. That's all they
go for now," said Tonio bitterly. " They want to brag they were
there the day Ildefonso was killed. They want to howl and yell
and follow the coffin to the station and read the obituaries and
tell how they *saw* it. That's what sells the ring out for Ildefonso's
fights ; even the football crowd buys tickets, for the fun of
seeing Ildefonso killed."

" He can't get killed, before the mano a mano. Have you
heard anything ? "

Tonio stuck out his lip.

" We're waiting for the telegram. Pasquale wants to fix it
after the feria at Salamanca, but Ildefonso's manager hasn't
come through. Paco's madder than a wasp."

At four in the morning, tired of sitting on a hard chair, Tonio
stetched himself out on the floor. Dawn was breaking when
Paco fell over him.

II

" The doctors say he'll be out in a week," Tonio told Aracea.

She stood by the hospital bed and Paco smiled sharply up
at her.

" It's got me out of that flea-bitten show at La Linea, anyhow."

" And got you a rest before Valencia. They say you'll be out
on Tuesday. I'll send Martín."

" Why go to the trouble ? Chano'll bring me down."

" The Alvis is much more comfortable, and Martín's a better
driver."

"You oughtn't to have bothered to come," he muttered shamefacedly; and, suddenly, grinned. "How's the little torero?"

"Fine." If the little torero could survive the fight at Talavera and Tonio's telephone message, he could survive anything. She brushed his forehead with her lips, and went out to Tonio on the broad white corridor. "You'd better come down with him on Tuesday, Tonio; I'm sending the car and I'll get a nurse in, to see to the dressings."

"Muy bien, señora."

"Pay the boys' wages up to the twenty-fifth and tell them we'll be at Valencia."

. . . It was Tuesday night. Martín had set off before dawn. The room was prepared, and the nurse installed.

At every sound, she went out on the gallery, and each time there was the patio, filled with moonlight, and the darkness of unopened doors under the archway. At two in the morning, the doors swung open, and the car rolled in, down a shaft of whiteness. She rushed down the stairs.

"No está." Martín sounded fed up.

"You—haven't—brought him?"

"He'd left by the time I got there."

"Left—for where?"

"No sé, señora."

". . . Pues," said Aracea, after a silence, "may you sleep well."

It took some time for her brain to grasp that this was happening to *her*. It happened, of course, to other women in her position; but not to *her*! She had guessed about the girl in Málaga, and assumed there were others, but a man does not put a public slight on his wife for the sake of a whore or a cabaret girl. That is to say, not a man like Paco, who knew how she and her world regarded those things, who, for all his faults, was caballero—and who, apart from respect, owed her so much!

Who was it? Tonio knew; that was as positive as that he would face fire and swords before giving his master away. Would he be equally invulnerable to money? She realised, with a shudder, that she could not lower herself to bribe Paco's servant. Whether or not she was successful, Paco would be bound to learn of it, and would be ready to kill her.

When she went down to the office, Carlos said, with a polite air of surprise, " So Paco didn't arrive." She knew in a flash that Carlos knew also, and would not give him the satisfaction of seeing her bewilderment and grief.

"They thought it would be better for him to have a few days in the mountains; it's cooler up there."

She would have liked to hit his amused, secretive mouth.

" Claro. Of course—it depends. He will naturally want to be in good shape for the mano a mano. Have they fixed the date? "

" I have not heard anything."

" There are some curious rumours : that Ildefonso is refusing it. That there's been a quarrel——"

A picture shaped itself in Aracea's mind : a hot day, in Sierpes, with the canopies stretched overhead. Paco, for once, accompanying her, she on a shopping expedition, he on his way to Don Pasquale's. A block in the narrow alley; all the tie-sellers, people with lottery tickets, town bloods and youths, with a gipsy or two, clustered round the open façade of one of the clubs. When a waiter came out, to disperse the crowd that was molesting the customers, there was Idelfonso, holding court; having his shoes cleaned, surrounded by a flattering côterie of distinguished admirers. His face of a damaged eagle was creased into something meant for a smile ; launching some jest in a thick andalu' that brought a roar of appreciation from the audience, he had his strange look of crucifixion. Christ jesting from the Cross.

As Paco and Aracea passed, his eyes, with their profound acquaintance with death, travelled across the space cleared by the waiter, and met Paco's. Paco's face lit, flashed into a smile, he lifted his hand.

" Olá, hombre ! "

And Ildefonso deliberately turned his head away. Paco

checked his stride, and Aracea instinctively laid her hand on his arm.

"Don't be silly; you can't make a scene when I'm with you." She resented the snub as sharply as Paco, but her one thought was to get him away before they were recognised by the crowd and friction developed between the partisans of the great rivals. Her brain swam in incoherence—yes, at least, even by the critics Paco and Ildefonso were accepted as rivals. "Because, by then, you'll belong to me" : crazy words, spoken by a borracho—forget them. Forget those unholy eyes.

"Sweet holy Jesus, he can't do that to me, with all these people looking on!"

"*Please* come."

She felt his eyes full of anger and suspicion turned on her, and knew what he was remembering. She said faintly :

"It's too hot—I feel ill—you'll have to take me back to the car."

". . . Is it true, that you and Ildefonso have quarrelled?" —It was the same night, in their bedroom. He turned on her.

"Oye. Quarrels between men are no business of yours."

"But what did you quarrel about?"—She knew she was being rash, but it was unbearable, not to know.

Paco let out a short, scornful laugh.

"Ildefonso's had a good time—and a long time. He doesn't like the feeling he's being crowded."

She thought, And he's still the maestro. She was flooded by an intolerable feeling of protection for Paco. She felt like crying, " Ah, don't waste yourself in jealousy! There are powers against which it is useless to fight "—and remembered, in a pitiful flash-back, the days when Paco was gay and confident and had no envy, even of Ildefonso, because he was so sure of himself. And now, when he was secure, when he commanded the respect of the great critics, when the best end of the afición was with him, it was not to be borne, that he should weaken himself with jealousy.

The last two seasons had produced a crop of young toreros who were all set for the high places, and offered plenty of competition, even to the Niño de Maderas. Paco took it with good humour born of confidence, and of his growing popularity in the profession. His generosity, both in and out of the ring, was by now well known. Yet all the popularity could not blind him to that jaded image, that ghost, moving always ahead of him, interposing its moonlit skeleton between him and his goal. They yelled for the Niño and crossed themselves for Ildefonso ; that was the difference. And until that ghost was laid, there could be no peace in his soul. At any moment, Ildefonso might depart into immortality, taking with him the unimpaired legend. It was a race against time, with nervous anxiety lengthening the odds . . .

The correo came in ; out of the sheaf of envelopes she picked up a postcard from Sylvia Brett Pawl. They were cruising in the Albacobacas' yacht round the Isles of Greece.

" Strange as it might appear, I'm getting bored with male society, and wish you and Paco were with us. The only other female on board is Tom's niece, whom I'm supposed to be chaperoning, and it's not my métier. Leo is here——"

She read it through twice, slowly : " bored with male society "—" the only other female "—and, with the instinct which is the blessing and the curse of wives, had the answer to her question.

III

Don Pasquale Basilio shared the anxiety of his client about the two-handed fight in September. It might easily be the last chance of bringing the diestros together, and the acceptance by El Aguilucho, of a mano a mano with his younger rival would elevate the Niño, for good and all, above the newcomers who were crowding him uncomfortably.

In two recent fights, Ildefonso had revealed to an awe-stricken public the imperishable quality of his art. Physically a ruin, his domination over the bulls increased, apparently, in proportion to the failure of his physique. At Linares, with Miuras, he gave a supernatural performance; the series of naturales he developed in the last act, which left the suit of lights crimson from chest to thigh, had never been equalled in the lifetime of any who witnessed it. He seldom killed well; at Linares he made no concession to the critics who invariably fell with delight upon this weakness in his performance. But those who had watched the breath-taking slowness of his cape-work and the fearful closeness between him and the bull—still, perhaps, hypnotised by these miracles—seemed unconscious of being cheated of their climax. A " milagro " indeed; a milagro of surgery and penicillin. A phrase coined by Pedro Santillana was shortened into a permanent epithet by the fans : " He Who Walks With Death." The plazas were crowded out for " The Paseo de la Muerte " as soon as the bills went up.

Only the young or ignorant rated the two seriously as rivals : Ildefonso, with his strange mansedumbre, his acceptance of Fate that avoided him time and again only by a hair's breadth—as though loath to destroy so willing a victim—and Niño de Maderas, with his flash and sparkle, his defiance, his showman-ship and his stunts that were only possible to one in full possession of his youth and strength. One of the younger writers attempting a comparison, wrote :

" When Ildefonso enters the ring, Death takes charge. At the entrance of the Niño, Death shrugs its shoulders, pulls a face, leans, bored, on the fence. This refusal by Death to accept its role in the Immortal Tragedy robs the valiant performances of Niño de Maderas of their tragic core.

" The great matador is he who brings into the soul of the watcher that sense of closeness to Eternity that is not to be evoked by any trick or sensation, unless the performer has within himself the sublime acceptance of his own place in the ritual of the fight : which is that of the vassal of Death. This sense of consecration is, so far, absent from the art of Niño de Maderas."

Laying down the article, Don Pasquale grunted and knitted his brows. Bullring literature left him, as a rule, with his tongue well in his cheek, but now and again—as though by accident—the note of truth sounded. In his opinion, the " sublime acceptance " was there, but was falsified by an affected bravado that antagonised the serious afición. The telephone rang.

He snarled, " Quién es ? "

" It's me—Paco."

" Where are you speaking from ? "

" Up in the Guadarramas," came the answer guardedly.

" How's the scratch going on ? "

" Well enough.—Oye, Pasquale : any news ? "

" Nothing of importance."

" Hell—nothing from Ildefonso ? "—The line crackled under the sudden high-pitched assault of Paco's voice.

" I'm expecting a ring from his agent ; you'd better let me know where to get at you."

" I'll ring back later," said Paco, evidently disinclined to give his address. " Madrid's been at me ; they've been holding a couple of dates and now they're getting fed up. It looks like the son of a whore's ducking it ! They took the tripes out of him at Alcala ; may be he's scared of the show-down ! "—The sneer gave away the state of the speaker's nerves ; Don Pasquale cursed inwardly, and wondered who the woman was ; whether there could be any truth in the rumour that had reached his ears and made him vaguely uneasy. It was part of the game, for a matador at the height of his career to be linked up with a member of the nobility, but even Ildefonso had not gone the length of helping himself to the wife of one of his closest friends. Paco's caginess about his present domicile suggested there was something in it. That wouldn't go down at Parral, where the Alba-cobacas were constant guests—or, if it came to that, with Tano. Tano was away, with the yacht, and it was well known the duquesa did not care for cruising. Paco was crazy ; a couple of people as much publicised as himself and Doña Remedios couldn't keep a thing like that quiet for long ; one of these days there would be an explosion . . .

" Oye," Paco was chattering. " You've got to get on to this. I've been hearing a lot about Ildefonso ; the Mexican season'll finish him. There's got to be this showdown, before he's retired—or dead. And Madrid's got to be fixed. You'd better get on the line to Gandara and find out what Ildefonso's card is, and then ring through to Madrid and let them know I'm on the job. That'll throw it back on Ildefonso, and it's up to them. Get on with that, and I'll give you a ring to-night at the Hermanos."

" Bueno." It was useless to point out that, if Ildefonso was not inclined to play, no one could force him.

" You got the book ? "—The voice sounded calmer.

" I got it," said Don Pasquale guardedly.

" It's grand. Wait till you see the pictures. It's coming out this autumn in New York, but you know what we're like here. You might have some more copies typed and get them to the papers. There's no harm in a bit of advance publicity."

The typescript lay under Don Pasquale's hand ; a barbaridad. Only a foreigner could have written it, and only a person drunk with self-satisfaction could have passed it for publication. People who might be impressed by that kind of stuff were not buyers or readers of books, and the publication as it stood would finish Paco with the intelligentsia crowd he had never conquered, and make him the laugh of the country. The story of the boy launched on the profession by money and influence was bad publicity ; what the public liked was the tale of the kid with an empty stomach, stealing out by moonlight to cape the bulls, serving an apprenticeship of misery—not that of the sleek scion of a prosperous ex-torero, given every advantage from the cradle, married to a rich wife, entertaining the nobility. But the worst part was the pompous exposition of the art itself. Even Paco, fascinated by the prospect of seeing himself in print, should have seen the impossibility of those chapters which laid down, with an air of novelty, precepts taken for granted by people who had never got nearer the bulls than the top of the wall during an encierro.

Something was taking place at the other end of the line, some kind of impatience. Paco said hastily :

" Hasta la noche "—and rang off.

After a moment of hesitation, Don Pasquale lifted the receiver and gave the number of Parral.

" Don Pasquale ?—Muy buenas," said Aracea's voice.

" Muy buenas, señora ; 'stá bien ? "

" Muy bien, gracias ; y usted ? "

" Is Paco there ? " said Don Pasquale, discreetly.

" No, he's having a rest in the mountains."

" A good idea. He'll be fit in time for Valencia. I got the book."

" Muy malo !"

He drew a breath of relief ; for once, she was with him.

" He says it's at the printers."

" The boy who translated it took it to a publisher without letting us know. I'm afraid Paco's signed some sort of a contract. —Don Pasquale ; what about the mano a mano ? "

" There's no news, yet, from Ildefonsó. His agent hasn't seen him for weeks. He won't write letters and won't come to the telephone. You know what it's like in September ; the subscription fights have started, and the managements naturally want to get things fixed up."

" Do—do you think Ildefonso doesn't want the fight ? "

" Quién sabe ?—Ildefonso's pretty sick. He's got a lot of work before the end of the season."

" But it means so much to Paco."

" Naturally." He might have added, And to me, as Paco's agent.

" Can't you get hold of Ildefonso ? "

" That's Gándara's business. I've talked to him."

" It's worth a lot of money to Ildefonso."

" Ya lo creo."

" And worth more than money to Paco."

" . . . Paco's got to kill his book."

" But the American edition ?—We've already had the date of publication."

" No importance—the American public. But it'll do him a lot of harm here."

" Well, can you do anything ?—I suppose we can buy him out of the contract."

" We'd have to get his signature."

" I'll see what I can do."

There were times, reflected Don Pasquale, as he replaced the receiver, when it was useful to have a woman of intelligence behind one. He got the number of Don Toribio Gándara.

" You managed yet to contact Ildefonso ? " he asked, after the preliminaries.

" No. I feel it much, but I've written twice. He must have had the letters, that I sent in facsimile to several addresses. It appears we shall have to cancel the project."

" In confidence, there is bad feeling between him and Paco ? "

" That is my impression."

" Come—you must know something ! "

" Hombre, you know as much as I."

" There's been much talk," muttered Don Pasquale. " It will not have a good effect on our reputation."

" Claro. I hope you do not blame me in the matter."

" Certainly not.—Do me the favour to write again."

" It is waste of ink."

" Hombre, a two-handed fight in September with Niño de Maderas and Aguilucho is worth a little ink ! "

" I agree with you. I will do my best."

" They're both booked for Mexico ; we don't want the City to reap the benefits of a show between those two ! "—And that, thought Don Pasquale, as he hung up, may set you to work. Gándara was an old-fashioned agent, with not much push about him ; you didn't need push, if you were handling Ildefonso García ; you could sit back and answer the correspondence. A nice, soft job, which Don Pasquale, a fighter, did not envy. His pride, as well as his credit, lay in building successes out of possibilities, and his eye was on a couple of beginners he would like to have on his books. But, first, he wanted to see his acceptance of Niño de Maderas justified, and, until the show-down took place, he could not feel that he had accomplished his task.

Not for a moment was it to be imagined that the Niño would outshine his great contemporary; but his public acceptance by the Idol of the Ring as a worthy partner would raise Paco to a level he might not reach in years. If, on the other hand, Ildefonso were killed, or withdrew, before the encounter took place, the Niño would continue under his shadow, always compared to his disadvantage with one no longer there to defend his title. Wise in the mental processes of his clients, Don Pasquale knew that the prestige of a hand to hand with Ildefonso might well provide Paco with the stimulus he, so far, lacked, and complete his translation on to a plane which, up to the present, he had rarely touched. No one knew better than Don Pasquale the critical point Paco had reached in his career, or how, at this point, a set-back might be fatal, and launch him on a course that might reduce him, within a few years, to the ruck of fighters who, from one cause or another, never confirmed the bright promise of their début.

IV

" You go to-day ?—But you don't fight until Sunday."

" That's so, chica; a couple of days to get over the effects of this—and this ! "

That trip into the Guadarramas had been a mistake. It was fun, going to bed with a duquesa, but, when you were worrying about other things, you didn't want to be obliged, the whole time, to concentrate on something else. She was lovely, and she was mad about him, and wonderful in bed—and that kind of high-pressure love-making was ruinous on somebody just recovering from a fortnight in hospital. So there was a row before he left for Valencia.

Tears, cajolery, reproaches and, finally, taunts. Paco lost his temper, and the scene resounded through the big empty vaults of the summer palace where Remedios swore they were safe, because it belonged to her family, she had been brought up there as a child, the servants were her slaves, and Tano hated and would never go near it. Paco's sympathies were, on the whole, with Tano; perched fortress-like on a spur of the mountains, it was as bleak as barracks and nearly as primitive; in the intervals of their lovemaking, Remedios herself never ceased to whine for the luxury of their place in the South, or to impress on Paco the devotion that caused her, for his sake, to submit herself to these savage surroundings. Well, it was her suggestion, not his, and Paco grew bored.

It was, also, somewhat surprising to discover that the only woman whose society he had been able to tolerate over an indefinite number of days and nights was Aracea; this not only surprised him, but afflicted him with a slight sensation of guilt, such as he had never experienced in his dealings with other women. It hardened his determination to have done with the present affair, which, as it could not be publicised, added nothing to his prestige, and was doing him no good in his profession.

That night he was on the train for Valencia. After they left Madrid, the train ground with the endlessness of cross-country journeys across the burned lands of New Castile. Through an uncomfortable night the place in his groin jagged, adding to his apprehensions of Sunday. At one moment, Ildefonso was standing out on the corridor, sneering at him. He jerked himself out of sleep and went to get some water. The water was tepid, and full of cinders. During the day the compartment filled itself with dry heat until it became a furnace. The guard came in, sat down without invitation and gave himself the pleasure of a conversation with Niño de Maderas. A young man invaded them with an autograph book. His head split with heat and fatigue and boredom. At endless last, the Estación del Norte, the cab, the blue Mediterranean glitter, the hotel.

On Sunday, after practically two days of sleep, he put on an uneven show. When it was over, Tonio rubbed him down, and a practicante who had attended him on other occasions came in to give him a massage. " Cuidado—lay off there—it hurts ! " He winced as the cold shower hit the inflamed area that should, by now, have been healthy. Tonio held out the clean shirt. There were three clear days before the next show ; that was good.

" Where do we go next ? "

He knew what Tonio was thinking.

" I haven't made up my mind. Perhaps I'll stop on here and get some sea bathing."—One of the rich fans had invited him to his villa at Segorbe, but he was not inclined to accept the invitation, as his host's wife was a relative of Tano's, and he wanted no more of that tie-up for the present. He finished dressing, and, while Tonio cleared up the bathroom, strolled out on the balcony. Through the hot darkness the trees, illuminated below by the lamps round the plaza, formed a net of transparent green, like the wings of ichneumen flies. All round the central garden cars were parked. He glanced down at them idly—and gave a jump.

" Tonio. Get hold of Chano. Say we're getting out to-night. Where's the wagon ? "

" In Chaves's garage."

" All right. Take the stuff along and load it up. Tell Chano to drive out on the coast road. There's a place at the Alcira fork, I'll pick you up there. And don't look like an owl with tin-tacks in its belly ! I'll be there."

" Where are we going ? "—There was still suspicion in Tonio's face.

" What the hell's it matter, so long's we are out of here ?— So long "—he drew Tonio on to the balcony and pointed downwards—" as that doesn't tail us."

Slowly and incredulously, the man's face cleared. So that took out the black bug. And none too soon, by the look of Paco. Good news for the boys.

" Better get yourself something to eat. Better eat out, so I can settle the bill here before I take the stuff over."

His heart lightened as, avoiding the management, he slid out by a side door, making for one of the places he knew about, over by the old port. He grinned, to think of Remedios, sitting in the car—waiting ! He laughed, wondering how long she would wait, before sending her wall-faced chauffeur into the hotel, to command his presence; and what she would say and do when she found out he had given her the slip!

He ordered steak and a bottle of red wine, and bought himself a puro. Waiting, his eyes narrowed behind the smoke, seeing Sevilla. It was important to get back there. All agents were alike: no good unless you kept on at them. Jesus and Mary, they'd got to fix that show in September. Any day now, word might come from Madrid that the dates had gone. Any day, Ildefonso might catch the horn that would finish him; they said he was already practically a corpse. That could be why he was reluctant to commit himself beyond the limits of his present bookings—but he'd *got* to do the show in Madrid.

The wine trembled over the lip of the glass as Paco lifted it to his lips. He had started, lately, to be shaky after fights. Usually he found a girl. . . . Through the smoke a face shaped itself; a face with moonlight behind it, a body clear and cool as crystal. He recognised it, with a sense of surprise, wondering why that particular face should rise now, to tease him. The kid from La Faraóna's; Luz, now the star of the Caverna, in Málaga. They'd be in Málaga, by the beginning of September.

Chapter Ten

I

So, thought Aracea, I'm now on a line with Concha. I at least know where my husband's fighting, but I am never told when to expect him. My business is to receive him with humble gratitude, graciously to accept the privilege of my position as the wife of Niño de Maderas—and ask no questions!

And you're the one to blame, she apostrophised the little torero. She had begun to have moments when she was filled with a dark resentment of the innocent cause of her separation from Paco, followed by compunction, and struggles to bring justice to bear on the unhappy situation. Was the separation, in any case, inevitable? Would it—instead of being forced on them by uncontrollable circumstances—have taken place in an atmosphere of rebellion, of recrimination and, perhaps, of hatred? Conceivably. Yet she felt she was a woman with a grievance that badly needed an outlet. The return of Mary would provide the outlet, and she looked forward to it with a mixture of childish longing and prepared anger.

Paco thought fit one morning to ring her. She controlled herself to speak lightly, though cramp ran up her arm from her grip on the receiver.

" Olá," said Paco, " how's the little torero? "

" Very fine—and enormous." She waited for him to ask after herself, and, realising at last the folly of it, continued quickly, " Any news, yet, of September? "

" We've lost the dates. The son of a bitch won't face up to it. Wait till the critics set about him! It's common gossip, he's on his way out. They gave him the bronca at Alcala, and the ring was only half-full on Sunday—at Cuenca, that calls itself ' The Town of Aguilucho'! May be the fans are sentimental; may be they'd rather not see their favourite give himself away. Anyhow, I'm well out of it. It would do me no good, to stand up for a mano a mano with somebody who's lost his cartel! "

Under the sarcasm and the violence, she could detect the bitter disappointment. She knew all about the fiascos at Alcala and Cuenca—and about the exhibition at Ronda when, as though in compunction for their recent abuse, the critics burst into a paean " No hay qué uno! " So long as Ildefonso could hold the cape, his cartel stood higher than any in the profession. Paco knew this as well as she, and it added to his bitterness—and to her pity for him; while in her heart she prayed that Ildefonso might carry his glory to the end. But it was hard on Paco. What had the other to lose, by granting that one favour to a former friend? There was no question of forfeiting his own position, but, rather of adding to it, by an act of public generosity to one who, in the natural course of events, must succeed to the throne.

What had become, she wondered, of all the humbleness and sweet loyalty which, in the long ago, had accepted unmerited punishment and unmerited abuse, for friendship's sake? Ay dios—and what career could put more twists and distortions into human character than that of the ring?

" Are you coming home? " she asked, after a silence.

" Probably—for a few days. I want to hurry up the printers. There ought to be a few copies ready to take out to Mexico."

" Has Pasquale said anything? " she inquired cautiously.

" A lot of cow-droppings! Much he knows about writing! " She heard his contemptuous laugh. " It's a pity you sent him the book before it got into print."

" It was your suggestion," she came back quickly.

" I thought he'd use it for publicity. It's plain enough, why that one isn't pleased : we haven't paid him enough compliments. If I'd buttered him up, it would have been Cervantes! But it will sell in New York, and the dollars will be useful if I stop there on my way back."

" But you don't like New York."

" We didn't know anybody then. It's different, now Wilbur's over there, and I can meet amusing people."

So from November, when he left for Mexico, she was unlikely to see Paco until the beginning of the Spanish season. As she put back the receiver, a fury beat up in her. How dare he treat her like that—as though she were a servant, to bear his children and run a home for his benefit! How dare he accept all the good things with which she had loaded him, and behave as though he had a right to them ; use her house as a place to entertain his guests, make strangers free of the resources of Parral, act as though he were its master, while disclaiming the responsibilities of the position! How dare he squander his own by now handsome earnings, and take it for granted that Parral would pay for extravagances over and above those to which his work entitled him?

She walked sharply along the gallery, to the anteroom which had once been Tía Carmela's ; where Olalla was now established, in charge of the secretarial work she—Aracea—had removed from Carlos's hands. Olalla was calm, she had method; in a few months she had made order out of the chaos created by the indolence of Carlos. It was seldom, now, necessary to go down to the office, which was used mainly, by Carlos, for the reception and entertainment of business associates.

She sat down to sign letters and cheques, soothed, as always, by the cool efficiency of Olalla. It was a surprise, when Carlos walked in.

" Con su permiso ?—I thought you would like to know "— he addressed Aracea—" that we have a visitor. Our friend Ildefonso."

" *What* ? "

Carlos laughed gently.

" I thought you would be surprised. He is, I fancy, a little embarrassed. De la Torre is here, with a party; Ildefonso is among them. They are at present looking at the lot for Los Fuentes."

" But—the marqués de la Torre—I must ask them to lunch," she stammered. The marqués was an old friend of Don Luis, a famous afícionado, an ancient and honoured guest of Parral.

" I imagined you would feel that way; so I came back to tell you."

" How many ? " she asked, after a pause.

" With Ildefonso—eight."

" One can hardly exclude Ildefonso," she said curtly, and turned to Olalla. " Will you arrange that ?—And," she added to Carlos, " you had better look after them in the big room, until luncheon is ready. I won't come down."

She went back to the sala, and propped her head on her hands. It was impossible, in loyalty to Paco, to receive Ildefonso under this roof; yet equally impossible to fail in courtesy to the old marqués de la Torre. What was she to do ?

The past rushed back on her : the day when she held the montera in her hands like a chalice. The dark and shameful moment when his eyes claimed her, and, like innumerable women, she visualised him, breathlessly, as her lover; when, possessed by a guilty excitement, and the drive of a sexual urge more formidable than she had ever known, she felt her own eyes reflecting the disgraceful message; submitting, accepting—like Leda conquered by the swan! But no snowy god-personification. Black, lean and evil, with poison in its plumes, and a horned beak of blood, it reared, and she offered herself to the killing, to the adulterous coupling that was like a killing. And afterwards told herself she was like the fool who falls in love with an actor, under the influence of the compound of false emotions created by the art of the theatre.

Then the encounter at the Casino; the statement—" By then, you will belong to me "—and, beneath a mechanical revulsion, the sense of helplessness it created!

You're pregnant; you're hysterical; you're creating a situation out of nothing. Calm yourself; remember your dignity, and the dignity of this house. You will make yourself look respectable. You will receive the marqués and his friends. You will . . .

The indrawn breath stayed suspended in the lifted cavity of her chest. Slowly, almost unconsciously, her hand went to her heart. She knew what she had to do.

Olalla found her in her bedroom, combing back the heavy black waves from her brow.

" They are on the terrace; but there will only be seven. Ildefonso excuses himself; he is going to see his wife, at Sanjorje."

" He has gone? "

" He is about to go. Carlos has ordered the car."

She was out on the gallery. There were several cars. Carlos was there—and another. She bent over the rail.

" Buenos días, Don Ildefonso."

They both looked up—Carlos with his perpetual, tedious air of ironic amusement. A face of death lifted itself from the wide shoulders of a light suit, from a linen collar and a hand-painted tie.

" Muy bueno', señora." His lips split over his teeth.

She descended the stairs with deliberate leisure; a curious calm enfolded her. She was conscious of her bulk; she aimed it at those ungodly eyes, which she avoided as she extended her hand, but she was unable to repress a shudder as she withdrew it from the claw-like touch.

" You don't accept the hospitality of Parral ?—I thought we would meet at lunch."

" Muchísimas gracias. I have a family, I don't have many chances of seeing them. The señora will understand."

" Naturally. But it is a disappointment." Her mouth ached with the smile she gave him. " There are many changes since you were here."

" Many," he agreed, laconically.

" You have seen the new room ? "—Taking for granted Carlos was following, she led the way under the gallery. " It doesn't look much like it was when we practised our capes down here as children, does it ? "

" Mucho cambiado. Muy elegante," he muttered.

" You will take a copita.—Carlos "—she turned, and found they were alone. Disconcerted, she went towards the bar. " There is sherry, or will you make yourself a cocktail ? "—The others were evidently having their drinks on the terrace, served by the boy who should have been on duty here. Ildefonso remained by the door, looking round the big, shining room. She gave him a quick look, and looked quickly away. Something— some aura—had deserted him ; it was just a skeletal figure in a flashy, expensive suit ; it was the little boy in ragged trousers, grown up, " made good," but momentarily awed by his surround- ings. She recovered her composure, and poured out a glass of sherry with a steady hand. " The archway's new, isn't it. It leads up to the comedor." She filled a second glass. " Here's your sherry—if you'd like it."

After a momentary pause, he paced towards her. Aracea knew that curious, cautious pace, like treading on sponge rubber, as she knew the pin-pointed pupil of the eye. Ay dios, it was true —all they said about Ildefonso. A gush of anger and pity carried away the last of her uneasiness. Ay dios—*you* ; to trade your godhead in that fashion !

" Salud," said Ildefonso, lifting his glass.

" Salud," she returned. " Those were good days ; I haven't forgotten them."

" Nor I."

Perhaps it was as well Carlos had left them alone. She stared at the golden contents of her glass.

" Then—I may ask a favour."

" Qué ? " he said—like a peasant. She knew the roughness was deliberate, that he could, when he chose, be as gracious as any noble. She felt her mouth dry up. There was a throbbing silence. Ildefonso said, with indifference :

" I was beaten for you once, for nothing. Do you remember that ? "

To her shame, she found she did not remember. He laughed dryly.

" You've forgotten. I haven't."

" When we were children—— ! " she stammered.

" Then—I dedicated two bulls to you."

" Ay, por dios—— "

" Te quiero. Lo sabe."

The insolence, the indecency of the avowal for the moment silenced her. What was there but contempt, for one capable of such betrayal. Yet, in some way, it increased her pity, and her sense of personal security. The dueña of Parral inclined her head.

" Don Ildefonso García does me too much honour." As he stood there, thunderstruck, with a look of blind outrage on his face, she continued calmly, " I asked you to grant me a favour." Still he was silent. " Give Paco his mano a mano."

" It's too late. The dates have gone."

She brushed aside the feeble excuse.

" Oh, come ! The name of Ildefonso can command—— ! "

" Ca ! Not the Monumental !—and it won't do Paco any good. Paco'll have it his own way next season, anyhow." He made a gesture of dismissal. " My card's full, and I want a rest before the season in Mexico. Maybe we'll fix up something out there."

" But that's no use for our public. It will provide the

aficiónados with a sensation and make a great climax to this season," she persisted.

He shook his head. " No," he said stubbornly.

She bit her lips.

There was enough Castilian blood in her to resent this pleading to the son of an Andalucían peasant, of a peón on her own land. When she addressed him as " Don " Ildefonso, she intended it as an ironic reminder of the difference in their status. It was a foolish thing to have done, and she must change her tactics quickly. She sat on the edge of a table, making a slight gesture implying that she accepted his decision, and invited him also to be seated. He hesitated, looking at her from the corners of his eyes, and sat on one of the stools at the bar, lolling, leaning his arm on the glass-topped shelf, looking at her. Suddenly it dawned on her that the slightly insolent attitude was not intentional, but an expression of an inner sense of insecurity, and it seemed strange that this public idol, this honoured guest of nobility, this favourite of poets, painters and musicians, should still have within him that little speck of weakness, of sensitivity, perhaps, to his present surroundings.

" Very well ; let us not argue," said she, affecting to dismiss the subject. She dropped the grand manner and gave him a broad, frank smile—the smile of Aracita. " But at least let me persuade you to change your mind about lunching with us. You know how much interest Papá took in your career ; his joy in your success ; his great admiration for you—when you had not yet reached the heights you've now attained ; his unalterable belief in your great future. How gratified he would have been, to receive you here, in this place which is your home ! Now come ; consider I am speaking for Papá ; do us this honour."

He shook his head again—but uncertainly.

" I feel the señora's graciousness very much——"

" Anda ! "—She dropped back to the casual speech of their childhood. " There was a time when I was Aracita and you were Ildefonso, and there was no ' señorita ' or ' señor ' between us ! —when we ate our merienda together, sitting on a stone wall, or we sneaked into the kitchen to coax bowls of soup out of Josefa ! Don't tell me you've forgotten those days."

" They were very long ago."

" And Aguilucho prefers to forget them," she said, with affected reproach. " I excuse myself, for reminding him."

" Mira "—he also spoke roughly, in the manner of " those days "—" I have a family. I don't often see them. Sanjorje isn't far from here, and what happens at Parral is always known in our village. The niños would feel it much, that their Papá had been so close to them and had not come to see them."

" Claro ; and they must not be disappointed. They are fine boys ; you are to be congratulated."

" But you have not seen them."

" Que sí ! I have," she smiled at him.

" You've seen Pepillo ? " he asked incredulously.

" Pepillo, and Marco, and Paquita, and the little Gregorio ; all the children. I have seen your fine house and I have drunk your wine and eaten your bread," was the triumphant answer. " So it is not friendly of you to refuse the hospitality of Parral."

A smile broke reluctantly on his face.

" I am drinking your wine."

" Bueno ; pour yourself another glass."

He did so, and drank, while she told him the story of the visit to Sanjorje.

" And it will soon be time for Pepillo to come and practise with the little calves."

" He's only just started to handle the cape ! "

" I must send him one of mine ! "—Only the other day, Olalla and she had gone through the chest in which were stored the " toys " of her childhood ; strange treasures, for a little girl. The minute capes, gradually increasing in size, which she soon began to despise because they were not " real," and rejected for one, actually much too heavy and too big for her, that was stained with the blood and torn with the horns ; the little muletas, with their sticks and the wooden swords ; a collection of banderillas, each carefully labelled with the date and the place where it was used ; the piles of scrap books, the albums of photographs which the little torero, si Dios quiere, would inherit. One of the capes : a present from the little torero to Ildefonso's son. They were looking at each other, now, steadily, with the quiet affection of their youth ; the tension, for the moment, had gone. Ildefonso drained his glass and set it down. Getting up, he held out his hand.

"Pues—muchas gracias, y hasta luego."

As she rose, the loose smock she was wearing—one that Mary had sent her from London—caught, and dragged across her body. She loosened it quickly, but it had caught his eye. His eye remained fixed on the betraying curve. She felt something shrivel between them, something die : the ease, the feeling of " old times " she had striven hard to establish. Her heart sank. No hope, now, for Paco.

"Tu eres embarazada."

"By the grace of God—yes," she flung back at him.

"It's Paco's ? "

"What a question ! "

He laughed shortly.

"Good luck—and give Paco my congratulations."

Indignation, fury and a sense of insult held her silent as they walked down the room together. Ildefonso halted before the portrait of Paco, leering from its gilt frame. He sneered :

"Muy Niño de Maderas ! "

"Just as much Niño de Maderas as that coloured photograph of you," she flung back at him.

"Eh !—That's a barbaridad. Concha likes it—as much as Paco likes this."

Startled, she realised that Ildefonso, the son of a peasant, knew the difference between art and atrocity. Of course he had sat for innumerable artists. The great English painter, John, had made a sketch, later elaborated, that was hung in some famous collection. There was the Zuloaga statement—at almost the beginning of his career—and at least a dozen artists, of Spanish or French celebrity, had left to posterity their records of " El milagro." Genius had its own freemasonry, to which Ildefonso belonged ; to which Paco had never penetrated. Angrily she told herself it was unjust; that envy and malice had withheld from Paco his dues . . .

When the car swept out of the patio, she found Carlos at her elbow.

"Prima mia; your guests are getting very hungry!"

She shot a look of hatred at the sly, smiling face, and turned towards the stairs.

"Very well; I am ready."

II

She was now in the sixth—nearly the seventh—month of pregnancy; taking all things—including previous mishaps—into consideration, it seemed a miracle. Since the third month she had had little discomfort, and, thanks to Olalla's care, had observed most of the régime prescribed by the doctors. Much to Olalla's disapproval, however, she continued to ride. "One might think this baby was yours, not mine!" she retorted, to the former's reproaches, when, on their expeditions, Bandera broke into her free, light trot over the shrunken grass.

"It is not mine, and not yours alone," replied Olalla. "It is the future owner of Parral."

"Oh-ho; and what's Parral got to do with you?" she mocked, and gave her companion a quick, suspicious glance. Parral and de la Cerna; they were too closely knitted up for her pleasure. And she was mortally bored with the family excitement about the coming event; the letters, the visits from relatives she barely knew; the old wives' tales, the advice with which she was loaded, the unconcealed disapprobation at her continuance to lead a " normal " life, instead of retiring modestly into semi-invalidism. She knew her conduct had furnished " un escándalo " to the Segovian family, and suspected Olalla of contributing to it. Thank God, Mary would soon be here, with her sensible, English ideas and her unemotional attitude to the commonplace of childbirth.

Her interest in the life of the ranch had sharpened during that long, slow summer; the dropping of the calves, the small, soft, long-legged creatures burrowing into their mothers' smooth flanks filled her with a tenderness that was new to her. There were two little deserted things that, owing to their mothers' sickness, she was bringing up by hand; crouched in the straw, her hand in the pail of milk, she felt the soft, sucking mouths on her fingers and the delicate roughness of the little tongues; she took the soft buffeting of hornless heads, she whispered their names into feathery ears. Soon they would be too strong and too rough for her ministrations—at any rate, for the little torero, who must be guarded.

As in the old days, she missed none of the functions: the branding and ear-clipping, the testing of the bulls and the cows. She rode round the feeding lots, casting an eye of knowledge over the animals, that were being readied for the ring, and sometimes exercised her right of veto over one that was not, in her opinion, up to Parral standard. She had many arguments with Carlos over that.

" But, cousin, there can't be perfection in every one, even of *our* bulls! We'd soon be running at a loss, if we conducted the business on those lines," he protested.

" You don't need to tell me that. And that one—Peleador—will be in fine condition in another week or two. He hasn't settled down to the feed; he's still hankering after the grass. How long's he been in? "

" A fortnight, like the others," muttered Carlos.

" Pues, give him another fortnight; he'll do us much credit."

She caught the glint of approval in Benito's eye; Carlos might try to double-cross her, but that one would see to it that her orders were obeyed. The moral effect of her continual presence was already amply visible on the ranch; Carlos was the manager, and all orders had to go through him, but she was Parral! Spurred by her presence to unwilling activity, Carlos was on the job, and was feathering his nest in plenty of trivial directions which she suspected, but which she was unable to check; under-the-counter dealings with the innumerable individuals who did business with the ranch. What did it matter, so long as the credit held? Paco could deal with such matters; not she—a woman, debarred by her sex from the long, smoky, surreptitious sessions in the office, the glances and " entendidos " and nods that clinched a deal. Well, if they were losing money, it was he—Paco—who would suffer, in the long run. She could, at least, protect the name.

One responsibility she had been obliged to relinquish; she could no longer watch the loadings. The risk of mounting to the top of the old wall was no longer to be undertaken. There was no place from which, in her condition, she could safely supervise the dispatch of the bulls to their various destinations. She must trust to Benito that there would be no last-moment juggling with consignments; and, in a test of cunning between Benito and Carlos, she was satisfied, for the present, that the former would win. There would be a " malentendido ": the bulls for Málaga, or Barcelona, would somehow find their way to some place with a raging afición, to contribute to the honour of a small management and the éxito of some astonished novillero with a hopeful eye on Madrid. Benito knew her ideas and respected them. Benito agreed that it paid better, in times of dire competition by a hostile interest, to build up the credit of a struggling ring, than to devote the whole of the famous produce of Parral to established centres.

Riding back to the house, half-listening to Olalla's happy small talk—she knew nothing and cared less about the bulls—she again looked forward to the arrival of Mary. A sudden loneliness swept over her, a longing for someone to confide in, someone not to be swayed by personal interest, someone capable, not only of affection, but of understanding.

As they rode into the patio, Antolín, Concepción's nephew, came out from under the gallery; that meant a telephone message. When they were all—herself, Olalla and Carlos, out of the house, it was Antolín's duty to answer the telephone. He sat gravely, a book of study in his hand, on the gallery, within earshot of the two telephones, the house and the office. It was Concepción's gentle pride, to see him sitting there; her nephew, who could read and write, and understand the awful mystery

of the aparato she, in her long years in the house of Parral, had
never dared to touch.

" There's a message, Antolín ? "

He approached, with the air of humble respect in which he
had been trained by his aunt.

" Sí, señora. Don Paco. He is arriving to-night."

Paco. Arriving. Paco, her husband—and the lover of
Remedios Albacobaca.

" Did he say he would be here in time for supper ? "

" He said nothing of the hour, señora. Only that he is
arriving to-night."

" Where was he speaking from ? "

" He did not say, señora." Antolín sounded distressed, as
one accused of failing in his duty.

She was so tired, by midnight, that she decided to go to bed.
She had been keeping early hours, for the sake of the little torero.
The wireless had droned, Olalla and she had sat, their heads bent
over their needlework, Olalla contributing occasional remarks,
unrelated to the subject on the air : " We have not yet decided
where the nurse is to sleep, when she comes. . . . Don't forget
Don Alejandro wants to see you on Thursday. . . . Don't you
think it would be a good thing if I moved my bed into the room
next to yours ? You might want to call me in the night."

" Por dios, I'm not likely to call you before October ! " She
glanced at the clock and rolled up the garment she was em-
broidering—a bed jacket for herself ; the nuns of Sanjorje had
begged for the privilege of making the layette. " Good night ;
sleep well. I hope Paco won't disturb you, when he comes in."
—Paco was wont to announce his arrival, at whatever hour of
day or night, with a long fanfaronade on the horn. All the
evening she had been wondering how she would receive him :
this Paco no longer hers, but another woman's. And why this
one should matter, and the others—for she knew there had been
others—not at all. Each time she looked up, against the pale
walls, and pale furniture, and vases of flowers, there was the
neat, pretty, false little head of Remedios, who had been so often
their guest, who had been photographed with them in this very

room—were they, even in those days, lovers ? No, that was not likely. Even after their first return from Mexico, Paco was still passionately her lover, and, though all that year, they were seldom apart.

She heard, through her drowsiness, the clock strike two, before Paco—for once without blowing the horn—swaggered into the room.

" Olá." He bent over the bed and gave her a possessive kiss, which she found herself mechanically returning.

" You're late ; where have you come from ? "

" I've been in town." He yawned consumedly, unknotting his tie. " Jesus, I'm hungry ! Is there anything to eat ? "

" You'd better call Antolín ; he'll find you something."

He strolled out on the gallery, and his shout for Antolín echoed through the still house.

" Por dios," he grinned, returning, " it's like a museum after closing time ! Where's Carlos ? What goes on here, when I'm away ? "

" We keep different hours. Carlos is probably in town. If you'd let us know what time to expect you, there would have been a meal for you."

" I bet there's a meal somewhere," he laughed, and went out, banging the door. Of course there was a meal ; whatever the dueña might say, someone, expecting the master, would be about.

His cool assumption of rights, in her house—the house he used only as a hotel ! Did he act like that in the house of Remedios ?—Probably ! And with more justice.

She was so exhausted that she fell asleep, and was roused by his return.

" Well, I've got news for you," he announced, while she struggled against the clasp of sleep. " The mano a mano's on ! "

She was suddenly, dazzlingly awake.

" Ildefonso's come across ! I guess he didn't like what the fans were saying : that he was frightened of the show-down. Pasquale heard from his manager this morning ; we've got on to Madrid, and it's fixed for the thirteenth. A rotten date," muttered Paco, " but it was the only one they'd give us. I'd like to know, exactly, what made Ildefonso change his mind."

" He was here, a few days ago." The words broke from her before she had time to consider their significance.

" *What ?*—Here ? " gaped Paco.

" He had a glass of wine, and went on to Sanjorje."

" That's a nice piece of impudence ! "

" He came with the marqués de la Torre." She was now fully awake. " A party of them came, to look at the bulls ; naturally, they stopped for lunch—but not Ildefonso." Sharply aware of danger, she chose her words. " He wanted, of course, to see his wife and family, at Sanjorje." Better he should hear it from her than from Olalla, or Carlos.

" So that's what made him alter his mind," said Paco, after a bitter silence.

" Al contrario. He said his card was full, and he was unable to take on anything more before the end of the season."

" So you discussed it ? "

" If you call it a discussion. We mentioned the proposal ; I said you were disappointed, and he regretted. There wasn't any more to say, was there ? "

" And this conversation took place with de la Torre and his friends ? "

Her mind worked quickly ; there was no point in lying, Carlos would certainly betray her.

" It was just before he left ; he took a drink, downstairs."

" You and he were alone ? "

" Hombre, for a few moments. The others were on the terrace," she stammered. " Carlos came out, to see him to the car. I happened to be on the stairs——"

" What luck for you both ! " he sneered. " So you fixed this up with Ildefonso."

" I have told you : nothing of the kind. He refused to discuss it."

" That's a lie, isn't it ? "

" I give you my word."

He looked at her hatefully.

" There are ways of refusal . . . that amount to acceptance."
She lifted her shoulders.

" I have nothing to do with those."

" And I suppose you've got nothing to do with it, when Ildefonso dedicates his bulls to you ? "

" That's ridiculous. And, on one occasion at least, you gave your permission."

" So, to oblige you, he gives me the mano a mano."

" I have told you ; he refused it."

" How long were you both together ? "
She lost her head.

" How long were you and Remedios in the Guadarramas ? "

He stood there, not looking at her, the bed-lamp cutting out the planes of his face in patches of black and yellow, snapping his fingers, then turned abruptly and walked through into the sala, not troubling to close the door. She heard the click of the receiver and the sound of dialling.

" Con quién hablo ?—Oye, it's Paco. You've got a coche ? Good ; send it now. Yes—now. To Parral. You'll come yourself ? That's fine. Hasta luego."

The receiver crashed back, and the farther door of the sala slammed. She heard his short, crisp steps tap along the gallery, and guessed he was going down to the big room. She crawled out of bed, brushed her hair and dragged on a peignoir, then went down the long passage to the comedor, and down the stairs, under the archway. The lights were on over the bar and the rest of the room in darkness. Paco was pouring himself a drink ; as he looked up at her, the liquor spilled and dripped over the glass ledge.

" You can't behave like this."

" Salud," he observed, over the lip of the tumbler.

" Do you know it's three o'clock in the morning—Come to bed."

He laughed. The record of the past months was written all over him—in his jerky movements, in the yellowed eyeballs and the nervous tic in his jaw. One season—enough to destroy all she had been at pains to build up.

" At this rate, you'll be useless by the end of the month."

" I've not done badly, so far," he boasted.

" Ya lo creo. But it's time you had a rest."

He flung off the hand she laid on his arm.

" I know what I want, without you telling me."

" Remedios ? "—She managed not to say it. " You want to get yourself in condition before the thirteenth. You've got three weeks, and only a couple of fights. Hombre, be reasonable. Take some time out here ; keep sensible hours ; lay off *that*—and let's enjoy ourselves for a few days."

" What a prospect ! " he jeered.

" It's months since you've been home, and I want your advice on a lot of things."

" Eh ?—What's the matter with Carlos ? You've got him to advise you ; or may be he's got tired of giving advice by now ? "

" Don't be ridiculous ! What's the advice of Carlos worth ? "

He gave her a dim, silly smile.

" Carlos is buena persona. I feel sorry for Carlos."

It was useless to talk ; he was hopelessly drunk. A sense of emptiness spread around her. She let herself slip into a chair. He scowled at her resentfully.

" Why don't you go back to bed ? "

" We don't see so much of each other. I'll wait for the coche," she murmured.

" Have a drink, then."

She shook her head. She said presently :

" Is that place on your leg better ? "

" It's fine."

There was no more to say. The lights round the bar made a small, glaring pool at the end of the long dark room that reflected them from polished wood and chromium. She sat with her head on her hand ; without looking at him, she was aware of Paco, filling and refilling his glass. He lurched and knocked off an empty bottle with his elbow ; it crashed on the floor and she looked without interest at a segment of glass that had lodged on the hem of her gown.

" Well," she said at last, " is this meant to be the end ? "

" The end of what ? "

" Of our life together. Of you and me, as husband and wife."

" Qué dices—We're married."

" If that's what you call it ! It's not my idea of marriage. Never seeing my husband——"

" Ay, qué lástima ! You oughtn't to have married a bull-fighter. You ought to have married "—he gave his foolish laugh—" Carlos ! And worn ' los pantalones' and——"

The tentative note of a horn sounded in the patio, Paco shouted, " Olá ! "

" Se puede ? "—The grinning face of the chofer appeared in the lower door. She got up quickly, drawing her gown about her, and left them to it. Red dawn lay on the house of Parral, when she heard the hired car grind out of the patio.

Antolín came while they were at luncheon, and called Carlos to the telephone.

" Well ? " said Aracea, when the latter returned.

" Eight bulls for Madrid, on the thirteenth." Their eyes met. " Congratulations," said Carlos softly. " You effected much—in a very short time ! "

Chapter Eleven

I

" HAVE A cigarette ? "

" No, thanks.—Do you think," said Mary with hesitation, " you're smoking rather a lot ? "

Aracea laughed and lit another ; that was two packets, thought Mary, in the course of the afternoon and evening. She tried to turn her reproach into a joke by catching Aracea's right hand and spreading out the narrow fingers. " Qué sucia ! " she pointed to the stained nail on the index.

" Olalla's been too busy lately, and I can't do my right hand."
She pulled it away, jerked the neckband of her gown away from
her throat and, lifting both hands to her head, dragged the hair
back from her brow so viciously that her eyebrows were slanted.
" Dios, this heat ! "

" If you would sit down for a while you would feel it less."
—The figure pacing the room reminded Mary too vividly of
Doña Leandra ; the endless, aimless pacing, the air of withdrawal, of holding her companion at a distance. Slowly, and to
her own dismay, Mary had begun to wonder if she had made a
mistake in coming back ; in spite of the correct warmth of
Aracea's welcome, and the attention shown to her comforts, she
had received an impression that she was not, really, wanted ;
that some kind of antagonism, for which, in spite of the most
searching self-examination, she could not account, had invaded
their relationship. She reminded herself that, as a child, Aracea
was always sullen when she felt ill and that women were often
irritable at this stage of pregnancy, and that she must certainly,
for the present, conceal her disquietude, which was only likely
to increase Aracea's defensiveness.

" You like heat. It will be hotter in Málaga."

" Málaga ? Are we going there ? "

" Carlos will drive you over on Sunday. I don't think it will
be much of a fight. When they have to pay out big money to
the espada they get it back on the bulls."

" Perhaps I won't go." She had no great desire for the escort
of Carlos, for his irony and his gossip.

" As you please. I thought you might wish to see Paco."

" Naturally. But I'm here, mainly, to see you."

" Oh, I'm rather dull these days. Having a baby makes one
stupid, I think."

" I don't think you're having enough company," suggested
Mary diffidently.

" Company ?—Por dios, if you knew the company I have !
One day last week, the whole Ribera family came over and sat
round this room, like owls, staring at me. After about two hours,
Carlos took the men away and the women started telling me all

about the things that happened to them when their children were born. And about a Maderas girl who gave birth to a baby with no mouth and an eye in its chest——! "

" Qué barbaridad ! "—Mary winced. " Why didn't you put a stop to it ? "

" I don't care. We've had various monsters born out here, from time to time.—Another day it was Tío Federico and his wife and the wife of the son who's just got married ; she's ' carrying,' too, and everything had to be shown, and I had to remember what it cost—— "

" But, chica, I don't mean that kind of company. What has become of all your own friends, the people who amused you ? "

" The De Gaulas ?—All the girls are married now, and they've gone up to their summer place at Hendaya."

" Do you ever hear anything of the Brett Pawls ? "

" I had a card from Sylvia ; they're wandering around."

" With the Albacobacas, I suppose. And what has happened about the book ? " Mary persevered.

" It is printing. There are the proofs of the pictures—if you like to look at them." She pointed to the table indifferently. Mary picked up the sheaf of slub.

" Leo Mond is really brilliant—the little horror ! " She laughed. " Ah—that's a beauty ! "—A white wall, with Paco's shadow silhouetted upon it, and, facing it, also in shadow, the lowered head of a Parral bull. " How on earth did he get that ? —Oh, montage, of course. A lovely profile "—she traced the young, arrogant line with her finger. How handsome the boy was. " That's the interior they published in *London and Paris*," she observed, lifting another page. " Very clever lighting ; very good of all four of you—but—— " She looked up—" this one is crossed out ; aren't you using it ? "

Aracea appeared not to hear. She was standing by the radio. A sudden blare of mixed news and flamenco poured into the room. Mary glanced at the next ; the one to which *London and Paris* had given a full page—the duquesa de Albacobaca and Niño de Maderas, smiling at each other. It, as well as the interior, carried a slash of red pencil from corner to corner. Mary laid the pictures down slowly ; she was beginning to understand.

Concepción came in, with coffee on a tray. She could just manage to support it to a table near the door, but it was one of the little offices to which she clung, because it gave her entrance to the sala and made an excuse for wishing her señora good night. Antolín carried the tray along the gallery for her, and opened the door, and put the tray into his aunt's hands, watching anxiously until it was safely disposed of. She stood there, with her white hair, her angelic face, her humbly folded hands ; her presence—thought Mary—an unconscious benediction.

" Does mi ama wish for anything more ? "—The grace of the antique title, so seldom heard in modern times, lay on her lips like a flower. Aracea's back was turned to her, her ears deafened by the roar of the radio. Mary went and touched her on the shoulder.

" Concepción ; do you want anything before she goes to bed."

Aracea turned slowly. Her eyes met those of the old servant ; exchanged some unfathomable, female message. She slowly crossed the room, until they stood face to face. Mary watched, with a strange sense of exclusion. She watched Aracea drop her head for a moment on Concepción's shoulder, and the old hand linger for a moment on the shining, dark hair. Something told her this was a nightly ritual—and Antolín, standing at attention in the open door, its acolyte.

" Good night, Concepción ; God keep you."

" God keep my mistress ; sleep well." She turned her sweet smile and the grace of her bent head on Mary. " That the señorita may sleep well too ; it is good to have her again under the roof of Parral."

With a respectful bow to both the ladies, Antolín stepped forward and gave his arm to his aunt. The door closed softly. Mary stood still, with a choking sense of emotion. The little ceremony had moved and, in some curious way, disturbed her.

It set her at a distance. Purposely or not, it underlined the change in Aracea.

" You'll have some coffee ? "—Aracea brought her the cup casually, dismissing, by her manner, the little scene.

" Thank you, chica." She spoke absently. " That dear soul —she's getting very frail, isn't she ? You'll miss her, when she's gone."

" Oh yes ; one misses people—for a while."

" Aracea ; what have I done to annoy you ? "

" Annoy ? "—The dark eyes met hers blankly. " But nothing. I hope I haven't been rude, Miss Mary ? " she said, with genuine concern.

" ' Miss ' Mary ! It was Mary, last time I was here."

" Excuse me ; I wasn't thinking. I mean—I was thinking, actually, about Paco. I left a message "—she glanced at her watch—" for him to ring me to-night. They want our bulls, on the thirteenth, in Madrid ; I thought he might like to know."

Mary felt ashamed of her emotionalism, and replied, as she stirred the sugar into her coffee :

" I should think he will be very glad, when you are able to travel about with him again."

" What—with a baby and a nurse ?—Oh no ! I've learnt my lesson," was the bitter retort.

" No, naturally, you'll have to spend most of your time at home. But you'll be able to go to some of the fights, and you won't have these long separations," she persisted. " By the time Paco is back from Mexico you'll be strong again, and able to enjoy the season."

Aracea twisted her shoulders impatiently, let herself down in a chair and beat the air with a fan ; her brows were gathered in a scowl, her eyes fixed past and beyond Mary.

" My marriage is in a mess ; I suppose you realise that ? "

" What has happened, chica ? "

" Just the usual thing," she shrugged.

" Perhaps," offered Mary, after a silence, " it will be better, when the baby is born. I remember your telling me, once, that

Paco loves children; he'll be very happy, won't he, to be a father ? "

" And what does that do for me ? " muttered Aracea.

" I'm not sure." Mary smiled. " Except—happy people are usually at their best."

" You said that," said Aracea slowly, " like a little girl ! What is it about the English ?—It is as though they never grow up."

" Perhaps," said Mary, after consideration, " it's a form of self-protection. Instinctive, not considered. We do think," she added, " that happiness is important ; perhaps that is childish, from your point of view." It struck her that it was strange, to be saying these things to Aracea.

" But *what* is happiness ?—It is an accident : no ? It is something one cannot command. It depends on innumerable things ; it is a flash—and gone ! One doesn't count on it."

" What does one count on ? " murmured Mary. Aracea stared ; it was evidently something she had never thought about. " The love of God ?—the love of those one cares for—— ? "

" I am not a religious," said Aracea brusquely. " Mi papá ; yes, I loved him—and he is dead. I think I love "—she hesitated —" this little worm inside me : which may love me, perhaps, later on——"

" And Paco."

She flung up her hands to cover her face.

" What is the use—— ? "

" Love," said Mary, " is not a matter of ' use.' What is the ' use ' to love one who is dead ? Yet—one doesn't stop loving."

" You've been in love—Mary ? "

" But naturally."

" What happened ? " asked Aracea, in a gentle voice.

" He was killed."

" In our war ? "

She bent her head.

" A Spaniard ? "

" Yes."

" I think—for you—it was, perhaps, a good thing he died."

438

" You're guessing. We loved each other—very much."

" . . . I think," said Aracea, " ' to love ' means something different to us, than to you." She looked at her watch again. " Paco won't ring now ; he's either out with his friends or in bed. We had better go to bed too."

Arm in arm, they went out on the gallery. The lights of the electric bulbs were reflected up in the deep gilding between the rafters ; the patio was a shadowy well. Mary checked her step to look down into it.

" What do you see ? "

" Only some little ghosts : the boys, and a bad child in her riding breeches, with sore hands ! " She smiled. " It seems very quiet, nowadays." The thought crossed her mind : Si Dios quiere, it won't be quiet much longer. A " little torero," and then, perhaps, another, and another. . . . Oh, be quiet, you maudlin old maid ! she apostrophised herself. " Did you hear about Mirry's wedding ? " she asked, to change the subject.

" Mirry—— ? "

" Mirry Scott ; she married a boy in the Air Force. I thought she might have written to you about it."

" Perhaps she did. I don't remember. Yes, I think I heard something—but I hate writing letters, and it's silly, to go on writing to people you never see."

" They were all asking about you at the Smogs' dance ; Viola Bruce was very anxious that I should persuade you to join the Guild ! "

" It would not make much sense, would it ? ' Smogs ' ! " She laughed. " It's so like them. I do not understand people wanting to get together and pretend they are still schoolgirls."

" Oh come, that's not quite fair. They're very fond of the school, and Reverend Mother and Miss Morgan ; it's not unreasonable, to enjoy going back to a place where you were happy, and talking about old times. You yourself had a very good time." As Aracea was silent, she added, " Didn't you ? "

" Are you going to stay there for ever ? " asked Aracea, ignoring the question.

" ' For ever ' is a long time ! " smiled Mary.

" Why do you stay there ? " persisted Aracea.

" Perhaps because I've got no other prospects—at present," said Mary, after a pause. Yes, it was a poor excuse, and an unconvincing one. " Perhaps I am lazy "—came nearer to the truth. That, and discouragement about the book on Spain, which had been refused by four publishers ; she had lost faith in it herself, and to lose faith in a thing over which she had laboured for so long added to the lethargy that held her at St. Margaret's.

" I think it is bad for anybody, to go on teaching in a school for a very long time," said Aracea slowly. " I think it is perhaps all right, if you are a nun, and you have the vocation. Besides, many nuns are very like children themselves and they are able to fulfil themselves in their work. But for people like you it is —what is the word I want ?—crippling."

" Do you feel I'm ' crippled ' ? "—The word startled her.

" Not exactly. But I feel—may I say it, Miss Mary ? "

" Yes, of course ; but please—not ' Miss ' Mary ! Tell me why I've become ' Miss ' again, after being ' Mary ' so long," she begged.

" It is a little difficult—and I didn't mean to call you ' Miss,' Mary dear ! " The pressure of Aracea's arm tightened, and Mary returned it quickly ; the first spontaneous mark of affection she had received since her return. " I really do not know how to say it all : but I feel—somehow—as though I were the elder, now, and you—and you——" She made a gesture of relinquishment.

" Does it affect your—feeling for me ? " said Mary, in a low voice. It's true, she was thinking ; I feel it also.

" It makes it—different," admitted Aracea.

" When did you begin to feel like this ? "

" I think, a little, at Easter. There was some kind of—change. It wasn't in your letters. It wasn't anything I could actually— describe. It made me a little unhappy," confessed Aracea.

" Chica, I am sorry. But why didn't you tell me then ? "

" I did not know how to. It took me by surprise. When we were at St. Margaret's, you were not at all like the other governesses ; I felt you were like me—we belonged to each other.

I would not have stayed one week in that place, if you had not been there ! It would have been impossible, impossible," repeated Aracea violently.

" What made it ' impossible ' ? You enjoyed so many things," Mary reminded her. " You were so much admired, so popular— it isn't very often, you know, that English girls become as fond of what they call ' a foreigner ' as they were of you ; our young people, on the whole, are very insular——"

" ' Our ' young people ?" Aracea checked her.

" I meant the St. Margaret's girls."

" Yes ; you belong to them, don't you ? "

" Of course I don't." Mary drew a breath of relief ; was it, after all, no more than a flash-back to childish jealousy ? " So far as ' belonging ' goes, I ' belong ' to you ; just as much as when I was with you here."

Aracea gave her a deep look of scepticism.

" All the same—it's different," she persisted. " Yes—I suppose St. Margaret's was fun, in a way. But it wouldn't have been, if you had not been there to talk to. It is very exhausting, to be always with people who think of nothing but school, and winning matches, and House competitions."

" I know; it gets very boring, at times."

" It is worse than boring ; it is bad. Girls should not be encouraged to put all their passions into such things, Mary. It gives them false ideas of importance, it interferes with their normal development. At seventeen or eighteen years old they are still children—and by the time they are thirty or forty, if they are not married, they are either fossilised into something which is not human, or they are rushing about, trying to get all the experiences they should have had before they were twenty. Excuse me, but I do not think Englishwomen are moral at all !—and I think it is the fault of the schools that train them in all the wrong things, and do not let them be feminine until, really, it is too late."

Mary did not repress her smile.

" There is a lot of truth in what you say, chica—and there is also some exaggeration. A good many people would say the training justified itself in the conduct of Englishwomen during the war."

"Caramba, are women, then, to be trained up for war?"

"It's not quite the same thing," pointed out Mary, "to train them in qualities of self-discipline and self-control that may come in useful, in time of war.—Why are we talking about this?" she said suddenly. "You know that I cared no more than you about games, except for the pleasure one got out of playing. Like you, I preferred riding and swimming and the things one does by oneself and for oneself, or in competition with one other person. The happiest time of my life was the time I spent here, with you——" She paused; the memory of that unforgettable, guilty happiness rose in her throat and choked her.

"But now you are contented to be at school, to let yourself become like Sister Mary Theresa, like Miss Gaylor, like Miss Burns——"

"God forbid!" cried Mary. "Do you mean"—she was genuinely shocked—"you think I am slipping back into that kind of—immaturity?"

"Of course you are not a fool, like Miss Gaylor, or an envious old virgin like Miss Burns. But—I think you will be offended——"

"Please say it, whatever it is."

"It was Carlos who said it. He said, since you were away, you have become as British as your own Government."

"But I am British; I never pretended to be anything else," Mary said, puzzled.

"'La primera inglesa andaluza'?—Ay Mary! I've seen you blush with pleasure, when you were called that."

"I was never such a fool as to take the piropo seriously!— At all events, Tío Federico's," retorted Mary.

"Sometimes it is intended to be taken seriously. I was very serious about that, because I loved you, and I loved Tío Federico, and it is very good when two people one cares about admire each other. And, you know, in spite of your funny pronunciation of the Spanish, Mary dear, I very seldom thought of you as English. You seemed so much one of us, because you liked all of our things ; no, it was more than liking—you understood them, you were part of them."

" But you surely do not feel that that is altered ?—Chica, you don't forget that I once made a choice, very nearly a disastrous choice, between my country and yours ? " said Mary quietly. " One can't go back on a thing like that. I lived for nearly nine years as a bad Englishwoman ; I tried to be a good Spaniard. Now I'm trying to remember I'm British—but that doesn't make me false to my former loyalty ; and how can it affect us—you and me ? "

" It would, if there were war between Spain and England."

" How could such a thing be ? " cried Mary : then realised what lay behind the childish-sounding words. " Ah—you are thinking of the present Government. It's true : no effort is being spared, to foment ill-feeling ; no lie's too gross to give the people, through your Press, as well as mine——"

" As it was in our war." They had reached Mary's room, and Aracea sank into a chair. " Tell me something, Mary : why is it the British have a way of choosing allies among their natural enemies, and of overlooking their friends ? "

" Caramba, I'm not a diplomatist, or even a politician ! "

" There shouldn't have been war between England and Germany, should there ? "

" Of course not. But the German people are very susceptible to mania. The first time it was *folie de grandeur* ; last time it was paranoia. Next time "—she shrugged her shoulders—" God knows. But an ally with that kind of susceptibility would be, at the very least, undependable."

" The French did not show themselves dependable, did they ? "

" We can't afford to be ' at outs ' with the French, because they are too near to us. It's a matter of expediency—like El Caudillo's acceptance of support from Hitler."

" Ah—that committed him to nothing."

" Because he is a brilliant statesman. But that," sighed Mary, " is difficult to explain to the English, although we benefited from it as much as you."

" So a Communist-riddled France is better than a loyal Spain. Doesn't your Government see that we must have a Western bloc against Communism ? "

" Considering that the Labour Government is very largely made up of Communists who have snatched the Party label to get themselves in power, and who backed the bogus Republic and Azaña's efforts to crush out the Church—its interests lie very much in the opposite direction," said Mary dryly.

" But, Mary, how do you have the patience to teach a lot of silly girls, when such things are going on ? "

" What would you have me do ?—I am at least attached to a Catholic community, whose activities, puerile as they may be, are directed to the propagation of truth. When the General Election takes place, of course I'll do all in my power——"

" And Winston Churchill ? What does he think about Spain?" persisted Aracea.

" He doesn't like the smell of Fascism ! "—She smiled wryly. " Churchill is a great man—the greatest of our age—with not a very fine nose for ideological distinctions. And you mustn't forget he's francophile ; that's enough, by itself, to prejudice him against El Caudillo."

" One of his family fought against us."

" Not a Churchill ! " said Mary hurriedly. " You mustn't take seriously the antics of a vain and irresponsible boy." Watching Aracea's lowered lids, her compressed lips, she realised, to her discomfort, the under-current of antagonism to England and all things English that took her aback and deeply distressed her. At least, she tried to comfort herself, knowing it is there, I am forewarned ; but how had it begun ? The Aracea she had known —who she had tried, very delicately and indirectly, to influence— had always shown herself lightheartedly indifferent to international questions ; too young to realise much of her own country's war, the European war had neither affected nor interested one whose mind was wholly concerned with her immediate surroundings. Bearing in mind the anti-British bias of Don Luis, Mary had felt it wiser not to direct her attention to matters that would involve partisanships, and, above all, discussions of the uncomfortable state of British diplomacy as regards Spain. She found herself unprepared for this disconcerting backwash, for which surely St. Margaret's—hot-bed of juvenile Toryism—could not be responsible. And suddenly she knew the answer: *Carlos.* " Carlos said . . . you have become as British as your own Government." A typical piece of " Carlos " mischief-making, of treachery. She should have seen it before.

" I think," she said carefully, " we have known each other too long, and too well, to allow ourselves to be affected by things like these, Aracea. Let us forget them—at least while I'm here ! Perhaps I'll be less ' British ' in a week or two—it takes a little while, to shake the dust of the schoolroom off one's feet ! And I promise not to talk about St. Margaret's—I really cannot imagine why I did ; I am only interested in you, and the bulls."

Aracea smiled slowly.

" I think I have been unkind," she said, as they kissed good night.

" Al contrario," was Mary's quick reply. " After what you have said, it is easier—for us both."

Yet it was long before she slept. There were lacunae in the explanation ; the veils, though thinned, were not completely withdrawn. And one sentence remained, written on the dark and into her dreams : " How do you have the patience to teach a lot of silly girls, when such things are going on ? "—Had Aracea actually said that, or was it an echo of her own conscience which had told her the same many times ?

II

" That one—and the one on the right ; that's Peleador, isn't it ? I told you he'd be a credit, given time."

Benito nodded respectfully ; the dueña was seldom wrong.

" And in the next lot," said Carlos, " is something."

The horses moved softly through the dust between the walls, leaving in their wake a reddish cloud that hung for a while, then, carried forward by an imperceptible current of hot air, settled on the shoulders, the thighs and the boots of the riders. The heat was like a furnace. On either side of the barriers, the pride of Parral ripened towards their great hour.

A head of steel raised itself from the feeding trough, distantly contemplated the human creatures and lowered its muzzle back to the grain.

" Qué preciosa," murmured Mary. It was, in truth, the perfection of a Parral bull, immaculate in proportion, in colour and formation. Perhaps a little over-large . . .

" What's that ? " asked Aracea in a sharp whisper.

" That's Hechicero, of the Capanegra line."

" No." She dismissed it with a shake of the head.

" It's a bravo, señora."

" We won't send that to Madrid.—What about the lot for Tierraplata ? "

" Over the way. We're loading them the day after to-morrow."

Mary spat dust out of her mouth and pulled the scarf up the nape of her neck ; although on the point of setting, the rays of the red sun burned like cinders. Was it wise for Aracea, to spend all these hours on horseback? But she had had her lesson, not to interfere. They moved on to the next enclosure. Aracea hitched her hat forward and muttered scowlingly under its brim :

" Take out the one over there, by the wall."

" What's the matter ? "—Carlos moved up beside her. " It's a good type—perhaps a little under weight—but look at the horns. There," he turned to Mary, " you have the true Parral horn, short, broad, curving forward more than out—the kind matadores pray for—— ! "

Aracea interrupted him irritably :

" She knows as much as you do, amigo, about the Parral horn! It looks to me like a manso ; I'd rather it didn't go to Tierraplata."

" If they only get one manso—— ! "

" Other places can afford a manso better than that, and I gave Don Pablo my word. Oye "—she turned to Benito—" put the Capanegra animal with this lot . . .

" Carlos is furious," she muttered to Mary, as they rode back to the house, and laughed a little. " He always resents it, when

I interfere in choosing the bulls. Unless Benito's smart, that manso will find its way to Tierraplata, in spite of what I've said." She drew her brows together, frowning across Bandera's ears.

" What had you against the other—Hechicero ? " Mary had the curiosity to ask.

" Nothing—except superstition."

" Capanegra ?—He was too big, of course ; but I thought this one was perfect."

" You may remember," said Aracea smoothly, " Capanegra had a brother."

" Ay, dios ; forgive me, chica——"

" De nada. That line has always been doubtful : monsters, or of evil character. I think Hechicero is neither, but it is better not to take a chance. I'm pleased, on the whole, with that Madrid lot," she admitted. " However the draw goes, Paco can be sure of honest animals, with the best of our blood in them. I wish I could watch the loading."

" I am sure you can trust Benito."

" You don't know how sly Carlos can be ! "—She gave a short laugh.

" He's got nothing to gain, has he, by going against your wishes."

" The satisfaction "—Aracea shrugged her shoulders—" of outwitting me."

" Surely a very petty satisfaction ? "

" People like Carlos get a great deal of pleasure out of petty things." She nodded wisely. " Have you noticed how old and shrivelled he is getting ?—He has quite lost his attraction for girls and he's very bitter about it. And, of course, he doesn't like it, now I am here all the time, and he can't have his own way over everything."

" Why do you suppose your father trusted him ? "

" Papá didn't ! " was the quick retort. " But Papá never expected to die ; why should he ? I am sure, right on up to the last, he hoped to have a son. If Mamá had died, I am certain he would have married again, with that object. He took Carlos into the business—well, almost as a joke ! He took care never to give him any responsibility, and they amused each other. They had a good deal in common, you know: muy andalu, very fond of la juerga and the old-fashioned way of living that has disappeared since the war. He admired Carlos's courage, and sympathised with the loss of his career. I think they must have made that contract on a night when Papá had had too much to drink and Carlos was sharp enough to take advantage of it——"

" What contract was that ? "

" Why, the one that made Carlos a trustee, and gave him all his present authority. I suppose he thought, between us, we would manage to run the business, until my brother was grown up," shrugged Aracea.

" But he wanted you to marry Carlos."

" It didn't much matter who I married, did it, so long as I had children ?—and, as Papá had made Carlos his assistant and was training him in the work, it was a practical idea. If God didn't choose to give him a son, at least his grandchildren would be brought up on the estate, and the name, instead of Parral y de la Cerna, would have been De la Cerna y Parral ! That's what's soured Carlos," said Aracea shrewdly. " He fully expected I would be forced, finally, to marry him; I think, after Papá's death, he imagined I'd give in, out of respect for Papá's wishes. That would have been tremendous éxito for him, and for the de la Cernas ! And now, for all the airs he gives himself, he is only the manager, and if the baby turns out to be a boy, he will have no importance whatever. So he tries to revenge himself by reducing our credit——"

" But surely, in that, he's reducing his own ? "

" That's of no importance to Carlos ; in the long run he's got no responsibilities. He has no legitimate children, and now, if he were to marry, I do not think he would have any.—Shall I tell you something I found out, after I settled down here ? "— Aracea swung towards her in the saddle. " Carlos was doing very well out of doctoring the horns."

" But that's illegal ! " cried Mary, genuinely shocked.

" Papá would have thrown anybody out for suggesting it !

The mayoral—the one I got rid of—was in on it; the pair of them were making a nice little sum out of some of the less particular managements, who were, of course, in with the matadores."

" What had Paco to say to that ? "

" Oh, he laughed. I think he and Carlos made a joke of it together."

" It would not have been so much of a joke for Carlos, or for Parral, if he had been caught and fined. I'm surprised he should think it worth while ; it could not pay anyone in his position—whatever it meant to the mayoral."

" That is just—Carlos. It amuses him to do sly things, to feel he is getting the better of somebody ; for him, it is like a game. He does not care about anything except spending money and having a good time. I am afraid there are many like him to-day. Perhaps he was a good soldier ; now I think he is more like a malicious old maid. Even the family is bored with him. He is a little evil—and he is also a little dangerous. I tell you this," concluded Aracea, " because I am sure you will hear a great many stories on the way to Málaga."

Mary smiled faintly.

" I'm not likely to pay attention to Carlos's stories ! Chica, I don't really care about going to Málaga ; I shall be more than satisfied with Madrid on the thirteenth. And even that I would enjoy much more if you were going with me."

" Naturalmente ; but I have to look after the little torero."

" And why shouldn't I stop with you on Sunday ?—I'd much prefer a quiet day here, to that long drive with Carlos."

" Quiet day, madre mia !—I'm expecting a pack of dreary people ; Don Alejandro's wife—did I tell you he married, a girl of sixteen ? She's bringing the children and the nurse. And the wife of the alcalde from Sanjorje, with her sister and their children. A busy day for Olalla, and much boredom for me ! "

" Then let me stay behind and help you."

They had slid from the horses. Aracea turned on the stairs and threw her arm with a laugh round Mary's shoulders.

" Querida Mary—siempre la más cariñosa ! " She dropped
a light kiss on the other's cheek. " Olalla likes to feel important,
and you, as a spinster and an inglesa, would certainly put a
check on the obstetrics ! " she grinned.

" Talking of obstetrics, I think you ought to have a rest."
Mary flashed a smile of gratitude at the girl ; during the last
hour they seemed, at last, to have drawn together ; for the first
time since her return, she had recaptured some of the happy
confidence of the former visit.

" Yes, I think I will put myself and the little torero to bed
for a while," complied Aracea, and turned in the doorway to
add, " And perhaps I will send for Olalla to come and do my
nails, so you won't scold me when I come down for supper ! "

Mary found Olalla placing a bowl of roses in her bedroom ;
she dutifully admired the frail, papery, scentless blossoms, so
different from the sweet, warm, English roses. The two women
exchanged smiles of appreciation ; somewhat surprisingly, they
liked each other. Mary had appreciated, at their first meeting,
the qualities of the sober, sensible young Castillana, and Olalla's
instinctive jealousy gave way, first to her delight in the prospect
of practising her not very expert English, and, later, to her
recognition of a character as staunch as her own.

" Aracea has gone to rest."

" That is good. I think," smiled Olalla, " you have very
good influence on her."

" I've been telling her, I'm not a bit keen on going to Málaga
on Sunday."

" But why ? You like very much the bullfight. Aracea tell
me often you are muy aficiónada ! Oi, qué barbaridad ! I am
Spanish and I have never saw a fight in my life. It gives me the
bad face to think of it," grimaced Olalla. " But Englishwomen
are muy valiente—no ? El sangre, las tripas they like—no ? "

Dismissing with a smile this sanguinary picture of an Englishwoman's tastes, Mary continued :

" I think I won't go. I can help you with the children, can't
I ?—At any rate, I can keep them out of the way. I'm sure
Aracea will be glad of your help, in entertaining her visitors, and,

as you're a señora, you won't be embarrassed by the conversation ! " she concluded with a laugh.

" Please, Miss Mary ! "—Olalla spoke quickly. " Excuse me —it is better you go. It will be o'right ! I look after the children. She have to make talk—there is no time to listen to the radio. Señora Gómez—she hate the bullfight as much as I do. It offend her very much if we put on radio to listen to the bulls. Señora Gómez—the alcalde——" She broke off confusedly, and continued in rapid Spanish. " You see, it is not merely a question of good manners ; it would be very bad policy, to offend the Gómez——"

Mary listened patiently through a long dissertation on local politics, and nodded her head.

" I see what you mean ; if she were by herself, she would be obliged to entertain her visitors. But I don't quite understand ; she herself seemed quite anxious for me to go."

" The poor child !—You have not seen Aracea, when Paco is fighting." It came out in a rush of confidence. " She is hysterical—quite mad—not at all like herself. And afterwards, she is ashamed. Ay, that is the most pitiful ! She hates us all, because we have seen her crying, walking up and down the gallery, calling on God and the Virgin to protect her husband." Mary was silent and aghast ; was this the Aracea who had always averred that her anxiety, in the plaza, was not for Paco, but for the credit of the bulls ?

" Well, last time, as God willed, Don Alejandro came, just while it was going on. He gave her an injection. The morning after, he called again. They were by themselves a long time. Before he left, he came to my office, and told me what—God knows !—it was unnecessary to tell any person of intelligence : that she was endangering the child, as well as herself, by these unhappy indulgences. Don Alejandro is old, and a little old-fashioned, but she has known him from her childhood ; she would listen to him, though to no one else—and, Miss Mary, she is making a great effort ! It is part of the effort, to insist that you go to Málaga on Sunday—and part of it, too, to receive these people, to whom she could easily have excused herself."

" Yes, now I understand," said Mary, slowly. It hurt, a little, that Aracea had not explained these things herself. " And of course," she added, " I will do what Aracea wishes."

" Please don't malentiend me," said Olalla, lapsing into English. " She adores you ; you are the Only One—except Paco. But she is afraid, because you are simpática. Sometimes it makes more strong, to be by oneself."

" I've felt, rather, that she didn't want me." Mary was ashamed of the admission, but it was drawn from her, against her will, by the other's candour. Olalla shook her head violently.

" No, no. You. are mistaken. Don't forget—she has our blood, the blood of Castile, as well as Parral." She spoke with the cold pride of Doña Leandra. " Ay, Miss Mary ! It was un desastre—that marriage of Leandra's. Many people were to blame. It is not the first time, in our generation, the women have been betrayed—through greed, or indifference," said Olalla bitterly. " But we have always our pride ! Pride is an empty thing, but many of us have to live on it. It is better than nothing. But Aracea has much more than that," she pointed out. " She is going—si Dios quiere—to give a son to the light, who will inherit this important property."

" You have a son—haven't you ? "

Olalla shrugged her shoulders.

" I have given birth to a son. I suppose I shall have him for a few more years. Then, if he isn't claimed by his father, he will be sucked into the family. He will be a priest, or an intellectual."

III

The faint, silken spread of the Mediterranean, hazy with heat, lay below them, and the pale bullring. In the corrales the bulls looked like insects ; somewhere, in darkness, were the bulls for the afternoon.

They lunched, extravagantly, at Gibralfáro. Throughout the long journey, which started soon after dawn, Carlos had preserved an impeccable discretion. A secret amusement possessed her, looking at him across the table. A glittering ruin. To him, no doubt, she appeared the same—only there had never been any glitter. Two middle-aged people—the definition was still, to her, a little startling, having so briefly tasted the wine of youth—contemplating, with polite irony, their partners in the " might-have-been." What an easy conquest! she thought, scorning herself as much as him. A sex-starved spinster, falling for a typical Andalucían rip—no, that, she decided carefully, seeking justification no less for herself than for him, did not precisely describe it. A girl—a woman—robbed by war of her lover ; desperately lonely, snatching at illusion. And on his side ?— God knew what. The allure, perhaps, of a relationship not wholly sexual ; the rare experience of meeting a woman who could talk and understood, as well as make love. Or—she reprimanded her own vanity—who was there, and was easy! That's more like it.

He was lifting the glass to her. She responded mechanically. Dios, what a face : with the black eye-patch, and the deep graving of dissipation, and the irony, and all.

" Salud," she observed coolly.

" Salud—to our past. I was very much enamorado," he had the impudence to tell her.

" I think we might find more profitable subjects of conversation." It sounded ridiculously prim, old-maidish.

" Oh, surely not ? " he grimaced. " There is, after all, nothing more edifying than to look back upon the temptations one has resisted——"

" To whose resistance are you referring ? "—This was really too cool !

" To yours, of course," was the imperturbable rejoinder. " Speaking for myself "—he wagged his head regretfully—" I have always mistrusted the virtues of resistance. Speaking academically, Miss Carpenter : do you find them rewarding ? "

" Certainly more rewarding than this silly conversation," said Mary tartly. " What a charming place this is ! " she turned her head to look across her shoulder at the sea under its sultry summer haze. Gibralfáro had been an empty red hillside, tufted with stunted olives, on her last visit to Málaga.

"You have an excellent profile," murmured Carlos. "With very little effort I could be enamorado again."

"Oh, for heaven's sake, don't give yourself the trouble! You seemed determined to spoil this outing, which I have been enjoying very much up to now," she sighed.

"I suppose you know you have altered a great deal?"

"I suppose you mean I am more British!" she flung at him —and had the satisfaction of seeing a glint in his eye before he flung his head back and roared with laughter.

"My dear Miss Carpenter, you were always as British as the Union Jack!—That, coupled with your devotion to Spain and the Spanish, was what made you dangerous!"

"Dangerous——?" she faltered. "I should have thought that was the last thing I ever was."

"Ni na ni na!" he mocked her. "I am not the only person, then or since, who found you very dangerous indeed.—Do you know what it is, Physalia?"

"One of the hydrozoans—that we call Portuguese man-of-war?" she offered, after a moment's thought.

"Probably. It is very pretty, and if you are foolish enough to touch it you may be paralysed. Or you may die of poisoning, I forget which," said Carlos nonchalantly.

"Thanks for the comparison."

"De nada. It is not quite correct," he admitted. "The thing of which I am speaking—it is a *slow* infection, but invariably fatal."

"More and more charming. I hope you are not infected."

"Not I; I discovered my prophylaxis in time! Others are, perhaps, not quite so lucky."

"Don Carlos"—she turned squarely towards him—"I wish to goodness I knew what you are talking about!"

"Please go on looking bewildered; you have no idea how becoming it is. It suggests something to me: how much the face of Venus de Milo would be improved by a touch of bewilderment—at finding herself there, pobrecita, without her arms and so exaggeratedly décolletée ! "

It was impossible not to laugh at his absurdity.

" Your arms are intact and your costume all that propriety and a good English dressmaker could desire, but you have several times reminded me, lately, of that poor creature at the Louvre——"

" Now, come ! I can't be Physalia and the Venus both at once ! " laughed Mary. " And I don't think my figure—— ! "

" You are very elegant, now that you are not so thin. Altogether," said Carlos, " the change is very impressive. There are things I could not say to you, then, that I could say now."

" Please don't," said Mary quickly.

He laughed quietly, and refilled her glass.

" Down there "—he gestured to the window—" are los toros. If people are a little mad about los toros—like you and I—strange things may happen ; strange approaches ; strange understanding."

" Don Carlos." She made a strenuous effort. " There's no question of ' approaches ' or ' understandings ' between you and me. Please let's be sensible. I'm looking forward to the fight——" Her voice died away. She found herself thinking of the journey home ; the long, dark loneliness, the endless, hypnotic kilómetros —with a companion cynical enough for anything. She pushed back her chair. " We're going to see Paco, aren't we, before the show ? I'll tidy myself. Con su permiso."

The car, in neutral, rolled down the winding road ; the sea flashed before them at intervals, was blotted out by the pink shoulder of a hill. Carlos touched the self-starter and eased in the gear.

" I think it will not be much of a show. Paco is saving himself for the mano a mano."

" What are his chances ? "

" In a show-down, between him and Ildefonso ? " Carlos laughed. " Perhaps," he continued, " Ildefonso is a little tired of that section of the public which sets up comparisons between the two. No doubt, it is very irritating."

"But surely—Paco's his nearest rival."

"As the horse who comes in ten lengths behind the winner is 'nearest' to winning the race! If Ildefonso is in form, Paco will be reduced to nothing at all. And that will finish him."

"Why?—Isn't everyone saying that Ildefonso will retire at the end of the Mexican season?"

"Oh yes," said Carlos easily. "And if Ildefonso happens to have a bad day on the thirteenth, and Paco is lucky, Paco may hold his own through another season at home. If Ildefonso has one of his days of 'transfiguration,' when Jesus and Mary and Joseph look after him, Paco will be knocked back among the ruck. There are at least two of the boys who took the alternativa this year and last who can show Paco the way, and beat him at the finish. To perform a series of naturales and kill with a flourish is not, as you know, the whole art of tauromaquía!"

"Oh come; Paco can do more than that."

"Certainly. I have seen him very good; very good indeed. Much emotion, mucho estílo," said Carlos seriously. "But he has not yet had time to find himself. He still does not know, absolutely, what he is doing, and he is very tempted to 'show off.' He has all the tricks; he is, perhaps, the greatest master of the adorno at present in the ring. But he has not yet found the Thing for which there is no name. Sometimes it descends on him—and he is as astonished as the audience. You can see his astonishment. But he cannot—like Ildefonso—command it. He cannot yet, at will, accomplish the transition between art and the more-than-art that gives people like Ildefonso—Manolete, and Belmonte, and Joselito and perhaps half a dozen others in this century—their pre-eminence. Paco's aware of it—without knowing, quite, what he is aware of; it makes him uncomfortable. His father, El Cigarrón, had a glimmer—not more; El Cigarrón was very nearly a first-class torero." Characteristically, he swung from seriousness to levity. "And the mano a mano will be an enormous sensation!"

"Naturally; wasn't the last one Manolete and Arruza?"

"Olé, la afiiciónada!" He laughed. "You perhaps don't know that, according to rumour, Paco and Ildefonso are at each other's throats ?—Not professionally ; Ildefonso—you know the saying—' No hay qué uno.' It's some kind of a personal quarrel —over a woman ; at least, that's the story. And Ildefonso accepted the challenge—so they say—to show Paco up. Craziness, on Paco's part ; of course, he's banking on the possibility, at the end of the season, that Ildefonso's played out. He's very stupid —Paco. Much more stupid than Aracita."

They skidded in to the kerb, outside a hotel in the heart of the town. The pavement was seething, it was like the entrance to a beehive. The excitement of before-the-fight caught hold of her. They thrust their way up the stairs, between innumerable people with claims, real or imaginary, on the hospitality of the diestro. Very different from a pension in a squalid side street of Madrid.

The upper part of his body naked, Paco was having the machos tied by Antonio.

" Olá ! " His hand burned in Mary's palm, his grin split his face. He was obviously jangling with nerves—and so was any torero, before the fight. Somewhere else in the town, two other boys were going through the same ordeal ; were holding their little courts, were perhaps envying Niño de Maderas, because he'd got all the Press and the smart afición and the big end of the business, crowding in on him at the Hotel Medina, and they just had their personal fans and a few gaping foreigners, who wanted to be able to boast they had watched a bullfighter getting into his clothes.

As people kept pouring in, and the air rattled with loud Andalucían voices and thickened with the smoke of cigars, Mary wished him Good-bye and " mucha suerte." Paco jumped up to kiss her hand ; she noticed the twitch of his shoulders and a muscle that jerked in his jaw, but he spoke with his usual assurance.

" It was nice of you to come.—Miss Mary ! " he shouted, as she turned towards the door. " You're coming to Madrid, aren't you ? "

" Si Dios quiere." Surely he was going to ask after Aracea.

" Mind you do ; you'll see something ! There won't be much

this afternoon; I'm not going to get a hole in the pants before the thirteenth."

" Perhaps you'll be home, before then ? "

" Quién sabe ? " He dropped his arm on Carlos's shoulder. " You'll be down here again before the end of the week ?"

" You're stopping in town ? "

" Sure. Come over one night and we'll fix a juerga. It's about time you got Parral dust off your boots ! " winked Paco.

" We've got to get those bulls of yours off; I'll come over and tell you about them," smiled Carlos. Paco's head jerked back and he laughed in his throat.

" Tell my wife I want them the size of beetles, with chiquitillo horns—nicely softened down ! "

An appreciative guffaw went up from the audience; it was the kind of joke Niño de Maderas could get away with.

Heat simmered along the Alameda, dripping in white spangles between the lances of the palms. Carlos found a parking place, and, as they were early, stopped a taxi. " We may as well go down to Martín's and have some wine ? " he suggested.

" I am rather in the way; you would have preferred to stay and talk with Paco."

" Qué chiste ! " he mocked her.

They sat for a while in a window at Martín's, the tide beating sluggishly on the pebbles. The beach was deserted; the small boys and the fishermen were all up near the bullring, getting a vicarious satisfaction out of the crowds assembled for the arrival of the toreros with their cuadrillas.

As they climbed the stairs, and then descended to their places on the barrera, Mary put on her sunglasses, partly because the glare across the sand was very strong, partly in self-defence. Would it ever desert her—the remembered thrill ? The time might come—and then, she thought, I'll know I'm old, and nothing will thrill me any more. She leaned forward, to watch the familiar routine in the callejón; the sword-handlers folding the capes and laying them over the inner fence; hooking the banderillas over the string; fixing the muletas. She felt herself part of the humming plaza as she looked over at the sol, where she had so often sat : where the crazy afición was, and sometimes the fights, and nobody cared about physical comfort so long as he could have his share in the glory of the afternoon.

The band had started to play—and there was a sensation of some kind up on the gradas. Mary turned her head. All the young men in light American suits and sunglasses were standing up with their backs to the ring, shouting Olés. At the top of the steps, against the dark background of a group of evident notabilities, stood a girl in a white dress, her mouth and teeth making a square of coral and ivory in her small golden face, her hair of golden copper flung back like a mane from a broad, square brow. Her descent, flanked by her escort, was the descent of a smiling empress ; all along the barrera people were rising, so Mary did the same. The girl brushed past, with a powerful scent of gardenia, and, in passing Carlos, observed, " Olá, amigo ! " The guests of the management, down in the callejon, turned round and lifted their hats ; the piropo, at its broadest, rose from below, and drew shouts of laughter and appreciation from those within earshot.

" Who is it ? "

" That ?—A very talented young person—in more ways than one ! " (Ah, thought Mary ; and you've not had the benefit of the " talents." Vamos, hombre ; you've had plenty of pleasure. Why, at your age, and mine, indulge in bitterness ?) " The señorita Luz, of the Casa Caverna, and a very particular friend of Paco's. And that," he added, " is why Paco *might* have bad luck at Madrid, the week after next."

The band broke into " La Morena de mi copla," and the paseo started out across the glittering sand.

Chapter Twelve

A STARING moonlight made the landscape as clear as day. From her window, between the silvered trails of morning glory, Mary could overlook the new avenue of young elms which, with their drooping foliage loaded with dust, looked as though they had been snowed upon. A distant light or two marked the taverna at the end of the village, and along the highroad a few figures drifted towards it. Out on the balcony, her view extended itself over the farm buildings, into the enclosed yards where now the great, half-savage watchdogs ranged, and where the night watchmen were posted with their guns. She leaned her head against the rejas which formed a cage over window and balcony, and when a step sounded within the room took it for granted it was one of the servants, to turn down the bed and bring water for the bath.

" Miss Mary ! "

" Olá, I'm here." She stepped back into the room, to face Olalla. " I've overslept, and my watch has stopped ; what time is it ? "—Writing letters, she had not taken her siesta until nearly sun-down, and by now it must be time for supper.

" Isn't Aracea with you ? " said Olalla, in a perturbed voice.

" No—— ? " She spoke calmly, on a note of inquiry, but caught the infection from the other's uneasiness. " Perhaps she's with Concepción—— "

" I've been to Concepción's room. I've been everywhere," said Olalla. " She is not in the office, or in the big room. No one has seen her. She has been so sick to-day ! Mucho fiebre ;

paseando, paseando—never still. Always looking at the clock, or the telephone. If he can't come," she burst out indignantly, " why can't he ring up ? Qué monstruoso !—But all men are monsters," she ended with a shrug.

To-night, thought Mary, the loading of the bulls for Madrid. It had been decided, Aracea told her, to load them in the cool of the evening, so that the first part of the long journey could be accomplished overnight. Telling herself it was preposterous, that Aracea, in her condition, would never have undertaken the long, rough ride up to the corrales where they held the encierros, she hurried along the gallery. Leaning over into the horses' patio, she found, as she expected, darkness in the stall of Bandera. She called, there was a rustle, and a sleepy figure stumbled out of the straw.

" The señora has gone out ? "

" Sí, señorita."

" How long ago ? "—A foolish question ; it elicited, as was to be expected, only a vague reply.

" Where to ? "

" No sé ; no me lo dijé nada la dueña."

" Was she by herself ? "

The man, taking fright, started to whine that it was not for him to ask questions, that he did as he was told—and she cut him short.

" Bring round one of the horses—the castaña—now, quickly." He gaped.

" Y la silla——— ? "

Don't be a dam' fool, she felt like snapping, as, forcing the smile of courtesy, she requested him to do her the favour of saddling the chestnut and bringing it to the foot of the stairs " en cinco minutos punto." She had got out of the habit of patience with the limitless stupidity of the peasant, and of the longueurs of politeness claimed by the inheritors of the tradition of " caballerismo," though both word and tradition might be obsolete in the class most jealous of its privileges.

" Ay, por dios ! "—Olalla caught the discarded peignoir and snatched a shirt from the back of a chair. " And only seven weeks before the child is born ! Qué locura ! She must be out of her mind."

As the chestnut pounded along the road to the village, Mary told herself, At any rate, she won't be so mad as to climb the wall ; Carlos won't let her. Sweet illusion—instantly to be dismissed. One word from Carlos would be enough to precipitate disaster.

When, slithering over the cobbles, they arrived at the barricades, she shouted to a couple of men leaning on the wall to let them down for her. The sides of the street and all the windows were crowded ; the excitement of the encierro was in the air. Against lighted interiors a dark frieze of bodies thrust out, to share in this preliminary diversion.

She stared down at the suspicious faces lifted to the moonlight.

" It's prohibido. They're loading the bulls."

" I know that. The señora has gone up, hasn't she ? "

They stared back at her ; newcomers to the estate, to them she was a stranger, and they had their orders.

" No la hé visto," muttered one.

She slid from the saddle and knotted the reins into the nearest reja. They were all crowding round her, yelling warnings, explanations, prohibitions ; poking her, catching at her sleeve. She threw them off and stood for a moment, with her back to the barriers, looking up the street down which she had just come. Suddenly she let out a shout and pointed ; the childish ruse succeeded, and while every head was turned away, she ducked under the wooden rollers, and was away, stumbling and gasping, up the narrow, stony lane. Under another set of rollers, and she was out in a space of weed and rubble, and caught her breath as she recognised, ahead of her, the ruined massif of the old pelota court. Its broken summit described a flattened arc against the sky. Thanks be to God, Aracea was not up there.

It was years since she had been near this place of ill omen ; on their rides, she and Aracea had avoided it. And she had no idea how to get round to the other side, where the trap was and the loading chute and the trucks with the boxes. She, who had no head for heights, had several times in the past declined Aracea's invitation to climb that crumbling structure, and had therefore never watched an encierro.

Crouched in the weed and shadow at its base, she strained her ears. A deadly silence, broken only by an occasional grunt, a muffled shout, the hollow donging of the steers' bells and the drum of a bull's feet, hung over the scene of the operation that required so much patience, and carried so many chances of mishap. Once there was a plunging rattle, followed by a slam of iron, and she guessed one of the bulls had been boxed.

It became intolerable, crouching there in shadow, unable to see anything, torn by foolish dreads, wondering where Aracea was, and of what folly she was capable—though surely Benito would see that his mistress did not get into trouble. The wall of the corral, which formed an extension to the frontón itself, was too high for her to look over, and she knew better than to climb it, to risk disturbing the work proceeding on the other side.

She was halfway up the frontón, her breath sobbing, her fingers clawed into the dried weed-growths, before she was aware of having started. She knew before she reached the top that she could not possibly stand up, at that giddy height, on that treacherous surface, and she was nearly choked by the beating of her heart when at last, she lodged her bare arms on the shelf, and dragged herself over the lip of the stonework.

Her head swam for a moment in the blazing moonlight, in the emptiness and space ; then she forced herself to look down at the grey and white and black pattern of the corrales, and the trap, and the iron tops of the boxes. She could see the people along the stirrup that ran along the outsides of the chute, and the boys crouching with the ropes in their hands that controlled the gates of the trap. All along underneath the farther wall of the corral, silent and motionless, figures were clustered ; they could see no more than she had seen, while on the ground, but they were sharing in the excitement of loading Parral bulls. Straining her eyes, she sought in vain for Aracea. A bare head and the black circles of sunglasses stood, certainly, for Carlos ; she recognised Benito's broad shoulders, he was on the stirrup, nearest to the box, with a pole in his hand.

Down in the corral a horseman waited, still as statuary. Then three steers, leading and flanking a bull, trotted in. Fighting the eddies of her brain, Mary looked down. They were absurdly small; foreshortened, they were like toys on wheels. The horseman, moving as though he were part of his own shadow, circled imperceptibly, and the steers swung obediently towards the trap. As the first one entered, the bull, horning its partner aside, broke away. Backing towards the middle of the corral he lowered his head, tearing back the dust with his feet; then, seemingly without preparation, launched himself at the base of the frontón.

Mary shut her eyes, waiting for the impact, which, however, did not come. There was the dull ring of bone, or horn, on wood, and she realised that down there, out of sight, there must be a barrier of some kind—but the yell that went up was like an obscenity in that still scene. What could have caused it? she wondered, as she opened her eyes. The bull was trotting out again, and the steers were patiently collecting it. Once more it was conducted to the gates of the trap; once more it halted obstinately, while its escort moved forward. Then someone flapped a hat, and it charged in. The steers circled sheepishly back to the opening, the gate closed after them. There was a bellow and a heart-stopping clatter, and the first stage was accomplished.

" Benito ; Benito."

" Sí, señora."

" Look at that horn ; is it damaged ? "

" Me parece qué no."

" Make sure before you box him."

Mary could hear none of the conversation, but she watched, with incredulity, the laboured run across the dust, and, with a hiss of indrawn breath, the effort it took, with the help of an offered hand, to mount the wall on the farther side.

Ignoring the muttered " Cuidado, Aracita ! " of one of the men who had known her since childhood, Aracea was working her way on hands and knees along the top of the wall.

" Get down, you fool ! " hissed Carlos.

" I'll get down when I know if that horn's all right."

" It will be worse by the time it gets to Madrid."—The bull, refusing the chute, was lunging and horning at the walls. Benito, who knew bull talk, was doing his best.

" No, it won't ; if it's spoiled already, we'll take it out."

" What nonsense ; you know what happens in the boxes."

" That's no fau't of mine ; but no bull's going off this ranch—*with my knowledge,*" she paused to emphasise, " that isn't sound."

Luckily, the moon threw her shadow away from this side of the trap. It was impossible to lie down flat, but she could stretch out on her side, and look down at Peleador.

The bull, puzzled and defensive, slid back floundering from the black opening towards which they were trying to decoy him. Four times he had repeated this manœuvre ; twice, with a bound, he had tried to escape the trap itself. Now he stood still to think, because his casta prompted him not to waste himself on futilities. He heard bull talk, and rejected it. The moon and the stars reminded him of the long cool grass of which he had latterly been deprived. Full of rich grain, his fighting blood simmered in him. He carried death between his horns, and he sought life, to destroy it. Rocking from side to side, he afforded, without knowing it, the full value of his unblemished horns to the one who lay watching.

Aracea lifted her head cautiously, and nodded at Benito. Peleador, in spite of that crack he had dealt the burlador, was all right. She chose a moment when the bull's back was turned to lower herself to the stirrup, to the ground. She let herself slip gently on her bended knees and sideways on the earth ; propping herself on her hands, she dropped her head and panted a little. She had fulfilled her duty to Paco, and the rest could be left to Benito.

" And now, prima mia, I suppose you consider you have helped to box the bulls ! "

" I haven't done anything of the kind ; but I've satisfied myself that eight Parral bulls have left this ranch in perfect condition—whatever happens between here and the ring ! "— Refusing help, she pushed herself clumsily to her feet. She began to stumble round behind the trucks, behind the vans, that shook and gave out a hollow thunder from their deadly load. She had left Bandera tethered at the far end of the old pelota court. It seemed like a very long way, farther still, the ride back to the house. She stood still, hearing from a distance the faint sound of her name.

She stared incredulously up at the old frontón ; at the figure waving between her and the stars.

" Jesus and Mary ; what are you doing up there ? "

As Mary clambered down, she held out her hand, to help her over the last stages.

" You're a devil ! " Mary was sobbing. " You shouldn't give us these scares. Olalla's distracted——— "

" Olalla's a tonta, and she hates everything to do with the bulls. But I thought you had more sense ! "

" Sense ! I was looking for you everywhere. Where were you ? "

" Just below you," she answered coolly, " behind the burlador. That was a fine crack !—did you hear it ? Dios, I thought the horn was certainly broken——— "

" Do you mean to tell me you were behind the burlador, when the bull hit it ? "

Aracea giggled weakly.

" There wasn't room for me and the little torero on the ledge behind the chute ! That's where I meant to be, but we—we couldn't accommodate ourselves ! I couldn't lie on my stomach on top of the wall, and I'm not tall enough to look over. I don't trust Carlos, at a loading, and Benito hasn't enough authority. And there was just room for us, between the wood and the wall. Ay," she gasped, " I'm tired ! "—and slid through Mary's arms on to the dry earth.

. . . It was past midnight, when Mary rang the Medina hotel. A grating voice informed her that Don Paco was not in.

" Oiga ; this is important. A family matter. Find out where we can get hold of him."

A long mumble. Hold the line. She held it—it felt like eternity. It was not Paco's voice that, eventually, answered.

" Don Paco—no está aquí."

" It's you, Tonio ? "—She drew a breath of relief. " This is the señorita María—la inglesa—speaking. I must speak to Don Paco ; where can I find him ? "

" It's difficult to say, señorita——"

" Oiga : his wife is ill. I've got to get hold of him."

" Pues—I will try to find him. I'll tell him to ring back.— La señora está mala ? "

" Listen, Tonio : I want to get Paco *now*. And I think you know where he is."

" Pues "—came after a long pause, with obvious reluctance— " you might try the Casa Caverna——"

When Paco came on the line, she knew by his voice he had been drinking.

" Olá !—This is Niño de Maderas speaking. Who wants him ? "

" It's Miss Mary. I think you had better come home."

" Qué pasa ? "

" Aracea. She's "—there was no point in exaggerating—" not well. I think you should see her, before going to Madrid."

" E' difícil. I've got a lot of business——"

" Well "—she forced herself to control her anger—" perhaps I should add that she's got ill attending to *your* business. She looked after the loading of the bulls to-night——"

" Why ?—What's happened to Carlos ? "

" I think she felt it was too important a matter, to trust to anyone else," said Mary carefully. " In her condition, you know, it was a great strain ; she fainted afterwards, and we now have her in bed. If you would come, it would be a very great help. I am sure she would pay attention to your wishes, and not insist on getting up, and doing foolish things."

There was a silence ; then he mumbled something. She could not tell if it was acquiescence or an excuse. He hung up. Mary clenched her hands. Damn him. *Damn* him.

So as not to disturb Aracea, she had put in the call from the office. Stealing up the stairs, Olalla met her on the gallery.

" I've just been in to see if she wanted anything ; she's

sleeping as peacefully as a baby ! "—The words were hardly out of her mouth before the telephone shrilled in the sala.

" Oh, what a nuisance "—she pushed Olalla aside and ran to answer it, but even as she lifted the receiver the door flew open from Aracea's bedroom.

" It's Paco, isn't it ? "

" Yes, it's Paco," said Mary reluctantly, as she passed her the receiver.

" It's you, Paquito ? "—Mary pushed a chair behind her, and went out closing the door. The connection seemed to be bad ; he went on shouting " Quién es ?—Quién es ? " angrily, and so loudly that she had to hold the receiver away from her ear.

" Hombre, don't deafen me. It's me—Aracita."

" There's a lot of noise this end." His voice sounded thick and muddled, its vibration was like a drum. " Pues—como está' ? "

" I'm fine ; we're both fine." The joy of hearing him had taken all the ache away, and the tiredness.

" They said you were ill."

" Who said—— ? What nonsense ! We've been out to-night, seeing your bulls off.—Who says I'm ill ? " she demanded.

" I forget—maybe I fancied it."

" Querido, that's not like you !—Well, how are you, after Sunday ? "

" Fine. I'm always fine."

" They said the bulls were bad."

" Regular, and bad."

" You seem a very long way off," she sighed, after a pause.

" I'm in Málaga." (As though she did not know.) " Oye : ' stá ' vien—verdad ? "

" Of course I am. What's molesting you ? "

" You'll get the doctor, if anything's wrong."

" Hombre, it sounds as if you're the one who needs the doctor ! "—She tried to make it sound like a joke, knowing now that he was very drunk.

" I tell you I'm fine. . . . The bulls are good, eh ? "

"I give my word for each one of them. Benito has gone with them himself."

"Gone to buy himself some fun in Madrid."

"That's not Benito. He's coming straight back, by plane. According to Benito, Parral can't run itself if he's away!"

She thought of the past, when they had burned up the wires with their whispers, their passionate longing to see and to touch, as well as hear. Yet, if he had completely ceased to care, would he have rung up, just to ask if she were ill?

"Had you got something in particular to tell me?"

"To tell you——?" He sounded puzzled.

"I wondered—perhaps—if you were coming home——" she faltered. She had not meant to say it, but in his fuddled state he might have forgotten the object of his call.

"Mucho trabajo"—she could hardly hear him. Then he cleared his throat and added more loudly, "I'm taking the boys out to the country to-morrow to work some cows."

"But, chico, why not bring them here?"

There was a long silence before he answered.

"All right."

"You mean, you will?"—Her heart leapt.

"Sí sí; mañana"—and it sank again. Pretending to believe him, she said coolly:

"You'd better let me know how many you'll be."

"Tonio'll fix it.—There's nothing the matter with you?" he repeated, with fuddled persistence.

"Nothing at all. You'd better go back to your friends."

"Pues—sleep well."

She waited to hear him hang up; she waited—and dropped the receiver back on its stand.

Mary was sitting by the bed-lamp, reading.

"What did you tell Paco about me on Sunday?"

"I? Nothing whatever." Prepared for recriminations, Mary was no less relieved than surprised that Paco had not mentioned the telephone conversation. "The room was full of people and we had no chance to talk."

Aracea laughed as she crawled into bed.

" I thought as much. He's got a papalina fenómenal ! "

" Well, is he coming home ? "

" He says, to-morrow."

Mary said, after a pause :

" There will be time enough to tell the servants, in the, morning."

" Quite time enough," was the dry response.

The receiver dropped, and clacked at the end of its string against the wall of the passage outside the toilets that stank of drains and disinfectants. The ceiling overhead shook with the noise of the rumba band. A reedy voice bleated into the microphone. In the cupboard called a dressing-room Luz cursed him for his delay.

Sweat was in his eyes and his head was a sponge soaked with griefs and grievances and resentments.

Aracita. Aracita in bed in the dark. Carrying the baby.

Ildefonso. Dedicating his bulls to the wife of his rival. Aracea, holding the montera, as if it was, as if it was the blood of Christ ! And the pair of them, plotting the mano a mano ; to show him up—Niño de Maderas !

. . . He and Ildefonso, caping the bull-calves at Parral : El Cigarrón and the dueño looking on. He the " espada " and Ildefonso the " cuadrilla " ! Ildefonso sneaking the show. It made him mad, because it wasn't good enough, to have the suit of lights, and the backing, and everything Ildefonso hadn't got, and be shown up in front of his father and Don Luis. The anger had not lasted more than a minute, and it was useful, because it made him work. It clinched his determination, to get to the very top. And the rivalry was good, for both of them ; there was no sort of jealousy, no bad feeling.

But he swallowed the dirt ; he let himself be guided—sweet suffering Christ !—into a dead end. Trapped like a bull. They all had their heads over the wall, laughing at him, until he saved himself, with that one, desperate bound ! And now he'd got them scared ; even Ildefonso—obliged, at last, to defend his title. Yes ; obliged. He hadn't taken that on to please Aracita.

That could be her view of it ; women like to delude themselves. As much as they like having the top man.

Genio's all right, but it takes more than genio, to handle three Parral bulls. You just can't do it, if your legs won't serve you, and you're not sure how near the bull is, or how far, and your joints are apt to lock at the moment you've most need of flexibility. Hombre, you're muy valiente but valour isn't enough. The bulls know it, as well as you. You were sure, and then you started to doubt. And you've waited too long !

I've got nearly a week to get in condition. I'm all right. Only too much drink, and . . . I'm all right. I'm fine. I'm going to show the whole fripping lot of them : the Aguiluchistas and the Press and—and Aracea. Let them frip themselves. I've got myself nervous. I've been imagining things. I'll have a couple of days with Mateo's cows, and Luz can chew her pretty nails . . . ay, Luz . . .

II

" It's a good thing we took your reservation so long ago." Olalla turned from the telephone. " That was the office, ringing up to confirm ; the Madrid plane's crowded out."

" All right ; ring back and tell them there's a cancellation. I'm not going."

" You're not—— ? "

The eyes of the two women met. There was a reluctant relief in Olalla's.

" But, Miss Mary—what will Aracea say ? She has made all the arrangements, and booked you in at the hotel——"

" Let me see to it. There's no need to say anything to Aracea, for the present."

" It's very kind—I'm sure, for you, it's a sacrifice," stammered Olalla.

Sacrifice ?—A mounting excitement, that gripped the whole of Parral, was presided over by Aracea ; a cigarette endlessly glued to her lip, she received visitors, she answered the telephone, she accepted condolences on her inability to be present at the great event. Sylvia Brett Pawl rang up from Madrid: "We've just flown over; stopping with Tano and Remedios. Do you know Remedios is going to have a baby? Tano won't let her go to the fight, and she's *furious*! She sends you her love . . ." "Give her mine—and my congratulations." She replaced the receiver, marvelling at the steadiness of her voice. She looked at the clock, calculating the hours.

When supper was over—they had it on trays in the sala—she turned to Mary.

"This had better be 'hasta luego.' I'm going to take one of my sleeping pills; I'll probably be asleep when you leave."

"Chica"—Mary hesitated; this was "it." "I've changed my mind; I'm not going."

"Why not?"—An instant tension flung up the barrier between them.

"I've seen a lot of bullfights; perhaps I'm getting too old for them. It's a long way, in the heat—and I always disliked Madrid," she concluded weakly.

"That's ridiculous! This isn't 'a bullfight,' and you've never seen a mano a mano. Perhaps it's your last opportunity of seeing Ildefonso; they say he'll retire, after the Mexican season."

"That's unfortunate, for me." She lifted her shoulders slightly. "But I've got plenty to look back upon. I've seen him, after all, at his best."

"I insist you go! I don't want you, or anyone else, in the house!" Her lips shook, quivers ran down her.

"I promise I won't come near you; Olalla and I will listen to the broadcast in the office, with the servants," said Mary, calmly.

"So you, too, think Paco——" She swallowed the end of the sentence, as one swallows a bitter draught.

Mary was silent.

"You know a great deal; much more than——"

". Ah, let's leave it," broke from her lips—" what I know or what I don't know ! I came here, as I came all those years ago, to look after you. Perhaps it's unnecessary ; but—here I am ! " She forced a laugh. " And I don't see how you can get rid of me without being rude ! We agree—I've made mistakes. But don't you think I might be allowed to make up for them ? "

" I don't see how it ' makes up,' not going to the bullfight," muttered Aracea.

" I know ; you'd rather I were out of the way. Well, I've promised, haven't I ? You shan't see me all day, if that makes you any happier."

Aracea got up quickly, and went to the door.

" You're very kind, Mary." The clock struck as she was speaking ; in silence they counted the strokes. Twelve. The day had begun.

" We used "—Mary moistened her lips. " Do you remember ? —We used to say our night prayers together."

Aracea came back slowly. They knelt down together. Angel of God, who art my guardian, enlighten, guard, direct and govern me . . . Jesus Christ, defend and keep me . . . Into thy hands, O Lord . . .

Aracea cast herself into her arms.

" Get up, darling ; you've been kneeling long enough."

" Oh, Mary, Mary ; don't go away. I'm so frightened——"

" Hush, chiquita ; God will look after Paco—and the little torero."

" I won't have my pills," said Aracea, as Mary drew the sheet over her. " I don't think they're good.—I suppose Paco is in bed by now."

" Without doubt ; Tonio would see to that."

" He had to do this, for the sake of pondonor."

" I know that, chica."

" It will be terrible for him, if——"

" He has much time, to recover his credit."

" And it will be terrible for all Spain, if Ildefonso——"

" ' No hay qué uno,' " Mary reminded her. " If the day favours one, and is unkind to the other, Ildefonso is always Ildefonso, and Paco, at least, is admitted as his rival." She felt ashamed of the trite conclusion, as she bent over the girl to kiss her good night.

It was a little after four when Aracea came to her room.

"I think something's happening; I've got pains like toothache down my spine."

Chapter Thirteen

I

Don Pasquale Basilio, who had taken the long journey to Madrid partly as a compliment to his client, but mainly because he, like every other informed person, had no intention of missing a historic occasion, was, on the whole, relieved to find his protégé in a state of blind nerves. It would have been like Paco, out of bravado, to be laughing, smoking, joking and entertaining a roomful of people. Don Pasquale—even he—had had difficulty in penetrating the barrier drawn by Tonio between his master and the mob on the stairs and corridor. Muy bien; Paco was taking this seriously—as well he might; it was either the beginning or the end of his career as a universally admitted star of the ring.

Paco, astride the knotted towel held by Tonio and the barber, was writhing into the taleguilla; his head down, his teeth clenched, he acknowledged with a nod the arrival of his impresario. There was nobody there but Chano, Tonio and the barber, and a character introduced as Don Fidelio Mora, who appeared from the adjoining bathroom, wiping his hands on a towel, and after a muttered conversation with Tonio, made his excuses. Don Pasquale did not care for the presence of Don Fidelio, and was satisfied at his departure.

Paco stood shivering and hugging his ribs, while Tonio lifted the nylon camisa, and held it for his master's arms.

" I'm thirsty," snapped Paco. " Get me a drink."

Chano brought a glass of cloudy liquid.

" What's that ? " asked Don Pasquale, out of curiosity.

Paco laughed harshly.

" Barley water ; you don't have to worry.—Get Don Pasquale his usual." He gulped feverishly.

Don Pasquale suppressed a start ; in his experience, the connotations of barley water were disagreeable. He, accepted, however, gin and lime, and turned his eye from the taleguilla to the jacket hung over the back of a chair ; both flesh-coloured, loaded with bullion of silver and gold. He murmured absently :

" Preciosa.—Listen, boy ; play it down to-day. The twenty-three thousand customers in front aren't looking for stunts."

Paco nodded.

" What's the time ? "

" You're all right ; nearly an hour before we set out."

Someone pounded on the door, and Paco jumped as though he were shot.

" Keep that bloody door locked ! "

" It's locked," said Tonio calmly, offering the shirt. He jerked it over his shoulders, shivering at the slimy contact with his flesh ; it was too hot to wear the thin woven vest he usually wore, to mop up the sweat.

" You look fine," said Don Pasquale uneasily. Paco looked like hell. " You don't have to worry about a thing."

Hadn't he ?

It had never happened before, and it had to happen now. Nobody knew but Tonio, who had fetched the doctor. Potassium permanganate and gallons of barley water. No liquor—and he was dying for a drink ; the glass in Don Pasquale's hand was sheer torture.

He turned his tormented eyes to the little image of the Macarena on top of the dresser : the small figure in coloured ivory, encased in purple plush, Aracea had given him, that went with him everywhere ; with the gilt socket for the candle. Holy Mary, Mother of Jesus, why'd this got to happen *now* ? Tonio knew, and Chano guessed, when he sent for him to say Chano could hang the sticks. Ever since getting over that last jab in the groin he had done his own banderillearing : the show the crowd expected from Niño de Maderas. And to-day, of all others—well, if you're taking three bulls, instead of two, it's commonsense to save yourself. He would see how he felt, before the last . . .

Somewhere in the town was Ildefonso—feeling the same way ?—sitting down to rest after the sickening effort of dressing, with death in his limbs and twenty-three thousand pink dabs dazzling in his brain and all the adulation and cruelty of the crowd singing in his ears ?—With a distinct picture of the horn waiting to get him in the belly, and the white slab and the stink of ether that, by now, was surely as familiar to him as his own breath ?

They said Ildefonso didn't care any longer, that he was disappointed each time they pulled him off the slab and sent him into hospital, instead of to the mortuary. But, Christ, I want to live ! I want to live to be the greatest matador in Spain, and to-day's my chance, and this had to happen, and because I'm not used to it—like Ildefonso—it's taking up all my thoughts and cutting down the one thing I was able to rely on.

Again came the pounding on the door. Tonio yelled :

" Quién ? "

" A telegram."

" Carájo—shove it under the door, or leave it outside." The blue slip with slips of white pasted on it appeared on the parquet ; Paco took it and jerked it open with his thumb.

> " Love thoughts confidence.
>   ARACEA & THE LITTLE TORERO."

He balled it up in his palm. His hand was shaking. I suppose I ought to have rung her up. I wonder if Ildefonso's had one too ? He heard himself laughing, and Tonio saying flatly :

" Here's your tie."

. . . He was dressed. The door was open, and Tonio had cleared the passage and stairs. Don Pasquale and Chano had gone—the former to his place of privilege in the callejón, and Chano to wait in the car downstairs. He walked stiffly to the dresser, knelt and crossed himself. His mind was perfectly blank; he could not remember one word. He waited a little, then got up, and walked along the passage, and down the stairs, and through the yelling crowd of kids and passers by, and into the car.

II

The hum of the plaza rose and fell in waves; sometimes it was like a muffled roar of wild beasts, sometimes it fell to the ominous buzzing of a hive about to swarm. Outside the hideous modern building mounted police controlled, to some extent, the crowds, and made way for the cars that put down their loads at the main entrance. It was not a fiesta, but, in compliment to Ildefonso, there were a few mantillas round the palcos, and a spattering of shawls, reduced by the vast space to the size and importance of gaudy postage stamps.

Posing for their photographs, the two diestros presented a notable contrast. Niño de Maderas, in flesh pink and gold, with the bright, artificial smile pasted on his face, was the fulfilment of the romantic—or feminine—conception of the matador. The early, wax-doll, almost foolish good looks had given place to something harder, more dangerous, more formidable; the faint muscular curve of the profile from hip to ankle was like a steel blade, and every line carried a purpose that was confirmed by the handsome, confident face. Separated by at least a yard from his companion, even the Press photographers did not ask them to move together; this was a battle, over which the Press was already licking its chops. They had not uttered a word to each other, and the cuadrillas, uncomfortably involved, stood bunched on opposite sides of the passage-way, turning their backs on each other, and pretending no one else was there.

Paco, as usual, had squared himself and taken up the classic stance at first sight of the cameras. Ildefonso, leaning against the barrier, his chin on his arm, looked across his shoulder, and made no effort to move. So he was taken, in an attitude that was a subtle insult to his rival. Paco saw it too late and bit his lip as he swung aside. Ildefonso turned to his contemplation of the invisible. It was a matter of indifference to him, that fools, or the uninformed might take him for a shabby member of his own cuadrilla.

He had no longer need to consider any of the things that had contributed to his rise from a thin, anxious boy with nothing but a rag of red cloth between him and starvation, to the top of his profession. In a few short, hectic years he had gone through fortunes—simply because he had not the least idea of what to do with money. Deprived in his youth, he had indulged all his appetites until his palate grew satiated. He had been careless and cautious and generous and mean, all at the wrong times, in the wrong places and with the wrong people. He had made himself an object of worship, even of superstition, and had profited by it, sensing advantage, but unable to understand what it was about. Life was some sort of a machine he had never learned to manage, any more than he had learned to drive a car.

When sufficiently drunk, he could enter with assurance into the world of rich and famous people, accept with cynicism their adulation, make on it; it flattered him, but, in the long run, it entailed too much effort. He grew bored with its restrictions and its formalities, he sank back to a society in which he could be at ease. Sick in body and soul, his one instinct was directed to the prolongation of his career—not because he loved life or feared death, but because it had come to be the only thing that mattered. Why, he could not have said; it was perhaps because it was the only thing that survived of his dire pilgrimage. Having lost faith in everything else in the world, he believed in himself; or, rather, in the image they had raised of him, in the legend of his own immortality. No ordinary being born of woman could have survived the things he had survived, and no one, unless borne up by some supernatural power, could still go into the ring and do the things he did—taking them for granted.

But the wreckage he dragged about with him was breaking

down fast; he knew it, if no one else did. And in the night he had made up his mind to tell Gándara the Mexican season was off. Poor old Gándara—who regarded him as a son; who was already crying in the callejón, as he cried from beginning to end of all Ildefonso's fights! Gándara, whose advice he had slighted and spurned and jeered at until, of latter years, he ceased to offer it.

If he had listened to Gándara, he might now own a banking account, a country estate and a couple of big cars; perhaps a flourishing wine business, or a dry goods store. Bullfighters usually did well when they turned comercios. The way things went, there would be a bit of worthless property at Sanjorje, his portrait in several collections and the sale of his postcards; his creditors would certainly swoop on the house, and Concha and the kids—may be they would make out, with Gándara's help. There was a manzanilla on the market, that was supposed to pay him for the use of his name, but he usually lost or forgot the cheques when they turned up, and, so far as he could remember, there was no agreement in writing.

Somebody—perhaps some of the rich fans—might raise enough to buy the sculpture by the Madrid boy; it wasn't sold yet. Too big for anything but a museum (or a cemetery; it might look good over the grave), it could be good or bad; he had given the boy something to pay for the stone and a few coñacs. It was just a big chunk of granite, until you went on looking, and then there was something like an eagle and something like a bull, and the eagle was smothering across the bull's head. . . . He liked it, he couldn't say why. And there was no rich family, to put up a thing like Joselito's. Nicer, somehow, to be represented by an eagle and a bull than by a stretched-out marble photograph with a lot of people in their fiesta clothes crying round the base.

That which passed for a smile smeared itself between the eagle-beak and the narrow jutting chin as he looked across the white-shining ring, and beyond, and beyond . . .

And now—Niño de Maderas.

The Niño was better than they made him out. Better than

anyone expected, who had seen him at the start of his career. He'd got what the young afición liked and he was as brave as they come. Whatever they chose to say about Sánchez and Léon and the Basque—the runners-up—he was going to be at the top for years. Only, to-day, he was going to have it. To-day—if it took the last of his broken intestines, and the tin and rubber inside his body—Ildefonso would show them. To-day he would leave something the Niño would never live down. And, if he had had a grain of sense, he would never have invited.

He was just out of hospital, when old de la Torre and his friends carried him down to Sevilla : another of his " phenomenal " recoveries ! He'd just been obliged to cancel a bunch of dates, but had instructed Gándara to confirm the last two big fights of the season. For the first time in his life, he had agreed to an empty fortnight, before leaving for Mexico. He had brushed off the Niño's agent, who had been plugging at him for months about the two-handed show in Madrid ; his card was heavy enough, without that. And that last piece of surgery, cutting across already ruined tissue, had acted as a warning.

But when he walked into the house of Parral, for the first time since the death of Don Luis ; when he came face to face with her, and the great painted daub of the boy from Maderas —and remembered that, but for his humility, he might have called himself the boy from Parral—the warning broke down.

Not immediately. All the time he was talking to her, in that fancy room with the flash bar, where the Niño showed off and entertained his high-class friends on his wife's money, his intention held good. There was Salamanca, and there was San Miguel, on the 28th, and for this last—perhaps his last show in the Monumental he meant to save everything. Not even she should persuade him out of that.

They'd been drinking on the terrace, and drink, latterly, had affected him in a curious way. As the wine slid down inside him, he seemed to dissolve, to float, to rise and soar out of his own body, with its faded urges and desires ; and, as the people around him receded, almost to invisibility, he had a sense of singular liberation from everything terrestial. When he met her at the foot of the stairs, this feeling was still with him—and her sudden appearance was like an intrusion.

The sharp stab of desire that tore him apart, as he crouched in the hole in the wall, was a memory, no more. The dedication of the bull : the first time, yes, that meant something. And the second, and the meeting in the Casino, was defiance. He wanted her ; across the alluring body of his companion that night, he wanted her. But he wanted more to assert himself ; to confirm the name by which, jokingly, she had called him when they were children. " Maestro ! " That was what he really wanted ; to show her what " maestro ! " meant.

Women, for him, were over ; so he told himself, when they sat in the big, downstairs room which he remembered as a cellar. " Te quiero " ; he said it mechanically, more as a test for himself than for her. It was too late. That last spell in hospital had finished all that. He could have left her drily and calmly, until she got up off the table. Until she showed him, deliberately, that she was carrying Paco's child.

It took him like the horn in the side of his head. It went down inside him, in long shivers, and he was walking down the room, and there, life-size, in the big gold frame, was Paco, grinning at him. Paco, who had everything from the start ; Paco, who, after fighting only when it pleased him, now strutted at the head of the profession—behind him, Ildefonso, but only a little way behind, crowding him insolently, sometimes getting between him and the sun. Paco who, not content with his other advantages, possessed this woman. Paco, who was now swaggering round the clubs and cafés, boasting that he, Ildefonso, funked defending his title !

. . . His long, narrow chin resting on his arm, Ildefonso smiled at nothing across the plaza. As the hum of the plaza, jagged by the cries of the water sellers, and the gaseosa boys, and the boys with trays of toasted almonds and peanuts, rose and fell, he waited, with the confidence taught him by the years, for the moment when something beyond his will and his valour would straighten out his crumpled body and launch him on another wave of glory. . . .

III

Tonio notched the stick into the red rag and laid open the leather case with the estoques and the descabello. He took out of his pocket a silk handkerchief, and wiped down the blades carefully. He glanced at the capes, neatly folded across the fence, and at the water-bottle; he ran his eye along the string of banderillas, with their frills of pink, green and yellow paper, and looked up at the clock. Farther along the callejón, Ildefonso's man was doing the same, and the boy who served the sobre-saliente, a young matador de novillos, Bailarinito Chico—said to be a descendant of a famous fighting family of the twenties. There was no communication between the sword handlers; the Chico's boy was too shy, too overwhelmed by the company in which he found himself. Tonio had too much on his mind.

The telephone call had come through ten minutes before they left the hotel; he was called downstairs to the office, and answered it impatiently, with an eye on the time.

" Quién es ? "

" It's you, Tonio ? "

" Sí, señorita." He recognised the voice from Parral.

" The señorita Mary speaking. You're by yourself ? "

" Sí, señorita."

" Don Paco is well ? "

" Very fine." What was he supposed to say ?

" Tell him to ring us when the fight is over. He'll be—si Dios quiere—a father."

" Y la señora ? " faltered Tonio.

" Well enough. Adios—y buena suerte."

The band blared out and a roar went up, as the paseo started across the sand. The Niño—pale and glittering like sugar icing, his rich young face lifted with a smile, brown as chocolate; the Other, dark, greenish steel, and the famous eagle-beak twisted in a grimace that might be a smile under the crammed-down blackness of the montera. A pace or two behind them, the sobresaliente, montera in hand—for this was his first appearance in the illustrious ring.

. . . Paco leaned on the barrier and watched Ildefonso winding the bull round him. Again, and again, and again. This, the great Ildefonso act, was beyond him, and he knew it, and resigned himself ; he had his own reprisals. Ildefonso had the crowd by the short hairs. Closer and closer—fourteen hundred pounds-worth of death with horns brushing his hip, gathered into the cape, dismissed and drawn back again. Preciosa. Paco contributed his Olá ! to the crowd's, as he took the cape in his teeth and, working his hands along the hems, stepped out and closed up with the cuadrilla. Some of the fans shouted ; he paid no attention, keeping his eye on the bull, and on Ildefonso. The young Bailarinito was out as well, hoping for a chance, but not likely to get it ; Moreno and Asiano, who pic-ed for Ildefonso, were two of the best in the business.

When the first horse went up in the air, Ildefonso went in, so quietly it seemed unnatural. The bull turned straight into the cape, too close to acquire momentum, so close to the fallen horse that it barely escaped the outstretched hooves. Accepting its direction, it followed the cape like a tame dog, while the crowd preserved a dissatisfied silence. The silence persisted, when, after a series of verónicas, Ildefonso passed the cape behind him and started slowly backward, butterflying the bull towards the centre of the ring. It appeared too simple; the domination of man over bull was too complete. The crowd grew bored, the air heavy with indifference. Paco thought, Jesus, I've got to wake them up. Ildefonso left the bull fixed. The cuadrilla moved in, to work it towards the second horse.

Released from magic, like a somnambulist coming out of sleep, the bull backed from the pink circle of the capes ; chose, charged, and galloped away round the tercio. Conscious of escape, it despised the attempts to lure it back, until, from the corner of its eye, it caught sight of the horse. Paco felt the vibration in the soles of his feet as it drummed past him, with the shiny patch of the first pic on its shoulder. It took the horse like a landmine ; he heard the pic yell as it heaved and burrowed, and partly withdrew, and bored in again. The pic had lodged infamously back, and the crowd yelled its fury with the lump of human misery, as it fell towards the barrera, and the horse rocked over towards the bull, and the bull, tossing it off, bored in again towards the man.

Paco slapped his cape across the bull's eyes as one of the peónes grabbed its tail. He reached out and grabbed one of the horns, wrenching the head round towards him, and danced backward, shaking the pink wing : " Ha, toro. Ha ha."

The bull came like a rocket. He hardly knew what he was doing as he swirled the cape over his left shoulder and the bull sheered out after it. From then on, everything that happened was a series of reflexes. There was no time to think, except about standing still ; rising on tiptoe, letting the horn graze his chest, holding his breath while the heat and the weight and the blood-smell beat into his nostrils. Doing it again and again, while the roar swelled and shaped itself into the Olés . . . and, sick and stinging, he found himself jerking back to the callejón, with no notion whatever of what he had done. Tonio held up the water-bottle and he gulped. By then he could grin at the crowd and be grateful for the lull, while Ildefonso's head banderillo and the sobresaliente were hanging the sticks.

Again, the excitement died down. A Madrid audience is not easily stirred. It was used to Ildefonso's estatuarios ; it took them for granted. The bull, after the second pic-ing, and the twisting with the capes, and the three lots of sticks, was so far reduced that there was nothing to gain by prolonging the act. When, after two failures, Ildefonso came down to the fence and took the third sword from the handler, the crowd yelled its abuse. He ignored them, and the cushions skidding on the sand, and drove the sword in. He left it to the cuadrilla, to fan the bull down on its knees. A poor show, for Ildefonso.

" Take it easy," Pasquale had said. The warning was in his mind, as he watched Gusano taking out his first bull. So far, there wasn't much to compete against. And this wasn't a " stunt," or tourist, audience.

From the start, everything went wrong. He had just begun

to get the bull under control, when the angry cries of the cuadrilla informed him that something was amiss. He swore as a ragged figure darted in front of him, snatching the bull's attention; running, dodging, evading all the efforts of Chano and Gusano to capture it. By the time they'd cleared out the espontaneo, the trumpet sounded, the horses were coming in, and one of his chances had gone. In disgust he turned to Bailarinito. "Go on; you can have the first quite." The boy looked at him in surprise but moved in eagerly. The crowd started to object; they had not paid double prices to watch a sobresaliente, but the Chico, making the most of his unexpected luck, started to cape the bull neatly over and left it presented to Curro. The bull put its head right down between its feet and whaled in with a big right hook, and all hell broke loose as Curro, executing perhaps the most dastardly shot of his career, sank the tope half-way down its spine, and, unable to extract it, lunged and yelled and lugged—with the mono doing his best— and the bull swinging out for another charge, dragging him, dragging him with it. As he hit the ground and the horns came scooping, the Chico's cape swung over them. For Curro, clasping his head with his arms, it was trampling and the huh-huh of the bull's breathing and the fumbling of the horn and a slum in Triana with a hungry litter of kids . . .

And that takes you out for good, thought Paco, you and your starving family—while the Chico went into his gaoneras, finishing with a serpentina that the crowd forgot to cheer, because they were still mad with the punishment of the bull.

Paco took the next quite; the bull, heavily punished again by Peral, was seeking its querencía, and the crowd was hooting cheerfully by the time the trumpet went.

Chano looked at him doubtfully.

"Go on; I told you, didn't I?"

"Matador!" they were yelling. "Matador!"—while Chano went out. He set his jaw. He should have offered the third pair, as a courtesy, to the Chico, but that one had had enough publicity already. "Matador! Matador!" Hard luck on Chano, who had planted a couple of pairs impeccably; but this was supposed to be the great act of Niño de Maderas. Suddenly he knew Ildefonso was looking at him. All right, you bastard; wait till the next bull, and I'll pin another look on your ugly face.

. . . The bull had settled in its querencía. Time went by, while he sweated, while Chano and the boys worked themselves to rags. He made himself ridiculous, by tempting it on his knees; this brought jeers from the crowd, and by the time he took the sword he was murderous. He squared and profiled; and the sword went in, with silly ease. It was over—and a duller spectacle had seldom been afforded by a torero of the first rank to a Madrid audience. Hoots and whistles and ribaldries proclaimed their awareness of it. Two bulls, between Ildefonso and Niño de Maderas, and not an ear cut!

IV

Such a thing had never been heard of: a woman, in the act of giving birth to a child, and listening to a bullfight on the radio! Expressing disapproval in scowling brows and pouting lips, the nurse sat sullenly upright in a corner of the room; her patient, who had just thrust her imperiously aside, continued between pains, to bend over the cabinet, impatiently twirling the knobs, filling the room at one moment with a blast of noise, at the next with demoniac shrieks and stutters, followed by brief interludes of clarity. What could the nurse do?—The doctor, Don Alejandro, was there; if he liked this sort of thing for his patient—so much the worse for everybody! "Don't molest yourself, señorita—the excitement will help!" A nice thing to tell an experienced woman, who knew her responsibilities. Never again, if God willed, would she take a case in a bullfighter's household, or in charge of a doctor who seemed to take more interest in the bullfight than in his patient. A nice thing to happen to a woman who hated the bullfight and thought it was a disgrace to her country and was engaged to the manager of a football team, Los Amarillos, in Valladolid.

Beside the window sat Mary, with a cigarette between her fingers. For the first time in her life, only a fraction of her attention was on the broadcast. Through the smoke of the cigarette her eyes were on Aracea ; now and again she rose, to wipe the girl's grey face, to sweep back the dark hair that matted in the sweat of Aracea's brow, or to offer her arm for the endless walking, walking that had gone on now, intermittently, for nearly fourteen hours. How much longer would the girl's strength hold out ? Even the formidable stamina of the daughter of Parral could not be expected to endure much longer. Was Don Alejandro's confidence a bluff ? Any English doctor would have had her under the anaesthetic by now.

Her brain had become a dark screen, crossed by moving bands of thought, sometimes parallel, sometimes interweaving, sometimes—when, seeking another cigarette in her pocket, her fingers touched the envelope from England—blotted out in a single thought : the thought of her own future. It seemed inevitable that the letter should arrive to-day, when her crowded brain was too full to deal with it. If it had been from anyone but the Reverend Mother she would have put it aside ; but there was something as compulsive about that black angular writing as there was about its author, and, during the lull of the midday meal, she had read it—at first incredulously, then more incredulously still.

It began with the statement that the writer had long recognised in Mary Carpenter talents for which a teacher's career afforded insufficient outlet, and went on to speak of the manuscript of her unsuccessful book, *Here Is Spain*, which, just before returning, she had given the Reverend Mother to read :

"I hope you will not think it a breach of confidence, that I passed on your manuscript to Monsignor Baring, who has shown it to Everard Dauncey——"

Dauncey : editor of *The European Review*, a new Catholic monthly which, in three or four issues, had gained for itself a reputation envied by its less fortunate competitors. Backed by the wealth and integrity of interested Catholics, it was published in four languages and prominently displayed in the better-class bookshops of all the Latin countries. With a tick of the heart, Mary wondered if they could think of serialising *Here Is Spain* in its pages and read on breathlessly:

"It appears that they wish to devote a certain amount of space to *informed* articles on Spain, and Monsignor Baring would like to hear if you are interested. From what I am told, I gather that this is not work that could be successfully combined with teaching, as it entails office hours and a very heavy correspondence. You will no doubt be given the details if you write to Mr. Dauncey.

"Much as your work at St. Margaret's is appreciated,"

—the letter concluded:

"—I feel it my duty, my dear Mary, to lay this proposition before you, for your serious consideration. I have no means of knowing what your private resources are, or whether it will appeal to you economically. But I think from our conversations, that it was what you would call '*A job that needs doing.*' You will, of course, realise that we would find it very difficult to replace you immediately, but in the course of any correspondence you may have with Monsignor Baring or Mr. Dauncey, you may consider yourself at liberty—if you wish to be—at the end of the Winter Term."

Eagerness and self-doubt, whirling in her brain, reduced Mary to silence for the rest of the meal. Impossible to think properly—certainly to come to conclusions—with all this on her hands, and mind. So there she sat, trying to thrust it aside, with an ear on the announcer's shouting voice and an eye on Aracea, or on the doctor. For the love of heaven, wouldn't he put a stop to it now?—The girl looked like death after the last lot of pains. He was—Aracea had said it herself, laughing—" a maniac about the bulls," but he couldn't be so irresponsible . . .

" Don Alejandro——"

" Ah, it is the intermission ! "—He straightened himself, beaming through his white beard, and nodded at his patient. " Papá torero—very good ! And now another paseito—for the little torero ! "

Aracea dragged herself up obediently ; her obedience, thought Mary, as she laced her fingers through the thin, cold ones that were slippery with sweat, was pathetic.

" Chica, hasn't this been going on long enough for you ? Wouldn't you like to get it over now ? " she murmured, as they went out on the gallery.

" Get it over ? Of course I'd like to get it over ! I am not enjoying any of this, let me tell you," muttered Aracea, through set teeth.

" I mean, finish it off in your sleep. I'm sure Don Alejandro will give you the anaesthetic now, if you ask him."

" What—and miss the rest of the fight ? "—She gave a hysterical giggle. " Qué barbaridad. Tío Alejandro would never forgive me." Heavy and weak, she continued to pace, on Mary's arm. From the office below came the roar of the intermission music ; the patio below was crowded with listeners, along the farther sides of the gallery the women were clustered, leaning on the rail, their eyes and their smiles on the dueña. " God watch over the señora. God send the señora many more beautiful children ! "

" One's enough for now," Aracea called back, raising a shout of delight, from the men below, as well as the women. What a day : the Niño fighting the mano a mano in Madrid, and his wife de parto ! " We should look well, if this were twins : two boys ?—or a boy and a girl ? Not two girls ; no, no, after all this trouble that would be too much bad luck." She went on jesting breathlessly. " To present Paco with two little female over-ripe plums—it would be a scandal. I'd be ashamed of myself."

" No, you wouldn't ; you would be as proud as Lucifero. But it's not twins, so the question doesn't arise.—It's not been very exciting, so far," said Mary, keeping up the lightness. " But we shall hear something, before the end!—I spoke to Tonio. He said Paco's 'fine.' "

" You spoke to Tonio—when ? "

" I went down to the office, about half an hour before the fight. Of course, I said not to tell Paco, until it's over."

" Paco—fine. And Ildefonso—— ? "

" Tonio wouldn't know, would he ? "

" Let's get back."

" Are the pains coming again ? "

She nodded. A groan broke from her. Supported in Mary's arms, she turned at the door, her nails biting into Mary's flesh.

" There's some sort of instinct. If you disobey it—— "

Mary felt herself recoiling from the wildness of her eyes.

" What do you mean ? "

" He didn't want to fight."

" What ?—Paco ? "

" Ildefonso. The bull that kills Ildefonso will kill a million people—— "

" Ay, chica, be sensible."

" And I shall carry in my heart the guilt of it."

V

The third bull—Ildefonso's—was one of the fabulous bulls that carry death or immortality between their horns. The crowd recognised it. With the waves of applause beating on his ears and on his heart, Paco looked on at something to which, he knew, he had no answer. Every sculptured line, every perfected movement carved itself into his simple, shallow brain that, for all its shallowness, could recognise the inimitable. This, with the unreduced animal, was the holy act of Ildefonso ; the beautiful, lethal business that only he could conduct, that set the whole keynote of the performance and prepared the audience for what was to come. Of all his contemporaries, only Ildefonso was capable, in this first act, of dominating not only the bull but the crowd, of imposing on the latter a kind of respect, amounting to something like reverence, that held in check even the faction that delights in showing off its own information and wit at the expense of the matador.

Paco's vanity began to set up resistance. No more " take it easy "; next time, by Jesus and Mary, he would show them something. He would pull out every trick in his repertory—things Ildefonso could never attempt. He'd knock the breath out of them—with the help of Mary Virgin and a Parral bull. He knew it all: the capework, and the things with the muleta, and the sword. He'd give them *everything*.

His quite went off well; he had profited in Mexico, where the act is taken more seriously than in Spain. The crowd screamed with delight, as he spun out in a farol; he actually felt the wind of the horn as it skimmed his temple. And his brain was still humming with the roar when he found Ildefonso opposite him. Offering him—he gaped—the two sticks frilled with paper.

" Go on, boy; these are yours."

The ring and the callejón and everything spun around him. The banderillas; his own suerte. That he'd had to give over to Chano and the Chico, because . . . So you think you've got me! You're so fripping certain, and you've got me.

" Go on. You had bad luck with your animal. This is a bull."

The crowd gave a half-hearted cheer as he went out on the sand; the Niño had lost favour; so far he had given them nothing they expected. They weren't paying those prices for a few tricks with the cape and one easy kill, with a half-dead animal. He felt their animosity reaching towards him across the waving sand, and across the bull which, still fixed, rode up and down on heaving waves of sunlight: as he felt the sneering confidence of Ildefonso—offering the sticks to an adversary already beaten! The cuadrilla was waiting, looking towards him.

An audible gasp ran round the tiers, as Chano ran out and clapped down the chair behind him. As he settled into it, there were some shouts, some jeers; it was a circus act, not belonging in that performance. He set his teeth in a grin and lifted both arms, as a sign to the cuadrilla. The head peóne started caping the bull down towards him, and cat-calls broke out. Apart from its inaestheticism, the stunt was an outrage—as though a clown stumbled on in the last act of Hamlet. It was dangerous, and magnificently showy—and Ildefonso's fans resented it. And to hell with their resentment, he thought, as he bent his arms and raised the sticks vertically towards the bull. The chair was not more than a couple of yards from the fence, and if anything went wrong the bull would rush straight through him and nail him into the planks. Paco crossed one knee over the other, in an attitude of insolent ease; that was the foot that would come down for the feint—and shouted " Ha, toro ! "

When it came off, the yells of disapprobation and the shouts of the fans were about equal. As he stumbled back to the callejón, he knew he had prepared himself a bad reception for his second bull; but he had given them a taste of what was to come, and now Ildefonso could get on with the old-time stuff and they could go on their knees and push their heads down and receive the sacrament as he chose to celebrate it ! And the critics could prepare their flowery pieces, and Ildefonso could be the messiah of the bulls—and perhaps half a dozen people might get the idea that, after all, bullfighting wasn't some kind of an esoteric act, taking place behind temple veils in an aura of mysticism, but a hard, plain thing that involved guts and blood and valour; a physical test, in which the advantage lay with the enemy, because the enemy was hampered by no rules, and had not to satisfy twenty thousand people who insisted on having their money's worth.

They gave Ildefonso the ear. The hysteria of the crowd had barely died down when the fourth bull, Peleador, slid into the ring, and Gusano and Camillo ran out, trailing their capes. Chano moved up beside him.

" It's an uncle; it's hooking both ways. Take it wide, and save up the fancywork till Curro's been at it."

Paco told him what to do with his advice, and edged through the fence. Each step he took made him feel sick, but he set his teeth and thought of Belmonte.

He had them shouting " No, no ! " before he tied the bull up with a rebolera. There were two loops of gold hanging down from the taleguilla, and twice, as the shoulder caught him, he had nearly lost his balance. An old trick—that of holding his breath—which he thought he had mastered, had revived, and as he walked away, his ribs were heaving, but he managed to pin the smile on his face. He'd got them at last; broken down their antagonism and their apathy.

During the next eight minutes, Niño de Maderas defeated the traditionalists by an exhibition which, for skill and valour, was not to be matched by any of his contemporaries. For the first time, Madrid settled down seriously to contemplate one who, so far, had never made much impression upon the most selective audience in the world. It was not Ildefonso; it was altogether another school of thought and of technique. It was cold, it was athletic, but it had its moments of pure artistry, and for suicidal daring, it had not been matched for years. Those who had feared, on the strength of his previous adorno, that the Niño would produce a succession of circus antics, were reassured by his gravity.

It seemed like a mile, back to the callejón. He drank more water. And this, Jesus and Mary, wasn't the end. For at least another hour he must go on, offering his flesh and blood up to twenty-three thousand people whose insistence had given Ildefonso the ear; who must be made to award him the same. There was three-quarters of a metre of bull's blood from his chest down on to the upper thigh. Tonio was on his knees, trying to stitch up the embroidery that had broken loose again. Cocking his leg for Tonio's convenience, Paco was reminded, and winced. If I get through this—never, never again! I'll take a vow, I'll have myself doctored, but, by Christ, I'm going to be the top bull-fighter in Spain.

He had not heard the trumpet, but Tonio was handing him the stick and sword. Now. Now.

The space between himself and the President's box seemed to prolong itself like elastic, but he was there at last. The tiers dazzled as he looked up at them, to receive the nod. As he turned away, emptiness and solitude folded round him like a wet cloth. Slowly he raised the montera, and, as he pivoted, the whole plaza became like pink snowflakes, dancing around him. Without looking, he tossed the montera backwards. Now.

As he shook out the muleta gently, and spread it with the sword, he saw Chano had the bull well placed. He moved up four short steps, chopped his heels down into the sand and called the bull. As it came thundering down on him like an express, he opened up his first pass.

The silence was unnatural. Flagging the bull from horn to horn, Paco's mind was very clear ; as soon as he had it in control, he would go slowly into the redondo, pulling it round to the right and then changing to the left ; then some slow, two-handed passes, finishing with the pase por bajo—and then start on his adornos : the stunts for which Niño de Maderas was famous, some of which he had copied and improved, and others he had invented. Time was the thing to be remembered. He was facing towards the big clock, and in the split second after the horn ploughed past his chest he glanced up to reassure himself.

He felt the bump, but did not realise until he took the slam behind him of the barrera that he was being carried on the horn. It was so simple, so sudden, there was no time for fear, until he heard the screams and, in a flash like lightning, saw the bull's head in front of his eyes : the muzzle going down, the great weapon of bone and hair between the horns—hardly less formidable than they, the hot gust from the nostrils—and something falling on the top of him and yellow and red and trampling and more yellow and red—and lying doubled up between the sand and the estribo, and a pair of human eyes staring into his. . . .

VI

Don Alejandro, rubbing his hands, hurried into the sala.

" A Dios gracias ! Fine news for all—a grand little torero ! And how are things going in Madrid ? "

" Ay, por dios—listen——"

The announcer's voice came cracking in a series of shouts :

" Niño de Maderas has been carried to the infirmary—his condition is said to be grave——"

Don Alejandro's jaw dropped, he gasped. Already the house of Parral was filling itself with wailing.

" Oh, Don Alejandro, for God's sake go and make them be quiet——"

" An act of exceptional valour was performed by El Aguilucho who, at the moment of the hit, leapt the barrier, and by clinging to the horns of the bull, averted the tragedy at the risk of his own life. The bull was eventually drawn off by the peóne de confianza, Chano Martínez, and is now being taken by the sobresaliente, the valiant and noble matador de novillos, Bailarinito Chico. He is preparing a superb péndulo. . . . Further reports on the condition of Niño de Maderas will be given as information becomes available . . ."

Everything was white—except the face that came close, then swam away, then approached and faded again. He moved his head impatiently ; he couldn't see the clock. He tried to say " What's the time ? " but his mouth felt loose and weak. And that blistering bull had yet to be killed . . . " La hora "—it just came out that time. A hiss came from somewhere : " He's speaking," and he repeated with fury, " *La hora !*—el clarín——"

Somebody laughed.

" You don't have to bother about that trumpet, boy. The time ?—Going on for midnight."

And then he remembered he had had the horn. Oh God, the horn on a day like this, with all depending on it.

He tried to remember where he got it ; there wasn't the least pain anywhere. Pain ?—There was nothing. As if they'd stripped him out of his body and put him in bed—put *what* in bed ? He tried to feel his arms, his legs ; God, there was nothing ! They couldn't have amputated everything.

His eyelids were still there ; they kept closing—he strained them open, and the face swam in again.

" Tonio——"

" Sí ; I'm here, hombre."

" Give me a drink."

Someone wetted his lips. More whiteness, flowing across his sight like a stream of milk. Somewhere, through it, the figure of Niño de Maderas shaped itself, the beautiful, shining figure— the great matador; the greatest——

" Go on; tell him."

" Paco. Paco. Are you listening, hombre ? "

He forced his eyelids up again. It was Tonio's face, very close, grimacing.

" Your wife says to tell you—you got a boy."

" He don't know what you're saying," said another voice.

He did not. His mind—what was left of it—was filled with that beautiful, shining figure, out there on the sand, with all the crowd cheering—for him. Of course, that was himself—Niño de Maderas.

Tonio's face disappeared. There was no more time.

The door opened. The men in the room turned their heads. Tonio was on his knees before the little Macarena he had brought from the hotel. They all got up.

" It's finished ? "

Ildefonso hesitated, then walked over to the bed. What lay on it was white and so completely quiet that he shrank back involuntarily, crossed himself and kissed his crossed finger and thumb. Tonio bent over quickly and laid his ear to his master's chest; looked up at Ildefonso, and shook his head; no, it wasn't finished, yet.

Ildefonso stood there. Presently the eyelids flickered. The dark eyes, already emptied of everything, opened. Saw, and remained seeing. As though drawn, Ildefonso bent a little towards them. The room was hot and still and moths spun round the light bulb. Tonio and Gusano and Camillo, in their dark suits, were cut out against the white wall. No one spoke. Then Paco said, very distinctly :

" No hay qué uno."

Chapter Fourteen

"I THINK, if you don't need me, I'll get on with my packing?"

"Can't the servants do that for you?"

"If I do it myself I don't have to look for things."

"As you please."

. . . Already, thought Mary, I am outside.

She had known it from the hour they brought Paco home; when they opened the lid of the coffin, so that his wife might look for the last time at the quiet, waxen face, so unlike Paco that it might have been an effigy. And on the day of the funeral. And during the last hour, when they all three—Aracea, Olalla and herself—buried Paco for the second time.

The encrustations of bullion had to be protected with pads of black tissue, thin rolls of cottonwool laid along the folds to prevent the silk from cracking, handfuls of dried lavender and orris root scattered through the sheaves of silk and satin to keep out the moth. There was no sound except the rustle of paper and a laconic word or two as the black stuff of the women's gowns laid its shadow on flame and yellow, on saffron and pink: the last shining teguments of a bullfighter.

As each of the suits was examined and folded, Tonio came forward and enveloped it in a square of linen, then took it in his arms and carried it to the open coffer which stood on its clawed and gilded feet in a corner of the room. His eye-sockets puddles of lead in his narrow face, he carried each one as though it were the body of his dead master. To each bundle as he laid it down he murmured, "Adios, Paco." At last the coffer was full.

" The swords, señora ? "

" I am taking care of those."

In response to a gesture, Tonio lowered the lid, swung down the clamps and slid the iron rod through the hasps. The key turned in the locks. Pero ya duerme sin fin . . . Paco had received his last interment.

" Is there anything else for me to do, señora ? "

" Nothing more. Many thanks to you. Go with God."

" With God," he muttered, as he hurried away. They heard him give a whining cry, like a bereaved dog, on the gallery. Then, at a sign from Aracea, Olalla brought the long cloth of brocade. Mary stepped back as the two women spread the purple web between them, advanced and lowered it slowly over the coffer. Borne down by the weight of its fringe, the pall settled on the gilt and the leather. Standing at either end, the women crossed themselves.

" Shall I put the lights out ? " asked Olalla.

So she asked if she was wanted, and receiving her reply, went to her room. Perhaps she had already stayed too long ; perhaps she should have left Aracea and Olalla and Tonio alone, to perform those final obsequies, in which she had taken part as a matter of course—as she had taken part in all the sad aftermath of the funeral arrangements, and the sable hordes that descended upon the house of Parral, to fill it with their formal mourning. All of that, with Aracea still in bed, had been left to her and Olalla ; it was not until Aracea was up and about again that she began to be conscious of her exclusion.

It was not that all the conversations were now conducted in Spanish, and all the small matters which she had made her particular charge now referred to Olalla. The latter, at least, was natural, as everything would be taken over by Olalla from the moment of her departure. But those long, dark and distant moments when Aracea, across the room, or across the babe she held in her arms, seemed to be studying her, confused and puzzled her. She wondered whether to challenge or ignore them ; what relation they bore to the conversation that took place a few nights after her arrival, and whether understanding, or partial understanding might again be arrived at by discussion : whether Olalla, who continued invariably to be pleasant, friendly and considerate, could, if asked, provide the answer to the riddle. Pride, however, and a sense of perhaps foolish loyalty, forbade taking Olalla into her confidence : as justice forbade her blaming the latter for a state of affairs that, patently, Olalla did not invite, and could not be expected to resist.

It was a fortnight since she had written to the Editor of *The European Review*, but as yet she had received no answer. For this Mary felt she was herself to blame ; she had written, she felt, too guardedly ; a fear of showing herself over-enthusiastic had sent her to the other extreme of coolness. Painfully aware that her Fleet Street record was against her, she had sent no references —while admitting that she was experienced in journalism. Well, if they wanted to know more, they could ask.

But as each post came in, bearing no reply to her letter, her heart sank lower and lower ; the shining confidence she had felt immediately after writing went out like a candle flame. She remembered that she had not given her address in England, or the date on which she was returning ; a miserable lapse for a person applying for an important situation. Now, if she cabled, it might look impatient, or too eager.

When her packing was finished, she went to find Olalla, to see if there were any jobs in which she could make herself useful. She found her in the old schoolroom, now converted into a kind of library, in which were stored many of the books that had crowded the walls of the sala, and Aracea's old lesson books, and some of her own old Tauchnitz editions, abandoned for lack of space when she went back to England after the war.

" Olalla ! What ever are you doing ? "

Olalla, who was bending over an open chest, straightened herself sharply, looked startled, then embarrassed ; her face flushed as she came quickly to Mary.

" I thought you were packing—don't trouble—I'm just finishing." She tried to prevent Mary's coming farther into the room.

" But why didn't you ask me to help you ? What are all those books ? Why are you putting them into that trunk ? "

" It is only some things Aracea asked me to put away—please don't——" Her pleasant face was crimson with distress.

" English books," said Mary, slowly. She put Olalla gently aside and went to look at the covers she had recognised. Leandra's English novels, her books of poetry ; Aracea's story books and the few textbooks of her schoolroom days, tied into bundles, packed tightly inside the wooden framework of the chest. " What is going to be done with them ? " she asked presently.

" It is just to make a little more room," stammered Olalla. " I was just told to put them away, until—perhaps until we have time to go through them, and see which are valuable, and which " —her voice died away. " Oh, you should not have come in," she cried grievously.

" It doesn't matter. So they're going to be destroyed. What a mess you're in." She looked dispassionately at Olalla's dusty fingers and dishevelled hair. " Go and get tidy, while I finish the rest for you. I suppose there'd be no objection to my taking one or two, if I wanted to keep them ? "

" I cannot bear you to be hurt like this."

" Where is Aracea ? "

Olalla dashed her hand across the back of her eyes and peered at her watch.

" She was giving Luisito his feed when I left her—it will be over now—perhaps she is in the sala. But—Mary—she did not mean—she will be so upset if she knows——"

" Don't worry. I'm not going to say anything about it. But I have to leave here very early in the morning ; I think I will say good-bye to her now, and ask if I may have my supper in bed."

" Of course you may, and I will go and order it now. Oh, I feel so much, that you are going ; we shall all miss you so much," said Olalla confusedly, as she hurried from the room.

The long table in the sala was loaded with letters and with the great black-bordered envelopes with their printed enclosures that Mary and Olalla had spent days in addressing to the family and friends of Niño de Maderas ; the letters of condolence were scattered everywhere. Aracea, her head bent over a sheet of notepaper, said, without looking up :

" I don't know when we are going to finish these things"

" Can't I do some of them ? "

Aracea lifted her small, mask-like face and hollow eyes.

" Oh, it's you. There is a letter here, somewhere, for you ; it came yesterday, or the day before. I am sorry I forgot it." She flung the papers aside, uncovering the envelope, which she passed to Mary, with a laconic, " Perdoneme."

At last : the one ! Her hand shook a little as she took it.

" Thank you. I'm glad it came before I go.—I came to say good-bye."

" But you're not going to-night ? " said Aracea quickly.

" No ; but I don't want to disturb you in the morning. I shall be gone before you and Luisito are awake."

" You had better come and say good-bye to Luisito." She rose and, followed by Mary, went through the double doors to her bedroom, and into the room behind it, where the heir to Parral slept like a prince in his high cradle of gilded basketwork, which had been his mother's, and in which, too briefly, had lain the sad procession of little uncles, whose tiny ghosts Mary felt, with a shiver, in the air. Not that there was anything ghostly about the small dark face, the prematurely intelligent dark eyes and mouth shaped like a rosebud round a rosy thumb.

" Guapo, guapísimo," murmured Aracea to her son. " Is he not the most beautiful baby you have ever seen ? "

" He is the image of Paco," smiled Mary, laying a finger tenderly to the down covering the tender skull.

" It is strange, that so hideous a little object can become so beautiful, in just four weeks." Nodding to the fat, proud girl who had risen at their entrance, Aracea led the way back to the sala, and closed the doors behind them. " Don Alejandro says it is because I have such good milk, enough for half a dozen ! " She laughed, and looked oddly at Mary. " It is a pity, is it not, that Luisito has no brothers or sisters ? "

" It is a pity," agreed Mary.

" You know that, but for you, he might have had them ? "

" What are you saying ? " cried Mary, aghast. In the darkness of Aracea's eyes she saw her own image, tiny and shrunken. Aracea moistened her lips and forced them into a smile.

" Oh yes. But I'm not blaming you, Miss Mary. It was Mamá, in the first place, who sacrificed me to you, and in my turn I sacrificed Paco. Of course I should have known better. By now we'd have several children, instead of one little baby——"

" I cannot let you say such things to me," whispered Mary, when she recovered her breath. " What have I ever done, to deserve it ? You can't speak to me like that without explaining yourself. It's cruel—and abominably untrue ! "

Aracea went to lay her head against the frame of the window —just, as it happened, where Leandra's weary head often had lain. Her profile, looking out at the garden, was suddenly that of a dark, dispossessed Leandra, daughter of de la Cerna, not of Parral.

" I am sorry if I am cruel. I do not mean it. And I do not blame you. It would have been better, I think, if you had been a silly old English virgin, like Miss Bax ! In the long run, you would have done much less harm."

" What harm have I done ? "

" I believed everything you said ; partly because I was fond of you, and because—how clever you were !—you never criticised us, or suggested in any way that our ideas were wrong. You just offered another way of thinking, and that's always attractive to young people, isn't it ? I was particularly ready to accept it, because you seemed to care about all the things that were important to me ; the bulls, the fight——"

" I ' seemed ' to care ? You cannot think I was pretending ? "

" Oh no ; and it gave you so much advantage ! It made me pay attention to you. It all led up so smoothly to St. Margaret's, and ' sport ' and ' keep yourself fit,' and ' a woman's duty is to interest herself in her husband's career,' and how to promote your husband's success—— ! "

" When did you ever hear such things at St. Margaret's ? "

" It may not have been there "—Aracea shrugged her

shoulders. " It may have been when I was staying with people,
who treated me as if I were grown up and were always talking
to me about getting married."

" Well, if they told you that," said Mary, after a pause, " I
do not see much harm in it."

" Excepting that it gave me the wrong ideas ; things that
could never work here, at home. If I'd never had a foreign
education, I'd have been perfectly contented. I'd have settled
down happily to have babies, and lead the normal life of a
married woman——"

" Would you ?—The average married woman isn't the owner
of a ranch ; if she marries a torero, she doesn't know enough
to follow his career."

" Or else she chooses between the nursery and the plaza !
Do you think I'd have been an exception ? I don't think it's
likely. I wanted to bear Paco's children. I wanted very much
a home where Paco would bring his friends. I wanted to be
on good terms with his family—though, apart from Don Amadeo,
I didn't like any of them much. But that is part of a wife's duty :
to welcome and be welcomed by the relations of her marriage.
And you, and Mamá between you, made all that impossible.
From their point of view, you turned me into a ' foreigner '——"

" You weren't ' a foreigner ' to Paco."

" Oh yes I was, sometimes, when he was angry with me ;
then I was ' la inglesa ' ! I was ' la inglesa ' when I had different
opinions from his, and when I argued about things I knew
more about than he did. He was modern enough, when we were
by ourselves, to enjoy arguing, but he hated it when other people
were there. And he never, never forgave me for making him
ridiculous in front of the cuadrilla and the afición."

" I cannot imagine you doing that, however much you might
quarrel in private."

" A matador's wife doesn't travel about with her husband.
She doesn't make him go dancing and swimming and playing
tennis with her—you knew that as well as I. You always knew ;
but you never warned me, did you ? "

" Would you have paid the least attention to a warning ?

From your letters I gathered you were happy; I hadn't the least idea that anything was wrong, until I came back here at Easter. You weren't any longer a child; I felt I had no right to interfere."

"But didn't you *see* what was happening?" persisted Aracea. "Did you realise that all the mistakes I was making were the things I'd learned from you?—' *Why* shouldn't bullfighters take as much care of themselves as British sportsmen?—*Why* should they increase their risks by foolish habits away from the ring?'" Her intonation set the phrases into ironic question marks. "'The perfect bull, the perfect horse, the perfect man, and so—the perfect bullfight!'" She began to laugh hysterically. "Caramba—it's like Miss Gaylor, lecturing the First Eleven at the beginning of the hockey season."

"You make it sound that way; but you believed it—once."

"I believed it because *you* said it, and because I was too young to know that you cannot train an artist as you train an athlete. And you cannot make a cross between two cultures as different as yours and mine and produce something that isn't diseased!—Look at Mamá; she was brought up in the English way, but when she wanted to be free, like English girls—perhaps to be a musician, and marry the person she was in love with, they would not hear of it. Poor Mamá; how wretched she was——"

"Yet she was anxious for you to have the same kind of education——"

"Oh yes; that was an act of faith in my grandfather's beliefs. In her case they'd failed; in mine, because I have a much stronger character, they would succeed: that was how Mamá argued. I know her mind so well!"

"Do you really believe you would have been contented, to live like a little fly, fixed in the amber of the past? I can't see you accepting the life of your Segovian cousins."

"Why not?—Girls of my age, who've been through the universities and got modern ideas, are nearly all miserable. I don't believe English girls, for all the freedom and sex equality there's so much talk about, are as happy or secure as we are, so long as we remain faithful to ourselves."

" Does that mean the rejection of all outside influences ? "

She saw Aracea flush.

" Spain is a jealous country, Mary ! It had preserved its integrity through its aloofness, and we who desert it are made to pay."

" Yet we've agreed there is much it might assimilate to its advantage, without forfeiting its integrity."

" I perhaps agreed with that when I was young. Now I am wiser. I know that whatever good comes to Spain must come out of itself. Our good must be our own good, our bad our own bad ; not imitations of a foreign pattern."

" Have I ever tried to weaken your loyalties ? "

" Not directly. But you showed me other ones. It—it is like blood transfusion : some groups belong only to themselves, others will mix. Spanish and English corpuscles don't—what is the word ?—congeal." She paused a moment, before adding, " That's what lost us our monarchy. That's what ruined Paco and me."

" Yet—long before I met you—I already had many close friends among the Spanish people."

" In our war ? That was different. Now we have recovered our security."

" In other words, you have closed your doors ? "

Aracea spread her hands.

" You know where your house is." The gesture, the formal phrase, cut Mary to the heart. She knew the meaninglessness of that silken hospitality.

" I know, at least, that everything's finished, between you and me."

There was a flash of darkness from the window ; Aracea's arms were round her.

" Oh no, no ! " she was sobbing.

" But—you hate me," said Mary stupidly.

" Mary, Mary, don't say such things. I have always loved you—I cannot bear that you go away. Don't you understand ?—

It's Luisito." She clutched Mary by the shoulders, holding her away at arm's length, to look into her eyes. " Luisito must never learn English : not, at any rate, before he's old enough to have established himself, before everything, as a son of Spain ; then as the son of Parral, and of Paco. He'll be brought up in all the ' wrong ' ways old-fashioned country people bring up their children—the way Papá was brought up ; he'll be horribly spoiled, and be rude and domineering and selfish for a while, and then, suddenly, almost overnight, he'll turn into a little caballero and he'll fall in love, probably, when he is fourteen or fifteen. He'll love everything that belongs to our Andalucían soil, because from the very beginning he will be treated as the master of Parral. He will take no interest in anything beyond the borders of Spain. He'll marry an Andalucían girl, and breed like one of our bulls, and he will never, never be disturbed by suggestions that there is anything in the world more important than our bulls, and strengthening the casta, and preserving our honour and the name of Parral "—she stopped to draw breath.

" Tell me just one thing, that is more important, even, than your caring for me. Do you hate England and the English, as a race ? "

" No, no, no." She shook her head vigorously. " One does not hate people for not understanding. And it is not our character, in the South, to hate very much ; we are too light, too easy—except, perhaps, about love."

" You won't teach Luisito to dislike us ? "

" No, Mary, I will not "—a faint spark kindled in her eyes—" palabra inglesa !—Mary, are you ill ? Do sit down."

" I am confused "—she put her hand to her head as she sank into the chair. " There's so much—I never realised—so much for you to forgive——"

" Here, drink this "—Aracea put a glass into her hand. " You don't forgive people for acting according to what they believe. One must always do that—no ? " She bent to pick up something from the ground. " Look, you have dropped your letter. Don't you want to see what it says ? "

Mary smiled faintly, recognising the old, childish curiosity about letters, and tore it open. She read it through calmly, waited for a moment to make up her mind, then, with steady fingers, tore it into strips.

"Then it wasn't important," said Aracea disappointedly.

"Very important. It would amuse you very much, if I were to tell you what it is about."

"Please tell me."

"It is from the Editor of an English magazine; he wants me to write a monthly article, on Spain."

"That is splendid! Of course you are going to do it?"

"I think," said Mary slowly, "I have been given grace to refuse."

"Mary, you cannot! Think of all the people who are writing nonsense about Spain : things that do us harm! What was it you said the other day—that no effort was being spared—that no lie was too gross—to make trouble between my country and yours. And you, who could tell the truth——"

"How much of the truth do I know?"—Her voice was sad and bitter. "I should think the answer is plain enough, after what we have just been saying. I know nothing."

Aracea opened her lips, and closed them again ; went quickly to a corner of the room from which the bookshelves had not been removed. There—perhaps as an act of piety—were preserved, among a few other volumes, the works of Don Ramiro de la Cerna.

"I tried, sometimes, to read my grandfather's books, but I can't understand them," she murmured, as she drew one out of the case and opened it. "Only a sentence here and there. But I've just remembered something—it's in his own writing—he must have added it after the book was finished. Here it is." She put the book into Mary's hand.

"'El principio del conocimiento es confesarse la ignorancia.' The beginning of knowledge is to confess ignorance—and only the fool," she continued with her translation, "says '*I know*.'"

GLOSSARY

Adorno: Embellishment, or stunt.

Afición: Fancy.

Aficionado-a: Addict, fan, amateur.

Alternativa: Graduation from *novillero* to *matador*, marked by a ceremony when the full *matador* presents his cape and bull to the *novillero*. The alternativa may be taken in any city, but must be confirmed in Madrid.

Ayudado: Any pass in which the *muleta* is " assisted " by the sword: by inference, a two-handed pass.

Banderillas: Barbed sticks used in the third* act of the fight, to correct the hook of the horns. 70 centimetres long, they should be placed in pairs high in the withers and close together.

Banderillero: Member of the *cuadrilla*, whose business is to place the sticks, unless the *matador* has a taste and a reputation for the performance of this particular act (e.g., Armillita was a great artist in hanging the sticks).

Becerro: Bull calf.

Becerrada: Benefit or amateur show, with calves too young to be dangerous.

Bragado: Bull of any colour, but with white belly.

Brindis: The dedication of the bull, to the president or to some person chosen by the *matador*, before the kill. In general, a toast.

Bronca: " The bird ": the noise made by the audience when a bull-fighter puts up a bad show.

Brujería: Witchcraft.

Callejón: The passage between the ring (on the ring level) and the stands.

Calzones: Breeches.

Cartel: Reputation, prestige, command of publicity.

Chaqueta: Bullfighter's short coat.

---

* *Fifth act (Conrad).*
second act (Hemingway).

Cojones: Male appendages.

Corrida: First class, full-scale fight.

Cornada: Horn wound.

Cuadrilla: Team of bullfighters under *matador's* orders.

Cursi: Flashy, in bad taste.

Desayuno: Breakfast.

Descabello: The final stroke by the *matador* which kills the bull after two or more *estocadas.* Often the most desperate moment of the fight, unless the bull is sufficiently reduced to have its head down and its feet together, as the sword in going in between the shoulder-blades may encounter bone, and be flung out by the bull's subsequent movements, to the great danger of spectators.

Devisa: The colours of the ranch.

Dondé estamos?: Where are we?

Espada: Literally, sword; synonym for *matador.*

Estoqué: The grooved sword used in the last act of the fight. It is slightly curved at the tip and ground razor-sharp about half-way up its length of 75 centimetres. The *descabello* sword is not curved but the point is wider.

Faena: A completed act—whatever. Has latterly come to apply to work with the *mulet*—to the *matador's* design for this penultimate act.

Farol: A pass with the cape (see note).

Fenómeno: A brilliant young bullfighter. Unfortunately the term has become discredited because any youngster with a sufficient financial backing can become a " *fenómeno* " according to the Press.

Flamenco: (adjective) Odd, original, foreign. (noun) A school of music (guitar), singing and dancing of which the principal exponents are the gipsies.

Fuera: Outside, away, not at home.

Loco-a: Mad, crazy, cock-eyed.

" La que lleva los pantalones ": " She who wears the trousers," i.e., governs the household.

Matador: A qualified bullfighter who has taken the *alternativa.*

Machos: The tassels on the lace-ups of the *taleguillas.*

Muy macho: Abundantly gifted with male qualities.

Mala suerte: Bad luck.

Mano a mano: Literally, hand to hand; a show-down between two *matadors* of the first rank.

Maricón: Sodomite.

Mayoral: Head herdsman.

Media-verónica: A pass with the cape: see note.

Muleta: Heart-shaped flannel cloth attached to a tapered wooden stick, used in the penultimate act to complete the domination of the bull, and to prepare it for the kill.

Nevado: A bull of any colour, scattered with small white spots (" snowed-on ").

Novio-a: Betrothed.

Novillada: Bullfight with inferior bulls (often bigger and more dangerous than those passed for the formal *corrida*). The danger is increased by the elimination of the act of the horse. This makes the *novillada* more acceptable to foreigners, but increases the apprehension of spectators who recognise the hazards of the fight. *Matadores* and experienced *aficionados* frequently refuse to allow their sons to fight in the *novilladas*, on account of the exceptional risks involved.

Novillero, or Matador de novillos: A bullfighter who has not graded as *matador*, or who fails to make a living in the top class, and chooses deliberately the regular employment offered by the second-class fights.

Novillo: Bull that does not measure up to the standards of the *corrida*.

Ola: Hallo.

Olé: Cheers, hurray, etc.

Ojalá: God grant it. (Moorish.)

Palabra inglesa: On the word of an Englishman—supposed to carry more weight than the word of a Spaniard.

Papalina fenómenal: A full-scale hangover.

Paso de pecho: A pass with the *muleta* (see note).

Persianas: Sun-blinds.

Puta: Whore.

Qué barbaridad: What a barbarity, i.e., outrage, rudeness, etc.

Qué disparate: Don't talk nonsense.

Qué fastidio: What a bore.

Qué miedo: What a fright.

Recorte: A sharp pass with the cape (see note).

Revolera: A pass with the cape (see note).

Santurrón: Pious humbug.

Suerte: Literally, luck or chance. A manœuvre in the fight.

" *Sabes que Carlos a ha dado calabazas a la novia muchas veces?* ": Do you know Carlos has jilted plenty of his girl friends?

GLOSSARY

Taleguilla: The breeches worn by the bullfighter.

Tanto mejor: So much the better.

Tertulia: Assembly, gathering, club.

Tienta: Testing of the young cattle.

Torero: Term including all classes of bullfighter. N.B. *There is no such thing as a " toreador " in the present vocabulary of the fight.*

Traje de luces: Literally, the suit of lights: the uniform of the bullfighter.

Verónica: A pass with the cape (see note).

Volapié: The approach for the killing (see note).

Zaguan: Vestibule.

NOTE

As this is a work of fiction, and in no sense a treatise on bullfighting, no attempt is made to translate technical terms, for which the reader is referred to specialists in the art.